PRECINCT

MICHAEL GRANT

Copyright © 2012 Michael Grant
All rights reserved.

ISBN-10: 1467939064
ISBN-13: 978-1467939065

DEDICATION

This book is dedicated to all police officers past, present, and future who have made the ultimate sacrifice, and to those who continue to serve and protect with valor and distinction.

ACKNOWLEDGMENTS

My special thanks to Sandi Nadolny and Elizabeth Grant for their sharp eyes and blue pencils

Chapter One

It was the day before Thanksgiving and the eight Assistant Chiefs who commanded New York City's five boroughs had been summoned to One Police Plaza. These men, the top of the NYPD's food chain, commanded thousands of police officers and civilians. These men were responsible for the protection and safety of the more than 12 million people who resided, visited, and worked in New York City. These men had risen through the ranks by successfully dodging bullets, surmounting political turmoil, and negotiating the bewildering labyrinth of department politics. These men had reached the pinnacle of their careers.

And these men were—*terrified*.

Not of guns or terrorists or a burgeoning crime rate, but of just one man: Chief of Department Charles T. Drum.

Charles Drum, the source of the borough commanders' trepidation, sat at the far end of the shiny conference table with his hands clasped tightly in front of him. At first glance he didn't look particularly terrifying. He was a man of small stature with a blotchy complexion that marred an otherwise nondescript face. He did, however, possess a set of pale gray eyes that were capable of boring holes through steel. Like many diminutive men he was afflicted with a chronic Napoleonic complex and was quick to take exception to any and all slights both real or imagined. He was almost fifty-nine, but he tried to look younger by dying his hair jet-black.

He fooled no one.

In his quiet, private musings with a tumbler-full of scotch in hand (when he was still drinking), Charlie Drum would dream wistfully of being a Roman general in command of legions of soldiers who would, without hesitation, carry out his every wish even unto death. Dreams notwithstanding, he had to settle for being the third highest ranking member—being superseded only by the Police Commissioner and the First Deputy Commissioner—of the largest and most complex police department in the United States, a position he'd obtained by employing a dubious combination of intimidation, bombast, and the smallest modicum of talent.

He fancied himself a born leader and rarely passed up an opportunity to take control of the troops. Be it a siege with hostages or a benign event like the St. Patrick's Day parade, Drum could be counted on to make his appearance, wrest command of the detail from the hapless officer in charge and proceed to screw up what was otherwise a well-run effort. He was a meddler, a vicious enemy when crossed, stunningly incompetent, and his bulldog aggressiveness cowered everyone in the department, including Bruce Randall, the ineffectual police commissioner, and his equally ineffective first deputy commissioner, Floyd Bollinger.

It was 10 a.m. and the anxious borough commanders huddled around a table in a conference room on the 13th floor of OPP, shooting furtive glances at each other and wondering why they were here and not back in their offices preparing for tomorrow's parade.

The Thanksgiving Day Parade was an annual event that required a level of preparation not unlike the efforts expended in planning the invasion of a small third-world country. But instead of putting the finishing touches on their parade plans, they were sitting around a conference table pretending that a PowerPoint presentation on the latest procedure for reporting civilian sick time was the most vital piece of information they could ever hope to receive.

There were only two men in the room who were not afraid of Chief Drum and the thirty-four-year-old captain who was making the PowerPoint presentation was one of them. Richard Leland was super-bright—he'd scored the highest marks on the sergeant's, lieutenant's and captains tests—and super-ambitious. From the moment he'd raised his hand to take the oath that first day, every move he made had been calculated with one goal in mind: to become the police commissioner of the NYPD by the time he was forty. That was only six years away, but he was confident he was on track.

Even without the presence of Charlie Drum, such an august assembly of powerful borough commanders would have intimidated most captains, but not the supremely self-confident Leland who knew it was only a matter of time before he, too, would command his own borough.

Leland was tall and runner-thin though he hadn't been able to run a single marathon since he'd come to work for Drum eighteen months earlier. Sixteen-hour days left little time for running. Or anything else for that matter.

He clicked the mouse and the last slide, the NYPD logo on a field of blue, filled the screen. His alert, hazel eyes swept the audience. "Any questions, gentlemen?"

Chief Drum should have been in the front of the room asking that question, but he never ran a meeting when objectionable new procedures were being presented. He preferred to sit at the far end of the table so he could covertly watch his subordinates' reactions—as he was doing now.

From his I-can-see-you-but-you-can't-see-me vantage point, Drum's laser-like eyes darted from face to face probing for that telltale twitch of anger, that fleeting flash of rebellion in the eyes, that unguarded frown of disloyalty.

Leland, too, studied the faces of the borough commanders. He knew they were furious at Drum for wasting their time, but, being crafty veterans of the Machiavellian machinations of the department, they knew better than to expose their true feeling. Instead, the commanders studied the NYPD logo with great interest and stone-faced inscrutability.

All except Lucian Hightower, the second man in the room who was not afraid of Charlie Drum. The Bronx Borough Commander and the highest-ranking black man in the department had the thickset build of a football player, which was what he'd been at Fordham until a blown-out knee ended the hope of a promising career as a linebacker in the NFL. Now, he fixed Leland with large bulging eyes that had earned him the nickname "Bullfrog."

"I have a question, Captain. Where the hell am I supposed to get the people to handle all this additional paperwork?"

Leland didn't take Hightower's stinging sarcasm personally. The borough commander's anger, he knew, was really directed at Drum, but assistant chiefs couldn't use that tone of voice with the Chief of Department.

Chief Drum folded his arms tightly across his chest and rocked back and forth, looking startlingly like a zoned-out schizophrenic patient in a mental ward. "Lucian," he said in a high-pitched nasal voice, "we all know every borough office has two or three people squirreled away who aren't doing a damn thing. Use them."

Hightower trained his frog-eyes on Drum and blinked once, slowly. "There may be a lot of people doing nothing in headquarters," he said pointedly, "but that's not true in *my* borough."

The other borough commanders, stunned by Hightower's confrontational tone, focused on the NYPD logo with renewed intensity. Drum and Hightower's dislike for each other was legendary and everyone knew it was just a matter of time before a difference of opinion resulted in a cataclysmic eruption. Still, no one wanted to be there when it happened and risk becoming an unwitting victim of collateral damage.

"Your highly efficient staff should be able to handle it, Lucian," Drum said with a smile that had all the sincerity of a funeral director. He looked around the table. "Are there any more questions?" The other men hastily shook their heads.

~~

In the outer office Assistant Chief Tom Spencer, the Queens North Borough Commander took Leland's elbow and pulled him aside. "Richard," he whispered, "thanks again for your advice on my State of the Command report."

"No problem, Chief. It's basically formula stuff. Every year there's a new priority. Last year it was narcotics, this year it's community policing. The trick is to know the priority of the year."

Spencer scratched his veined-lined cheek. "Sometimes it's hard to know what they're looking for."

Leland studied the white-haired chief. In nine months, he'd reach the mandatory retirement age, but he still worried about things like the State of Command reports. Leland imagined the old chief would worry about the job long after he was out. It was a quality Leland liked and admired in the man.

Spencer leaned close and whispered, "Richard, would you mind if I have one of my planning people call you? Maybe you can explain to him exactly what the chief wants in these new civilian tracking reports."

"Sure, Chief. Have him call me."

Spencer was the first to ask, but before the day was over Leland would be getting calls from all the others—except Hightower. The crusty Bronx commander would rather cut off his right arm than ask advice from one of Drum's minions.

After every meeting, the other borough commanders routinely called him for clarification of what had just happened because they were reluctant to ask questions in front of Drum, who delighted in making the questioner appear stupid or inept. Leland didn't mind the calls because every favor bestowed was a favor owed. And in his eighteen months in the Chief's office, he'd built up an impressive reservoir of owed favors, all of which would serve him well in the future.

When Leland got back to his desk, John Wallace, a jovial, ruddy-faced sergeant, was waiting for him. Wallace did not fit the profile of good headquarters-administrative stock. For all his fifteen years he'd been a street cop, but a year earlier his wife had contracted cancer and he'd been given a personal hardship transfer and assigned to headquarters so he could work steady days. Unfortunately for Wallace, he'd been assigned to the Chief of Department's office and his irreverent attitude had put him on Drum's shit list from day one.

Despite Wallace's sacrilegious attitude toward the department, Leland had taken a liking to the iconoclastic, wisecracking sergeant and he'd risked the ire of Drum by taking him under his wing. For the past year, admittedly without much success, he'd been trying to turn Wallace into an acceptable headquarters staffer.

Wallace watched the group of borough commanders clustered around the elevator. "Just one hand grenade," he said to Leland out of the side of his mouth, "and we all move up eight slots."

"From your lips to God's ears."

Wallace absentmindedly flipped through Leland's in-basket. "Hightower looked pissed."

"He always looks pissed. Stop snooping in my basket."

"He's got a chronic case of *Drumitis*."

"Go away, Johnny. I have work to do."

"Hey, boss, a bunch of us are stopping off after work for a pre-holiday drink. You gonna join us?"

"Yeah, sure."

Leland opened the calendar on his smart phone and a knot tightened in his stomach. Tomorrow was Thanksgiving, the beginning of the dreaded holiday period. Last Christmas, the first since his divorce, had been a long, painful season. Like a latter day Scrooge, he'd raged through the season begrudging every Christmas carol, every brightly wrapped Christmas present, and every smiling couple he saw.

But this year he'd vowed he would not subject himself to that again. He'd booked a week in St. Thomas and was looking forward to getting away from the holiday season. No snow. No cold weather. No Christmas lights. And no damn Christmas carols. It would be a glorious non-Christmas celebration with just him lying on a hot sandy beach drinking rum-and-whatevers and thinking about absolutely nothing.

He opened a drawer and once again studied the colorful brochure displaying white sandy beaches, turquoise oceans, and deep blue skies. He was lost in the photos when he heard his master's voice.

"Richard!"

Charlie Drum never used the telephone intercom. Wallace was convinced it was because he didn't know how. Whatever the reason, when the chief wanted someone, he stood at his office door and bellowed his name.

"Yes, sir," Leland answered.

"In my office."

~~

Leland sat down across an expansive desk teeming with legions of miniature Roman soldiers. It was Drum's only hobby, but one that bordered on creepy and obsessive. There were miniature Roman soldiers everywhere.

"What can I do for you, Chief?" Leland asked.

Drum folded his arms and rocked back and forth. "It's not what *you* can do for me," he said, sounding vaguely presidential. "It's what *I* can do for you."

Leland fought to keep the excitement from showing in his face. Christmas was a traditional time for promotions. Had it finally arrived? Was Drum going to promote him to deputy inspector? Admittedly it was a little soon, but he'd been a captain for almost two years and for the past several months he'd been dropping hints.

"How long have you been a captain?" Drum asked.

"Twenty-three months, sir."

The chief nodded gravely. "You're doing a fine job, Richard. As I've told you many times, the key to success in this department is to keep moving forward. You don't move, you're a sitting duck."

Drum had never said for whom he might be a sitting duck, but Leland dutifully nodded and said, "Yes, sir."

Drum's eyes darted about the room and alighted everywhere except on Leland. That, the young captain realized with a sinking feeling, was not a good sign. Drum never made eye contact when he was delivering bad news.

"You don't have very much patrol experience, Richard."

Leland's heart thudded in his chest. *Patrol!* That dreaded word was anathema to him. Patrol meant the mind numbing everyday drudgery of a precinct and dealing with complaining civilians, unruly cops, lazy sergeants and insubordinate lieutenants. Patrol was a veritable minefield that could in the blink of an eye blow up a promising career. *His* career.

"Oh, well, perhaps not as much as some," he muttered. "But I did work in the Three-two for almost a year and a half…"

Drum waved a hand in dismissal. "As a cop. I'm talking about supervisory experience, Richard. Since you've been a boss you've spent all your time in headquarters."

Leland's face was a mask of diplomatic neutrality, but inwardly he bristled at Drum's implied criticism. *The hypocritical bastard had spent less time in the field than he had.*

As though reading his mind, Drum said, "Times change, Richard. Anyone hoping to move up in this department must be well-rounded. You need more patrol experience."

Leland heard a whooshing sound in his head. It might have blood rushing through his veins—or the sound of a guillotine plunging toward his neck. "What do you suggest, Chief?" he asked bleakly, knowing, and not wanting to know, the answer.

Drum grinned, displaying crooked, yellowed teeth. "I'm gonna do you a favor and give you that patrol experience," he said casually.

Drum's telephone rang, giving Leland a chance to get his breathing under control before he hyperventilated. While Drum berated a Brooklyn division commander for poor arrest stats, Leland desperately tried to think of a way out. The chief's suggestion—totally unexpected—had thrown him into turmoil. When he'd come to work for Drum he'd struck a Faustian bargain with himself and—he thought—Drum. He'd give the chief everything he had and in return Drum would promote him without the prerequisite patrol experience. He hadn't come to work for Drum because he liked or respected the man—no one liked or respected Charlie Drum. It was simply a quid pro quo arrangement. Drum would get an intelligent, dynamic, career-oriented captain with great report writing and interpersonal skills. In return, Leland would get a "hook," a "rabbi"—a high-ranking member of the department who could move his career forward. Leland had lived up to his part of the bargain. He'd given Drum everything he had, including countless nights and weekends and maybe his marriage.

While it was true that the promotional career path usually required patrol experience, Leland had hoped—no, damn it, *expected*—that Drum would make an exception for him. He was the best administrator in the building—even Drum admitted that. And now, was this to be his thanks? The very thing he'd done his best to avoid in his twelve years in the department? *Patrol?*

Being a precinct commander was fraught with danger; not physical danger, career danger. He would never forget what a precinct CO who'd had a career-death experience had told him: "Every day I went to work an imaginary box sat on my desk waiting for me, Richard. You know what was inside that box? A shit bomb ready to blow my career all to hell. I carried that box around with me all day. At the end of the day I left it on my desk and went home, grateful because it didn't blow up. But the next morning when I went back to work, there it was, waiting for me. Sooner or later I knew it was going to blow and finally it did."

Of course the captain had been blind drunk at the time, but he wasn't exaggerating. Leland had seen, first-hand, careers go up in smoke because of corruption investigations, excessive use of force allegations, or stepping on the wrong political toes. In many of these cases, the commanding officer had had no knowledge of the event—indeed some of them weren't even present when the event occurred—but it didn't matter. Chief Drum, the one who frequently brought the axe down on the head of the shell-shocked commanding officer, had a set speech he trotted out for these occasions, which the staff referred to as "Getting Drummed."

"*You* are the commanding officer," he'd point out to the victim. "*You* are responsible for everything, I repeat, *everything*, that takes place in your precinct. So if you didn't know about it, you should have." Leland, and Drum, knew that was a crock. It was not possible for the commanding officer of a couple of hundred cops and civilians to know *everything* that went on in a precinct.

Leland stared numbly across the desk at Drum and one question kept running thorough his mind: *How can he expect me to risk my career in that environment?*

Drum, who had the disconcerting ability to turn emotion on and off like a light switch, slammed the telephone down and instantly the scowl and harsh tone vanished. "Well, Richard," he continued as thought there had been no interruption, "what do you think?"

"Well, sir, I'm still working on that department vehicle survey and—"

"Someone else can handle that." Drum fondled a miniature Roman centurion. "The way I see it, you have two choices. You're welcome to stay on here, but"—the yellow teeth flashed—"you'll remain a captain for the rest of your career. On the other hand you can go to patrol as a precinct commander for a couple of years, make deputy inspector, and be on your way up the ladder."

Leland nodded thoughtfully. "I see." Inwardly his mind screamed: *A couple of years!*

"It's your choice, Richard."

What choice? Drum abhorred people who lacked ambition and drive. If he turned this opportunity down, it would only be a matter of time before the chief lost interest in him and cut him loose.

"You're right, sir," Leland said numbly. "It is a good career move. Thank you for thinking of me."

Drum waved a hand in dismissal. "It's nothing."

"Um, do you have any idea what precinct I'll get?"

Drum swiveled in his plush leather chair and studied the large city wall map with the casual indifference of a man trying to decide if he wants a turkey sandwich or a tuna fish salad for lunch. "I think the One-sixteen," he said finally.

The imaginary guillotine that had been hurtling down toward Leland's neck came to a sudden and abrupt halt. *The One-sixteen? Yes!* He had to force himself not to jump up and pump his fist in the air. If he had to go to patrol, Queens was the place to go. The One-sixteen was a quiet precinct and best of all Assistant Chief Tom Spencer was the Borough Commander. And Spencer owed him. Hadn't he done him favors in the past? Hadn't he just a moment ago promised to do him another favor? Things were going to work out after all.

The telephone rang and Drum grabbed it. "Chief Drum here." As he listened his face grew redder and redder. Then he growled, "I knew that sonofabitch was as useless as wings on a donkey."

He slammed the phone down. "Change of plans, Richard. Sperling got an unsatisfactory rating from Inspections. He's out. You're in."

"But... but Sperling has the Five-five," Leland whispered bleakly.

"Had. Now you have it."

Leland could hardly absorb the swift and brutal change of fortune that had just befallen him. A moment ago he was going to a country club precinct in Queens, and now—and now he was going to the *Five-five!* There were two major problems with the Five-five. The first being that it was in the Bronx—the domain of Chief Lucian Hightower!

Drum scrawled his signature on the bottom of a report and tossed it in his out-basket. "The Five-five isn't as bad as it used to be, Richard."

And *that* was the second problem. The Five-five was even *worse* than it used to be. It was the precinct that cops called *Fort Frenzy!* It was the precinct that HQ brass—including Drum—called *Camp Fuckup!* In short, the Five-five was the precinct from hell.

Drum reached for another report. "Your transfer will be effective 0700 hours Friday."

"*This* Friday?" Leland's voice cracked.

Drum's beady eyes ricocheted around his eye sockets. "Is there a problem?"

Leland recognized the tone, a tone that said there had better be no problem. As a new precinct CO, there was no way he'd be able to get Christmas off, especially with Lucian Hightower as his boss. "No," Leland said, wondering if he'd be able to get his money back on the airline tickets. "No problem, sir. None at all."

~~

Wallace was waiting for him when he got back to his desk. He took one look at Leland's ashen face and said, "Jesus, Cap, did the rabbit die?"

"I'm getting a precinct," Leland mumbled.

Wallace slapped him on the back. "No shit! That's great."

Leland stared at Wallace incredulously. "*Great*? How can you say that?"

Wallace leaned close. "It'll get you away from these headquarter pussies," he said out of the side of his mouth. "Be the best thing ever happened to you."

Leland picked up the travel brochure, took one last, sorrowful look at the lovely beaches and the blue skies, tore it up and dropped it in the wastebasket

Chapter Two

John Wallace's spur-of-the-moment pre-Thanksgiving party quickly morphed into a wake. The HQ Bar & Grill, just three blocks from One Police Plaza, was usually jumping, but at four-thirty in the afternoon – the lull between lunch and the cocktail crowd – it was deserted. The gloomy silence added a funereal pall to what was supposed to be a pre-holiday celebration.

Leland and Wallace sat at the end of the bar while a steady stream of cops and civilians came by to offer congratulations and advice. Leland found it hard to concentrate on what they had to say. Maybe it was because he was still in shock—or maybe it was the three martinis he'd downed in the past fifteen minutes.

Helen Gerber, a Senior Police Administrative Aide who'd worked in headquarters for twenty-six years, patted his hand. "Captain," she said summing up the feelings of most of the people in the office, "I'm very happy for you, but I'm very sorry for me. I've worked for a lot of bosses in my time and you are one of the best. I'm going to miss you." She planted a wet kiss on the cheek. "God bless you."

As she hurried out of the bar, Deputy Chief Denny Fowler, a large barrel-chested man, came in lugging a Macy's shopping bag. Since his heart attack, Denny Fowler had been assigned to the Chief of Department's office awaiting the Pension Board's approval for a disability pension. Most men would have jumped at the opportunity to get a three-quarters, tax-free pension, but not Denny Fowler. Even though he was only three years from mandatory retirement age, he wanted to stay, and he'd been trying – to the amazement of all – to get the Board to *deny* him a medical pension.

He slammed a *Patrol Guide* and an *Administrative Guide* on the bar. "It's all here, Richard," he said in his deep, resonant voice. "Everything you need to know about running a precinct is in these books."

Leland eyed the two six-inch-thick blue-covered tomes. Fowler wasn't exaggerating. These guides covered in great detail just about every contingency possible. They were called guides because they were supposed to be just that – guides. But most cops thought they should have been called *Bibles*, because failure to follow their Byzantine procedures was a mortal sin and you would burn in hell for all eternity.

Fowler thumped the books. "These guides have served me well for thirty-eight years, Richard, and I want you to have them."

"Thank you, Chief," Leland said, genuinely touched.

Not one for emotional display, Fowler slapped him on the back gruffly. "I can't say I'm too impressed with the 'new breed' that's been coming along, but you're a good man, Richard. You'll do fine. Remember," he said, gently putting his big hand on the thick books, "these are the procedures to be followed, but don't ever forget that it's people who carry out those procedures."

"I'll try to remember that, Chief. Will you have a drink with me?"

Fowler frowned. "I'm not supposed to be drinking, but what the hell."

Fowler threw down his drink—a shot of Black Label—in one gulp and pounded Leland's back again. "I've got to be going. Good luck, Richard, and God bless you."

Leland watched the big, proud man walk out the door and realized that he was seeing the end of an era. The 'new breed'—and Leland was one of them—would soon be running the department. He stared into his half-empty martini glass and wondered what cops would think of *him* thirty years from now.

"A real gentleman," Tim Frazer said, bringing Leland out of his reverie.

Lieutenant Tim Frazer, who'd worked for Leland for the past two years, was on a career path that almost mirrored Leland's. Although he was three years older and hadn't ascended the ranks quite as quickly, he was smart and just as ambitious. When Frazer had first been assigned to the office, Leland had taken him under his wing and had initiated him into the arcane workings of headquarters politics.

Frazer resumed the conversation that had been interrupted by Fowler's appearance. "It's a good career move," he said.

Leland speared an olive with a toothpick. "That's what Osama bin Laden said about his move to Pakistan."

"No, really, Richard, it's the beginning of your run up the ladder. You're on the fast track. Two years in the Five-five and Drum will move you along. Hey, you can be my hook."

"You won't need me for a hook, Timmy. You're on your way already."

Frazer shrugged modestly. "I hope so. I expect to get promoted by the summer."

Wallace grunted. "Just don't make any vacation plans, Loo."

Frazer shook his head. "That was a tough break, Richard. Maybe if you explain it to Hightower he'll …" He stopped when he saw the expression on Leland's face. "Yeah, I guess not. So what's the first thing you're going to do when you get there?"

Leland studied himself in the mirror behind the bar. He was beginning to get fuzzy and he intended to keep drinking martinis until he was a complete blur. He glanced down at Fowler's guides and shrugged. "I guess I'll follow Denny's advice and go by the book. Can't go wrong doing that."

"That may not be as easy as you think," Frazer said. "From what I hear about the Five-five, nobody goes by the book."

Leland nodded glumly. "I know the precinct is a loose cannon, but I'm gonna change all that. There's no discipline in that command and discipline is the key." Then a comforting thought occurred to him. You know, maybe if I whip them into shape quickly, Drum will give me a reprieve on my two year sentence."

He squinted at himself in the mirror and wondered whether he believed that or was just trying to convince himself. He downed the dregs of his martini and ordered another. "I'm gonna have to do something to get their attention right away," he said more to himself than to Frazer.

"Like what?"

"I don't know. I'll think of something."

"You've got plenty of time," Wallace said, draining his Bud. "You got all day tomorrow to think about it."

Frazer looked at his watch. "Gotta go. Listen, Richard, keep in touch. Anything you need, just holler. Okay?"

"Yeah, Timmy, I'll do that. Have a good Thanksgiving."

As Frazer was leaving, Harry Wolfe came back from the men's room. Leland didn't like the short pudgy captain when he was sober and three martinis hadn't altered his opinion. Wolfe was the quintessential headquarters bureaucrat whose forte was backstabbing and petty gossip.

The captain's entire life revolved around the dozens of useless projects he dreamed up every year, a practice that had more than once saved him from being "Drummed" by Drum. A year earlier, Wolfe had been offered the same choice as Leland, but he'd declined the opportunity to go into the "trenches," telling Drum he was perfectly satisfied to remain a captain for the remainder of his career. From that moment, Drum developed a love-hate relationship with Wolfe. He hated Wolfe's lack of drive, but he loved the captain's talent for generating complex statistical projects. It didn't matter to Drum that most of these projects were all bells and whistles with little substance. He liked to use Wolfe's convoluted statistical analyses as a weapon to flog out-of-favor borough commanders and hapless precinct commanders.

Wolfe climbed back on his stool. "So you're going into the trenches. You poor bastard." He could barely suppress a grin.

Leland knew that all the people who had come to have a farewell drink with him had come in friendship— all except Wolfe. He'd come to gloat and Leland was determined not to give him that satisfaction. "Yeah, it oughta be fun. Hey, Harry, I need an exec. You wanna come?"

Wolfe recoiled. "No, thanks. Unlike you and Timmy Frazer, I have no lofty career aspirations."

Leland studied the captain. He was only in his mid-forties with plenty of time ahead of him. Leland didn't understand people like Harry Wolfe who had no drive or ambition. "Why do you stay in the job?" he asked.

"They pay me very well to do very little. I can't think of a better deal than that."

"How about welfare and food stamps?" Wallace asked, signaling for another beer.

Wolfe ignored the impudent sergeant. "So, Richard, how do you plan to deal with the infamous Reverend Kawasi Munyika?"

Leland, who was about to take a drink, slowly lowered his glass. *Munyika!* In the shock of his new assignment, he'd completely forgotten about the Reverend Kawasi Munyika, the head of the People's Freedom Legion. At least once a month the flamboyant, rabble-rousing reverend made headlines supporting one dubious cause or another, and if there was no cause readily available, he made one up. Munyika and his band of malcontent followers demonstrated all over the city, but mostly in the Five-five because that's where the People's Freedom Legion headquarters was located. So far he was only a local irritant and a world-class pain in the butt to the NYPD, but he had aspirations of breaking onto the national scene.

"No problem," Leland said with more bravado than he felt. "If I can face a roomful of borough commanders, I can certainly handle Kawasi Munyika."

Wolfe's smile was all teeth and no warmth. "Good luck. If anyone can torpedo your career, it's the Reverend Munyika."

"Thanks for the encouraging words, Harry."

Wolfe slipped into his trench coat. "Well, I must be going. Richard, keep in touch."

"Yeah, Harry, you, too."

Now there was just Leland and Wallace. In the middle of the fifth martini it occurred to Leland that Wallace might be staying with him just to keep him company. "Hey, Johnny," he said. "You must have something better to do than hang around with me on Thanksgiving eve."

"No problem, Boss. My sister and her husband are staying with us for the holidays and to tell you the truth I'd just as soon not spend too much time with my brother-in-law."

"Why?"

Wallace screwed up his face. "He's a social worker. Jesus, I've never heard so much bleeding-heart bullshit from one guy in all my life. What he needs is a week working a radio car in Bed-Sty. That'd straighten out his priorities."

"How's your wife doing, John?"

Wallace's easy smile faded. "We're taking it one day at a time." He looked at his watch. "She's going into chemo right about now. I always go and see her when she's done. Most of the time she's asleep, or if she's awake she's sick to her stomach. But, I like to be there anyway..." His voice trailed off.

Leland felt a sudden stab of shame. Considering what Johnny Wallace and his wife were going through, what right did he have to feel sorry for himself? A line from a poem jumped into his head: *I cried because I had no shoes, then I saw a man who had no feet.*

Hey, Boss," Wallace said, changing the subject. "Did you mean what you said before about going by the book and tightening the screws?"

"I guess so. Why?"

Wallace scratched his chin and looked uncomfortable. He wasn't used to giving smart guys like Leland advice. "Boss, I'm sure you know what you're doing, but I've spent most of my time on patrol and I've seen COs come and go. The ones that come in like gangbusters usually have the hardest time. A precinct is like a family, ya know? Guys may fight and bitch all the time, but there's a real closeness that comes from working with the same people day in and day out. A new CO is kinda like a new stepfather. Sometimes there's a lot of resentment in the beginning. I don't know if it's such a good time to tighten the screws right away. You know what I'm saying?"

"Yeah, I do, Johnny. Thanks for the advice."

Leland knew Wallace meant well, but the sergeant was talking like a cop not a boss. The transition from police officer to supervisor involved more than just passing a competitive exam. It required a distinct change in thinking. Cops had their own agendas that usually revolved around taking care of number one. To be an effective supervisor, one had to recognize that the department came first. There were many who never made that mental transition from cop to boss. Leland had had no problem, but for people like Wallace it was impossible. Johnny Wallace might wear sergeant stripes on his sleeve, but he'd always think like a cop. Leland didn't hold it against him, but he knew that with an attitude like that, Johnny Wallace had no future in the police department.

Wallace's jovial mood returned. "Before I go, Boss, did I ever tell you about the time me and my partner filled a drug dealer's gas tank with bubble bath soap?"

For the next half-hour Wallace regaled Leland with war stories. With every wacky, hair-raising story, Leland became more and more despondent. Wallace was describing the screwball things that precinct cops did to fight boredom and fear, but from Leland's perspective, every one of those stories was a potential career-busting disaster.

Leland remained after Wallace left to go to the hospital. He lost track of his martini count because the bartender cleared away the toothpicks. As the evening wore on, more and more people emptied out of the surrounding office buildings and soon the bar was filled with a raucous crowd of young people intent on kicking off the start of the holiday season with a bang.

Leland watched the young women and dark-suited men—many of them his own age—engage in the delicate dance of "hooking up." At one point he caught sight of a beautiful girl with long, raven hair who reminded him of Marilyn and he decided it was time to go before he engaged in a episode of dialing-while-drunk. The martinis hadn't made him drunk, as he hoped they would. Instead, they'd made him melancholy. He was already despondent and didn't need to start thinking about his ex-wife. He paid his bill, tucked Fowler's books under his arm, and went home to his small apartment in Flushing.

Chapter Three

Richard Leland spent all of Thanksgiving Day alone in his cramped apartment immersed in Denny Fowler's Patrol and Administrative Guides. His one concession to the holiday was ordering in a turkey sandwich from the local deli.

He didn't get much sleep that night and at exactly 7:45 a.m. Friday morning he found himself sitting in his car glumly staring at the station house that was going to be his home—and his responsibility—for the next two years.

Like some ancient Crusader castle, the 55th Precinct station house dominated the surrounding terrain of row upon row of scarred and neglected tenements. Unlike her more contemporary sisters in other parts of the city—unimaginative brick structures that could pass for anything from a prison to a library—the 55th Precinct building had been built by the WPA during the Depression and was designed to make a statement about the power and majesty of the law.

It had once been a majestic edifice, built with the care and attention to detail that characterized building construction in a time when carpenters and stonemasons were craftsmen who took pride in their work. But eighty years of neglect had turned it into a gloomy, hulking affair.

The wide, front entrance was flanked by two massive Corinthian columns that supported a stone lentil bearing the words "Tenth Precinct" carved in bold Romanesque letters. The architect, perhaps believing in a more permanent world, had erroneously assumed that the precinct's numerical designation would never change.

The narrow, high-arched windows were reminiscent of a fortress—probably something else the architect had intended. The roof's parapet, extending three feet out from the façade and running the entire length of the building, had once been covered with intricately designed relief carvings, but most of them had fallen off and those that remained were rendered indecipherable by time, weather, and pollution.

With a jaundiced eye, Leland inspected the gothic-like structure that vaguely reminded him of the apartment building in *Rosemary's Baby*. The evidence of neglect and decay was palpable and it suddenly occurred to him that the sullen building was the perfect metaphor for the attitude of the people who worked within its walls. One of the two green lights flanking the entrance was out and the other was missing panes of green glass. Most of the windows, opaque from years of accumulated dirt and grime, were missing window shades and the few that were still there were ripped or hung at haphazard angles.

A movement at street level caught his eye. A black, battle-scarred cat, missing the tip of one ear, carefully picked its way across the tops of a half dozen open garbage cans in front of the station house. He sniffed at a pizza box and pawed at it. As it fell to the ground, the box opened and a handful of pie crusts and three empty Budweiser cans spilled out. Leland opened a small spiral notebook and began taking notes.

When he finished, he looked up and saw a thickset man with kinky gray hair and a cigar stuck in his mouth step in front of a second-story window and yank the window shade. It came down on his head in a cloud of dust and cigar sparks. Wrestling with the shade, the man opened the window and hurled it out, shouting a string of profanities as the shade crashed down on the garbage cans. The startled cat screeched and dove under a parked car. Leland made another note.

A minute later, two radio cars turned slowly into the block and stopped at the far end of the street to talk to three cops who were huddled in a doorway smoking. Leland looked at his watch. The late tour didn't end for another ten minutes, which meant all these officers should still have been at their assigned posts. Leland jotted down the radio car numbers.

Then, an unmarked car, with dome light flashing, came speeding down the block and rocked to a halt in front of the station house. Two scruffy cops wearing jeans and sweatshirts jumped out. The driver, a hulking mountain of a man, pulled the handcuffed prisoner out of the back seat and half-dragged, half-carried him into the station house. Leland made another note and closed the book. He'd seen enough.

He studied himself in the rear-view mirror, hoping to see a confident, take charge, precinct commander. Instead, all he saw staring back at him was a frightened face that looked a lot younger than thirty-four years. A couple of months earlier he'd started to grow a mustache, hoping it would make him look more mature. But so far the sparse hairs hadn't done much. He'd give it one more month and if it didn't thicken, he'd shave it off. It was itchy as hell anyway.

He got out of the car and the cold November wind made him hunch his shoulders as he hurried up the steps. He pushed open a deeply scarred oak door, and stepped into a gloomy, cavernous muster room that was at least forty by fifty feet. The eighteen-foot high ceilings swallowed most of the light coming from an inadequate number of fluorescent lights—several of which, he noted, were burned out. As he approached the elevated massive oak desk at the far end of the room he saw a woman and three children sitting on the floor in a corner eating McDonald's happy meals. Against the far wall he counted three sawed-off parking meters, one Cadillac bumper, and five new tires. It looked as though someone was setting up a flea market.

He stopped in front of the desk and waited for the lieutenant, a florid faced man in his early forties, to look up. But the lieutenant was busy writing and waved a hand. "Be with you in a sec," he said.

Leland read the man's nametag. "Lieutenant Hanlon," he said sharply, "what's more important, giving your attention to a citizen or doing whatever it is that you're doing?"

The lieutenant looked up and studied Leland with the red-rimmed eyes of a man who never quite got used to working late tours.

"Hey, pal, I gotta get this report to the borough in thirty seconds. Unless your hair is on fire or something, you think you can give me a minute?"

Leland reddened. This was just the sort of blasé attitude that gave the Five-five precinct a bad reputation. He'd been looking for some way to make a quick impression, something that would set the tone of his stewardship. Now, thanks to this incompetent lieutenant, he'd found it.

"*Lieutenant Hanlon.*"

The lieutenant looked up again and the weary smile was gone. "Hey, pal, I told you—"

Leland held up his shield and ID card. "I'm *Captain* Leland, your new commanding officer."

The lieutenant muttered an oath and dropped his pen. "Jeez, I'm sorry, Cap, but..."

Leland flipped open his spiral notebook. "Before you finish *your* report, you can give *me* a report telling me who's in RMP 2059 and 2015 and why they're parked up the street and not patrolling their assigned sectors."

"Sure, Cap, but the borough—"

"First me, then the borough, Lieutenant."

Leland smiled to himself as he walked toward a door marked "Commanding Officer." Just one minute in the precinct and he'd found an issue he could use to set the tone of his command. Fortunately, it wasn't all that serious. The tour was almost over anyway, but he could use it as a learning tool to jack up supervision. And supervision, as the management textbooks told him, was the key to running any command.

As he was walking past the staircase toward his new office, he heard shouts and the scuffle of feet on the stairs. Out of the corner of his eye he saw a blur hurtling toward him and turned. It was the prisoner he'd seen being dragged into the station house. Only now he wasn't handcuffed and he was heading directly at *him*—the only obstacle between the escaping prisoner and freedom.

Instinctively, Leland reached out to grab him, but the prisoner threw a punch and caught him squarely on the mouth, knocking him to the ground. The first pursuing cop, a short, wiry man, tripped over Leland's prostrate body and went sprawling across the tiled floor. Right behind him, the big cop Leland had seen drag the prisoner out of the car, hurdled over both Leland and his partner and caught up to the prisoner just as he reached the door. The prisoner threw a punch, but the cop blocked it and connected with a thudding right hook. The man bounced off the door and slid to the floor. The big cop flipped him on his stomach and snapped on handcuffs.

By now, a dazed Leland was back on his feet dabbing at his bleeding and rapidly swelling lip with a handkerchief. Before he could say anything, the gray-haired man he'd seen throw the window shade out the window brushed past him.

"You *scumbag*—" He grabbed the prisoner by the throat. "I'm gonna—"

"*Marvin*," Lieutenant Hanlon shouted, "I don't think you've met the new CO."

The man looked over his shoulder, but didn't let go of the prisoner's throat. "Sergeant Seidel," he said in a gravelly voice. "I got Anti-Crime."

The sergeant cocked his arm to throw a punch at the prisoner, but Leland grabbed him. "Sergeant," he said sharply, "that's enough."

Seidel blinked. "Huh?"

"I said, that's enough. The man is handcuffed and under control."

Seidel took the cigar stub out of his mouth and jabbed it in the direction of the prisoner. "You know who this scumbag is? A contract killer."

Leland gingerly dabbed at his throbbing lip and studied the short, slightly built prisoner. He, too, wanted to smash the smirking, defiant face, but that was out of the question. "How'd he get away?" he asked the Anti-Crime sergeant.

"We're printing the skell... Next thing he's bolting for the door."

"Who's responsible for this escaped prisoner?"

"What escaped? We got him before he got out the door."

"Sergeant, let's not play with semantics. He *escaped* from his arresting officer."

Seidel ran his hands through his kinky hair in exasperation. "Whaddaya talking about? We *caught* the guy before he made it out the door. He didn't—"

A tall man with white curly hair stepped between them. "Captain, why don't we get that cut cleaned up."

Leland looked at the fifty-something man with white hair and the angelic face of an ex-altar boy. "Who are *you*?" he demanded.

"Lieutenant Jack Barry, your Operations Coordinator. You're bleeding all over your shirt, Captain."

Leland looked down and saw that blood was dripping on his shirt *and* his brand new silk tie. *Damn!*

Barry led Leland into the captain's office and showed him the bathroom. "You'll need some paper towels," he said. "I'll be right back."

Leland turned on the faucets and murky sludge sputtered into the rust-stained porcelain bowl. "Lieutenant, hold the outgoing platoon. I'll want to say a few words to them."

Barry appraised Leland's disheveled appearance. "You sure you want to talk to them looking like that?"

Angry at being punched in the face, angry at an insubordinate sergeant, and angry at just being here, he snapped, "Yes, Lieutenant. Hold the platoon."

Barry shrugged. "I'll tell the sergeant."

Leland stared at himself in the mirror. Christ, he *was* a mess. There was blood all over his shirt and tie and his lip that was still swelling. He tenderly dabbed at it and said out loud, "Good morning. I'm your new commanding officer. I just want to say..." He stopped and shook his head. It was no use. He couldn't address the troops sounding like Alfred Hitchcock with a toothache.

Barry came back and handed a package of paper towels to Leland. "The platoon is waiting, Captain."

Leland tore the package open. "Never mind. Tell the sergeant to post the platoon and then come back in here."

By the time Lieutenant Barry returned, Leland had written out a list of every violation and deficiency he'd observed in his first fifteen minutes as the new commanding officer of the 55th Precinct.

He slid the list across the desk to his Operations Coordinator. "I haven't prioritized it, but I want answers and explanations for everything on that list. Furthermore, I—"

The telephone rang. Barry picked up the receiver and quickly held it away from his ear. The voice on the other end of the line was so loud that Leland could hear it from where he was sitting. And it was a familiar voice.

"Yes, sir. One moment." Barry held his hand over the receiver. "Chief Hightower's on the phone and he's madder than hell. He's looking for an Unusual. Did you tell Hanlon to hold off on that?"

Leland paled. An "Unusual" was a special report prepared for any newsworthy occurrence, ranging from the mugging of a prominent person to a triple homicide. If Hightower was looking for it, it had to be important—certainly more important than a list of cops who were off post.

Leland took the telephone from Barry, who quietly slipped out of the room. "Good morning, Chief. This is Captain Leland."

"*Leland*," Hightower roared through the telephone, "what in the *hell* are you doing? Are you looking to break the record for the precinct CO with the shortest tenure?"

"No, sir, I—"

"I gave a direct order to your lieutenant to send me the Unusual on that murder arrest *forthwith*, but I'm told *you* countermanded my order."

"Not exactly. I—"

"Leland, let me tell you something right up front." Hightower's voice dropped to almost a whisper, but even without the volume it was just as menacing. "Drum put you here over my objections. The Five-five needs a man with a hell of a lot more experience than some headquarters... *groupie*! But what's done is done. Just let me give you a piece of advice. You do what *I* want first and if there's any time left over you do what *you* want. Do I make myself clear?"

"Yes, sir. I—" He winced as the telephone slammed down on his ear.

Leland jumped up as Barry came back into the office. "Lieutenant, get that Unusual to the Borough immediately—"

"Done. I forwarded it myself." Barry scratched his pink cheek. "Captain, the *Daily News* was on the scene when Anti-Crime busted that guy. They've been calling the borough for more information. The chief doesn't like to be in a position where he doesn't have all the answers."

Leland slumped back into his chair. The pain of his throbbing lip coalesced with the pain of his throbbing headache and the synergistic effect multiplied the result tenfold. "I know that. It's just that... I didn't know the lieutenant was writing an Unusual for the chief."

"Captain, if I may offer a word of advice. I've never worked in headquarters so I don't know how things are done there, but a precinct is a lot like a fast moving merry-go-round. If you try to just jump on board too fast, you get knocked on your duff. The best way is to run alongside. When you get up to speed, it's easier to hop on."

Leland studied the lieutenant's face for signs of sarcasm or insubordination or ridicule, but all he saw was a pleasant, compassionate smile. "I know there's a parable in there somewhere," he said ruefully.

"I guess what I'm saying is, when you come in at the beginning of a tour, you might want to take the time to find out what's going on before you start issuing orders."

Of course the lieutenant was right. He should have known better, but he'd been in such a hurry to make his first impression. He'd made an impression all right, but not the kind he'd hoped for. "Thanks for the advice, Lieutenant, I'll try to remember that."

The clock on the wall said it was 8:15 a.m. He'd been here for less than half an hour, but it felt like a week. He was drained, exhausted. He turned to the wall map outlining the precinct's boundaries. "Why don't you give me a rundown on the precinct."

Barry stepped up to the map and using a pencil as a marker began. "The Five-five is approximately six-point-eight square miles with a population of about eighty-five thousand people. The breakdown is twenty-six percent Caucasian, fifty-eight percent Afro-American, fifteen percent Hispanic, and the rest miscellaneous. As you know, Cap, some precincts are country clubs and some are shithouses. The Five-five is the worst of both worlds. The northeast quadrant of the precinct, what we call the 'Hill,' is where the yuppies, the guppies, the dinks—or whatever they're calling themselves these days—live. They're well educated, outspoken, and politically astute. In short, a real pain in the ass."

"Why is it called the Hill?"

"The topography of this part of the Bronx is all hills and valleys," Barry explained. "You can't see it on this map, but this area is a hilltop. Below that, to the south, we have 'Death Valley.' As you can see, the precinct station house is in the middle of Death Valley. Below Death Valley—this little appendage here—is the 'Bulge.' Over here to the west is the 'Flatlands.' It's half commercial and half residential. Not too many problems out that way."

Leland studied the map. "Why is it called Death Valley?"

"Because it's in a valley and that little chunk of real estate accounts for eighty percent of our calls for service and more than ninety percent of our arrests. Some real bad people live down there, especially in the Bulge."

Leland found Barry's terminology disturbing. Chief Drum had a cause-of-the-month, and last month's was *Code Words For Racial Slurs*. Anyone caught using terms like "skell" or "mutt" around him risked immediate transfer; never mind that these were words he frequently used himself. He'd sent out a memo to all the borough commanders instructing them to be on the lookout for *Racial Slur Code Words*. Against Leland's advice, he'd even included an appendix of suspected code words, which turned out to be a big mistake. The memo was the cause of much merriment in the precincts and sparked a blizzard of unauthorized radio transmissions from bored late tour cops who amused themselves by shouting the more common slurs over the air, plus some new ones made up especially for the occasion.

Leland read aloud from his notes. "The Hill, where the rich people live, Death Valley, where the ghetto criminal element live, and the Flatlands, where nondescript people who stay out of trouble live." He looked up at Barry. "At best it sounds insensitive. At worst it sounds racist. Don't you think so, Lieutenant?"

Barry's smile was tentative, as thought he weren't sure if Leland was serious or not. "Racist? No, Cap, I don't think so. You know cops. They all have a warped sense of humor."

"Lieutenant, are you familiar with the Chief of Department's memo regarding code words for racial slurs?"

"No, sir."

Leland wasn't surprised the lieutenant knew nothing about the memo. There were probably dozens of department directives that he knew nothing about. It was just another example of the general sloppiness in the Five-five Precinct. "Lieutenant, the kind of terminology you used to describe the areas of this precinct could be construed as code words for racism. I'm going to issue a memo prohibiting our personnel from referring to the precinct in those terms."

Barry scratched his head. "You sure you want to do that, Captain?"

"Yes, I am." He made a notation in his spiral notebook and sat back. "Okay, let's talk about the community. How do we get along with them?"

"Which one? Each area has its own community group with its own agenda."

"Let's start with the Community Board."

The Community Board, the most important and influential political group in any precinct, was Leland's greatest concern because a precinct commander's career hinged on his ability to get along with its members.

The Community Board concept had been created to address the inherent problems of trying to coordinate the plethora of city agencies responsible for enhancing the quality of life in a given community. Traditionally, each city agency, often a fiefdom unto itself and answerable to no one, arbitrarily carved up neighborhoods into crazy-quilt boundaries with no thought given to coordinating services. This haphazard division of neighborhoods had given rise to chronic buck-passing and bureaucratic obfuscation. In 1975, the City Charter was amended to correct this condition and co-terminality came into being. Agency boundaries were reconfigured to accommodate the jurisdictions of police, sanitation, social services, and other city agencies. Now, finally, all these agencies—responsible for the same area—could work together. At least that was the theory.

A Community Board didn't have the power to make a city agency do anything, but politics dictated that any agency, especially a community-sensitive one like the police department, go along with a Board's "suggestions." This arrangement sometimes caused a clash of personalities, but Leland knew that any clash of wills between a precinct commander and the Community Board could be fatal. In such an encounter, the backroom workings of city politics guaranteed that a precinct commander came out second best. More than one career had been derailed as a result of just such a confrontation, and Leland was determined not to run afoul of this most important group.

"We have the usual hassles with them," Barry said. "Not enough cops on the street, double parking on the main drags, rowdy behavior at bar closing time; that sort of thing. Heidi Vancamp runs the Board. All in all, we get along with her very well. The Board is the least of our problems. I guess you know about Munyika?"

"Everybody in New York City knows all about the Reverend Kawasi Munyika. What's he been up to lately?"

"The usual professional agitation. No cause too small. No cause too ridiculous. Last week a kid was suspended from the local junior high for bringing an AK-47 to school. I guess he was tired of bringing the same old stuff to show-and-tell. In less than fifteen minutes, Munyika had twenty-five pickets carrying signs accusing the white principal of racism."

"Is it safe to assume that the precinct doesn't have a good working relationship with him and his group?"

"Like a Zippo lighter and a gallon of gasoline. Our biggest headache is manpower, Cap. Every time he pickets in the precinct we have to scramble to find enough people to police the detail."

"What about the borough?"

"Nope. The chief's policy is that each precinct handles its own demonstrations, unless it's really big or protracted. We breathe a lot easier when Munyika takes his traveling circus on the road."

Leland made a note to meet with Munyika as soon as possible. He was sure he'd find a way to finesse the troublesome reverend. After all, interpersonal relations was his forte. "Who are the other groups?"

"The Hill... I mean the north side has a group called CUT—Community United Together. It has a lot of influence with the mayor and the local movers and shakers in the Bronx."

"What's its agenda?"

"Keep the riffraff in Death Valley and off the Hill," Barry said with a straight face. "That's a direct quote."

Leland rubbed his temples. That sounded like trouble. "Who else is there?"

"There's a Bronx-wide organization, CROC, headed up by—"

Leland looked up from his notebook. "Crock?"

"Citizens to Regain Our Community."

"Well, at least it sounds like they have a sense of humor."

"Believe me, Cap. None of these groups has a sense of humor."

"Who runs it?"

"A community activist lawyer named Gloria Perez."

"How do you get along with her?"

"She means well, but she's a real pain in the ass. She spends a lot of time harassing city agencies, especially us, and she doesn't let up until she gets what she wants." The lieutenant pointed to the map. "Look at the Bulge—I mean this little section of the precinct. She wouldn't quit until Hightower agreed to add another radio car sector down there. I gotta hand it to her," Barry said with grudging admiration, "anyone who can talk Hightower into adding radio cars to an area that small has to have her act together. By the way, she'll be in to see you as soon as she finds out we have a new CO." Barry's light blue eyes twinkled. "You married, Cap?"

"No. Why?"

"She's one good-looking woman."

Leland grunted. "Activist lawyers aren't my type. Who else do we have?"

"A handful of block groups, but I've told you about the big ones."

Leland flipped his notebook closed. He was beginning to get a clearer picture of the Five-five's unique problems. Most precincts had one predominant profile: business, residential or ghetto. But the Five-five, with its peculiar mix of wealth, business, and poverty, had them all and that guaranteed a host of problems, and each problem, he knew, would come with its own special interest group wanting its problems solved first.

"Okay, thanks for the briefing, Loo." He pointed to the list in Barry's hand. "Get started on those right away."

Barry skimmed the list and smiled. "New panes of glass for the front light? I'm afraid not, Cap. This is a real old building. Building Maintenance said they stopped stocking that type of lamp fixture in 1947."

"How about the other one?" Leland said gently. "They still stock light bulbs, don't they?"

Barry's eyes twinkled. "You got me there, Boss. I'll have that taken care of right away." He looked back at the list. "Most of these house cleaning problems are because we've been without our cleaning attendant for the last three months."

"What happened to him?"

"He took a drug bust."

"Not in the station house I hope."

"No. A social club in his neighborhood."

"How about a replacement?"

"I've been trying. Personnel says they're working on it."

"For *three* months?"

"You know how those headquarters jockeys are. It takes that long to open the mail. They—" He stopped, suddenly remembering where Leland had come from.

"Never mind," Leland said dryly. "*I'll* call them. The boss there owes me a favor."

Barry read from the list. "Window shades are back ordered."

"How long?"

"Two years."

"*Two?*"

"You know the city, Cap. Never any money." He looked back at the list. "We're out of luck on the garbage can lids."

"Dare I ask why?"

"Quartermaster said we've exceeded our quota. They won't give us any more."

"How many have you ordered?"

"This year? Twelve."

"*Twelve?* What happened to them?"

"The kids steal them. They make good shields for their gang wars."

"They steal from *us*?"

"Yep. We're the only ones in the neighborhood with good garbage can lids—or any lids for that matter."

Leland was about to tell Barry to post a cop outside the station house, but he stopped himself. He could just imagine Hightower's reaction if he found out that his new precinct commander had assigned a cop to guard garbage cans.

"Who is that woman outside in the muster room with the children?"

"We busted her husband for assault on her yesterday. He made bail and she's afraid he'll come after her."

"What about social services?"

"They told her to come back next week. She's scared and she has no place to go. We bought her and the kids breakfast. When Social Services opens, we'll bring her over there and make sure she gets someone's attention."

"That's all very commendable, Lieutenant, but that's not the job of the police department."

"No, it's not, but no one else is doing it. If we put her out, her husband may find her and then we'll have a homicide."

"Perhaps," Leland persisted, "but the police department is not here to – "

"Cap, think about it this way. We're like those Indian forts in the old John Wayne cavalry movies. Remember how the settlers came in for protection? Well, it's the same here. We have people camping out here every night because they have no place else to go or because they're afraid to go home."

"Is that why it's called Fort Frenzy?" Leland asked sarcastically.

Barry's blue eyes turned cold. "No, sir. We call it the Five-five."

"I'm sorry, Lieutenant, that was uncalled for. What about all that stuff lying around outside?" he continued. "The muster room looks like an auto junk yard. Why isn't it secured in the property room?"

"Because the property room is temporarily the sergeants' locker room."

"What's wrong with their locker room?"

"It's under water."

Leland studied Barry's placid face. "You're putting me on."

"No, sir."

"I see. Of course you've called Building Maintenance."

"Oh, yes. They told me *El Niño* causes the flooding. They said *El Niño* should be gone by the end of the year and we can move back into the basement when it dries up."

Even Leland had to smile at that one. It was funny, and it would have been even funnier if Leland weren't the precinct commander. But it was also symptomatic of the uneven relationship between precincts and support units. The support units were physically removed from the precincts so it was easy for them to make excuses, especially when the precinct mentality had become such that they readily accepted lame excuses. The story about *El Niño* was someone's amusing way of saying they were not going to fix the leaky basement. Leland looked at his lieutenant. He seemed like a good man, but Leland wondered if he was up to the challenge of helping him turn this precinct into the kind of command that would get him promoted.

"So you took 'no' for an answer," he said.

Barry's pink cheeks reddened. "Captain, I've been on the job for almost thirty-five years, the last seven right here. If I took all this nonsense seriously I'd have a stomach made of PVC pipe and I'd be living on a diet of Melba toast and skim milk. Sometimes you just gotta roll with it."

Leland winced inwardly. Probably everyone else in the command shared the lieutenant's lackadaisical attitude. "Not any more, Lieutenant," he said quietly. "This is *my* command now and we're not going to 'roll with it' any more. We're going to take everything very seriously."

Barry's face was neutral, but he couldn't hide the frustration in his voice. "Captain, there are a lot more serious things happening in this precinct than a flooded basement and broken panes of glass."

"Perhaps, but we shouldn't have to work in a building that looks like a slum. How can I expect my sergeants to act like professionals when they're forced to change their clothes in the property room? You're going to hear me preach a lot about professionalism because I believe in it. And I also believe that a professional has the right to work in a professional environment."

Barry nodded stiffly. "Whatever you say, Captain."

"That's it for now. Oh, by the way, tell Sergeant Seidel to give me a full report on that escaped prisoner."

Barry, who was on his way out the door, stopped. "Cap, are you sure you want to do that? The prisoner didn't actually—"

"Lieutenant, I've been here for less than an hour, but everything I've seen so far tells me this place is running on automatic pilot. That is going to change. The officer responsible for that prisoner will be disciplined. Hopefully, that will send a message that everyone will be held accountable for his or her actions."

Barry nodded curtly and left.

~~

Leland spent the rest of the day wading through the mounds of reports, forms, and memos that constitute the paper-trail DNA of a precinct, hoping to get a clearer picture of life in the precinct. He read the Inspections Division evaluation that had caused Captain Sperling's downfall and the report clearly showed low productivity and sloppy administrative procedures.

Leland tossed the report aside and went to look out a window encrusted with the grime of decades. It had started raining and the rain, absorbing most of the light, cast a gloomy pall over the street. Idly, he watched the pizza box float down the sidewalk on a cascading stream and thought about what he had to do to survive here. The way he saw it, he had two major problems to contend with. The first problem, the precinct's sloppy administrative procedures, would be the easiest to deal with. Administrative problems were something he'd dealt with his whole career. It was the second problem that worried him. Low production figures were indicative of poor morale and he wasn't looking forward to re-training a precinct full of obstinate cops.

He watched the black cat—the same one who'd stalked the pizza box—take off across the street after a rat that was almost as big as he was. He turned away from the window and wondered for the third time in as many days if he was up to the challenge.

It was almost six o'clock when he closed the last folder. He was about to leave when Sergeant Seidel came in puffing on a foul-smelling cigar. "You wanted to see me, Cap?"

Leland had forgotten all about the Anti-Crime sergeant. He looked at his watch in alarm. "What tour are you working?"

"Seven to three."

The Inspections Division report had been critical of Sperling's failure to control overtime. "You're not authorized to work overtime, Sergeant."

"I'm not putting in for OT."

Seidel's response threw Leland off guard. "Why not?" he blurted out. "If you work overtime you should get paid for it."

"Cap, before I made sergeant, I was in the Bureau for nineteen years. We never put in for OT. If you had work to do, you did it, period."

"Well you're not in the Bureau now. When you work overtime put in for it."

Seidel looked nonplussed. "All right, I'll put in for three hours."

"You can't."

"Didn't you just say—"

"*Authorized* overtime, Sergeant. You weren't authorized to work overtime *today*." Leland had the giddy feeling he was doing a Who's-On-First skit. "What I mean is," he said more calmly, "you should put in for overtime when it's authorized, but you can't put in for these three hours."

"Okay, I won't." Seidel's puffed on his cigar furiously. "I think that's what I said in the first place."

Leland studied the short, grizzled man. He was probably in his late fifties, but his disheveled, unkempt appearance made him appear older. "Do you have the report on the escaped prisoner?"

Seidel tossed it on the desk.

"Who was the arresting officer?"

"Stan Quigley."

Leland scanned the report. "Tomorrow, I'll give him a command discipline." A Command Discipline—a CD—was given to cops by supervisors for minor infractions of the rules. It was up to the CO to decide on the proper punishment, which could range from loss of time to removal from a sector car. I won't take any time away from him, I'll probably just—"

"He won't be in tomorrow, Cap. Quigley and his partner went sick."

Leland's head snapped up from the report. "*Both* of them? Why?"

"Quigley hurt his back when he tripped over you and Kohler sprained his hand pun— I mean recapturing the prisoner," Seidel said with a straight face.

Leland studied the sergeant. They both knew what this was really about. Neither cop would have gone on sick report if Leland hadn't insisted on treating it as an escaped prisoner incident. *His first day in the precinct and he was at war with two cops! Maybe the whole Anti-Crime team! Maybe the whole precinct*!

"Turns out Pagan had a couple of outstanding federal warrants," Seidel continued. "He iced a couple of guys in Puerto Rico last year." The sergeant squinted through a cloud of cigar smoke. "A very bad dude." He looked around for some place to dump his ash. When he didn't see an ashtray, he flicked the ashes into his rumpled sports coat pocket. "Is there anything else you wanted, Cap?"

Leland's mind was reeling from his tactical blunder. He could only imagine what the rest of the cops were saying about him in the locker room, but he couldn't worry about that now. "This morning I saw you destroy department property," he said abruptly.

Seidel took the wet, soggy cigar out of his mouth. "That little hump, *Pagan*? He's not department property."

"I'm talking about the shade you threw out the window."

Seidel thrust the cigar back into his mouth. "That goddamn shade attacked me for the last time. At least three times a month that sonofabitch comes down on *my* head. I'm the only one it attacks. The other guys pull it, yank it. Nothing. I just walk by and *bang*! It's on me like a fly on shit. Look at my tie. Look at my shirt." He pointed at several small burn holes. "I coulda got self-immolated for chrissake."

Leland ignored Seidel's theatrics. "Sergeant, I expect my supervisors to treat department property with respect. This building looks bad enough. I don't need you making it worse."

Seidel's bushy eyebrows went up in genuine surprise. "Hey, Cap, in the big scheme of things it's only a worn-out window shade."

"It's not the shade, Sergeant. It's what it symbolizes."

Seidel's eyes narrowed. "What does it symbolize?"

"If supervisory officers don't respect department property, how can we expect our police officers to?"

Seidel's eyes narrowed to mere slits. "You *are* serious, aren't you?"

Leland met Seidel's squinty gaze. "Yes, I am."

"Okay, okay. I won't pull down any more shades."

"Or grab handcuffed prisoners by the throat."

"Yeah, that too."

By the expression of Seidel's face, it was clear that he didn't quite know what to make of his new commanding officer, and that was fine with Leland. Keeping the sergeant off balance was a good way to get his attention. He wanted to talk to Seidel about his attitude in general, especially about the way he handled prisoners, but he would review his folder first. "Okay, Sergeant," he said. "That'll be all."

At the door Seidel stopped. "Oh, by the way, Pagan says he's got AIDS."

"*What!*" Leland's heart thumbed in his chest and he prayed that none of the blood spattered on him belonged to Pagan.

Seidel exhaled a thick cloud of smoke. "I wouldn't worry about it, Cap. Twenty years ago every mutt I locked up claimed to be a Vietnam vet. Today, they all claim to have AIDS. He's probably full of shit."

Lt. Barry was behind the desk when Seidel came out of Leland's office. "What did he want, Marv?"

"He wanted to tell me I shouldn't grab prisoners by the throat and I shouldn't throw malicious window shades out the window."

Barry didn't know whether to laugh or cry so he just shook his head in dismay.

Seidel lit a cigar. "Jack, we can't afford another asshole like Sperling," he said in exasperation. "They'll close the fucking precinct down. You gotta keep a tight rein on this guy."

"Easier said than done," Barry said, thinking about how hard it had been to convince Leland that he shouldn't turn out the platoon. "Easier said than done."

Chapter Four

Leland was at his desk before seven the next morning. It was a habit he'd gotten into working at OPP and it had served him well. Most of the brass didn't get to work until ten and those three quiet hours gave him time to get a lot of work done without interruption.

But there was no such thing as quiet time in a precinct—especially the Five-five. Since he'd arrived this morning a steady stream of telephone calls and supervisors who needed something signed or approved had interrupted him.

Now it was after eleven and he'd hardly put a dent in the prodigious piles of memos, arrest records, and complaint reports that he'd planned to review. It made for boring reading, but buried somewhere in those piles of reports was the key to understanding the workings of the Five-five and the quicker he got a handle on it, the better off he'd be.

Barry stuck his head in the door. "Captain, Gloria Perez is outside. She'd like to say hello."

"Who?"

"Gloria Perez? CROC?"

"I don't have time, tell her—" He stopped when he saw Barry's eyebrows rise. "What?"

"Are you sure you want to do that?"

"Oh, all right. I guess I can spare a couple of minutes. Send her in."

Leland remembered what Barry had said about her looks, but he wasn't prepared for the woman who walked into his office. Gloria Perez was strikingly beautiful and the simple dark blue business suit she wore couldn't conceal the well-proportioned body underneath.

Her handshake was firm and she looked him right in the eye with a pair of large luminous black eyes. "Captain Leland. It's a pleasure to meet you."

He mumbled a reply and motioned her into a seat.

Gloria crossed her well-shaped legs. "I know you must be busy getting used to the precinct, so I won't take up much of your time. I just wanted to tell you something about what my organization does."

Leland smiled. "CROC?"

She returned the smile and her white teeth stood out against her light olive skin. "I had nothing to do with that name. My predecessor chose it. But as the name implies, we're in business to wrest the neighborhoods away from the drug dealers, the numbers men, and the petty street thieves. We do that by setting up block watcher groups, speaking at local schools, and getting people jobs."

"That's very commendable. I want to assure you that we will do everything we can to help."

She looked at him quizzically. "If you do, you'll be the first."

"Pardon?"

"Your predecessor, Captain Sperling, and *his* predecessor—I've forgotten his name—gave me the same spiel, but when push came to shove, they weren't much help."

Leland bridled at her characterization of his sincere offer of help as a "spiel." "Why wouldn't I cooperate?" he asked.

The puzzled expression remained. "You haven't been in patrol long, have you?"

Leland felt himself reddened. "What has that got to do with it?"

"It's been my experience that we—my organization and yours—have very different agendas. We shouldn't, but we do. For instance, I may ask you to put more cops some place and you'll tell me you can't because of manpower shortages or it doesn't fit the precinct's priorities."

Her know-it-all attitude was starting to irritate him. "Where," he asked curtly, "do *you* think we need greater police presence?"

She pointed at the precinct map on the wall. "For openers, you don't need three sectors on the Hill. That's just window dressing to placate the pompous asses who live there. You need more sectors in Death Valley, especially the Bulge."

He was astonished that she used the same pejorative terminology to refer to the precinct that the cops did. "Ms. Perez, I've issued a memo to all my officers instructing them to stop using those words to describe the precinct."

"Oh, please. What's wrong with them? It's a perfect description of Death Valley—both physically and psychologically. It *is* a valley and a behavioral sink—an area where chronic overcrowding exacerbates all kinds of pathologies."

"I took sociology 101, too," he said icily. "Nevertheless, my officers will not use that terminology."

She brushed her long, black hair out of her eyes. "You gotta be kidding. You've got criminals running wild in the streets and you're cranking out memos about semantics."

She stood up. "It's been nice meeting you, Captain. At least I know where you're coming from."

"By the way, Ms. Perez, where do you live?" he asked.

"On the Hill with the other pompous asses," she said with a grin.

Before he could think of a response, she was out the door, leaving behind only a lingering fragrance of perfume.

Leland stood back from the window so she wouldn't see him and watched her climb into her battered Volvo. She was an exasperating woman, but there was something about her that he found intriguing.

Just as he was about to turn away from the window, five cars pulled up across the street and twenty men piled out.

Leland had seen the Reverend Kawasi Munyika only on TV. In person, he looked even more imposing. In spite of the forty-degree temperature, the full-bearded Munyika wore a lightweight, multi-colored Dashiki and a neck full of various sized gold chains. His gaunt frame made him look even taller than the six feet, seven inches the press reported him to be.

Leland grabbed the phone and dialed Barry's number.

The lieutenant answered on the first ring. "I see them, Cap. I'm just about to call the borough."

"Good. Come into my office when you're finished."

~~

Leland and Barry watched the demonstrators from the window in Leland's office. "Does he have a permit to demonstrate?" Leland asked.

"Nope."

"Does he ever ask for one?"

"Never."

"What do we do about it?"

"Police the demo. No arrests. No hassles. Borough orders."

Leland was getting weary of his Operations Coordinator's casual attitude about proper police procedures and made a mental note to do something about it as soon as possible.

Leland read their signs and was puzzled by their generic nature. Some said *People's Freedom Party;* others said *Stop Police Brutality* and

Stop the Madness. "I don't get it," he said. "What exactly are they demonstrating about?"

"The arrest the Anti-Crime people made yesterday. They keep the signs non-specific so they can use them for other demonstrations."

"Was that prisoner connected to the People's Freedom Party in any way?"

"Nope. It's been a quiet week for Munyika. Any demonstration is better than none, I guess."

Leland had ordered all sector cars to respond to the station house. As the cars came in, Leland watched Lt. Hanlon assign police officers to positions around the growing group of demonstrators.

"Is the borough task force on the way?" he asked Barry.

"No."

"*What?*"

"It's like I told you yesterday, Cap. Chief Hightower's policy is for the precinct to handle all Munyika demonstrations. I call anyway, but they always say no."

Leland had never heard of a precinct being responsible for handling demonstrations by someone as high profile as Munyika. But he had the feeling that in his tenure here he would be hearing a lot of things he'd never heard of before.

Leland studied Munyika, who was standing on an overturned trashcan and bellowing orders through a bullhorn. "I guess it's time I met the Reverend Kawasi Munyika," he said halfheartedly.

~~

Outside, the crowd was even louder. Munyika shouted through the bullhorn: *"Stop police brutality. Stop the madness now,"* and the crowd picked up the rhythmic chant.

Leland threaded his way through the picket line and stopped in front of Munyika. "Reverend Munyika, I'm Captain Leland, the commanding officer of this precinct."

Munyika, pumped by his oratory, stared down at Leland, not seeing him for a moment. Then his eyes focused and he smiled. "Have you come here to arrest me or to protect me, Captain?" He had a deep resonant voice that sounded remarkably like Barry White.

"We're here to keep the peace."

"Then I suggest you arrest the police officers who beat up..." he turned to one of his aides and snapped, "What's the name of that dude was busted yesterday?"

The aide shrugged. "I don't know."

"You ought to arrest the cops that beat up what's his name," an indignant Munyika said to Leland.

"He wasn't beat up," Leland explained patiently. "He was trying to escape and only necessary force was used to affect the arrest. I was there and personally witnessed it."

Munyika grinned down at Leland. "Then while you're at it, go ahead and arrest yourself." That got a loud round of guffaws and chuckles from his entourage.

Leland turned away in frustration. There was no sense in talking to him. Lt. Barry was right. Munyika wasn't here to protest the arrest of "what's his name." He was here to get whatever publicity he could get.

Chapter Five

Carol Mazzeo jiggled her eight month-old son in her arms and watched the shiny apple-red Camaro roar up to the front of her house. She turned from the living room window and called out, "Peggy's here."

Twenty-six-year-old Eddie Mazzeo came out of the bedroom holstering his 9mm automatic. "Okay. Gotta go." He kissed his wife's cheek and the top of the baby's head. "Whew," he said wrinkling up his nose. "He stinks of talcum powder."

Carol patted down the sparse hair on the baby's head. "Better than something else."

"Yeah, I guess."

At the front door, she inspected him. She was almost a foot shorter than her six-foot-two husband and had to reach up to brush a piece of lint from his shoulder. She asked the traditional question that all cops' wives asked their husbands as they're going out to work. "You got everything? Gun, shield, wallet?"

And Eddie Mazzeo, following the traditional cop's ritual, patted his body to make sure he had the three critical items. "Yep. See you later."

"Eddie, you going to be home on time tonight?" She bit her lip. The question had come out sounding like a plea. Since the baby's birth, he'd been making a lot of arrests, and that meant a lot of time in court. She knew he was doing it for the extra money, still, she would have preferred that he spend more time at home with her and the baby.

"Don't know," he said. "If I make a collar, I'll be late. Don't wait up."

Eddie Mazzeo's small ranch home was in a middle class town in Westchester—in an area dubbed "civil service alley" because the reasonably priced homes attracted an inordinate number of police officers, firefighters, and other civil service workers.

Eddie skipped down the front steps and ran across the lawn that was his pride and joy. In summer he saw to it that the grass was lush and neatly edged, but now it was yellowed and withered by a late autumn frost. At the first sign of spring, he would be out with the fertilizer and grass seed and by June the lawn would once again be the best on the block.

Carol yelled after him, "Eddie, be careful."

He waved, but didn't look back.

The driver of the Camaro, a pretty girl with short auburn hair, rolled her window down. "Hi, Carol. Hey, that baby's getting bigger and bigger every day."

Carol half turned so Peggy Garrigan could get a better look at the baby's round face. "Yeah, and every day he's looking more and more like his father." Without thinking, she added, "Peggy, take care of him." Then she reddened. Eddie didn't like her to say that to his partners, especially a female partner.

They'd been married for three years but she still couldn't shake the feeling of dread every time he went to work. She watched the red Camaro pull away from the curb and disappear down the tree-lined street and wondered if she ever would.

~~

Peggy Garrigan, flicked her eyes away from the road and said, "That baby's adorable. He looks just like you."

Mazzeo ran his hand through his curly hair. "Yeah? You think so?"

She stopped at a traffic light and looked at him. "Definitely. He's got the same big brown eyes, the same nose." She ran her finger across his mouth. "And the same lips." She leaned across the seat and kissed him.

He pushed her away. "For chrissake, Peggy. Not here. What if someone should see us?"

She playfully tugged his ear. "Touchy, touchy."

The light changed and a horn sounded behind her. She flicked her middle finger at the impatient driver and stomped down on the accelerator, pulling away with a neck-snapping jump.

The Camaro was her toy. The salesman had recommended an automatic transmission, but she'd insisted on a stick. She loved the feeling of power that came from revving the engine through the gears. Sometimes on her day off she made the two-hour drive to the Catskill Mountains just to put the car through its paces on winding mountain roads. It was a good thing she was a cop or she would have lost her license a long time ago.

"What's been happening at the precinct since I've been off?" she asked.

"They dumped Sperling."

"We get a new CO yet?"

Mazzeo grunted. "Yeah. Some guy named Leland."

"*Richard* Leland? I remember him. He gave a lecture when I was in the academy. Hey, he's cute."

Mazzeo made a face. "He looks like he's sixteen for chrissake, even with that rat's ass mustache."

"What do you know from cute."

"I know he set a new precinct record. Just two days in the command and he's made the shithouse wall."

"Oh, no. What's his handle?"

"Captain Chaos."

"What'd he do?"

"What'd he not do? He wasn't in the precinct five minutes when he got his clock cleaned by an escaping prisoner."

"He get away?"

"No. Kohler caught him at the door."

Peggy shook her head. "What a welcome to Fort Frenzy."

"He's been pumping out memos like he gets paid by the page. Must have put out a dozen already."

"About what?"

"You name it. No more calling the Hill the Hill. No more calling Death Valley Death Valley."

"Why?"

Mazzeo shrugged. "He says it's racist."

"Jeez, what a jerk."

"And he's on a housecleaning kick, too. He even used his own money to buy a half dozen garbage can lids."

"You gotta be kidding. The kids swipe 'em?"

"The next day."

"What a doofus."

"He's got poor Jack Barry talking to himself."

"Old father Barry will calm him down. He always does."

"I don't know, Peggy. This guy's a professional Plazanoid. The word is he hasn't been on patrol since he was a rookie."

"He get dumped from headquarters?"

"The scuttlebutt is that Charlie Drum is Leland's hook. Drum sent him out to get a little patrol experience so he can make him a deputy."

"If it's experience he wants, he's come to the right place."

Fifteen minutes later Peggy pulled into a parking spot around the corner from the precinct station house. She started to open the door, but Mazzeo leaned over and kissed her. She didn't resist, but she whispered, "What if someone should see us?"

He pulled away. "Peggy, don't break my chops."

She checked her lipstick in the rear view mirror. "Eddie, lighten up."

~~

Mazzeo heard Billy Lafferty's high-pitched voice even before he walked into the locker room. Lafferty, a pinch-faced man in his early thirties, was the precinct's resident psycho. Every command has at least one cop who straddles the line between irreverence and insolence; courage and recklessness. More times than not, Lafferty crossed the line into the red zone. His often stated personal goal was to lock up "every scum-sucking skell in New York City." Trouble was, by his definition, anyone who broke the law, thought about breaking the law, or who even looked like he might break the law, was to him a scum-sucking skell. In the pursuit of his goal, he'd been known to push the envelope of legality to its limits. As he'd say to anyone who'd listen: "If the fucking skells don't obey the law, why should I?" Most of the cops, including Mazzeo, were convinced that Lafferty's recklessness was born of a self-destructive streak and because most cops didn't share his self-destructiveness, Lafferty had rapidly worked his way through a succession of partners. His latest, Charlie Reece, seemed to have a calming influence on him. So far, in the two years they'd worked together, neither one had been arrested.

Lafferty strapped on his protective vest. "Hey, Eddie, you hear the latest on Captain Chaos?"

"What'd he do now?"

"The first morning he was here he did a little snooping and caught two sectors and three footmen coming in early from the late tour. He gave 'em all command disciplines."

"*Seven* CDs! Sperling didn't give that many out the whole time he was here."

"Hey, Reece," Lafferty shouted over the top of his locker. "You're the PBA delegate. What are ya gonna do about this bullshit?"

Charlie Reece, a jowly man with a big belly, stuck his head around the locker. As PBA delegates went, Reece was unique. A lot of cops ran for the position because it gave them an excuse to get off the street and into an office job. But Charlie Reece had been a street cop for eleven years and was content to remain one. Three years earlier, he'd gotten fed up with day-job delegates who were never there when a cop got jammed up on a late tour. He campaigned on a promise to be a street cop delegate who would work around the clock and had won in a landslide.

"I got a meeting with him later," he said in a confidential whisper, even though what he was talking about wasn't confidential. "This guy's coming on like gangbusters and I gotta cool him down."

"What else did he do?" Mazzeo asked.

"He's treating that bullshit the other morning as an escaped prisoner incident," Reece said.

Lafferty banged his nightstick against his locker. "How can he do that? The guy never got out of the station house!"

Reece patted his partner's head. "Everyone knows that except Captain Chaos."

"The guy's got no balls either," Lafferty muttered.

Mazzeo strapped on his vest. "Why do you say that?"

"The prisoner busted Leland in the chops. Not only didn't Leland do anything about it, he stopped Seidel from tuning the guy up."

There was a moment of silence as the men pondered that scenario. Leland had violated an unwritten Five-five precinct rule: If a prisoner punches a cop, he has to be punched back. That wasn't police brutality; it was simply behavior modification.

Reece broke the silence. "Bottom line is he's gonna give Quigley a CD. I gotta get this guy to ease up."

Torres, a small, wiry man with a wide infectious grin, put his arm around the fat PBA delegate. "What if he don't ease up, Charlie?"

Reece lowered his voice and spoke out of the side of his mouth. "Then we might have to pull an unofficial job action."

"You mean a work slowdown?" Torres patted the PBA delegate's ample stomach. "Charlie, you slow down any more, you'll be going backwards."

Reece slapped Torres's hand away. "Up yours, you little wetback. Say what you want, but remember last year when Sperling was breaking balls about vacations? We went dead on summons activity for two weeks and he suddenly saw the light."

Mazzeo buckled on his gun belt. "I don't know, Charlie. I don't think this guy Leland is going to be the pushover Sperling was."

Reece shrugged. "They all got their Achilles heel. You just gotta find out where it is."

Torres looked at his watch. "Hey, we don't get down to roll call, there's gonna be another rash of CDs."

Lafferty slammed his locker. "Who's working tonight?"

"Friar Tuck," Reece answered.

"Let's give him a break," Mazzeo said. "You know how upset he gets when we show up late."

On the way down the stairs, Torres elbowed Reece. "Hey, Charlie, when you talk to the CO don't take no shit from him."

"I won't. Why'd you say that?" Reece asked.

Torres grinned. "'Cause I think if you break Leland's chops, he's going to have you transferred."

"You sound like you like the idea."

"I do. I wanna run for your job and get fat."

Reece playfully grabbed the smaller man in a headlock and threw his cap down the stairs. "You little spic bastard. You couldn't get elected cuchifrito-taster at the fucking Puerto Rican Day parade."

Sergeant Henry Engle stood in front of the platoon of thirty-four men and women and patiently waited for Mazzeo, Reece, and the others to fall in.

He was called "Friar Tuck" because of the ring of wispy gray hair surrounding his bald head and because in his youth he'd done time in a seminary. He was a mild-mannered man who seldom raised his voice and who had never been heard to utter an obscene word.

Engle looked up from his clipboard. "Torres, we're still getting complaints about the Joy Lounge. What are you doing about that place?"

"Short of nuking the joint, there's not a whole lot that can be done," Mazzeo muttered.

"That doesn't sound like the proper proactive entrepreneurial spirit to me," Lafferty deadpanned.

"That'll be enough of that," Engle said.

"I'm keeping my eye on it, Sarge," Torres said from the back of the ranks of much taller men and women. If there had been a height requirement when Torres took the police test, he'd still be driving a UPS truck. He claimed to be five-six, but Lafferty and Reece had grabbed him one day and stood him up against the measuring stick the detectives used for prisoner photos. Torres was barely five feet. But what he lacked in height, he made up for in heart.

He'd come to New York City from Puerto Rico when he was ten, but he'd never forgotten the poverty in his country and he'd been forever grateful for the opportunities available to him in the United States. He'd become a cop because he wanted to give something back to the country that had given him so much.

"Be careful," Engle cautioned Torres. "That bar is a bucket of blood. You have any problems, make sure you call for a backup."

"No problem, Sarge."

Reece goosed Torres with his nightstick. "That's a tough post, Shorty. You'd better take my stick too."

Torres whacked the stick away. "Stuff it up your fat ass."

Reece was making light of it, but the PBA delegate, paternal by nature, was truly concerned with Torres's safety.

From the day the Joy Lounge opened five years earlier, it had been a constant headache. Gin mills like the Joy Lounge were magnets for drug addicts, drunks, pros, and other assorted flotsam and jetsam. Fights between patrons were nightly occurrences. The frequent, and often violent, confrontations were a welcome sideshow to patrons so anesthetized to the normal highs and lows of life that only a cutting or a shooting could give them a rush. And these patrons had little use for the precinct cops' irritating habit of interrupting the bloodletting to make arrests and cart the losers off to the nearest emergency room.

Most of the time the objections were verbal in nature—with the occasional beer bottle thrown for rhetorical emphasis. But on occasion when temperatures were running hot, the objections escalated and the patrons had been known to take on the police. Thus, the Joy Lounge had earned the sobriquet cops used to describe such despised establishments: *a cop-fighter bar.*

Engle continued the roll call. "We're short tonight. Mazzeo and Garrigan, you'll double up. You've got Sectors Larry and Mary."

Mazzeo looked up from his memo book. "How come we got the Bulge again, Sarge? What about Reece and Lafferty?"

Lafferty looked down the row of cops between him and Mazzeo and grabbed his crotch. "Quit bellyaching, Mazzeo and do what the sergeant says."

Engle tried to look stern. "Mazzeo, I read the captain's memo at last night's roll call. We're not supposed to refer to parts of the precinct using that terminology."

There was a chorus of *"oohs"* and *"aahs"* from the ranks.

Mazzeo grinned. "Okay, how about we call it the infected appendix of the precinct?"

"How about the swollen scrotum?" Lafferty offered, grabbing his crotch again.

Engle reddened. He was an old-fashioned man and embarrassed easily when that kind of language was used, especially in front of women police officers. It didn't matter that those same female police officers often said things that made him blush as well. "All right, all right, that's enough with the smart remarks. Button up and look sharp. The CO wants to address you in front of the desk."

Earlier, when he'd been informed that Captain Leland wanted to turn the men out, Engle had rushed back to his locker to consult the *Patrol Guide* as to the proper procedures. In his four years in this precinct he'd never formally turned a platoon out in front of the desk; usually the platoon was informally dismissed from the sitting room.

Now, Engle, who'd been nervously rehearsing the proper commands in his mind, yelled in his best military voice. "*Attention.* Platoon, right face."

The snickering platoon did as they were told and turned toward a blank wall. A flustered Engle yelled, "About face." The four ranks made a ragged about face and this time, mercifully, they were all facing the door.

Leland, wearing a starched white uniformed shirt with gleaming gold captain's bars on his collar, stood behind the desk and studied the thirty-four police officers standing in front of him with mild trepidation. They were a sea of unknown entities. Who were the good cops? Who were the foul-ups? Which ones were the shirkers who did as little as possible? Which cops could be counted on to get the job done? In time he would learn the answers to these questions, but for now these police officers were unknown quantities, total strangers. And each one had the potential to bring an abrupt and ignominious end to his career.

He cleared his throat. "As I suppose all of you know by now, I'm your new commanding officer. Over the next several days and weeks, I will personally meet each of you individually. But in the meantime, I just want to give you a brief idea of what my policies are. I expect each of you to be and act like the professional police officer that you are. And that begins with looking good." His eyes swept the shoes in the first rank. "Apparently some of you have gotten the principle of the shine mixed up. Your *shoes* are supposed to be shiny, not your *trousers*."

He smiled, but the deadening silence and malevolent looks told him his attempt at humor had fallen flat. Hiding his embarrassment, he quickly added, "What I mean is, when you *look* good, you *feel* good."

Someone in the ranks muttered, "*Give me an A-men, brother.*"

Leland swallowed hard. The words weren't coming out the way he intended, and then he remembered what an old comedian he'd met at a retirement racket had once told him: "Making people laugh isn't easy," he'd explained. "First, you gotta get them to like you, otherwise you're gonna lay an egg. An audience don't laugh at someone they don't like."

In the thundering silence, punctuated only by the occasional squawk from the desk's radio, Leland realized that these cops didn't like him, and he was surprised at how much that bothered him.

He continued. "Language is an important part of our image. Foul language and racial epithets are counterproductive to our mission. There is no place for either in the vocabulary of a professional police officer. The department has spent a considerable amount of time and money training you and I expect you to put all that good training to proper use."

He had more to say, but their stony looks told him that this was clearly not the time or the place. Besides, he had a borough conference to attend in less than an hour. Frustrated at his poor beginning, he said abruptly, "All right, Sergeant, post the platoon."

Sergeant Engle was caught off guard. He had a fifty-fifty chance of getting it right, but he needed better odds than that. Before he had a chance to collect his thoughts, he shouted, "Platoon, right *face*." The platoon turned once again toward a blank wall. Flustered, he shouted, "Right face," two more times in rapid succession, which resulted in an equipment-clanging, leather-squeaking dance with grinning cops facing all directions.

"*Attention!*" Leland shouted above the laughter. The mingling crowd turned toward him. "Platoon, left *face*." They tuned to the left, toward the door. "All right, Sergeant. Take over."

The nonplussed Engle actually shouted, "Aye, aye, sir," before he blurted out, "Platoon, forward ho."

Leland could hear the chuckling and whoops of laughter as they filed out the front door. He hadn't wanted to usurp the sergeant's role, but obviously, Sergeant Engle didn't know the proper procedures for posting a platoon. He made a mental note to write a memo regarding that deficiency.

Outside, Billy Lafferty summed up everyone's impression of Captain Leland: "*What a fucking dork!*"

~~

Leland arrived early for his first borough commander's conference and walked into a room filled with zone commanders, precinct COs and their XOs. He recognized most of the faces by sight, but he didn't know many of them personally.

One familiar face stepped out of the crowd and came toward him. Leland had first met Inspector Warren Mann when they'd worked together on the planning committee for the last Democratic Convention. In the three months they'd been together, he'd been impressed with Mann's refreshing pragmatism and his ability to quickly absorb huge amounts of information in a short period of time. He knew that Mann was on the fast track and being groomed for a deputy chief slot.

Mann shook Leland's hand. "Richard, welcome to the Bronx. Come on, grab a cup of coffee and I'll introduce you to some people."

Leland poured a cup, but turned down a jelly donut. While he sipped his coffee, Mann introduced him to the group standing nearby. Each man offered congratulations or condolences, depending on how he viewed Leland's assignment.

"So," Mann said when there was a lull in the introductions, "Drum sent you up here for some patrol experience?"

"Yeah, and it's certainly been an experience so far."

Mann shook his head. "The Five-five. You really pulled the short straw on that one. It's the worst precinct in the Bronx. The city for that matter. When I first got here, Hightower gave me the tenth zone. There are five precincts in that zone, including the Five-five, but I wanna tell you, I spent most of my working time—and I don't know how many sleepless nights—worrying about your precinct."

"What makes it so bad?"

Mann shrugged. "You've got it all: high crime, politically astute community activists, Kawasi Munyika, and a lot of crazy cops." He leaned forward and lowered his voice. "And it didn't help that the last three COs were weak administrators. They let the cops and the PBA push them around. Now the inmates are running the asylum. The Five-five needs a tough boss. I guess that's why Drum put you there."

Leland stared into his coffee cup. He didn't have the heart to tell the inspector that there had been no grand design to his assignment. It was nothing more than the wrong phone call at the wrong time. "How do you like working for Hightower?" Leland asked, changing the subject.

"A lot of people here are afraid of him. He's tough, and he has little patience with incompetence, but he's a good boss. You do your job and he stays off your back. You'll have no problem with him."

Leland wished he shared Mann's confidence. He was about to ask another question when a deputy chief pulled Mann away to talk about an upcoming demonstration. "Richard," he called out over his shoulder. "Once again, welcome aboard."

"Thanks, Boss."

While Leland had been talking to the inspector, he'd been aware of a short, chunky captain standing in the corner glaring at him. He'd never met the man, but he knew him by reputation. Gregory Tyler was a "captain for life"—a derisive term used to describe a captain who, because of incompetence, bad luck, or a combination of both, was condemned to spend the remainder of his career as a captain with no hope of promotion.

In Tyler's case, bad luck had nothing to do with it. He'd achieved his terminal status by sheer monumental incompetence. In his fifteen years as a captain, the man had gone through a half dozen commands. As quick as he got one, he lost it. The wonder was that he kept getting another one. That thought must have finally occurred to someone in Personnel because his latest transfer was an assignment as an executive officer, a step down the career ladder.

"Apple Cheeks," as he was known because of the two vermilion patches on his chubby cheeks, walked up to Leland and put his pudgy hand out. "Greg Tyler."

"Richard Leland."

He smirked. "Yeah, I know. It must be a real shock for a headquarters hotshot like you to be dumped into patrol. Now you're going to see what *real* police work is all about."

Leland kept his smile. "Tyler," he said softly, "a captain doesn't get dumped *into* a precinct, he gets dumped *out* of a precinct."

Tyler's red cheeks glowed. "Listen, Leland. I've filled in at the Five-five a couple of times. Let me give you a piece of advice. You got a lot of problems in that command. That bitch, Gloria Perez, for one, is a real ball-breaker. You've got no supervisors worth a damn, and that Anti-Crime sergeant Seidel, ought to be committed. And the cops—well, they don't call it Camp Fuckup for nothing."

Leland couldn't help smiling. He was getting advice from a "captain-for-life" about how to run a command. "Thanks, Tyler, I'll try to remember that."

Just then, Chief Hightower came into the room and an expectant hush fell over the group. He was an imposing man whose mere presence could bring a room to full quiet.

"All right, gentlemen," he said, "let's get on with this meeting. I'm sure you have other important things waiting for you back in your commands." He looked around the room. "First, let me introduce you to the newest commander in our borough, Captain Leland. Dickie, stand up and let everyone see you."

Leland, wincing inwardly, rose. The only thing he hated more than being called Dick was being called Dickie. It had taken him a long time, with constant correction, to get everyone, including Chief Drum, to refer to him as Richard. He thought about correcting Hightower but, looking at the sea of faces staring back at him, decided this wasn't the time or the place.

When Leland sat down, Hightower pointed at a captain seated in the first row. "John, tell us what you've been doing to keep the lid on the Four-four."

For the next half hour, each precinct captain rose to deliver a mini state-of-the-command speech that was not much more than a commercial for the speaker. Leland noted that several captains, in describing what they were doing, subtly knocked other precincts in their efforts to make themselves look good. Apparently One Police Plaza wasn't the only place where politics was spoken. Still, he understood their reasons. Each man was competing for a limited number of promotional slots and if one could advance one's cause at the expense of a rival, what was wrong with that?

When the show-and-tell was finished, Hightower turned to his clerical sergeant. "Ralph, let's see the stat charts."

A PowerPoint slide came on showing the crime trends in all the Bronx precincts. The COs in the audience glanced at each other uneasily. Hightower's legendary "statistical inquisitions" were well known throughout the department and Leland was curious to see if the stories were true.

They were. For the next half hour, Hightower reviewed the complex sets of figures for each precinct, citing previous year's figures and percentages from memory. Leland was astonished at Hightower's ability to deal with such a huge amount of data. Each commander was in turn praised or castigated depending on the upward or downward direction of the red, green, and black lines on the graphs. When he came to the 40th precinct chart, he jabbed at an upward spike on the robbery line. "Captain Tyler," he said.

At the sound of his name, Tyler jumped up as though his chair was electrified. "Yes, sir."

The chief trained his frog-eyes on the pudgy captain. "I know you're not the CO, but you are in charge while Webb is on vacation." He waved a newspaper in the air. "What's this I read in the *Bronx Free Press* about a crime wave in the Four-oh?"

Tyler's red cheeks glowed as though he had a flashlight in his mouth. "Crime wave? There's no crime wave, Chief."

"Liquor store holdups." Hightower got up and began to pace the room. Leland noticed that the chief limped slightly. " How many have you had this year?"

Tyler squinted up at the ceiling as though he expected the numbers to appear there. Several COs glanced at each other and rolled their eyes. Apple Cheeks had no idea how many holdups had occurred.

"*Sixteen!*" Hightower's voice boomed. "It says it right here on page one, Tyler. How come the *Bronx Free Press* knows more about crime in your precinct than you do?"

Tyler's mouth opened and closed a couple of times like a beached fish, but nothing came out.

Hightower glared at the hapless captain in disgust. "When does Webb get back?"

"Tomorrow."

"Sit down. I'll talk to him."

Hightower's half-closed eyes scanned the faces seated before him. "Crime wave." He slapped the front page with a massive hand. "Gentlemen, there's no such thing as a crime wave. It's a fabrication of a bored, manipulating press. They concentrate on reporting one specific type of crime and damn if you can't find a crime wave. Crime wave is a *fiction!*" he shouted. "Unless,"—his voice dropped dramatically— "unless there is a pattern. *Then* it is a crime wave.

"If every time a perp holds up a liquor store he bites the owner's ear or only takes twenty dollar bills or pisses in the cash register—*that's* a pattern. And that means the same perp is doing all the robberies and I don't like that," he said almost in a whisper. "I'm a reasonable man, gentlemen. I know it's hard to stop sixteen perps from holding up sixteen liquor stores, but by God, you'd better be able to stop *one* perp from holding up sixteen liquor stores."

Hightower slammed the newspaper in the wastebasket with such force that it spun and fell over. "The bottom line is that I do not wish to read in the *Bronx Free Press*, or any other newspaper, that there is a crime wave in my Bronx. If you're paying attention to your crime stats, you should see a pattern develop long before some damn newspaper reports it. Do I make myself clear?"

There was a murmur of voices accompanied by vigorous head shaking. "All right. That's all I have for you."

As Hightower was leaving the room, he said over his shoulder, "Captain Leland, stop by my office before you go."

~~

Leland took a seat in the chief's cramped office and nervously studied Hightower as he signed a report for his administrative lieutenant. The office was small with one window that looked out on a plain brick wall. The chief's desk was a clutter of reports, memos, and statistical printouts. On the wall behind him were photos of the chief in the football uniforms of Boys High and Fordham. More than a half-dozen trophies crowded a shelf on the opposite wall.

The chief sat back in his high leather-backed chair and studied his newest precinct commander. "You're a bright man, Leland," he said out loud. But to himself he wondered how Leland could possibly work for a moron like Charlie Drum. "And you're a good staff man."

"Thank you, sir." Leland started to relax. Maybe he was going to get along with Hightower after all.

"But, you're not working in the Puzzle Palace anymore," Hightower said pointedly.

Leland sat up. "No, sir."

"You're in patrol. In the Bronx. In the Five-five precinct—the most difficult precinct in the entire city."

Leland nodded solemnly. He needed no reminder of that. All he thought about all day long—and through many sleepless nights—was the Five-five and how difficult it was.

Hightower thumped his ham-fist on his desk startling Leland. "In OPP crimes like homicides and robberies are simply lines drawn on a chart. But in patrol, they are life and death issues to be dealt with daily under the harsh white light of TV cameras, a prying media, and vigilant community groups."

"Yes, sir."

"Patrol is where the real police work is done, Dickie." Hightower's voice took on the passionate tone of a coach exhorting his men to go out there for the second half and do the impossible. "It's the crucible in which a man's true character and abilities are revealed. Patrol is the front lines where the real battles are fought."

"I understand, sir," Leland said gravely. But he didn't understand. *Where the hell was the chief going with this?*

"In my thirty-seven years in the department," Hightower continued, " I've seen many rising stars soar in the rarified, non-realistic atmosphere of One Police Plaza only to fizzle out in the cold, damp reality of patrol." He sat back and studied Leland, wondering if this hotshot captain was up to the challenge.

"How are you adjusting so far, Dickie?" he asked in an almost fatherly tone.

Leland was about to ask the chief to call him Richard, but the stern look on Hightower's face told him this wasn't the right time. "Fine, sir. There's a lot to learn, but I'm working on it. Chief... about that delayed Unusual..." Hightower waved a hand in dismissal. "Past history. I allow all my COs one mistake the first day in the precinct. So tell me. Have you made any innovative procedural changes yet?"

"Um, actually, no." Leland was furious with himself. Usually he had no problem with one-on-one conversations, but he was sounding like a tongue-tied dolt. He suddenly remembered his memo on precinct description terminology and blurted out, "I did write a memo forbidding my people to refer to parts of the precinct as the Hill and Death Valley."

Hightower's bulging eyes blinked once. "Why?"

"Why? Ah, because that kind of terminology could be construed as... racist." When Hightower continued to stare at him without saying anything, Leland added tentatively, "As you'll recall, Chief Drum sent down a memo regarding racial slur code words and—"

Hightower's face contorted in disgust. "That memo was such bullshit, I didn't even pass it down to my precinct COs."

"Oh, really? I thought—"

"Captain, the first thing a good CO does is get his priorities straight. If writing memos about suspected racial code words is high on your list of priorities, you're living in la-la land."

"Yes. I mean, no, that is, I thought..." Leland let the sentence die because at the moment he was so flustered he didn't know what he thought.

Hightower rummaged around on his messy desk and picked up a piece of paper. "I got your report on the escaped prisoner, Captain."

"Oh, good."

"I have just one question.

"What is that, sir?"

"Why?"

"Why what, sir?"

"Why did you make it an escaped prisoner incident?"

"Because the prisoner got away from the arresting officer and—"

"He never got out of the station house."

"Well, technically that's true, sir." *What is going on? Leland asked himself. Am I the only one in the world who believes the prisoner actually escaped?* "I saw it as a good opportunity to make an example of sloppy police work," he added lamely.

"So you gave the cop a command discipline."

"Yes, sir."

"I understand the arresting officer and his partner went sick."

"Um... yes." Leland wondered how Hightower knew all this. Was there a spy in his command? Barry? Seidel? He made a mental note to find out who the spy was. He didn't need someone in his command running to Hightower every time something went wrong in the precinct.

Hightower flipped open a folder containing a thick printout. "Captain, do you have any idea what your sick report stats are?"

Leland reddened. The command sick report was just one of dozens of memos and statistical data reports that he still hadn't found time to read.

"The command's sick report summary is on my desk, but there's been so many other—"

"Did you read it?" Hightower snapped.

"No, sir."

"The Five-five has the highest sick report rate in the entire borough and it would appear that your handling of a questionable escaped prisoner incident has added to those dismal figures."

"I didn't know. That is, I—"

Hightower leaned forward. "Captain, let me remind you again, you're not in Kansas anymore. Your job is not just to shuffle forms and reports around all day. You're dealing with cops. Surely in one of the many management books you memorized for your promotion exams you must have read something about human psychology. You must know that for every action there's a reaction. In the future, before you take an action, consider the reaction."

"Yes, sir," Leland mumbled.

"That is all." Hightower reached for a report in his in-basket, signaling that the meeting was over.

As Leland was going out the door, Hightower said, "Captain, one more thing. I demand high standards of performance from my precinct commanders and I will hold you to that standard." He paused and then added, "Regardless."

"Yes, sir." Leland understood the implied threat. If he screwed up, Hightower wouldn't hesitate to dump him—Charlie Drum or no Charlie Drum.

Chapter Six

A black Mustang with dark tinted windows slowly drove down Glendale Street. Marvin Seidel, crouched down behind the wheel of his battered Honda Civic, whispered into his portable radio, "Heads up. The Mustang is back."

The dashboard radio said it was 1:45 a.m. Seidel kneaded his stiff knuckles. The early morning December chill was playing hell with his arthritis. "Come on you sonsofbitches," he whispered. "Snatch it so we can all go home and get some sleep."

For the fifth night in a row, at Captain Leland's direction, Seidel and four members of his Anti-Crime team had been sitting on stakeouts at various locations, hoping to catch an auto theft team that had been working the precinct.

While he sat shivering in a car that was as cold as a tomb, he recalled the bizarre conversation he'd had with Leland after he'd casually mentioned that a car theft ring was operating in the precinct. He'd thought the captain was going to take a heart attack.

"*How many cars stolen?*" Leland asked, actually rising out of his chair.

"Seven in the last two months," Seidel responded.

"Do you realize this is a crime wave?"

"I wouldn't call seven stolen cars a crime wave."

"But these are not just stolen cars. You've described a pattern. Newer, expensive sports cars; all stolen after midnight; always during the week."

Seidel studied the hyper captain from behind a blue smoke screen. "I guess you could say it's a pattern. So?"

"Sergeant, are you aware that there have been sixteen liquor store holdups in the Four-oh, since the beginning of the year?"

"I can't say that I am, Cap. I tend to just pay attention to crime in the Five-five."

"All with the same MO," Leland added. "Which means the same guy did all sixteen."

"Okay, if you say so." Seidel had no idea where Leland was going with this.

Leland paced the office. "There's an MO here, too. Obviously, the same person or persons are stealing these sports cars."

"Captain, thousands of cars are stolen in this city every year."

"But not in my precinct. And not when there is clearly a pattern that could be misconstrued as a crime wave."

"Who would call seven stolen cars a crime wave?" an exasperated Seidel asked.

"Chief Hightower," Leland whispered, looking around as though he expected the chief to fall through the ceiling. "That's who."

Now Seidel got it. Captain Leland was on the verge of a nervous breakdown because he was terrified Hightower would get wind of this. "What do you suggest we do?" he asked, knowing what the answer would be.

"I want you and your Anti-Crime people to start doing stakeouts all over the precinct."

"Cap, I only have four men available right now."

"I don't care. I want the stakeouts to start tonight."

And so, starting that night, they had begun the stakeouts. For the first four nights nothing happened and it got to the point where Seidel hated to go back to the station house because Leland was always there waiting for him.

"Anything tonight?" he'd ask with a desperate look of hope.

And Seidel would shake his head and say, "No, Cap. Nothing."

And the desolate captain would wander back into his office. It was pathetic.

Now Seidel, shivering from the chill, kneaded his knurled fingers. He hated stakeouts. Proactive by nature, he found stakeouts boring and tedious. He preferred stalking his quarry, but the MO of car thieves precluded such tactics. It was just like in the old movies when the Great White Hunter was called in to shoot the rogue lion. "I can't chase the lion," the hunter would patiently explain to the frightened villagers. "I can only set the bait and wait for him to come to me."

In this case the bait was a brand new Porsche Boxster S. Why anyone would park a sixty-thousand-plus dollar sports car on Glendale Street without an armed guard watching over it was beyond Seidel's comprehension. Still, he was grateful to the asshole owner for providing the bait.

When the Mustang had passed through the block ten minutes earlier, he was certain they were the team. But when they didn't come back, he was just as certain they weren't. Now, with a satisfied smile, he watched the Mustang's tail lights flash on and off as the occupants slowed to get a better look at the Boxster.

Police Officer Paul Carrington, the youngest member of the Anti-Crime team, peered out from a darkened doorway halfway down the block and stamped his feet to ward off the night chill. "You run the plate, Sarge?" he whispered into his radio.

"Nope. Dirty plate. Couldn't see the number."

Police officer Stan Quigley and his partner, Tom Kohler, whose bulk took up most of the van's front seat, sat parked at the opposite end of the street. Quigley keyed his mic. "How many in the car?"

"Dunno," Seidel muttered. "I couldn't see shit through those fucking tinted windows. There oughta be a law about that."

Quigley grinned in the darkness at his partner. Even though they were operating on a confidential channel, department procedures forbade profanity. But Marvin Seidel wasn't big on procedures.

"Sounds like he's really pissed, Tommy."

Kohler grunted and concentrated on the headlights slowly approaching.

The Mustang stopped alongside the Porsche and a squat figure, wearing baggy pants and a Knicks jacket two sizes too big, jumped out.

Police Officer Al Soika, who was standing in a doorway across the street from Carrington, whispered into his radio. "Hey, we got a Knicks fan, boys and girls. Male, black, twenty."

"Probably stole the jacket," Quigley said.

"Knock it off," Seidel hissed into the radio.

Knicks jacket walked up to the car, took a quick look up and down the block, and pumped the right front fender up and down several times.

"Bingo," Quigley said.

Kohler nodded. The man was rocking the Porsche to make sure it didn't have a tilt-activated alarm system.

From his end of the block, Seidel caught a glint of metal as the man slipped a "Slim Jim" out from underneath his Knicks jacket. "Wait until he gets in the car," Seidel whispered into the radio.

From the van Quigley and Kohler watched the man efficiently work the thin strip of metal down between the door and the window. In less than ten seconds, the door was opened.

"Damn," Quigley said with grudging admiration. "It takes me longer to get into my own car using a key!" He saw the amused expression on Kohler's face and said, "Don't say it, Tommy. Don't say it."

Knicks jacket quickly jumped into the Porsche.

Seidel started his car and pulled away from the curb, " Okay," he said. "Let's take 'em."

Kohler gunned the engine. The tires screeched and the van sped up the block going the wrong way. It took the Mustang's driver only a second to realize they were cops. He jammed the Mustang into reverse. Then he saw Seidel's car coming down the street from the other end and hit the brakes.

For just a moment the Mustang stood still, its engine roaring. With its black body and darkened windows it looked like a sleek mechanical beast capable of leaping to the nearest rooftop. Then, without warning, the driver floored the accelerator and the Mustang, leaving a trail of burning rubber and smoke, jumped forward—toward the van and Quigley and Kohler.

The Mustang and the van, both traveling at top speed, were quickly closing on each other. Quigley grabbed the dashboard. "Holy shit!" he shouted in his high, squeaky voice. "The crazy sonofabitch is playing chicken!"

With unconcerned determination, Kohler firmly gripped the wheel with his big hands and concentrated on the rapidly approaching car whose oncoming headlights loomed larger and larger. When Quigley was sure they were going to collide, he closed his eyes. He tried to think of a prayer, but he couldn't remember one. At the last second, the Mustang veered to the left and catapulted onto the sidewalk exploding garbage cans in all directions.

Kohler slammed on his brakes and, before the vehicle had stopped its forward motion, threw the van in reverse and stomped down on the accelerator. The van quivered as the wheels spun to gain traction. Then the tires gripped the asphalt and the vehicle shot backward. Even in reverse, the van managed to keep pace with the fishtailing Mustang because it was slowed by continuous collisions with clusters of garbage cans and parked cars. Quigley opened his eyes. The Mustang was almost at the corner.

"If they make it to the avenue, they're home free," he shouted. "There's no way this old van will keep up with that new Mustang."

Suddenly the Mustang tilted at a crazy angle and a plume of sparks shot out from underneath the car as it mounted a garbage can and skidded into a fire hydrant. A geyser of water shot up, mixing with the steam from the Mustang's ruptured radiator.

Quigley jumped from the van and dove for the cover of a parked car. Squinting through a fine mist of water and steam, he trained his gun on the tinted windows. Then his jaw dropped when he saw Kohler's hulking shape sprint around to the driver's side of the car. The big man swung his heavy six-battery flashlight and the side window shattered. As the driver revved the engine in one last futile effort to dislodge the car from the garbage can wedged in the under-carriage, Kohler slammed the flashlight into the side of his head. Before the dazed man knew what was happening, Kohler yanked him through the broken window as though he were a rag doll.

The other door flew open and a wild-eyed man stumbled out with his hands held high. "Don't shoot," he said to Quigley. "Just keep that crazy motherfucker away from me."

When Knicks jacket had seen the van coming down the street he'd jumped out of the Porsche and sprinted up the block toward Seidel. The Anti-Crime sergeant abandoned his car in the middle of the street and tried to head him off, but the much younger man was too fast for him. As Seidel puffed and chugged his way up the street in pursuit, his two Anti-Crime cops, Carrington and Soika, blew past him as though he were standing still. Paul Carrington had been a varsity runner in high school, but even he couldn't keep up with the fleeing perp.

Seidel, plodding at a pace only slightly faster than a walk, wheezed an oath as he saw the perp disappear around the corner. By the time he stumbled up to the corner, he saw Carrington and Soika frantically shining flashlights in doorways and under cars.

"I'm too old for this shit," Seidel muttered, hugging a No Parking sign pole for support. "Forget it, guys"—his voice cracked from lack of oxygen—"he's gone."

"*Officer...*"

Seidel looked up. An elderly woman was sitting at a window on the third floor. *What the hell was she doing looking out the window at this time of night?*

"He ran into one of those buildings," she said, pointing to three identical tenements across the street.

Seidel unholstered his gun. "Come on," he said, forgetting about his impending heart attack. "We'll each take a separate building."

Seidel disappeared into the first building and Soika went into the second.

Carrington moved toward the third building. He told himself his heart was pounding from exertion, but he was a young cop and too inexperienced to admit that the pounding was as much from fear as from physical effort.

With a gun in one hand and a flashlight in the other, he cautiously nudged the first vestibule door open with his foot. Beyond was a second door. Through a broken window pane he could see the hallway was pitch black; something not uncommon in a ghetto tenement. Residents sometimes stole the light bulbs for their own use. On the other hand, it was possible that the perp had broken or unscrewed the bulb.

He gingerly nudged the second door open with his foot, but it didn't open all the way. *Something was stopping it.* Before his mind could register what that might be, the door slammed back at him knocking the flashlight from his hand. It smashed on the tile floor and went out, plunging the hallway into blackness. A fist came out of the darkness catching him on the side of the head and driving him back against the wall. Pinwheels of light floated in the darkness. As he bounced off the wall, a flurry of punches rained down on him. Throwing his hands in front of his face, he kicked out and felt the satisfying feel of soft flesh. His unseen assailant, exhaling sharply from the kick, bounced off the wall and hurled himself at the young cop with renewed vigor.

In the darkness, most of the wildly thrown punches missed their target, but one caught Carrington in the nose and he immediately felt the salty, iron-rust taste of blood in the back of his throat. Instinctively, he threw a punch with his gun hand and there was a startling explosion and a blinding flash as the gun went off.

The man screamed and fell to the floor. *"I'm shot! Motherfucker... you shot me."*

As Carrington frantically groped on the dirty tile floor looking for his flashlight, the first vestibule door banged open and the hulking figure of Tom Kohler loomed behind the beam of his flashlight. The light flicked to Carrington's bloody face. *"Sweet Jesus! Are you shot?"*

"No... I shot him. I think."

Kohler turned the light on a frightened, wide-eyed kid no more than eighteen or nineteen. He lay slumped against the wall groaning and holding his neck as blood trickled through his fingers and on to his Knicks jacket. Kohler bent down and pulled the hand away. There was a small wound at the front of the neck.

"I guess that's where the bullet went in," Carrington said wide-eyed.

The kid groaned louder.

Kohler turned the kid's head and saw another slightly larger wound. "Here's where the bullet came out."

The kid groaned even louder.

Kohler stood up. "The bullet went in and out. It's barely a graze. Unfortunately, he'll live."

The kid had been certain he was going to die, but when he heard Kohler's favorable diagnosis he reacted immediately. His life was not going to end in this dirty dark hallway after all. In fact, it was just beginning. He sprang to his feet with a renewed sense of purpose. He would start a new life outside this dirty hallway. It would be a new beginning.

But he made the mistake of trying to start his new life by going through Tom Kohler. The big cop grabbed the kid's throat with one massive hand, brought the six-battery flashlight down on his head with a resounding crack, and the kid crumpled to the floor unconscious.

While Carrington was cuffing his prisoner, Seidel and Soika came rushing into the hallway. "What've you got?" The sergeant's tone was flat and professional, but there was deep concern in his eyes. Marvin Seidel's Anti-crime cops were his kids.

"No problem, Sarge," Kohler said. "Paul had a little tussle with the perp. He shot him, but he's only grazed."

Seidel peered at the bleeding gash on the man's forehead. "Where'd he get that?"

Kohler shrugged. "When he found out he wasn't going to die, he tried to get away, shouting something about a new life."

Soika peered over Seidel's shoulder and winced at the gash on the perp's head. "He should have quit while he was ahead."

Seidel turned his attention to Carrington. The young officer's chest was still heaving and, although it was cold in the hallway, his brow was beaded with sweat. Seidel had shot and killed two men in his career. He knew exactly what the young cop was going through. Every new police officer imagines he knows what to expect if he has to shoot someone. He knows there will be heart-pounding fear followed by breath-catching elation. But there's another surprising emotion that only a cop who has actually shot someone experiences: Guilt.

It had taken Seidel a long time to figure out why he felt guilty about shooting someone who had tried to kill him. In his years as a detective he'd interviewed dozens of murderers and had seen more remorse from people who had accidentally run over a cat. But the difference between murderers and him, he'd learned, was that he—and most other cops—were decent human beings who valued and respected life. It was that value system that triggered guilt. But even knowing that, the little, nagging guilt never went away. After the department medals were awarded, after the congratulatory drinks were drunk, and after the soothing words of friends and loved ones faded away, one troublesome question would remain forever: *Could I have handled it another way?*

Seidel had seen many good cops driven from the job because of that guilt and he was determined not to let that happen to any of his men. He would keep an eye on Paul Carrington and look for the telltale signs.

He put his arm around the young cop. "Paul, you did good."

Carrington reddened at the extravagant praise from his sergeant. "Thanks, Sarge," he said, wiping the blood from his nose with his sleeve.

When they came out of the hallway, Quigley was sitting behind the wheel of the van keeping an eye on his two manacled prisoners sprawled on the floor in the back. "The Five-five Anti-Crime team strikes again!" he shouted gleefully.

"What the hell are you so happy about?" Seidel snapped. " I wouldn't exactly call this a textbook example of how to run a stakeout."

An exuberant Quigley unbuttoned his jacket and spread it open revealing a sweatshirt that showed a cartoon of an old log fort bristling with arrows. Under the drawing were the words in bold lettering: THE 55TH PRECINCT- WELCOME TO FORT FRENZY! "Hey," he said, "we're only living up to our name."

Seidel squinted at the grinning cop. "Captain Leland will be real happy to hear that."

~~

As Seidel walked through the precinct's massive oak doors, he collided with Captain Leland who was rushing out. "I was just on my way to the scene. What happened? Who got shot? Who got hurt?"

Seidel squinted at his CO through a cloud of smoke. "Everything's under control, Boss. We collared the auto theft team. Three under arrest. One perp shot, but nothing serious. Carrington got busted in the nose, but he's okay, too. They're both at the hospital."

Leland exhaled in relief. "That's it?"

Seidel studied the ash at the tip of his cigar. "Except for a little cleanup that'll be needed on Glendale Street."

"Cleanup? What cleanup?"

"The perps tried to get away by driving on the sidewalk."

"And? "

"And they sideswiped a few cars."

"How few?"

"About a dozen."

Leland felt a headache coming on. "Is that it?"

Seidel took a puff. "Yeah, that's it. Except for the fireplug."

"*What fireplug*? Sergeant, stop spoon-feeding me bad news."

"The perps hit a fireplug. It's still gushing."

Leland was already composing the Unusual in his head. It would involve hospitals, the Fire Department, and the Department of Public Works. He still had a long night ahead of him and his tour was supposed to have been over an hour ago.

Leland fought to keep his voice calm. "Sergeant, why is it that everything you and your Anti-Crime people do turns into a major disaster?"

"Captain," Seidel said patiently, "we made a good collar. Sometimes, things get broken."

Leland could only look at the grizzled sergeant in amazement. He made a mental note to get Seidel and his team additional training. A lot of additional training.

"I have to get to the hospital," Leland said, and brushed past Seidel.

Slowly, Seidel hobbled toward the desk with the gait of a man who's just gotten off a horse.

Lt. Hanlon, who'd been listening to the exchange between Leland and Seidel, said, "Marv, why are you walking like you got kicked in the nuts by a mule?"

"Don't ever get into a foot race with a teenage perp."

"That was a good collar, Marv. I didn't hear the captain say thanks."

"Captain Chaos wouldn't know good police work if he tripped over it." Seidel rubbed his sore calves with his sore hands. He was tired and just wanted to go home, but he still had to go to the hospital and see how Carrington was doing.

"I wonder how the brass at One Police Plaza selects precinct COs?" he asked Hanlon.

The lieutenant grinned. "Very high tech. Something involving a monkey and a dart board."

Seidel shook his head sadly. "Jesus, I hope so. I'd hate to think they picked Leland on purpose."

Chapter Seven

"I can't do it, Richard. Out of the question. I've got work backed up till the next millennium. Maybe in a few months."

"You owe me, Vinnie."

"Whoa! You used to be a hellava lot more diplomatic when you were in OPP."

"I don't have time to be diplomatic. My sergeants are using the property room for a locker room."

Leland was speaking to Captain Vinnie Spinoza from Building Maintenance, but he was looking at Lt. Barry, who was sitting across the desk from him slowly shaking his head as if to say Leland was wasting his time.

Leland decided to play his ace. "Vinnie, remember the final exam in captain's school?"

Spinoza's voice dropped to a whisper. "Jesus, Richard, don't bring that up on the phone."

"Vinnie, no one taps Building Maintenance telephones. When can I expect your people?"

"I don't know. Next week at the earliest. I'll see."

"Tomorrow at exactly 0800 hours I'll be standing on the steps of the station house to greet your people as they pull up."

"That's impossible."

"Coffee and donuts will be provided free of charge."

"All right. All right."

"Thank you, Vinnie."

"Fuck you, Richard."

Leland hung up. "Cross that problem off the list," he said to Barry. "Building Maintenance will be here tomorrow morning."

Barry shook his head in admiration. "I gotta tell you, Boss, the last three COs broke their asses trying to get them up here. I was beginning to doubt that Building Maintenance actually existed."

"I guess there's some benefit to being a Plazanoid, huh, Lieutenant?"

Barry started to laugh, and then caught himself.

Leland smiled mischievously. "It's okay, Loo. I know they call me that."

"You know how cops are."

"Yeah, I know how cops are."

And he did. He'd been in the precinct for just two weeks, but he was beginning to get a feel for it. Seidel's Anti-Crime team had made a great arrest, although at the time he'd been too distracted thinking about the wake of destruction they'd caused to notice. But the next day, he'd called Seidel and his team into the office and personally thanked them for a great job. Quigley, the cop he'd given a CD, was there and he didn't seem to be holding a grudge. Maybe there would be no war. Maybe the cops had begun to accept him.

Or maybe not.

~~

The next day, Eddie Mazzeo and Peggy Garrigan came out of the station house and gingerly stepped over two large hoses that ran from the basement to the street. Muddy, malodorous water pulsated from the hoses into an open manhole.

"I got to hand it to Leland," Peggy said. "He's really got things hopping around here. Two days ago we got a new cleaning man. Now this."

"This has nothing to do with Captain Chaos," Mazzeo said. "Barry has been asking for Building Maintenance and a new cleaning man forever.

"Eddie, give the man credit for something."

"I will. As soon as he does something useful."

"Like shaping us up?"

Mazzeo unlocked the radio car door and grinned at her. "Not a chance."

Peggy looked at him over the roof of the car. "Ten bucks says he does."

Mazzeo laughed, but he didn't take her up on the bet.

Eddie Mazzeo steered the radio car into Catherine Street, a narrow, concrete canyon lined with grim tenement buildings. At one time these buildings with their stately rectangular courtyards and ornate facades had been the proud homes of blue collar workers, but now the once scrubbed brick walls were covered with the spray-painted "handles" of graffiti artists and the "tags" of neighborhood street gangs.

During the summer, especially on hot nights, the thousands of people who lived in these cramped buildings flooded into the streets to escape the oppressive heat of the poorly ventilated apartments. On nights like that, cops held their breath because heat and ill-tempered people were an explosive combination. But tonight the weather was on the side of the law. A gusty December wind had driven almost everyone indoors.

Peggy's eyes locked on two teens shuffling up the street with that hip-hop, ghetto-walk they all worked so hard to master. Two sets of eyes glared back at her with a burning hostility that was palpable even from this distance. Peggy ignored the "fuck you" looks and instead concentrated on their body language. When she was satisfied they weren't "dirty," she looked away.

Mazzeo, who'd also been closely watching the pair, resumed his conversation. "Why do you stick up for Captain Chaos all the time?"

"I feel sorry for him."

"Sorry? Lafferty is right. He's a dork."

"Give him a break, Eddie. He's still new."

"When you look good, you feel good," Mazzeo wailed in the exaggerated tone of an evangelist preacher. "He has us mixed up with the honor guard at the Puzzle Palace."

"He wants us to look good. What's wrong with that?"

"I'd like to see how good he'd look if he spent his day chasing skells through dirty cellars and across rooftops. I'll bet he's never made a collar in his life."

Peggy rolled her eyes. "Eddie, this is me you're talking to. Don't try and make it sound like you spend every waking minute of your time rolling in the streets with felons."

"You know what I mean."

"I know what Leland means. Look at Lafferty. His uniform always looks like he got caught in a mudslide."

"Don't use that slob as an example."

"Okay, how about you, hotshot? Look at your shoes."

Mazzeo reddened. He took great pride in his appearance, but his shoes were a mess. "Hey, I was out in the rain for two hours last night with an overturned truck."

Peggy poked his side. So since last night you haven't found time to shine your shoes?"

Mazzeo threw up his hands in resignation. "Okay, okay. Enough already."

"All I'm saying is cut the captain some slack."

Mazzeo turned onto Longview Avenue. "Why? He's here for only one reason and that's to get his ticket punched and get promoted. He doesn't give a shit about you, the precinct, or me. He's gonna do his time here and crack the whip on us so he can look good to the assholes downtown. Then he's outta here; another deputy inspector to wander the halls of One Police Plaza."

"My, aren't we bitter."

"Not bitter, just realistic."

Peggy looked at her watch. They were halfway through the tour. "Pull over," she said. "It's my turn to drive."

A half-hour later they were driving down Holland Boulevard. Peggy glanced in the rear-view mirror and saw a radio car with lights flashing speeding down the wrong side of the avenue. "You hear anything on the radio?" She asked Mazzeo.

"No, why?"

There's an RMP coming up behind us in an awful hurry. She pulled to the side and the other car screeched to stop alongside them. Lafferty was behind the wheel. "You won't believe this shit," he said. "I just gave some guy a summons for running a light."

"You're right," Mazzeo said. "I don't believe you gave out a summons."

Lafferty's face scrunched up in a tight grin. "Hey, I give one out every now and then just to keep in practice. So listen to this. The guy goes, 'You can't give me a ticket, I'm an ex-government official.'"

"What'd you do?"

"I stuck it up his ass. What else? When I hand him the summons I go, 'What kind of government official were you?' I figure maybe I bagged an ex-Secretary of State of something. 'I worked for the Post Office,' he goes. You believe that shit? The guy delivered mail and got pissed on by dogs for chrissake. Ex-government official my ass."

Peggy stared at Lafferty in disbelief. "You sped the wrong way down a crowded avenue to tell us *that*?"

"Yeah, it's funny, don't you think?"

She looked at his partner, Reece. "How do you put up with him?"

Reece rolled his eyes. "Every tour I do with this man is worth a thousand days plenary indulgence. I figure by the time I die, I get to pass Purgatory and go straight to Heaven."

The four of them paused to listen to a radio transmission. When it wasn't for either car, Mazzeo said, "Quiet night."

"Yeah," Reece said. "I hate quiet tours because I have to listen to Billy's whacky ideas all night. I could go for a nice exciting bodega holdup right about now."

"Yeah, right," Lafferty said. "By the time you got your fat ass out of the car, the perp would be in Jersey."

Reece put his hat on and pulled it down over his eyes. "Resume patrol. You're giving me *agita*."

~~

The next two hours were relatively quiet with just the routine calls—past burglaries, reports of stolen cars, and the usual assortment of the sick and dying. Peggy turned onto Gates Avenue—the dividing line between the Hill and Death Valley—and looked at her watch. "Another half hour and we head back to the barn. You going straight home?"

Mazzeo was silent for a moment. "No, I'll go back to your place."

"Don't do me any favors," she said, bristling at the patronizing tone in his voice.

"What's the matter with you?"

"Nothing."

In angry silence, she mechanically steered the car up and down the streets of their sector and thought about their "relationship"—whatever the hell that meant—and her ambivalence toward it. She knew the pluses by heart: He was good looking, funny, gentle and compassionate. There was only one minus: He was married. How the hell, she thought for the umpteenth time, did I get mixed up with a married man?

The radio squawked a message: *"Sector Adam, respond to a 10-52 family disturbance."* She listened to Reece acknowledge the job and smiled. He was probably glad to have something to do besides listen to that maniac Lafferty.

A family disturbance. That was how it all started just a little over a year ago. She and Eddie had been working together for less than three months. Like a lot of female-male partnerships, there was a certain uneasiness, things left unsaid, but understood nevertheless. Most male cops were convinced that women couldn't handle themselves in the street and, recalling the actions of some of her contemporaries, she had to admit there was some justification for that opinion. She couldn't understand why some of these women became cops in the first place.

They were terrified of the street, terrified of guns, terrified of being—a *cop*. They did everything in their power—including getting pregnant—to get off patrol and into a cushy clerical assignment.

Not her. From the moment she'd heard her first war story from her father, a retired homicide detective, she knew she wanted to be a cop. Two months after her twenty-first birthday she was sworn in. Academically, she was in the middle of her Police Academy class, but she was in the top ten percent of her physical class, and the third best marksman. When she and another woman were given their assignments to the Five-five, she was ecstatic. The other woman threw up. Even in the Academy the Five-five had a reputation as the busiest and craziest precinct in the Bronx. Who wouldn't want to work in a place called Fort Frenzy? As far as she was concerned, it was the perfect steppingstone into the Detective Bureau.

In the beginning, Eddie was cool. Clearly, he didn't want to work with her. But all that changed the night they responded to that first family disturbance. Statistically, a family disturbance is the most dangerous call a cop can respond to. The atmosphere is often a witch's brew of raw emotions, potential violence, ambivalent family ties, and an undercurrent of fear or hatred of the police that can escalate from a shouting match to a homicide in a heartbeat.

While they were still climbing the stairs they heard shouting. When they got to the apartment, Mazzeo said, "Do you remember what they taught you in the Police Academy?"

Peggy, stung by the condescending tone in his voice, snapped, "Yeah, do you?"

Mazzeo rolled his eyes and banged on the door with his nightstick. A heavy-set woman, bleeding profusely from a cut on her forehead, opened the door.

Following the prescribed tactic—separate the combatants—Mazzeo led the drunken man, who was taller and heavier than he was, into the living room, while Peggy remained in the kitchen to calm the woman. When Mazzeo judged the man had cooled down sufficiently, they returned to the kitchen.

As Mazzeo was explaining the legal options to the woman, she suddenly turned toward her husband and without warning kicked him in the testicles. Enraged, he lunged for her. Mazzeo stepped between them and jabbed the man in the stomach with his stick. The man doubled over and went down. The woman, inflamed by the attack on her husband, snatched up a frying pan and slammed it into the side of Mazzeo's head.

His knees buckled and, as he was going down, the man grabbed for his holstered gun. Peggy lunged at him, but he backhanded her and she slid across the kitchen table and onto the floor.

Stunned by the blow from the frying pan, Mazzeo struggled to fight off the taller and stronger man, but the man was in a drunken rage and ripped the gun from his holster. Peggy got back on her feet in time to see the man fumbling with Mazzeo's weapon, trying to pull the trigger. She'd drawn her gun, but she couldn't shoot because she was afraid of hitting Mazzeo. She swung her nightstick and it came down on the arm holding the weapon. There was a dull snap and the man, screaming in pain at his broken forearm, dropped the gun. She drove the pointed end of her stick into his solar plexus. His eyes rolled up into his head and he slid to the floor gasping for breath.

Mazzeo, still shaking off his grogginess, snapped handcuffs on him. Peggy spun toward the woman, who was reaching for the frying pan again. "Listen, bitch," she shouted in voice raspy with fear and anger, "you just *twitch* and so help me God I'll lay you out."

After Peggy processed the arrest, she rushed to the hospital and waited outside the emergency room while Mazzeo was treated for his head wound. When he came out his head was shaved and they'd applied a bulky dressing. "How're you doing?" she asked anxiously.

He shrugged. "X-rays were negative. All I've got is six stitches and a world-class headache."

They stood on the sidewalk outside the hospital and babbled about meaningless things. They were both pumped by their shared brush with danger and neither of them wanted to go home. Finally, Mazzeo said, "How about I buy you a drink?" He looked at her curiously. "You saved my life."

With a start she realized she had saved his life—and probably her own. "No, I didn't," she mumbled, "but you can buy me a drink anyway."

They stopped at a bar across the street from the hospital. With each drink and with each retelling of the story, the incident went from scary to funny. By the time the bar closed, they were laughing so hard they had tears in their eyes.

Outside on the sidewalk, they reverted to talking about trivial things and she sensed that he, like her, was still too keyed up to sleep. "Would you like to stop by my place for a nightcap," she blurted out.

"What the hell," he said. "We're off for the next three days. There's plenty of time for sleep."

Back in her apartment, as they sat in the living room listening to her favorite Patsy Cline album, she studied him in the dim light. He no longer looked like the same man she'd turned out with at the beginning of the four-to-twelve tour tonight. But neither was she. They'd become different people. Tonight's events had forged a bond between them—a unique, strong, bond that seldom develops, even between a husband and wife. He looked like a vulnerable little boy with his partially shaved head and bulky dressing.

All she did was touch his cheek.

~~

It was early the next morning when he woke her with a kiss. She rolled against him and muttered into his chest, "What time is it?"

"Four-thirty. I gotta go." He paused, as if unsure what to say. "Peggy—"

She put her finger to his lips. "Don't say anything, Eddie. I'll see you in a few days. We'll talk."

They did talk, but not about that night, at least not right away. Finally, after three weeks of them both pretending nothing had happened that night, he said he wanted to see her again. To her amazement—and not a little shame—she agreed.

And in this way she entered into a dubious relationship with uncertainty and ambivalence.

Another radio transmission brought her back to the present. "Eddie," she said, breaking the silence, "what do you tell Carol when you don't go home?"

Mazzeo was looking out the window, intently watching four men standing in a doorway where crack was sold. "That I made a collar and got hung up in court."

Neither spoke for a long time after that.

~~

Police Officer Hector Torres came out of the tenement building feeling optimistic. He'd spent the first half of his tour knocking on doors trying to convince people that together they could do something about the Joy Lounge across the street. He'd been met with fear, disbelief, and ridicule by some; but others expressed anger because they were afraid to let their children play outside the building. They wanted something done about the Joy Lounge and it was these people that he planned to organize into the nucleus of an ad hoc tenant group.

He was standing on a stoop across the street from the Joy when a man came rushing out of the bar. "Yo, officer," he shouted to Torres. "There's a problem inside. You best check it out."

As Torres hurried across the street, he thought about putting out a call for a backup, but he quickly dismissed the idea. He told himself he'd check out the "problem" first. But the real reason was that Torres, like most cops, was reluctant to call for a backup. In spite of the training, many cops still clung to the old Texas Ranger mentality that said: "I can handle this alone."

Inside, Aretha Franklin was shrieking out a soul tune on the jukebox. People stood three deep at the bar, pretending they didn't see him come in, but no one came into a bar like the Joy Lounge without being sized up carefully. Failure to spot an irate husband, boyfriend, wife or girlfriend coming through the doors could be, literally, fatal.

He yelled over the music's din. "What's the problem?"

The bartender gave him a blank look and shrugged. Just then he heard sounds of shouting and chairs being knocked over in the back room and he went to investigate. To the encouraging shouts of onlookers, one man was holding another over a pool table and beating him with a broken pool cue. Torres knew the combatants and recognized most of the spectators. He'd arrested almost all of the Joy Lounge regulars at one time or another. He stepped forward to grab the pool cue and never saw a man step out of the crowd behind him and smash a full bottle of beer over his head.

Suddenly, he was on his hands and knees, blinking down at the beer-soaked tile floor through a very long narrow tunnel. He looked up just in time to see a well-aimed kick coming toward his face. There was a blinding red flash and he felt himself rolling on the beer-slick floor. An instant uproar of voices filled his ears, reminding him of angry surf.

And it triggered a memory.

He was a kid again, riding the waves in Coney Island. A rogue wave caught him and rolled him like a rag doll, filling his ears with the terrifying sound of the surf as it ground his body into the coarse sand and sharp seashells. His searing lungs sought a gulp of air as he tumbled in the belly of the beast. He thought it would never end. He thought he was going to die. Finally, the wave spit him out on the beach, coughing and gasping for breath.

But this wasn't Coney Island, and it wasn't the sea and sand that were punishing his body; it was fists and feet. Through a red haze, the pool table loomed before him. Doing his best to ward off the punches and kicks raining down on him, he crab-crawled toward its shelter. He slithered under the table and reached for his radio, but it had been ripped away from his belt. Suddenly, grasping hands clawed at his legs and he felt himself being dragged out from under the table.

And the terrible, awesome surf pounded down on him again.

~~

"Ten-thirteen, assist police officer, in the Five-five... 421 Sumter Avenue... what units responding?"

"Christ!" Mazzeo said, grabbing for the mic. "That's the Joy Lounge."

Peggy flipped on the lights and siren and stomped on the accelerator. As the car leapt forward, Mazzeo keyed the mic, "Sector Larry on the way." Other units responding quickly followed his transmission.

The New York City Police Department uses dozens of radio codes, but none has the heart-thumping impact of a Ten-thirteen. A Ten-thirteen means a cop, one of their own, is in trouble and the "trouble" can range from having a difficult time subduing a prisoner to being shot. You never know until you get there. And that's what cops do. Get there. Fast.

Peggy Garrigan, concentrating on the traffic in front of her, skillfully weaved around stopped vehicles and accelerated past the ones that ignored the lights and sirens. Mazzeo leaned forward and strained to hear the radio over the unrelenting wail of the siren, praying for the dispatcher to come on the air and say that the call was unfounded. At Sumter, Peggy took the turn on two wheels and the RMP roared down the block. They could see flashing lights of other radio cars already on the scene.

"Good Christ... !" Mazzeo muttered as they pulled up.

Even on a quiet night the sidewalk in front of the bar teemed. But now in the glare of revolving dome lights, at least two-dozen men and women swirled around a half-dozen cops who were flailing and jabbing with nightsticks. A handful of women, wearing everything from skin-tight sequined dresses to jeans and tank tops, joined the men in pelting the cops with bottles and rocks.

Three bottles caromed off the radio car's windshield as Mazzeo bolted out the door and plunged into the screaming crowd. An unseen hand grabbed for his gun. He spun around, swung his nightstick, and felt the sharp crack of wood against bone. The hand let go of his gun. He pushed forward and was blindsided by a punch to the cheek. He saw stars and his knees buckled, but he forced himself forward. He couldn't fall down. Not here.

A shrieking woman, who'd lost one of her stiletto heels, knocked his hat off and it was instantly trampled underfoot. Ignoring the gobs of spit and flying bottles, he swung his stick at the hate-twisted faces in front of him.

Suddenly, Reece was beside him. "What's going on?" Mazzeo shouted over the shrill screeching of *"Police brutality"* and *"Off the pigs!"*

"Torres is inside," Reece said, his chest heaving with exertion. "We gotta get to him." He chopped with his stick and a handful of people parted.

Mazzeo, fending off blows, helped him open a path. At the door, Mazzeo and Reece met four other cops and together they charged the door. A group of snarling men with eyes and minds blurred by alcohol tried to stop the cops, but the momentum was theirs and they burst into the bar.

Most of the patrons had already spilled out into the street; some to join in the mayhem going on out front, but most because they knew it was a very bad idea to be caught in a bar where a cop had just taken a beating. The few patrons who'd chosen to stay took one look at the wild-eyed cops coming through the door and realized they'd made a very big mistake. As they scrambled to get out, the cops, now in a white-heat rage, flailed wildly at every passing head. In seconds the bar was empty except for a surly bartender holding a sawed-off baseball bat.

Mazzeo moved toward him menacingly. "Drop the fucking bat," he shouted.

The bartender smiled scornfully and tossed the bat on the bar.

"Where is he?" Mazzeo asked.

"I didn't see nuthin'."

"Where the fuck is he?" Mazzeo snarled.

The bartender nodded toward the rear of the bar.

Shoving tables and overturned chairs out of the way, the cops rushed to the rear. Mazzeo was the first to reach him. If he hadn't been told it was Torres, he wouldn't have recognized the blood-spattered body sprawled among overturned chairs. Gently, Mazzeo turned Torres over. His face was a raw, bloody pulp and his ripped uniform hung from his skinny frame in tatters.

A shaky hand clawed at Mazzeo's sleeve. One eye was swollen shut, but the other eye, wide with terror, stared out from a bloodied face. "Help," he whispered hoarsely. "Help... "

"It's okay, buddy," Mazzeo said soothingly. "You're going to be all right, Hector."

Mazzeo heard a voice behind him. *"Mother of God!"*

He turned and looked up into the ghost-white face of Sgt. Engle. "He's hurt bad, Sarge. We gotta get him to a hospital right away."

Engle took one look at Torres and knew immediately that there was no time to call for an ambulance. He spoke into his portable radio and his voice was surprisingly calm. "Anybody in an RMP outside the Joy?"

Peggy Garrigan, who'd been using the car to herd people off the street and on to the sidewalk, answered. "Garrigan. What do you need, Sarge?"

"I need a car at the front entrance. *Now.*"

There were a few dozen people between her and the door, but she nudged the car forward. Instantly, a screaming mass of angry faces closed in on her. Hands and faces pressing against the windows obscured her vision. She had the bizarre sensation that she was underwater, piloting the car through a sea thick with frenzied humanity. As the mob pummeled the car with fists, feet, and bottles, one man climbed up on the hood and tried to kick out the windshield. She tapped the accelerator and then stomped on the brake. The man cartwheeled off the hood and disappeared into the crowd.

Suddenly, the car began to rock. *They were trying to tip it over!* She jammed the shift lever into neutral and floored the accelerator. The roar of the engine scattered the people in front of her. She snapped the gear into drive and the vehicle jumped forward. Through the spittle-covered windshield she saw a group of cops beating a path toward her. As the way opened in front of her, she gingerly tapped the accelerator. Then something crashed against her side window and it shattered in an explosion of glass chips. Hands reached in and grabbed for her. She felt a sharp pain as an earring was ripped away. She gunned the engine and left the terrifying, grasping hands behind.

She drove the radio car up on the sidewalk and stopped directly in front. Mazzeo and three cops carried Torres out and gingerly handed him into the back seat. Mazzeo stayed in the back, wiping the blood from the unconscious cop's face. Engle jumped into the front seat. "Let's go, Garrigan," he shouted. "Cortland Memorial."

As they drove off the sidewalk, a dozen bottles rained down on the radio car. Peggy flipped the windshield wipers on to clear the spit and shards of glass. Fortunately, the windshield held.

~~

A trauma team was waiting when the radio car screeched to a stop in front of the emergency entrance. Engle, Garrigan and Mazzeo helped the staff lift the unconscious cop onto the gurney. Engle followed them inside, leaving Garrigan and Mazzeo alone.

Now that they were away from the mêlée, Peggy's hands began to shake uncontrollably. To give herself something to do, she took a handkerchief and tried to wipe Torres's blood from Mazzeo's uniform.

He pushed her hand away angrily. "Those motherfuckers!" he shouted, savagely kicking the side of the dented radio car. "Those mother-*fuckers!*"

"Take it easy, Eddie."

"*Take it easy?*" Did you see what they did to him?"

She'd never seen him like this and it frightened her. His face was chalk-white with anger and he looked at her with eyes that weren't focusing. "It's okay, Eddie," she said soothingly. Hector's going to be fine." She prayed she was right. "It's over."

He glared at her and slowly his eyes came back into focus. "It ain't over," he said in a voice constricted with rage. "It ain't fucking over *yet*."

She opened the car door and pushed him in. "Come on, let's get back to the station house. The tour's over."

~~

Within minutes of Garrigan and Mazzeo leaving the hospital, Leland arrived. He ran into the emergency room and found Sgt. Engle talking to a dark-skinned Indian doctor.

"How is he, Doc?" Leland asked.

The doctor turned a serene face to Leland. Like most emergency room doctors who serviced neighborhood ghettos, he had long since stopped being distressed by the carnage he saw daily. To protect his own sanity he'd learned to blur the distinctions between patients: Cops, felons, children, old women were all the same to him. He did his best to help each one of them, but he never allowed himself the luxury of wondering who did, and who did not, deserve his help. His only concern was that there was enough blood, oxygen and beds to handle the never-ending tide of dying and near-dead that daily swept through the doors of his emergency room.

Dealing with patients was one thing. Dealing with their loved ones was another. Early in his career, he'd learned to rely on the jargon of medicine to insulate himself from the pain felt by friends and relatives. Saying a patient's vital signs were worsening was preferable to saying a patient was dying.

"The officer," the doctor said in a clipped British accent, "came in with a fast pulse and high blood pressure. We are doing a CAT scan to ascertain the full extent of his injuries, but the most obvious injuries appear to be to the head and the eye, which has swelling in the area of the zygomatic arch. His right pupil was dilated; signs of an epidural bleed, and it was necessary to make a bore in the left temporal area to prevent brain herniation."

Leland, impatient with words he barely understood, snapped, "Is he going to be all right?"

"It's too early to tell, Captain. The epidural bleed has been compressed for now. Thanks to the burrholes, the right pupil is responding, but the left eye looks compromised."

"What does that mean?"

"The pupil appears blown and it looks like he has a blow-out fracture of the left orbit. He'll require maxillo-facial surgery, as well as ophthalmology and neurosurgery." The doctor hesitated. He believed in revealing the true condition of his patients, but sometimes that had to be balanced against the ability of a loved one to handle the truth. But this captain who was asking all these questions was not a member of the patient's family and there was no need to pull punches. "The right arm and leg are flaccid," he added.

"Meaning?"

"Possible brain damage. We'll know more later."

As the doctor was heading for the elevator, the doors flew open and a grim Sergeant Seidel strode in chomping on a cigar. A nurse pointed a finger at the offending cigar and said sternly, "I'm sorry, but there's no smoking permitted in here."

Seidel scowled at her. "Go away," he said in a gravelly, menacing voice.

The nurse opened her mouth to speak, but she saw the intense look in his eyes and thought better of it.

"How's he doing?" Seidel asked Leland.

"He's getting X-rayed. The doctor says it's too soon to tell."

Seidel grunted. "I just came from the scene."

Leland had all but forgotten the Joy Lounge. When he'd gotten the report of the Ten-thirteen, and the subsequent street brawl, he'd commandeered a radio car and was on his way to the Joy. But then he heard Engle on the radio making a request for a trauma team. Technically, he should have gone to the scene of the disturbance first, but he decided the welfare of one of his cops was more important. "I'd better get over there right away," he said starting for the door.

"No need, Cap. It's over. The street has been cleared. Everything's cool."

"What happened?" Leland asked.

"For openers, Torres's gun is missing. Not too surprising. The mutts never miss a chance to steal a piece. As best we can tell, Torres was called into the bar to break up a fight. For some reason they turned on him. We don't know if it was a setup or what."

"Why would it be a setup?"

"The crowd at the Joy Lounge has a reputation for cop fighting. Henry, how many times has a cop been hurt there this year?"

"At least five," Engle answered.

"Five?" Leland repeated incredulously. "Why hasn't the SLA closed the place down?"

"The State Liquor Authority can be very selective about these things," Seidel said, carefully watching the captain.

Leland caught his meaning. "You mean friends in high places?"

"Yeah, but we don't know who those friend are."

Leland looked toward the double doors at the end of the tiled-floor corridor and his jaw tightened. Somewhere behind those doors a police officer—one of *his* police officers—was fighting for his life. "I'm going to close that bar," he said softly.

Seidel grunted. "Good luck, Cap."

Chapter Eight

The "four-to-twelve" tour was held on reserve in the station house until almost one-thirty in the morning. When Leland was certain that there would be no further flair-ups at the Joy Lounge, he called the borough office and received permission to dismiss the platoon.

Upstairs in the locker room, a charged silence hung in the air as men, exhausted and high-strung, changed into their civilian clothes and left one by one.

Lafferty slammed his nightstick against the side of his locker. The resounding crash made the already tense men jump.

"Knock it off, asshole," Mazzeo snarled.

"*Five* cops," Lafferty shouted. "Five cops hurt in that fucking bar this year and now Hector. This shit's gotta stop."

"What do you have in mind, Billy?" asked Jim Elliot, a lanky black cop, who was examining a ripped sleeve.

"I say we teach those mothers a lesson."

George Oliver, another black and Elliot's partner, picked a piece of glass out of his blue riot helmet. "How do you figure on doing that?" he asked.

"We go back to the Joy Lounge and kick some ass."

Oliver rubbed an angry bruise on his left cheek. "Don't sound like a bad idea to me."

Elliot grunted. "Hell, sounds like a damn *good* idea to me."

Lafferty studied their weary, smiling faces and realized that they didn't think he was serious. "Hey, I'm not kidding. I say we go back there and kick some serious ass."

Every cop in the locker room stared at Lafferty in silence. They weren't smiling now because what he was proposing was crazy—even for him. Still...

"Whoa, guys," Reece said, sensing the mood changing. "Don't even think about it."

"Why not?" Lafferty said.

"Because it'll bring us nothing but grief, asshole. IAB will come down on this command like a ton of shit."

"Screw Internal Affairs," Lafferty snarled. "Let 'em come."

A young redheaded cop named Victor Martin spoke up. "That's easy for you to say, Lafferty, but I'm on the sergeant's list and I don't need IAB on my ass."

"Hey, Martin, fuck you *and* the sergeant's list okay? Either you're a Five-five cop or you're not."

Martin flushed at the implication that he was afraid, started toward Lafferty. "Hey, asshole, I've been in this command as long as you have. Don't tell me—"

Mazzeo stepped between them. "Take it easy. We got lumped up enough for one night. We don't need to beat up on each other."

"I'm telling you we can't let these mutts get away with this shit," Lafferty said, unwilling to let go of his idea.

"I took some lumps tonight, too," Reece said. "And I'd like to tune those guys up same as you, but as your PBA delegate I gotta tell you it's wrong. Vic is right. IAB will come in here and rip us all a new asshole."

Lafferty hurled his bloodstained uniformed shirt to the floor. "The job doesn't give a shit about us. Even our CO wimped out. Captain Chaos ran to the hospital so he wouldn't have to get his nice clean white shirt dirty at the Joy."

"That's bullshit," Reece said. "Leland went to the hospital to see how Torres was doing."

"Yeah, right. What is he, an MD? He didn't show up because he was protecting his ass. Pure and simple." Lafferty sat down between Elliot and Oliver. "You guys saw what they did to Hector."

The two cops busied themselves buttoning their shirts.

Lafferty stood up and paced in the aisle. "I'll tell you one thing," he continued. "If we don't do anything, pretty soon we won't be able to put a footman *or* a sector in that area. The mutts will own it."

There was a crushing silence in the locker room as the men pondered what they pretended they didn't hear Lafferty say. Lafferty broke the silence. "I say we go back there. Who's with me?"

Lafferty looked at Elliot and Oliver. "How about you guys?"

"All right, I'm in," Oliver said without hesitation.

Elliot buried his face in his locker. "I would," he mumbled, "but the sergeant's test is coming up and—"

"Man, will you stop that shit?" Oliver said. "You use that lame excuse for everything. Since you've started studying for the exam, you've become a real pussy."

"Up yours, George. Just because you're too stupid to pass the damn test—"

"Save the anger for the Joy," Lafferty said. "You in, Jimmy? Yes or no."

Jimmy Elliot looked at his partner and shook his head in disgust. "All right. I'm in."

Lafferty put his arm around Reece. "How about you, pard?"

"As your delegate, I'm telling you this is wrong."

"How about as my radio car partner?"

Reece studied the slightly built cop and sighed. "You hump. If I don't go, who'll protect your skinny little ass?"

"Wait a minute. What if there are innocent people there?" Vic Martin asked.

Lafferty snorted. "In the Joy? Gimme a break."

"I don't know about this," Martin said. " I expect to be made with the next batch of sergeants."

Lafferty slammed his locker door shut. "So what? Oliver has a chance to go to the Bureau. Elliot wants to be a sergeant. I want Anti-Crime. We all got things we don't want to jeopardize. Are you in? Yes or no?"

Martin looked around at the rest of the men for some hint of what they were thinking, but they avoided his eyes. "All right," he said softly. " I'm in."

Tom Kohler had said nothing during this whole discussion. The big Anti-Crime cop was a born-again Christian, but before his conversion—a miraculous event that had shocked and dumbfounded everyone in the command—he'd been the toughest, hardest drinking cop in the precinct. Even crazier than Billy Lafferty. Now the six-foot-seven cop had become a model of forbearance and a Bible-carrying, gentle giant.

Lafferty poked Kohler with his stick. "Hey, Tom, I know you're a holy roller and all that shit, but the way I see it, this is a simple case of good versus evil. Whaddaya say?"

Kohler snapped his combination lock shut and turned to look down at the diminutive Lafferty. "Billy," he said in a gentle voice that belied his size, "I think we must all do what Jesus taught us."

"Which is?"

"Turn the other cheek."

"Turn the other cheek? Wait a minute. Didn't he also say 'an eye for an eye'?" Lafferty smiled smugly at the others. He had the big man there.

"No, he didn't, Billy."

"He didn't? Well, who the hell said it?"

"God the Father."

"What's the difference?" Lafferty said in frustration. "God the Father, Jesus, and the other guy—what's his name? —they're all part of the same trifecta or something, right?"

Reece smacked the top of Lafferty's head. "Show a little respect, you ignorant atheist bastard."

"It's okay," Kohler said in a compassionate tone that only frustrated Lafferty more. "Jesus also teaches forgiveness."

Lafferty grabbed the big man's arm. "Tom, listen to me. Jesus never worked the Five-five, okay? If he turned the other cheek here, he'd have been DOA before he even made it to Calvary."

Kohler patted Lafferty's cheek with a massive hand. "I pray for you every day."

"Ain't nuthin' worse than a whacko religious fanatic," Lafferty shouted, after he was sure the big man had left the locker room. He turned to Mazzeo. "You're the last one, Eddie. You in or what?"

Mazzeo had been listening to Lafferty and the others with mixed emotions. He wanted more than anything to go back to the Joy Lounge and exact some street revenge on the people who had beaten Hector Torres. But Reece had a point. Trashing the skells in the Joy would bring the wrath of the department down on them.

He looked into the five faces of those who had agreed to go and he knew that they, like himself, didn't want any part of Lafferty's hare-brained scheme. Still, Mazzeo had been a cop long enough to know that the people who had beaten Torres would never be brought to justice. And that wasn't right. Maybe street justice wasn't the answer, but what else was there? "Okay, I'm in," he said quietly.

Lafferty pumped a fist in the air. "Way to go. That makes six and that's enough to handle the skells in the Joy."

Mazzeo slammed his locker shut. "You got a plan, Billy, or do we just go in and kill everyone?"

"Of course I got a plan." Lafferty reached into his locker and pulled out a paper bag. "This is something I saved from last Fourth of July's contraband."

He spilled the contents of the bag—a half-dozen M-80 firecrackers—onto the bench. "We stick these on the ledge of the shithouse window at the back of the bar. When it blows, the bar will empty out and we'll be waiting outside."

"Lafferty, you are one crazy sonofabitch," Reece said, studying the M-80s."

"Hey, I do my best."

Elliot waved a blackjack in the air. "Jacks only. Agreed?"

Everyone nodded. Lafferty looked at his watch. "It's almost two. The Joy closes at four. We'll hit them around three."

"That gives us time to get a couple of beers at Corr's," Reece said. "I could use a drink."

Lafferty stuffed the M-80s in his pocket. "Damn, this brings back memories of my gang days."

Jim Elliot slipped up behind Lafferty. "Who were you with, Billy?"

"The Astoria Falcons."

"Shit." Elliot sneered. "I was with the Harlem Zombies. We ate white-ass fairies like you for breakfast."

"You're playin' with your puddin', Elliot."

~~

Peggy Garrigan was waiting for Mazzeo outside the station house. "Go ahead," Mazzeo said to the others, "I'll catch up."

Peggy looked puzzled. "What's up? Aren't you coming with me?"

"No, I'm going to stop with the guys."

"Eddie, you said— "

"I know. Listen, I'm all keyed up. I need to unwind. Have a couple of beers."

"I have a couple of beers in my refrigerator," she said coldly.

"Peggy, why don't you just go home."

Tears welled up in her eyes. "Eddie, I was there, too. I'm still shaking. I *need* you tonight."

Mazzeo wanted desperately to go with her, but now that was out of the question and he certainly couldn't tell her the real reason he was staying. He put his hands on her shoulders. "Peggy, tomorrow night I promise—"

She pushed him away. "Fuck you. There isn't going to be a tomorrow night."

As he watched her walk away, he almost ran after her, but then he remembered Lafferty and the others. Reluctantly, he turned and headed for Paddy Corr's bar.

Paddy Corr's, the precinct's watering hole, had all the prerequisites for a cop bar. It was close to the station house and the civilian clientele, reflecting the ethnic mix of the neighborhood, was made up of hard working blue-collar blacks and Hispanics. Not much chance of a cop running into a former client here.

When Corr's opened in 1940, the Five-five precinct had been a mostly Irish neighborhood and Corr's bar was just one of dozens of Irish saloons that occupied strategic street corner locations. But after the war, the young men and women who grew up in crowded tenements wanted something more for their children. The allure of fresh air, tree-lined streets, and the lush sprawling lawns of suburbia pulled them away from the Bronx in droves and they moved to distant communities with strange sounding names like Levittown, Hicksville, and Tarrytown.

As they abandoned the old neighborhood, the Irish bars began to close or were taken over by the new inhabitants. Clancy's became Players. Noonan's became the Paradise Lounge. And the Shamrock became Reverend Moses Goodfellow's Evangelistic Church of the Heavenly Waters of Life.

By the '90s, Paddy Corr's was the only one left; the dinosaur of Irish saloons. It, too, would have gone the way of the others if it wasn't for the steady, if modest, flow of income from cops in the Five-five. The bar barely turned a profit for Paddy Corr, but he was a widower in his seventies and what he made from the bar was enough to pay the bills and have a little left over to make the annual pilgrimage to the Old Country.

Mazzeo stepped through the door and was immediately assailed by the smell of stale beer and cigarettes. He recognized most of the regulars by face, but he didn't actually know any of them. There was an uneasy truce between the cops and the neighborhood clientele, and nodding at each other was as close as the two groups ever got.

The Five-five cops usually congregated at the far end of the bar so they could keep an eye on the front door, but tonight they had secret things to talk about, criminal things, things that they didn't want anyone else to hear, and they'd retreated to huddle in the back room.

Paddy wiped a glass with a dirty bar rag. "Hello, Eddie," he said with a thick brogue that sixty years in this country couldn't erase. "What'll you have?"

Lafferty insisted the brogue was phony. He claimed that if you woke up old man Corr in the middle of the night, he'd talk just like everyone else. And one night, after too many beers, he had to be physically restrained by the others from driving up to old man Corr's home in Westchester and testing out his theory.

Mazzeo tossed ten dollars on the bar. "Gimme a beer, Paddy."

The little man with his large, pointy ears, tiny squinty eyes, and a massive head covered with white curly hair, looked like a leprechaun sprung to life. He slid the bottle across the bar. "I heard about Hector Torres. A terrible thing that. God take the dirty bastards that did it." He shoved Mazzeo's money aside. "The first one's on me. To Hector."

Mazzeo held up his bottle. "I'll drink to that." The cold beer had a soothing effect on his parched throat, made hoarse from all the yelling. He wanted nothing more than to sit with Paddy, listen to the old man rant about the IRA and the bloody English, and get smashed. But there was something that had to be done tonight and he couldn't do it drunk.

In the back room, the others were talking in uncharacteristically hushed and subdued tones.

"I just called the hospital," Reece said, pulling out a chair for Mazzeo. "Hector's still in the operating room. The Chaplin and Hector's wife are at the hospital now."

Lafferty slid into a chair next to Mazzeo. "Check this out." He held up his handiwork, a cluster of M-80s with all the fuses twisted together. "I put this on the window sill attached to a half-smoked cigarette. In a couple of minutes, *boom*! And the fun begins."

Reece eyed the lethal package. "You missed your calling, Billy. You should have been a terrorist."

Lafferty grinned. "It ain't too late. Maybe after I retire."

For the next hour they drank in silence. Usually after a four-to-twelve the conversation was a non-ending stream of funny, tragic or just plain whacky stories about arrests, asshole complainants, and unusual aided cases. But tonight, no one had much to say because they were thinking about Hector Torres—and what they were about to do at the Joy.

At two-thirty, Lafferty broke the uneasy silence. "Okay, it's time."

"Listen up," Mazzeo said quietly. "Whatever happens tonight, we weren't there. We didn't do it. We don't know who did. Agreed?"

Everyone nodded solemnly.

As they all stood up to leave, Vic Martin said, "Wait a minute, guys..."

All eyes turned to him.

"I... can't go."

Lafferty slammed his bottle on the table. *"Jesus Christ!"*

Martin looked flustered. "I'm sorry, guys. I can't risk... you know... the promotion and all."

Mazzeo was furious at the young cop. If he'd said that in the locker room, it might have changed the minds of some of the others and he'd be in Peggy's apartment right now instead of the back room of Corr's planning a crime. He grabbed the redheaded cop's sleeve. He wanted to tell him he was a shithead. Instead he said, "Vic, you don't know anything about this. Understood?"

Martin pulled his arm away. "Yeah, understood."

Reece broke the strained silence in the wake of Martin's leaving. "I got something for you guys." He reached under the table for a shopping bag.

Lafferty peeked into the bag and pulled out a handful of woman's pantyhose. "What the fuck are these, door prizes?"

"You wear it over your face so you won't be recognized, dickhead."

Oliver picked one up and examined it. "Where the hell did you get these?"

"The trunk of my car," Reece answered.

Lafferty shook his head. "All this time my partner's a cross dresser. Who knew."

"My wife and I sell these things at the flea market on weekends," Reece explained. He saw the grins on their faces and added, "Don't laugh. There's a hundred percent markup on this shit. We do pretty good."

"I'm glad," Lafferty said. "Now you'll have a fallback career when IAB fires your ass for trashing the Joy."

"Don't even kid about that," Reece snapped.

~~

The five cops filed out past a dismayed Paddy Corr. Considering what had happened to Hector Torres, he was expecting a good night at the register. From long experience, he knew that cops drank the most when they were sad or angry. And this lot was *both*.

Quietly, the cops came down Sumter in ones and twos and slipped into darkened doorways across the street from the Joy. Lafferty melted into an alley to deliver his package. Minutes later he was back on the street. Reece waved him over to the doorway where they'd gathered.

Lafferty pulled the pantyhose over his head. "Couple of minutes, no more," he whispered. "I took a peek inside. Maybe ten or twelve guys. The usual scumbags."

Lafferty tapped his jack in the palm of his hand. "The bartender is mine. That scumbag said he didn't see nothing when Hector was getting beat. Well, he's gonna be seeing fucking stars in a couple of minutes."

They waited tensely in the doorways for the explosion, but four minutes went by and nothing happened.

"Maybe the cigarette went out," Oliver offered.

"Nah, it'll go any second," Lafferty said confidently. "Keep your shirt on."

When two more minutes past, Mazzeo said to Lafferty, "Go back and find out what the hell went wrong. Set the damn thing off yourself if you have to."

"What? And miss all the fun?"

He scurried out of the doorway and was half way across the street when a tremendous explosion almost knocked him off his feet.

The off-duty cops poured out of the doorways and rushed the front door of the Joy. As the shell-shocked patrons stumbled out of the smoke-filled bar, they came up short at the bizarre sight of a group of men with weird faces blocking their way. In the darkness, they couldn't see that the faces were distorted by tight-fitting pantyhose. The cops waded into the group swinging jacks and throwing punches.

The bartender came out swinging a baseball bat. Lafferty ducked a wild, vicious swing and drove his jack into the man's testicles. The bartender's eyes widened like a frightened horse and he crumpled to the ground. Lafferty dove on top of him and came down on his head with the jack again and again. The next thing Lafferty knew, Reece had him in a bear hug and was pulling him off the bartender, who'd been beaten into bloody unconsciousness.

As Reece dragged him away, Lafferty surveyed the scene with satisfaction. They'd done what they'd come to do. Three men lay sprawled on the street. The rest had managed to run, crawl, or stumble away from the enraged cops.

In the distance, they heard the sound of fire engines. "Let's get the hell out of here," Reece shouted to the others.

As a parting shot, Lafferty picked up a garbage can and hurled it through the front window.

Chapter Nine

At 5:30 a.m., the jangling telephone woke Leland from a restless sleep. It was the borough office and the message was brief and succinct: Report to Assist Chief Lucas Hightower forthwith.

In today's vocabulary the word "forthwith" is old-fashioned and seldom used, especially in conversation. But it is still an important word in the lexicon of the New York City Police Department. There are a couple of rules regarding its use: Whether written or spoken, it is to be used only by a superior issuing instruction to a subordinate, and the word, connoting immediacy of action, is never used lightly. The other rule is that the speed of compliance with the word 'forthwith' is in direct proportion to the rank of the superior using the word.

Leland, literally tripping over himself, showered, dressed, and made it from his Flushing apartment to the Bronx in record time. He was still shaving with his battery-powered razor when he pulled up to the borough office.

Now he sat in Chief Hightower's office, warily watching the Chief pace his small office with a linebacker-intensity that in the old days had struck fear in the hearts of opposing quarterbacks.

"What the *hell* kind of operation are you running over there, Leland? You got a bunch of vigilante cops running loose. What next? They gonna burn a cross in front of the borough office?"

Leland was at a distinct disadvantage. He didn't know what Chief Hightower was talking about. He'd thought the forthwith had something to do with the Torres assault and it wasn't until he arrived at the borough office that a clerical sergeant told him about the second incident at the Joy Lounge. He'd immediately called the precinct to get more information, but the desk officer's update was cut short when Hightower bellowed from his office, "*Leland*, get in here."

Leland cleared his throat. "Do we know for a fact that Five-five police officers did this?" he asked tentatively.

"Who else could have done it, Attila the Hun?"

"I don't know sir. But I intend to find out," Leland said forcefully.

"Yeah, well you'll have to get in line. IAB has already begun a full-scale investigation." He pointed a thick finger at Leland. "And *that's* confidential, Captain."

"Yes, sir."

Hightower sat back in his swivel chair and read from the Unusual. "Twelve assault charges filed... setting off an explosive device... attempted arson... criminal mischief..."

He threw the report on his desk in disgust. "Leland," he said in a low, menacing voice, "I have to tell you, your début here as a precinct commander has been something less than auspicious."

Leland tugged at his stiff starched collar. He was only too aware that he was screwing up by the numbers. For some reason—unfathomable to him—he couldn't seem to get in sync with running a patrol precinct. He wanted to tell Hightower the delay of the Unusual that first morning had been a misunderstanding. He wanted to tell him that it wasn't his fault that a bunch of crazy cops went rampaging through the precinct. But he didn't tell Hightower any of these things because, to his dismay, he realized that in just slightly more than his two weeks' tenure as a precinct commander, events were controlling him instead of the other way around. What he said was: "I'll try to do better, Chief."

Hightower's voice was low and raspy with anger. "You do that, Leland, or so help me God, I'll drop kick your ass out of the Bronx so hard your grandchildren will feel it. Now get back to your command and see if you can regain control of it."

~~

The mood at the station house was even more sullen than usual. Cops glared at him as though he were responsible for what had happened at the Joy Lounge. Still, he had to admit there was cause for anger. Internal Affairs, and the wrath of the borough commander, was about to descend on the precinct. A blood bath was imminent. It was just a question of when and how many casualties.

Lieutenant Barry followed Leland into his office "I hear IAB has started an investigation."

Leland looked at him inquiringly.

Barry shrugged. "I got a friend," he said vaguely.

Of course he did, Leland thought. Everyone had a friend somewhere. That was how the department functioned. Nobody relied on official channels for information; either they were too slow, or they didn't tell you enough, or they told you nothing. Unofficial channels—composed of networks of friends, acquaintances, and people who owed favors—were the preferred method of gathering information in a notoriously secretive organization like the NYPD.

"How's Torres doing?" he asked.

"He came out of surgery a couple of hours ago. He's in Intensive Care."

Leland looked at his watch. "Six hours?"

Barry nodded glumly. "There were complications."

"Like what?"

"Something to do with an epidural bleed. They had to bore a hole in his head to relieve the pressure on the brain. He's still unconscious and there's still no movement in his right leg."

"Meaning?"

"Possible brain damage."

"Is Torres going to die?" Leland asked straight out.

"I don't know, Captain. But he's in bad shape."

"Keep checking with the hospital. I want to be kept apprised of his condition."

"We're calling every half hour."

"How's Torres's wife?"

"Doing as well as can be expected. The PBA and the Chaplin's office are taking good care of her."

"Does he have children?"

"She's pregnant."

Once again it occurred to him that he knew absolutely nothing about Police Officer Torres or for that matter anything else about the two hundred men and women who worked for him. He was the commanding officer. He should know who was married, who was divorced, who were the gamblers, the drinkers, the workers, and the malingerers. But the men and women he saw at roll calls and in the hallways and in the radio cars were still nameless faces with no histories. He made a mental note to start reading the command's personnel folders. *As soon as he got the time.* He felt like the circus performer who keeps plates spinning on the top of bamboo poles by rushing from one pole to another. It was funny as a circus act, but it was one hell of a way to run a precinct.

Leland studied Barry. This was someone else he knew nothing about. Was he married? Did he have children? Could he be trusted? Even more importantly, was he a competent Operations Coordinator? It was up to the commanding officer to staff the precinct with qualified people and that meant evaluating his key people. But how could he do that when they were all strangers to him?

"I want the names of the men who attacked the Joy Lounge," he said to Barry.

The lieutenant's placid demeanor remained unruffled. "We don't know that our cops were involved, Cap."

"Oh, come on. You know as well as I do that our cops were responsible. It had to be the guys on the four-to-twelve tour." He picked up the previous night's roll call and scanned the names, but of course they meant nothing. He tossed the roll call on the desk in frustration. "Well, Lieutenant?"

"If our cops were involved, it could have been anyone on the four-to-twelve. Torres is a very popular guy."

Leland was disturbed by Barry's use of the word "if." Either he didn't trust his commanding officer enough to confide in him or he was employing the cop's traditional stonewall tactic of ignorance. Either way, he didn't like the lieutenant's attitude. An Operations Coordinator occupies a critical position in the precinct; he was the commanding officer's right-hand man. Leland made a mental note to look for someone with a better commitment to loyalty. But who would be loyal to him? Loyalty wasn't something that you commanded. Loyalty grew out of trust, and trust developed over time. Glumly, Leland wondered if he'd be in the precinct long enough to build that trust.

"All right, Lieutenant, that'll be all. Would you ask the desk officer to get me a sector car? I want to tour the precinct."

"Sure. Oh, by the way, Gloria Perez is outside. She wants to see you."

Leland rubbed his temples. It was only ten minutes after eight, but he could feel a headache coming on already. "Send her in."

There was nothing sexy about her. She wore a dark blue suit and sensible pumps and her hair was pulled back in a severe bun. Still, as soon as she walked into the office, Leland felt—something.

"Good morning, Ms. Perez," he said, trying to sound perfectly disinterested and failing miserably. "Please sit down."

"I won't be staying." She put her hands on her hips the way a frustrated teacher might address a class of unruly students. "Captain, your command is out of control. You've got a bunch of crazy cops who think they're Rambos. If you have any hope of connecting to the people who live in this precinct, you'd better rein in those nut cases."

"Wait a minute. We don't know that police officers were involved," he sputtered in protest.

"Unless you still believe in the Tooth Fairy, you know damn well it was your cops who went back to the Joy Lounge last night to exact their pound of flesh for Officer Torres."

She was right of course, but he wouldn't give her the satisfaction of telling her that.

"You're entitled to your opinion, Ms. Perez."

She shook her head the way one does when dealing with someone who's clueless. "You've spent way too much time in OPP. There's no time for a learning curve here. You've got to find out what's going on around here now and take control."

She was sounding just like Hightower. "Thank you, Ms. Perez," he said, stiffly. "I'll take your advice under consideration."

"I hope so."

She turned and walked out of the office, leaving him to consider his career—a career that seemed so promising just a week ago and now appeared to be on the verge of total collapse.

~~

Sergeant Marvin Seidel stood at his office window and watched Gloria Perez get into her Volvo. He heard Kohler and Quigley come into the Anti-Crime room and, without turning, called out, "Get in here."

The two cops came in and sat down. Seidel turned away from the window. "That Perez broad has one great pair of pins."

Quigley grinned. "Yeah, we passed her on the way in. Kohler was so busy watching her, he tripped over that pile of tires and almost broke his freakin' neck."

Kohler reddened. "Those tires shouldn't be there anyway," he muttered.

Seidel lit another cigar and studied his two Anti-Crime cops. They weren't the perfect team, but they were the best he had. He didn't hold it against Tom Kohler that he was a born-again Christian. Usually, fanatics of any stripe made him nervous, but Kohler never proselytized in the office so Seidel didn't care if he wore a hair shirt at home and slept on a bed of nails. He was a good cop.

Quigley, on the other hand, was much too hyper for Seidel's tastes. The little cop reminded him of a yapping wire-haired terrier on speed. Still, he had the instincts of a good cop.

Tom Kohler and Gene Quigley were the perfect Mutt and Jeff detective team. Kohler, a hulking six-foot-seven, was a man of few words. But given his height, and the zombie-like stare he could turn on a suspect, he didn't have to say very much. Quigley, on the other hand, never stopped talking. It was said his hapless suspects confessed just to get him to shut up.

Before Seidel made sergeant three years earlier, he'd been a First Grade detective. Making First Grade was the pinnacle to which most detectives aspired. But that wasn't good enough for Marvin Seidel. More than anything, he wanted to command his own detective squad and the only way he could do that was to take the sergeant's exam. He studied, passed the test, and cultivated a "hook" who could get him back into the Detective Bureau as soon as his probation was up. He had it all lined up and everything was proceeding smoothly—until the night before he was to be promoted. Under the influence of too many scotches, he made the career-death mistake of calling the Chief of Detectives an asshole to his face in front of a bar full of detectives. When the apoplectic Chief regained his voice, he declared Seidel anathema and vowed to move heaven and earth to see to it that Seidel would spend the rest of his worthless career wandering in the wilderness of patrol.

But Seidel was, if nothing else, a survivor. Within six months of his assignment to the Five-five, he'd convinced the CO to put him in charge of the eight-man Anti-Crime Unit. Disregarding the *Patrol Guide's* job description of anti-crime duties, Seidel turned his Anti-Crime Unit into a quasi-detective squad, conducting investigations, interviews, stakeouts, and other assignments that were supposed to be conducted by the precinct detective squad. The CO—and all subsequent COs—turned a blind eye to the Anti-Crime sergeant's operation because Seidel and his men made a lot of arrests and kept the crime stats down.

Seidel studied Quigley and Kohler through a cloud of blue cigar smoke. Despite their flaws, he was proud of his creation. He'd molded them, trained them, coached them, yelled at them, and now they were almost ready to become real detectives. If he couldn't be a detective squad commander, at least he could train cops to become detectives.

"What'd you find out?"

Quigley popped three sticks of gum into his mouth. "A dozen complainants claim they were all beaten up by cops. I still don't know what blew up the shithouse window. "

"Firecrackers," Seidel said. "I called a buddy in the lab. Probably cherry bombs or M-80s."

"From the damage I figured plastic explosives."

"What kind of damage?"

"Took out the whole freakin' window and a chunk of the wall."

"Anybody hurt bad?"

"Nah, the usual contusions, intrusions and protrusions. Nothing a few stitches can't repair." Quigley grabbed his crotch and winced. "But one of the scumbags was taking a whiz at the time. He damn near ripped off his willy when the bomb went off. He still can't hear shit, but the doctor says he should be all right in a week or so."

"Can any of these mutts make an ID?"

Quigley feigned disappointment. "Nope. They say the perps were all wearing stocking masks."

"Stocking masks, huh?" Seidel flicked an ash into a hubcap full of cigar stubs. "Clever bastards."

"Master criminals, no doubt."

"Did you talk to that hump, Alvin Tatum?"

"Yeah. Unfortunately, he'd left early last night and missed all the excitement."

Seidel puffed his cigar furiously. "I know he don't own the joint and I'd give my pension to know who does."

Quigley nodded in agreement. "I'll tell you one thing. Whoever owns it has a lot of weight. OCCB and Narcotics have tried to close them down for years, but they can't. That joint has more lives than a cat."

"The boy wonder downstairs says he's gonna close it," Seidel said.

Quigley chuckled. "He keeps screwing up with Hightower, he'll be looking for a job as a bartender there."

Seidel chomped down on his cigar and looked at his watch. "I'm going over there to talk to Alvin."

"About what?"

"Torres's gun. I want it back."

"One more gun on the street isn't gonna make a whole lot of difference," Kohler observed quietly.

Seidel glared at the tall cop through a cloud of blue smoke. "It's the principle of the thing, Tommy. No one takes a cop's gun in *my* precinct."

"You think you can get it back?" Quigley asked.

Seidel crushed his cigar in the hubcap. "Fuckin'-A."

~~

Workmen were nailing plywood sheets across the front window when Seidel pulled up in front of the Joy Lounge.

Inside, a lanky bartender was telling a joke to three customers. As soon as Seidel came in, all conversation stopped and the four men shot hard, silent stares at the sergeant.

Seidel scowled back at them. "Where's Alvin?" he asked the bartender.

"In the back, but he don't want to be disturbed."

"Well, hell, I don't either, but I'm here ain't I?"

He walked down a short, dark corridor. Alvin's office was opposite the men's room and the pungent odor of gunpowder still hung in the air. He pounded on the locked door. "Open up, Alvin."

After a considerable clanging and rattling of locks and chains, the door opened and a grossly fat black man with small pig-like eyes stood blocking the entire entrance. "What you want, Seidel?"

Seidel pushed him aside and stepped into the messy, cramped office. "We gotta talk."

"The cops was here already. They talked to everyone."

Seidel swept a pile of skin magazines onto the floor and flopped down on a ripped leather chair. "I got something important to talk about."

Alvin squeezed his fat frame around his desk and sat down. "And I got somethin' important to talk to *you* about. I wanna know who be bustin' up my place and beatin' on my customers?"

"We're working on it, Alvin. These things take time."

"Dozen of my customers beat. That is some *shit*," Alvin said, working up a real case of indignation.

"This is a dangerous neighborhood, Alvin," Seidel responded with mock seriousness. "There's a lot of muggings going around."

The fat man screwed up his face in disgust. "*Twelve* guys get mugged. *All* at the same time! Outside my bar? Who you shittin'? Was cops what did it."

Seidel feigned shock. "Police officers? New York City police officers? Don't be ridiculous, Alvin. That's against the law."

Alvin pointed a sausage-like finger at Seidel. "I don't give a good flyin' fuck what it's against. *They* did it. *You* knows it and *I* knows it."

Seidel shook his head. "Alvin, you'd make a lousy cop. You just can't go around accusing people of crimes. You need proof. Evidence." He fired up a cigar and blew a thick cloud of smoke toward Alvin. "If anyone can ID them, we'll be glad to hold a lineup."

"Shit," he muttered, knowing Seidel was shining him on.

"But that's not why I'm here, Alvin."

The fat man looked at Seidel suspiciously. "What you want?"

The sergeant studied the ash at the tip of his cigar. "The police officer's gun."

Alvin grinned and his little pig eyes disappeared behind two mountains of cheek fat. "I ain't got it."

Seidel leaned forward. "I don't give a rat's ass who's got it. I want it back."

Alvin's hearty laugh made his whole body quiver. "You playin' wit yourself, my man. That gun be long gone."

"Alvin, you look like the kind of man who likes a challenge. I'll give you till tomorrow night to get it back."

The grin vanished and the pig eyes reappeared. "Don't threaten me, cop. You can't do shit to me."

Seidel leaned close. "How about putting you out of business for starters?" he whispered softly, as though the room might be bugged. "Your 'customers' who beat up that cop last night made a big mistake. Cops got their own agendas; some concentrate on drug collars, others gambling, others drunk drivers, and some even get off on writing traffic tickets." Seidel jabbed the wet, chewed-up end of the cigar at Alvin. "But nothing focuses a cop's attention like another cop getting beat up. If I call for a full-court press, you're gonna have cops climbing up your asshole. That means no more drug deals in the bar, no more pros working the bar, no more numbers, no more… nothing."

Alvin's smile was gone, but Seidel could see he still wasn't completely convinced. He pulled his trump card out of his pocket—a semi-automatic—and slammed it on the desk. "And the first one to take a fall will be you."

Alvin eyed the gun warily. "What's dat?"

"That's your gun."

"The hell it is."

Seidel patted the gun. "It's yours if I say it's yours."

"You can't arrest me for no gun that ain't even mine," he said, sounding not at all convinced.

"It's a cruel world." Seidel stood up and put the automatic back in his pocket. "You got until tomorrow night. You give me the cop's gun or—I give you your gun."

When he came out of the office, he heard a man taking action over a pay telephone outside the men's room. When the bookie saw Seidel, he quickly hung up and scurried back to the bar. Seidel ripped the telephone off the wall and hurled it to the ground.

As he was leaving, he said to the bartender, "Hey, pal, your phone's out of order."

~~

It was late afternoon by the time Leland opened the ham and cheese sandwich that had been brought to him three hours earlier. He was so busy he'd forgotten all about it until his grumbling stomach reminded him that he hadn't eaten in almost twenty hours.

Just as he was about to bite into the sandwich, he heard the sound of chanting and went to the window. Outside the station house thirty men and women, carrying signs that said 'People's Freedom Legion' and 'No More Police Brutality' chanted, "Stop the police state. The cops are out of control."

Barry came in to the office. "I called the borough. They said we should handle it."

Leland watched Munyika get out of a car. Someone handed him a bullhorn. He turned away from the window. "Why are they picketing?"

"The Joy Lounge."

Leland looked at his sandwich in his hand. Suddenly, he wasn't hungry any more. He tossed the uneaten sandwich in the wastebasket. "I guess I should go outside and talk to him."

Munyika saw Leland approaching and shouted at him through his bullhorn, "Have you come to protect me or arrest me, Captain?"

"I just want a peaceable demonstration," Leland said wearily.

"Then arrest those renegade cops who assaulted the innocent patrons in the Joy Lounge."

Leland pushed the bullhorn aside. "I can hear you without that. The matter is under investigation."

"A pat answer signifying nothing." He held the bullhorn to his mouth and shouted to his followers, "We will stay here, day and night, until this so-called 'investigation' is concluded and those cops go to jail."

A roar of approval went up from the crowd.

Back in his office, Leland kept an eye on the demonstration from the window. When the press showed up at three o'clock the picketers became more animated and obligingly cranked up the volume for the benefit of the cameras.

A young woman with a blow-dried hairdo that looked like a helmet interviewed Munyika. Fifteen minutes later the reporter and the TV trucks were gone. Five minutes after that Munyika was gone, and by five o'clock the remaining picketers had drifted away.

Barry came into the office. "I called the borough to let them know it's over."

Leland rubbed his temples to alleviate his pounding headache. "You think they'll be back tomorrow?"

"I doubt it. Munyika got his face time on TV. That's all this is about."

"So you think we're done with him?" Leland asked hopefully.

"Until another opportunity presents itself."

Leland hoped that opportunity would never come. Munyika frightened him. Professional agitators were career-slayers. Their sole purpose in life was to attach themselves to causes and it mattered not whether the cause was great or small, just or ill advised, as long as they got the media exposure they craved. And that media attention was sure to come at the expense of Leland and the Five-five precinct.

Chapter Ten

In spite of a little voice inside his head that warned him to stay away from Munyika, Leland knew he would have to go see him. With a little bit of luck, maybe he'd be able to get Munyika to agree to some ground rules for future demonstrations.

Harry Wolfe had been right about one thing: If anyone could torpedo his career it would be Kawasi Munyika. Leland had witnessed others lose their commands because of their inability to control activists like Munyika. He remembered with trepidation the scorn and invective Drum heaped on Captain Sperling every time he failed to police Munyika's many demonstrations in the Five-five precinct.

If Leland was to survive his two years in the Five-five, it was imperative that he establish a working relationship with the man. If he could get Munyika to agree to talk to him before a demonstration, he was convinced he'd be able to set ground rules that both he and Munyika could live with. That seems simple enough, he thought, as he pulled to the curb in front of Munyika's headquarters. But somehow, he suspected, it wouldn't be that easy.

The Reverend Kawasi Munyika's headquarters was housed in a rundown storefront in the heart of Death Valley. Leland climbed out of the car and looked up at the large red-and-black-lettered sign across the top of the storefront:

THE REVEREND KAWASI MUNYIKA'S
HEADQUARTERS OF THE PEOPLE'S FREEDOM LEGION

Even though it was a chilly forty-five degrees, three burly men, whom Leland assumed to be Munyika's bodyguards, sat outside on milk crates seemingly unaffected by the cold. As he walked past, they said nothing, but there was no mistaking the hostility in their sullen eyes.

Inside, a thin, studious man wearing thick wire-rimmed glasses, looked up. "Yes?"

"Captain Leland. I'm here to see Reverend Munyika."

The man motioned to a row of folding chairs lined up against a wall. "Have a seat," he said and disappeared through an unmarked door.

Leland sat down and nodded to a young woman who was cutting articles out of a newspaper. She ignored him.

The cramped room was sparsely furnished with second-hand office furniture. On one wall, fastened with thumbtacks, was a large black, green and yellow Black Nationalist flag. Next to it was a poster of Malcolm X.

The door opened and the man reappeared. "Go in," he said curtly.

Munyika's spacious and well-appointed office was in marked contrast to the Spartan outer office. A customized chrome-and-glass wall unit, containing a 60-inch LCD TV and a well-stocked bar, dominated the room. The other walls were covered with photographs of prior demonstrations and street scenes. Some showed the police in blue riot helmets, others featured beleaguered politicians, while others showed wide-eyed throngs of people. And all the photos had one thing in common. The Reverend Kawasi Munyika was the center of every photograph.

With a smile that was more patronizing than sincere, Munyika uncoiled himself from behind a gleaming mahogany desk. The only words Leland could think of to describe Munyika were *big* and *charismatic*. The gaunt-thin man's head almost touched the ceiling. His jet-black skin with the sheen of polished ebony was in sharp contrast to his reddish modified Afro hairstyle. He wore a black and red Dashiki set off by gold chains around his neck and thin gold bracelets on both wrists. But his most striking feature was his wide-set eyes that seemed to glow from some inner vision. There was also something vaguely familiar about the man's appearance, but Leland couldn't quite put his finger on it.

"Good morning, Captain." Munyika extended a huge hand to Leland. "Have a seat."

Leland sat down on a plush leather couch and Munyika folded himself back into his oversized chair. It didn't escape Leland's notice that the activist was much more cordial and polite in private.

"Well, Captain, what can I do for you?"

"We met earlier, but I thought I'd stop by and introduce myself formally."

When Munyika said nothing Leland continued. "I just want you to know that I'm here to help you in any way that I can."

Munyika regarded Leland with undisguised amusement. Since he'd gone into the community activist business, he'd had numerous dealings with the police, other city agencies, and politicians. Long ago he'd learned a secret that few people knew. It was a secret that to a great extent had been responsible for his success. And that secret was: Government workers and politicians, at whatever level, live in a chronic state of fear. They are afraid of losing the next election; afraid of losing the next promotion; afraid of being labeled racists and bigots. Once he understood that verity, he realized that the best way to exploit that fear was through confrontation, and the more violent the better.

Clearly, this young, inexperienced captain was fearful. Like his incompetent predecessor, Captain Sperling, this young man had come here hoping to find a way of avoiding future confrontations, as though that was possible or even desirable.

"Help me? How do you propose to help me?"

"I'd like us to work together. If there's a particular problem, I'd appreciate you coming to me first. I'm sure you'll agree that it's easier to settle little problems than to deal with bigger ones later on."

"I don't follow you."

"For instance, if you're going to picket, I could meet with you in advance and we could work out the ground rules and—"

"Ground rules?"

"Yes. How many pickets, where they'll stand. That sort of thing."

Munyika flashed a wolf-like grin. He was having a good time toying with this fool. "You don't understand, do you? I don't follow no ground rules, Captain. I do what I want when I want."

"Don't get me wrong," Leland said, struggling to remain solicitous in the face of the man's irritating arrogance. "I have no desire to deny you your Constitutional rights. But the police department has an obligation to provide for the safety and welfare of everyone concerned. All I'm suggesting is that we get together and work out the ground rules ahead of time so there's no misunderstanding."

Munyika stood up. "Captain, your job may be to provide for safety and welfare, but my job is to get the message of the People's Freedom Legion out to the world in whatever manner I see fit. And I ain't gonna get that message out following no damn ground rules."

A chagrined Leland left the office with the sound of Munyika's bellowing laughter still ringing in his ears.

~~

Peggy Garrigan and Eddie Mazzeo came back to the station house to eat lunch and pulled in behind a police department Quartermaster truck.

"What's going on?" Peggy asked the two men who were unloading boxes.

One of the men, a sweating, heavy-set man looked up. "Window shades," he puffed.

Peggy eyed the pile of large boxes on the sidewalk. "These are all window shades?"

"Yeah. We got orders to replace all the window shades in the station house." He pulled up his sagging pants. "Someone's got a lot of weight around here. I don't deliver this many shades in a whole year."

Peggy grinned at Mazzeo. "Window shades. A dry sergeant's locker room. You're next, Eddie."

"Mazzeo pushed through the oak door. "Like hell I am."

~~

Leland looked at the wall clock and rubbed his bloodshot eyes. He'd been at his desk since six this morning, but besides being humiliated by the Reverend Munylka, it felt as though he'd accomplished very little in the intervening twelve hours. Still, his daily "To Do" list said otherwise. He had crossed off fifteen items, but an important one remained: *Close the Joy Lounge*.

His best friend, Steve Janssen, had invited him to dinner and he was due in less than an hour, but he wanted to finish off this last item. He dialed the number for the State Liquor Authority. The SLA was the agency that had given the Joy Lounge its license. If the SLA could giveth, it could certainly taketh away.

It took him the better part of fifteen minutes to work his way through a bureaucratic maze of departments and sections and now he found himself talking to Irwin Traub, a mid-level supervisory drone in the enforcement section of the SLA, who was doing his best to build a stonewall between his agency and the police department.

"Mr. Traub," Leland asked in frustration. "When can you inspect the Joy Lounge?"

"Captain"—the man's monotone voice had given way to testiness—"we have thousands of licensed premises in this state. As I'm sure you're aware, Albany has cut our budget. We simply don't have the manpower to inspect a premise just because the police department asks us to."

"In how many of those thousands of premises have six police officers been assaulted?"

There was a silence on the other end of the line and Leland

continued. "I'm not asking you to inspect this bar on a whim. There's prostitution, gambling, narcotics, cops assaulted—you name it, in that place. It's got to be shut down."

"Captain, you show me a record of arrests or summonses for that activity and maybe we'll be able to expedite an inspection."

"You want activity? I'll give you all the activity you need." Leland said, slamming the phone down.

He grabbed his coat and rushed out of the office. He had just fifteen minutes to get to Queens. As he was heading for the door, Lt. Hanlon put his hand over the mouthpiece of the telephone receiver. "Cap, before you go I think you'd better hear this."

Reluctantly, Leland turned away from the door.

~~

Leland rang the bell and glanced at his watch uneasily. He was over an hour late. A man, the same size as Leland but a good twenty pounds heavier, opened the door. The smile on his face said Leland wasn't too late.

"About time. I was going to put out an A and P on you."

"APB. Do I come in or do you plan to feed me in the hall?"

Steve Janssen slapped Leland on the back and dragged him inside. "Pam," he called into the kitchen, "fire up the roast again. He's here."

A frowning Pam Janssen appeared in the kitchen doorway wiping her hands on a towel. She was a petite blonde with large horn-rimmed glasses. "Nice of you to stop by, Richard. I hope you like cremated roast beef."

"I'm sorry, Pam." He kissed her cheek. "Something came up at the precinct." He handed her a bag. "I brought red and white. I didn't know what you were having."

"The condition the roast is in, we may never know."

He patted her stomach. "Six months, huh? It looks like you were due a week ago."

"Thank you, Richard. I really do appreciate that. Steve, why don't you two go inside and have a drink while I do a CPR on the roast."

"Good idea. What'll you have, pal?"

"The usual. Make it a double."

"That kind of day?"

"It's always that kind of day."

While Steve made drinks in the kitchen, Leland went in and flopped down on a mushy sofa overrun with fluffy pillows. The living room was small, but Pam had made it appear larger by a skillful use of undersized, but tasteful, furniture. Since he'd been here last, they'd covered one wall with an assortment of photographs. He got up to examine a black-and-white photo of Steve and him in their St. John's track team uniforms. Both had been adequate distance runners, but neither had set any speed records. Steve had gained quite a few pounds since the picture was taken, but Leland felt great satisfaction knowing that he weighed exactly the same.

Steve came in carrying two glasses. As though he'd been reading Leland's mind, he said, "I gained twenty-five pounds since that picture. Can you believe it? He looked at Leland's flat stomach with envy. "I'll bet you haven't gained an ounce. Right?"

"Yeah, but it ain't easy, especially since I haven't been to the gym in over eighteen months."

"Hell, I go to the gym three days a week, but it doesn't seem to matter. How come I don't see you there?"

Leland fell into the soft armchair. "One Police Plaza kept me busy, but the precinct is even worse. I hardly have time to eat. There's always one more fire to put out."

"How long have you been there?"

"Two weeks going on twenty years."

"It doesn't let up?"

"Nope. If anything, it gets worse. There's always something happening. You have no idea, Steve. I get calls at all hours of the day and night, including my days off."

"You should have stayed where you were. At least you kept regular hours."

"It was time to move on," Leland added vaguely. He hadn't told his friend the real reason behind the transfer. Steve—or any civilian for that matter—wouldn't understand the department's Byzantine politics and promotional procedures.

Steve clinked glasses and sat down on the couch. "Good old Richie. Always climbing the ladder. I never met a guy with more ambition than you." He regarded his friend pensively. "You got way better grades than me. With your brains and drive you could have really gone somewhere in the private sector. Why'd you become a cop?"

Leland winced inwardly. He knew Steve meant well, but the implication of his remark was that being a cop or a captain, or probably even the police commissioner for that matter, wasn't really a career. It was just another civil service job—like driving a bus or picking up garbage.

"Because I want to fight for truth, justice, and the American way," he said.

Steve swept the cushions onto the floor and flopped down on the couch. "Bullshit."

"You never met my old man, Steve. He worked for a Fortune 500 company for more than forty years. I can't tell you how many times he got passed over for promotions because of office politics, and then, later, because of his age. I saw what it did to him and I swore I would only work some place where I could rise to the top on my talents and effort alone. One of my profs, an ex-cop, suggested the police department. He said promotions were based strictly on examinations. Sounded good to me, so I took the test." Leland smiled ruefully. "He neglected to mention that you only take exams through the captain's rank. After that, it's supposed to be merit, but it's really politics. So, ironically, I'm in the same position as my old man. The difference is I know how to play the game."

"I guess you know what you're doing, but you were damn good at marketing."

"I hated marketing."

"Hell, so did I."

"So why did you go into it?"

Steve ran his fingers through his thick, unruly black hair. "I don't know. You take some courses, you commit to a major, next thing you're in marketing."

"You like it?"

Steve shrugged. "It's a job. The money's good. Lord knows I'm gonna need it with a baby coming." He looked around the small room. "We gotta get outta here."

"What are you going to do?"

"Pam wants a house."

"Can you swing it?"

"It'll be tight, but I think so—if I can pick up a handyman special at a good price."

Leland laughed. "What are you going to do with a handyman special? You can barely screw in a light bulb."

Steve grinned slyly. "Pam's pretty handy."

Pam came into the living room with a glass of sparkling water in her hand. "Did I hear my name taken in vain?"

"Yeah." Leland grinned. "Your husband says you're going to be in charge of fixing up the dilapidated house you're going to buy."

She rolled her eyes. "I don't want to talk about this on an empty stomach. Come on, dinner is served."

On the way into the kitchen, Steve patted her stomach. "It doesn't look empty to me. It looks like you got two or three in there."

She smacked his hand away. "You silver-tongued devil."

Pam had exaggerated the condition of the roast. It, and everything else she put out on the table in the crowded dining area, was cooked to perfection.

When they were seated, and Leland had toasted the impending arrival of the new baby, Pam said, "So tell me, Richie, how come you were late?"

"We had a bias incident just as I was leaving."

"And you had to personally respond?"

"Yep. That's why they pay me the big bucks."

"What happened?"

"Four black kids from the Valley went up to the hill, spray-painted racial slurs on the walls of a Jewish Temple and beat the hell out of some Jewish kids who objected."

"The Hill? The Valley? Sounds like you're talking about Afghanistan," Steve said.

"Sometimes I feel like that's where I am. Guys, you wouldn't believe the tension between ethnic and racial groups in my precinct. Even the minorities have subdivisions. The Nigerians don't like Haitians. The Haitians don't like American-born blacks, and none of them likes Hispanics. And then there's the wealthy people who live on the Hill. They don't mix with anyone but themselves."

"And I suppose they all have their special agendas?" Pam asked.

"Oh, yeah. And I'm the one who's supposed to placate them all."

"Gee, that sounds like fun. Pass the potatoes, Solomon."

During the rest of dinner, the conversation moved from the police department to politics to current events and each topic erupted into an argument between Pam, the liberal, and Steve, the arch-conservative.

When dinner was done and they were working on the last of the second bottle of wine, Pam decided that Leland was mellow enough to bring up the touchy topic of Marilyn.

The four of them had met in the Hamptons five summers earlier. Steve and Richard, who'd known each other since elementary school, had a time-share in a house with five friends. Pam was in a time-share house with Marilyn and six girls, none of whom she knew because they'd met through an ad in the *New York Times*. Over the next fourteen weekends Pam and Marilyn had become friends.

One hot afternoon while they were taking advantage of a two-for-one happy hour in a crowded bar on Labor Day, they met Steve and Richard. Pam had been attracted to the more flamboyant and outgoing Steve and Marilyn had been attracted to Richard, the better looking and more serious one.

For Pam and Steve, it was love at first sight and they were married the following year. It took a little longer for Richard and Marilyn. They took turns backing away from marriage, and then, suddenly for reasons neither quite understood, they got married. And then, just as suddenly, it was over. Although they were good friends, Marilyn had never told Pam why she and Richard had divorced.

Pam, feeling terribly nostalgic, poured more wine into Leland's glass. She loved him like a brother. He hadn't changed in the five years she'd known him. He was still good looking, especially with those serious, dark hazel eyes. Secretly, she harbored a belief that one day he and Marilyn might get back together.

"So tell me," she said, trying and failing to sound casual, "have you heard from Marilyn?"

Steve choked on his wine. "Pam, for crying out loud. "

"It's okay, I can talk about her," Leland said, looking at Pam in amusement. "You never would have made it in the diplomatic corps."

"I'm direct. I'm sorry, but it's part of my charm."

He put his hand on her arm. "Please, don't apologize. To answer your question, no, I haven't heard from her."

For a while after their divorce he did hear from her from time to time. It had been a civilized divorce—no hard feelings, etc., these things happen, etc., the only logical thing to do, etc., let's keep in touch, etc. But as time went on, they spoke less and less and in a very short while, they didn't speak at all.

"How about you, Pam? Have you heard from her?" He hated himself for asking the question.

"No, not for a long time. I got a birthday card a couple of months ago, but that's it. She moved to Washington. She's working for some congressman from Michigan."

Steve broke the strained silence. "Pamela, dear, are there any other conversation-stopping questions you'd like to ask? Perhaps you'd like to know if Richie has leprosy?"

"Don't be gross. These things interest women. If it were up to you, you'd never mention Marilyn. You men are such insensitive clods."

"May we change the subject?" Leland asked.

Pam patted his arm. "Sure, what do you want to talk about?"

"Wine." He held out his empty glass to Steve. "Please sir, may I have some more?"

Steve splashed some wine into Leland's glass, spilling some on the linen tablecloth. He wasn't much of a drinker and the combination of scotch and wine was going to his head.

Pam shot him a dirty look, but said nothing.

"I saved your life, pal," Steve said, taking no notice of the spreading burgundy stain on the tablecloth.

"How's that?"

"Pam was gonna set you up with some old maid she knows."

"Steve—"

Leland turned to Pam. "I asked you not to do that." He was smiling, but there was exasperation in his voice.

"In my defense, I want to set the record straight. She's no old maid. She happens to be a very beautiful young woman."

Steve slammed his hand on the table and the glasses jumped, spilling more wine on the tablecloth. *"The kiss of death!* When a woman says another woman is beautiful, you know she ain't."

"And why is that?" Pam asked through clenched teeth.

"Because women don't know what looks good to a man. That's why."

She remained unflappable. "Of course we know."

"Oh, yeah? Richie, she thinks Megan Fox is a dog."

Leland's eyebrows went up. "What? Pam, I have a big poster of her in my bedroom. Are you kidding?"

"I didn't say she's a dog. I said she's kind of... generic. And for the life of me, I don't know why she's on the cover of every magazine except *Mad Magazine*."

"Pam," Leland shook his head. "Megan Fox? She's ... hot."

Pam frowned. "You really think so?"

"I'll tell you what. You set me up with Megan and *I'll* cook the dinner."

She stood up and started to clear away the dishes. "Men," she muttered. "You know nothing."

Steve jumped up. "No, no, my dear. I'll clean up. You cooked us a lovely dinner. Go inside and entertain our guest."

She patted his cheek. "Isn't he sweet?" She grabbed Leland's arm. "Come on inside, Richie, and tell me all about cops and robbers while hubby does the dishes."

Leland was in the process of telling a wide-eyed Pam about a double-homicide when there was the sound of a dish breaking. She jumped up. "I'd better get in there before that jerk breaks all my good china. As she was leaving, she turned. "Richard, tell me the truth. Do you really have a poster of Megan Fox in your bedroom?"

Leland considered stringing her out a little while longer, but she looked so disappointed. "Nah, I was just kidding."

"What a relief. I thought you were turning into some kind of pervert."

A moment later, a smiling Steve came into the living room with two drinks. "I did that on purpose. Broke an old dish. It always gets her back into the kitchen." He touched glasses. "Cheers."

For the next half hour they talked, or more accurately argued, sports. Steve liked the Yankees; Leland the Mets. Leland liked the Giants; Steve the Jets. They couldn't even agree on a hockey team. Leland liked the Rangers; Steve the Islanders. Each in turn, getting louder and louder, quoted statistics and game strategies trying to convince the other of the error of his ways, but of course to no avail. Finally, the impasse was broken by Pam, who came into the living room carrying a tray of coffee cups and pastries.

"What's the rule?" she said handing a cup to Leland. "The louder you are the more right you are?"

"This guy's hopeless," Steve said. "He'll never know anything about sports."

Before Leland could retort, she held up her hand. "Enough. No more sports."

The conversation assumed a more reasonable tone and moved on to politics and current events. Around eleven, Pam stood up and stretched her back. "It's time for me and whatsit to turn in."

Leland stood up and kissed her cheek. "Thanks for a great dinner. It's the first dinner I haven't eaten out of a cardboard box in weeks." He patted her stomach gently. "Do you know what it's going to be?"

"Steve and I have decided we don't want to know." She leaned close to Leland and whispered, "The jerk bought a football already. You believe that? What's a girl going to do with a football?"

As she headed for the bedroom she said, "Richie, don't be a stranger. I promise I won't spring an old maid on you." She stopped and turned around. "Megan Fox? I'll see what I can do."

After she'd gone, Steve leaned forward. His eyes were red and slightly out of focus. "So what's going on in the Bronx? Anything good I should know about?"

Steve was a closet cop-junkie who always started asking questions about police work when he was drunk. In the past, Leland, with his string of uninteresting headquarters assignments, had few exciting experiences to relate. Now he had plenty of stories, but few he wanted to repeat. Steve would have loved to hear about the Joy Lounge, but Leland had no intention of discussing that with anyone outside the department, even if it was his best friend. But he did tell him about the escaping prisoner who punched him in the mouth. Now he could even laugh about it.

It was almost two in the morning when Leland stood up and said, "Time to go, Steve. I gotta get up early."

At the door, Steve's red eyes looked troubled. "You know, Richie, secretly, I always wanted to be a cop. But after listening to you, I'm kind of glad I'm not."

Leland was stung by the remark, but he wasn't sure why. "So being a marketing guy isn't so bad after all," he said.

Steve chuckled mirthlessly. "I wouldn't go that far."

As Steve was closing the door, he yelled down the hallway. "Hey, Richie, I forgot to tell you, you're going to be the godfather for whatsit. When the time comes I don't want to hear about you having to work. All right?"

"It's a deal. Thanks, Steve."

~~

When Leland got home, his answering machine was blinking. He didn't want to answer it. It was late, he was tired, and right now, he wasn't in any mood to hear more bad news from the 55th precinct.

He climbed out of his clothes, sat on the edge of the bed, and stared at the accusing, insistent blinking red light. He sighed and hit the play button. He never thought he'd be so happy to hear a message from a time-share company offering him a free weekend in Florida.

He slipped into bed, but he wasn't tired anymore. His mind was filled with troubling thoughts and images. Seeing Steve and Pam together was a forceful reminder of the sorry state of his own social life. Tonight was the first time he'd been out since his assignment to the precinct. He had no "serious woman" in his life at the moment. He'd been dating a couple of girls, but since he'd been transferred to the precinct he'd had no time to call them.

Earlier tonight, Steve had spoken enviously of the single life: the Sunday afternoon softball games followed by the camaraderie over a few beers in a neighborhood saloon; the freedom to just take off for a long weekend; a check book with a positive balance. Except for the positive balance, Leland had none of that. His time was not his own. He couldn't just go away without leaving a forwarding address and telephone number with the borough. And his checkbook showed a positive balance only because he didn't have the time to turn that balance into a negative number.

Somewhere, deep down, he was beginning to wonder if what he'd decided was to be his life was going to be enough. He'd pushed everyone and everything out of the way—including Marilyn—in his quest to become a captain, and so far he'd accomplished everything he wanted. In terms of his career he was right on schedule. So why did he feel so— hollow? *If he and Marilyn hadn't divorced...*

The funny thing was, he never saw it coming. For over a year every night after he came home from work, he'd hole up in his den to study for the captain's exam. One night Marilyn came in, threw a pillow at him, and told him that he could sleep with his books.

And that had led to a terrible fight with both of them hurling accusations that would have been better left unsaid. Later, she retreated to the bedroom in tears, leaving him feeling angry and perplexed.

In the silence of his den, he tried to sort out why he was feeling so angry and the answer, when it finally came to him, stunned him. He wasn't angry because she'd banned him from their bed. He wasn't even angry about her accusations that he was a lousy husband. What made him most angry was that she'd taken time away from his studies.

The next morning she went to work early. When he went into the bedroom to get dressed he saw the made bed and it filled him with a sudden sadness. There was a pillow on her side and none on his. The indentation reminded him of an amputation.

For the next several weeks they barely spoke; hurt and pride wouldn't let them. Then one morning she handed him the divorce papers.

If he and Marilyn hadn't divorced...

He rolled over and angrily yanked the blanket up around his neck. After the divorce he'd promised himself that he would never use the word "if" again.

Before he fell into a fitful sleep, one thought did manage to penetrate his troubled mind: He'd put all his eggs in one basket. His police career was everything. His life. It was a conscious decision on his part to do so; it was what he wanted to do. But now the question was: Was it the right basket?

∼∼

While Leland was tossing and turning in his bed, the four-to-twelve cops were sitting in the Paddy Corr's discussing the Joy Lounge in hushed whispers.

Marvin Seidel sat on his usual barstool at the "civilian" end of the bar watching them. He didn't subscribe to the "us against them" mentality shared by most cops. While the Five-five cops sat at their end of the bar, he sat with the "civilians." He'd heard all the cop war stories—some real, some made up—ad nauseum. Besides, he enjoyed talking to the "civilians" and, as an added bonus, he often picked up information about what was going on in the precinct.

After the last of the civilians, a congenial maintenance supervisor for Con Ed, left, Seidel picked up his scotch and came down to the cops' end of the bar feeling an equal mixture of rage, anger, and sorrow about Hector Torres.

Lafferty drained his bottle. "They'll be no joy in the Joy tonight, right Sarge?"

"No, there won't." Seidel blew a thin line of blue smoke in Lafferty's face. "But in my opinion, whoever came up with the idea of trashing the Joy is a world-class asshole. Wouldn't you say so, Lafferty?"

"Well, I dunno, Sarge. I mean—no."

Mazzeo said, "I think they deserved it for what they did to Hector."

Seidel pushed Lafferty off his stool. "Let an old man sit down." He looked around at the young faces. They were all angry about what happened to Hector and for that he couldn't blame them. But he'd never forgive them for their stupidity.

"On the other hand, I gotta admire the guys who did it," he continued. "They had balls."

Lafferty visibly puffed up. "You think so, Sarge?"

"Absolutely. Think about it. These guys committed felonious assault. If they get caught they face arrest and imprisonment. They face losing their jobs, their pensions. But they risked all that without a thought about their wives and families. I want to tell you it takes big balls to be willing to let your kids see you do the perp walk on the evening news."

He took pleasure in seeing the uneasy glances that passed between them. "And then there's the cost of hiring a lawyer," he continued. "Only guys with big balls wouldn't worry about that. You know these shyster lawyers charge twenty-thou just to say hello? Can you imagine what it must cost to hire them for an entire trial? I guess they could always tap into second mortgages and the kids' college fund. I know I wouldn't have had the *cojones* to do what those guys did."

There was a silence as each man considered what Seidel said. Then, Mazzeo said, "What about justice for Hector, Sarge? You know nothing will be done to the mutts who beat him."

Seidel puffed on his cigar thoughtfully. "You're right, Eddie. There will be no justice for Hector and that's a goddamn shame." He drained his glass. "But there is an alternative."

"Like what?" Reece asked.

"When I was a young cop in Harlem, we had trouble with a cop-fighting bar so we gave them special attention. They couldn't shit without us hammering them with arrests and summonses. We tossed people, we tossed cars, and we came up with drugs, guns, and all kinds of contraband. Within six months the joint closed because everyone was afraid to go near it."

He saw Quigley come into the bar, stand at the door and motion to him. He stood up, left a couple of bucks on the bar, and pocketed his change. "And we did it legally," he concluded. "We didn't risk our jobs or our pensions." He fixed his steely gray eyes on Lafferty. "I don't know who had the bright idea to go back to the Joy, but he gave you guys some real bad advice. Internal Affairs is gonna beat on this precinct like a rented mule and some good cops are gonna get hurt. And that's a real shame, too."

~~

Seidel followed Quigley outside. "Whadda ya got, Stan?" he asked.

"Alvin wants to see you."

Boyer Street, a dead-end street sandwiched between a derelict park that no one used and a factory that went dead after five o'clock, was the quietest and most isolated street in the precinct. Because of its remoteness it had, in the past, become a favorite dumping ground for organized crime hit men. One year they deposited a record-breaking six stiffs. The new precinct commander, terrified that they might leave a seventh, designated it a crime-prone location and ordered radio cars to patrol it regularly—much to the irritation of hit men who were forced to clock the additional miles all the way to the marshes of Bayonne.

Seidel turned into the darkened street. The only car on the block was Alvin's lavender Cadillac. Seidel pulled up behind it, got out, and climbed in next to Alvin.

"What's with all this secret meeting bullshit, Alvin?"

"What am I gonna do, invite you to the Joy Lounge?"

"I don't mind."

"I do. I got enough trouble as it is." He picked up a newspaper on the seat next to him, underneath was Hector Torres's automatic.

Seidel knew Alvin would get it back, but he was surprised he'd done it so fast. "I don't suppose there's any prints on it?"

Alvin laughed so hard the car rocked. "That gun ain't never been so clean."

Seidel picked it up and stuffed it in his pocket. "You do good work."

"Okay, you got what you want. Get out."

Seidel opened the door. "Oh, Alvin, just one more thing. Who really owns the Joy?"

Alvin started up the engine. "Don't push your luck, cop. You got the gun, leave it go at that."

Seidel got out of the Cadillac. He leaned down and looked into the window at Tatum. "We'll talk another time."

"Not if I can help it," Alvin said, roaring away from the curb with screeching tires.

Chapter Eleven

Lieutenant Ronald Hanlon, the day-tour desk officer, peered over the top of his reading glasses and muttered an oath under his breath when he saw the two men come through the doors. One was tall and slender, the other short and stocky. Other than that, there was nothing distinctive about them, but Hanlon knew who they were.

Perhaps it was the way the taller man looked at the car tires stacked against the wall with such haughty distain. Maybe it was the way the shorter man's eyes darted about as though it was his mission in life to uncover all wrongdoing. Or it might have been the cheap, off-the-rack Sears sports jackets and ties. Whatever it was, Hanlon knew who they were and he wasn't happy to see them.

He took off his glasses and rubbed his eyes. It was almost the end of the tour and he just wanted to go home. The last thing he needed was a visit from Internal Affairs.

The tall one produced ID. "Captain Ingersoll, IAB." He inclined his head toward the short one. "And this is Lieutenant Segal."

"What can I do for you?" Hanlon asked, trying very hard to sound cordial.

The captain slid a typed list across the desk. "We're going to search the lockers of these police officers. Any of them working now?"

Hanlon's expression never changed, but inwardly he sighed in relief. Once, when he'd been a brand new lieutenant working the desk, IAB had come to arrest a cop. When they snapped the handcuffs on him, the cop had cried like a baby. Hysterical, he'd begged Hanlon to call his wife and tell her what had happened. Hanlon said he would. But how do you call a cop's wife and tell her that IAB just arrested your husband? It had been the toughest thing he'd ever done and he never wanted to go through that again.

He scanned the list. "No. They're all doing a four-to-twelve." He suspected the dour-faced captain knew that.

"We'll need someone to witness the search," the captain said.

~~

Lieutenant Barry led the way to the police officers' locker room on the third floor. He glanced at his list of combination numbers and hoped they were up to date. Each officer was required to have his combination on file, but locks broke and were replaced and some cops never corrected the records. Normally it was a minor irritation—unless IAB wanted to open a locker.

The lieutenant opened the first three lockers and gave them a cursory search. Barry stood to the side watching silently. It was pointless asking them what they were looking for.

They came to Lafferty's locker. After several tries, the lieutenant turned to Barry. "I don't think it's the right number. You wanna try?"

Barry tried the combination, but he couldn't get it to open either. "It's probably a new lock," Barry explained, silently cursing Lafferty.

The IAB captain took a bolt cutter out of a canvas bag and handed it to the lieutenant. He turned to Barry. "Lieutenant, we're going to cut the lock off. You will be responsible for securing the officer's property."

"I know my job," Barry snapped, rankled by the captain's condescending tone.

The hostile staring match was interrupted by the sound of the lock snapping.

The lieutenant patted down the hanging uniforms and poked into a shoebox containing a year's accumulation of *Patrol Guide* amendments and copies of arrest reports. The short lieutenant had to stand on the bench to see into the back of the top shelf. Using a flashlight, he rummaged around and withdrew a crinkled oil-stained paper bag. Barry caught the fleeting glance between the two IAB supervisors: A glance that said they had found what they were looking for. Barry knew that firecrackers had been used at the Joy Lounge and he prayed that there were no firecrackers in that greasy bag.

The lieutenant peered into the bag and looked up at the captain. "Gun cleaning equipment," he said.

Barry found his tone of obvious disappointment grating. These guys took too much pleasure in their work.

Just as the lieutenant was about to close the locker, he saw another bag on the floor behind an old pair of shoes. He opened the bag and pulled out a large hunting knife with an evidence tag attached to the broken handle.

The captain examined the tag and looked at Barry with just the hint of a self-satisfied smile. "This is evidence from an arrest over two weeks ago. It should have been returned to the Property Clerk's office."

Barry took the knife. "I'll take care of it."

The rest of the locker searches went without incident. Barry crossed the last name off the list. "Well, I guess that's it."

"One more," the captain said. "Peggy Garrigan. Where's the female locker room?"

~~

Barry stood behind Hanlon and watched the two IAB supervisors leave the station house. "They find anything?" Hanlon asked.

Barry tossed the knife on the desk.

"Who—?" Hanlon read the name on the evidence tag. "Lafferty! That dumb sonofabitch."

"Log it back in, Ronnie. I'll leave a note for the CO. He's gonna love this."

~~

"Those *motherfuckers*!" Lafferty hurled his broken lock across the room. "They didn't have a warrant. What right did they have to search my locker?"

"It's in the *Patrol Guide*, asshole," Reece yelled over the locker.

"But I wasn't even here."

"They don't need you to be present."

"*Bullshit*! What am I, a fucking wetback? The Constitution says I've got a right to life, liberty, the pursuit of happiness, and a locker safe from the prying eyes of IAB scumbags."

"I don't think I've ever seen that exact wording in the Constitution," Elliot said.

"Get over it." Reece came around the row of lockers. "And another thing, jerk off, the *Patrol Guide* says you're supposed to turn in all evidence forthwith."

Lafferty waved a hand in dismissal. "So I forgot. So sue me."

Eddie Mazzeo, buckling his gun belt, said, "They won't sue you, but you can bet Captain Chaos is gonna stick one up your ass."

Lafferty's face grew even more pinched. "You think so?"

Reece patted Lafferty's cheek. "Shmuck. Of course he's gonna zing you."

Lafferty pushed his hand away. "Oh, I get it. They can't tie me to the Joy Lounge, so they're gonna burn me with a bullshit white socks complaint."

Lafferty was referring to tactics used in the old days by IAB. It was common practice to charge a suspect cop with some minor rules infraction if they couldn't find anything more serious. An officer was out of uniform if he was wearing white socks.

Jim Elliot said, "Don't compare white socks to violation of evidentiary procedures."

"*Evidentiary procedures?*" Lafferty repeated in a mocking tone. "You're studying for the sergeant's exam, aren't you?"

"Yeah. Why?"

"Because you're beginning to sound like a hard-on boss. That's why. I hope I don't ever have to work for you."

"You better pray to God you don't, because I guarantee you by the end of the first tour you'll be studying for the Fire Department test."

"Up yours, Elliot." Lafferty buried his head in the bottom of his locker. "Where the hell are my shoes?" he said in a muffled voice. "Those sonsofbitches stole my—" He backed out of his locker red-faced, holding his shoes. "I wouldn't put it past them," he muttered to the grinning cops around him.

He slipped into one unshined shoe. "Who's turning us out?"

Reece slammed his locker shut. "Labonte."

Lafferty's eyes widened. "Labonte?" He hobbled toward the door with unlaced shoes. "Whoa! We gotta get downstairs. That man would give the pope a zinger."

Lafferty, Reece, and Elliot barged into the sitting room as Sgt. Labonte started the roll call. He shot them a withering glance as they sheepishly slipped into the ranks. Labonte finished the roll call and said, "All right, take your posts."

"How's Hector doing?" Peggy Garrigan asked.

"You're the PBA delegate," Labonte said to Reece. "What have you heard?"

Reece stepped in front of the platoon. "Hector's still in a coma and there hasn't been any movement in his right side. But last night he kinda squeezed the nurse's hand."

"That's good isn't it?" Peggy asked.

Reece shrugged. "The doc says it could be simple reflex action."

Peggy asked the question that was on all of their minds. "What's gonna happen to him, Charlie?"

Reece's expression was bleak. "They don't know. The best we can do is pray for him."

Sgt. Labonte broke the somber silence. "Okay," he said quietly, "take your posts."

~~

Peggy climbed into the radio car and slammed the door. "Those *bastards*!"

Mazzeo started the car. "Who?"

"IAB. Did you know they searched my locker?"

"They searched a bunch of lockers."

She went on as though she hadn't heard him. "I feel so... so violated. I'll bet those perverts put their hands all over everything."

Mazzeo grinned. "What the hell do you have in there?"

"That's not the point. They had no right."

"You're starting to sound like Lafferty."

"There's a big difference between me and Lafferty—and *you*."

"You're female?"

She stared straight ahead through the windshield. "No, not that. *I* wasn't at the Joy Lounge."

Mazzeo pulled away from the curb. "Neither was I, babe. Neither was I."

~~

In the two days since the attack on the Joy Lounge, Hightower's hatchet men—borough captains whose sole mission in life was to ferret out any and all wrongdoing on the part of precinct cops—had descended on the Five-five like a biblical plague of locusts, laying waste all in their path.

Infractions that were normally considered minor were now treated as serious violations. The intent of the borough supervision was to punish the command for what they had done. But the result was that it created a bitter siege mentality, causing cops to hunker down and become even more wary and defensive of anyone outside the precinct.

Leland studied the command discipline log while Barry sat across the desk from him. "Eight CDs last night—off post, improper memo book entry, improper uniform, officer out of radio car without hat on?" He tossed the log on the desk.

Barry flipped through the pages. "And ten the night before that."

"What's the reaction from the troops?"

"About what you'd expect, Cap. They've gone dead. Arrest and summons activity is in the sewer. By the way, Reece wants to see you later."

"I wonder what about."

A furious Leland studied the list of minor infractions. This was Hightower's doing. It was his heavy-handed way of letting the cops know that they'd made a big mistake attacking the Joy. The only problem was that the entire command was paying for the idiocy of a handful of cops.

Leland slammed the book shut and slid it across the desk to Barry.

"Lieutenant, I want to see Chief Hightower. Call the borough and set up an appointment."

Barry scratched his chin, "Cap, you sure you want to do that?"

Leland knew the question was Barry's way of warning him that he was about to do something stupid—and he probably was—but he was in no mood to heed the warning. "Yeah," he said evenly. "I'm sure."

A few minutes later, Barry stuck his head in the door. "The chief will see you at two o'clock."

As Leland was leaving for the borough office he saw Sgt. Engle behind the desk and pulled him aside. "Sarge, I was just looking at your squad's summons activity. It's abysmal. What are you going to do about it?"

Engle was stunned by the unaccustomed belligerent tone in Leland's voice. "I'll get the men to pick up their activity," he said, having no idea how he would make that happen.

"Good. I want to see results starting tomorrow."

~~

At precisely two o'clock, Leland walked into Hightower's office. Since this morning he'd had time to cool down and now that most of his anger had dissipated, he began to have second thoughts about asking for a meeting in the lion's den.

Hightower looked at his watch. "I've got to be downtown in less than an hour. What did you want to see me about?"

On his way over to the borough office, Leland had been trying to think of a diplomatic way to broach the subject, but he couldn't think of one. Now, to his consternation, he heard himself say, "I want to talk about the unwarranted supervision my command is getting."

Hightower's frog-eyes blinked once. Slowly. "*Unwarranted?*"

"Before the Joy incident borough supervisors averaged three CDs a month in my command. In the past two days they've given eighteen command disciplines. I'd call that unwarranted, sir." He was glad he'd remembered to add the "sir," hoping it softened the harsh, accusatory tone in his voice.

Hightower sat back and folded his arms across his massive chest. "Captain, has it ever occurred to you that when a group of cops run amuck like they did at the Joy Lounge that maybe, just maybe, the supervision in the Five-five might be too lax?"

"Chief, I've been in this precinct less than three weeks. How can I be held responsible for what happened at the Joy Lounge?"

Hightower slammed his ham fist on the desk. "A precinct captain is responsible for everything that goes on in his precinct."

"That doesn't make sense," Leland shot back. And as soon as he said it, it occurred to him that up until this very moment, he'd endorsed that concept, at least in principle. Hell, he'd even written an impassioned memo for Drum defending accountability under all conditions. Now, to his dismay, he realized he was wrong. It sounded good on paper, but how could you hold a man responsible for something that happens when he wasn't even there?

"What I mean," Leland added hastily, "is that what has been going on at the Joy Lounge has been going on long before I arrived at the precinct."

Hightower grimaced and rubbed his knee. "Sounds to me like you're hedging, Captain. Hardly what I'd expect from a headquarters-trained supervisor."

Leland refused to be baited by the sarcasm in his tone and remained silent.

Hightower continued. "So you think you're capable of reining in those lunatics in your command?"

"Yes, I am," Leland said with more confidence than he felt. Hightower was scowling at him and he wondered if he'd gone too far.

After a long pause, Hightower said, "All right. I'll pull my supervisors out of your precinct. I'll let you whip your command into shape all by yourself. Is that all?"

"Yes, sir," a stunned Leland muttered. "Thank you, sir."

On the way back to the precinct Leland's elation at his first victory over Hightower was short-lived when a disturbing thought occurred to him. Hightower had given in too easily, and that wasn't like him. He wondered if the chief had seen that he was right or if he was just giving him enough rope to hang himself.

~~

Sgt. Engle walked out of the station house, pondering ways to get his squad to pick up their summons activity. He knew why they'd went dead and he had no idea how he would be able to get them to get back to normal activity.

A voice called out, pulling him out of his funk. "Hey, Henry, is this where you've been hiding?"

Sergeant Craig Heller, a thickset, balding man, who had been Engle's partner in the Youth Division and had gone to be a detective in the Organized Crime Control Bureau, climbed out of an unmarked car.

Engle shook the big man's hand. "What brings you to the Five-five, Craig?"

Heller glanced around furtively. "We've been sitting on a wire on an organized crime joint over on Camaron Avenue."

"Which one? We got a few over there."

"Pete's Pizza," Heller said out of the side of his mouth.

"Get anything?"

"Mostly bullshit. We just shut the wire down. But they did have a lot to say about you precinct humps."

"Like what?"

"A lot of pissing and moaning about giving free pizzas to the sector."

Engle suddenly had an idea. "Craig, I'd like to hear that tape."

"No can do, Henry. It's evidence and—"

"Craig, you know I can keep a secret."

Heller studied the placid face of his old partner and knew the man was incapable of lying. "All right. I got a couple of minutes. Get in the car. I'll play it for you."

Heller fast-forwarded to the proper location and hit the play button. Engle heard a husky voice, which he recognized as Carlo, the owner's son.

"Another free pizza for them scumbags. Merda! Every day it's somethin' else: a pizza, a calzone, a hero. Marone! Don't these fuckin' cops ever eat Chinks?"

"What's the difference?"—it was the voice of Pete, the father—*"costs us a few pennies. For that the dumb bastards don't break our balls about the parkin' out front."*

"Fuck'em is what I say. For all the food we give them cheap cocksuckers, they should be parkin' the cars for us."

Heller stopped the tape in the middle of the old man's belly laugh. A worried Engle looked at Heller. "They're talking corruption. Is this going to be trouble for the precinct?"

"Nah. This is a fed operation. They could care less about free pizzas."

Engle knew it was a long shot, but he was desperate to get the captain off his back. "Craig, I want to borrow the tape."

"Are you out of your mind? I'm gonna deep-six this tape. You spread this around and for sure IAB will hear about it."

"I just want to play it for some guys. I'll have the tape back to you in fifteen minutes."

~~

A few minutes later, Lafferty and Reece drove into Cawley Park, a small, rundown vest-pocket park on the edge of the Valley. Reece pulled up next to Sergeant Engle's car. "You called. What's up, Sarge?"

Engle got out of his car and climbed into the backseat of their radio car, pushing nightsticks, briefcases, and an empty Pete's Pizza box out of the way. "I want to talk to you guys about your summons activity."

Lafferty rolled his eyes. "Sarge, we're out here fightin' crime and boredom. We don't have time for bullshit summonses."

"What's your excuse, Charlie?"

Reece jerked a thumb at his partner. "I write more than this hump does."

"That's not saying much. Lafferty doesn't write any."

Reece squirmed. "Sarge, there's not a whole lot of summons activity in our sector."

"How could there be?" Lafferty added. "The cars are usually stolen before the time runs out on the parking meter."

"What about Pete's Pizza?" Engle asked. "I see cars double-parked there all the time."

The two partners exchanged quick glances. "Come on, Sarge, the guy's gotta make a living," Reece said cautiously.

"Yeah, that's right," Lafferty added hastily. "There's no place to park legally."

"I had no idea you two were such humanitarians," Engle said. He was enjoying watching them squirm. "Do you guys know Pete and Carlo?"

Lafferty screwed his face up in concentration as though he'd been asked to name the seven dwarfs. "Pete and Carlo? I think that's the owner and his son."

"They're good people," Reece said.

"Salt of the earth," Lafferty added.

"That's funny. They don't speak that highly of you."

Both men turned around in their seats to face the sergeant. "Why do you say that?" Reece asked. He was getting more and more uncomfortable with the way the conversation was going.

Engle took the tape recorder from his briefcase. "I want you to listen to what your two 'salt of the earth' buddies have to say about you." He punched the play button and sat back to watch their expressions.

As the tape played, Lafferty looked at Reece wide-eyed and mouthed the word "scumbag" several times. Engle turned the tape off right after Pete's belly laugh. "I'm surprised at you guys," he said, slipping the tape recorder back into his briefcase. "Good cops should be a better judge of character."

Reece's face was ashen. "Sarge, is this an IAB tape? Are we in deep shit or what?"

Engle paused for a moment to let them think about that. Then he said, "If it was an IAB tape, they'd be playing it for you." He picked up the empty pizza box. "I don't get it. Why would you guys risk your job for a lousy pizza? Or is there more to it than that?"

"No, Sarge," Reece said emphatically. "I swear to God food is the only thing we ever took."

"I didn't think so, Charlie," Engle said softly. "Because if I did, I'd call IAB myself."

Engle got out of the car and leaned down to look through the window at the two frightened cops. "You both just learned something that I've known for a long time. When someone does a cop a favor, it's not because he likes him. It's because he expects to get something in return. I don't ever want to hear that you two took something for nothing." His expression was kindly, but his voice was like steel. "If I do, I swear to God I'll put you both out of the job. Are there any questions?"

There were none.

~~

When Engle came back to the station house at the end of the tour, Lt. Hanlon pulled him aside. "Henry, what the hell did you do to Lafferty and Reece?"

"Why?"

"They came in here earlier and signed out two summons books apiece. Twenty minutes later, I get a call from the guy who owns the pizza joint on Camaron. He's screaming about a couple of cops running amuck outside his business hanging paper on every car in sight. What the hell did you say to them?"

Engle shrugged modestly. "I just gave them a little pep talk."

Hanlon put his arm around Engle's shoulder. "Henry, if your pep talk can do that to Lafferty and Reece, you're wasting your time in the police department. You could be making a fortune selling timeshares in Kabul."

~~

Leland had learned early in his career that one guaranteed key to success was to find out what the boss wanted and give it to him. He still hadn't quite figured out exactly what it was that Hightower wanted, but he knew one thing: Hightower would not forgive a precinct commander who did not recognize—and do something about—a crime wave.

Immediately after that first borough meeting where Hightower had delivered his threatening tirade about crime waves, Leland had scheduled a meeting with his Anti-Crime sergeant to get a handle on crime in the precinct. But something always came up and the scheduled meeting with Seidel had been postponed several times.

Now, almost two weeks later, he finally found the time to meet with Seidel. The sergeant sat across the desk from him puffing on his ever-present cigar.

Sergeant Marvin Seidel was not Leland's ideal image of an Anti-Crime sergeant—or any sergeant for that matter. He was irreverent and disrespectful of rank, he smoked the most God-awful smelling cigars, and was in his opinion—although Leland would never say it out loud—too old to be an Anti-Crime supervisor.

"Tell me about the street crime in the precinct, Sarge."

Seidel squinted through a cloud of cigar smoke. "We're holding our own, Cap. Homicides are up a couple of ticks, but that's a citywide trend. Rape and robberies are down. But if we don't catch the Poet Bandit soon, he's going to screw up our stats."

Leland stiffened. "The poet—*what*?"

"Some nut job. He leaves a poem every time he does a robbery."

"*Every time!*" Visions of a ranting Hightower danced in his head. "How many 'every times' are there?"

"Three so far. He don't say nuthin'. Gives 'em a note telling them what he wants. On the other side of the note is a poem."

Bleakly, Leland recalled Hightower's fire-and-brimstone speech about crime waves. "How long has this been going on?" he asked in a tone barely above a whisper.

"Four months."

"*Four?* What did Captain Sperling say about this?"

"He said to keep it quiet."

"Keep it—" He stopped when he realized he was sounding like an idiot, repeating everything Seidel said. "What have you done to catch him?"

Seidel shrugged. "The squad is up to their eyeballs in sixty-ones. They don't have time to chase this guy."

"Sergeant, do you realize this is a pattern crime. This could be a crime wave! Is there any evidence? Any leads?"

Seidel squinted at Leland through a haze of smoke and thought: *Not that crime wave bullshit again!* "Nada," he said. " Other than the poems, there's no real MO. The first robbery was a fast food joint. Then he hit a supermarket. Three weeks ago it was a liquor store. Different times. Different days of the week. I wanna tell ya, it's the kind of case that gives a detective *agita*."

Leland, crazed by Seidel's casual attitude, jumped up and started to pace the office. To Seidel it was just another series of annoying crimes, but to Leland, it was a pattern crime and that could cost him his command. He took a deep breath and forced himself to calm down. "How about the poems?" Are there any clues in the poems?" he asked desperately.

Seidel opened a folder and slid three photocopies across Leland's desk. "Take a look for yourself."

Leland sat down and read the first note:

I have a gun. Do not ask me any questions. Give me all your money. Wait ten minutes before calling the police.

He turned the note over and read the poem printed in neat block lettering:

> *Barrels of trash on the ground*
> *Cries in the night, a terrible sound*
> *Shallow remarks in the hall*
> *do it tonight or not at all*

Leland looked up. "What does it mean?"

"Beats the hell out of me. I took the three poems to my friend, Irving Heisler."

"Who's he?"

"The Chairman of the English Department at Fordham."

"What'd he say?"

"Bad poetry. This morning I went to see another old friend of mine, Sydney Guidron. He's a shrink who lives up on the Hill. He says the first poem indicates the guy lives, or used to live, in a ghetto."

Leland looked at the four lines. "That's it?"

"From that one. Read the second one. This was a supermarket heist."

Leland read the second poem:

> *Find a man with a mind*
> *One and one or two of a kind*
> *Flip a coin if you choose*
> *Step aside if you lose*

"What's he say about this one?"

Seidel blew a cloud of smoke toward Leland and glanced at his own notes. "The guy has something called a value system deficit. He sees all of life's choices as a flip of a coin. According to Guidron, with an attitude like that, he's potentially dangerous."

Leland picked up the third poem. "And this one was from where?"

"A liquor store."

Leland read the poem:

> *Sun going down stops the lark*
> *No more time it's getting dark*
> *Colored leaves on some trees*
> *Come and go as they please*

Leland shook his head. "I don't get it."

"Guidron says the guy's getting desperate. Maybe homicidal."

Leland reread the poem. "Where does it say he's homicidal?"

"Apparently some psychos equate autumn with death." He answered Leland's puzzled expression with a shrug. "Hey, what do I know, I'm only a cop."

Seidel's casual attitude was driving Leland to distraction. *Has this man no idea how serious this is?* "And you say there are no leads?"

"Zip. Like I said, his MO is all over the lot. The squad dusted for prints. Nothing. We don't even have a decent description. He's been described alternately as white, Hispanic, and Mediterranean—whatever the hell that is. Height ranges from five-eight to six feet, age from twenty-five to thirty-five. About the only thing the three witness agreed on is that he's a bearded male. Oh, and the eyes. They all say he has these dark, luminous eyes that stare right through you." Seidel chomped on his cigar. "Eye witnesses! They're about as useful as an electric fork."

"Anyone ever see a gun?"

"He keeps his hand in his pocket. No one's actually seen a gun."

"Maybe he doesn't have one?" Leland asked hopefully.

Seidel squinted through the smoke. "You wouldn't wanna bet your life on that."

Leland reread the poems. "Where did he get the title, Poet Bandit?"

"Who knows? These handles just pop up."

"Don't use that title anymore."

"Why?"

"The media," Leland explained. "They love stuff like this. For them it's great headlines; for us it's nothing but headaches."

Once again, Leland thought about Hightower's tirade about pattern crime waves. Ruefully, he had to admit the Chief was right. In his time at One Police Plaza he'd personally seen the devastating effect adverse headlines had on the department brass. He was so certain of the inevitable dynamics that he could draw a flow chart outlining the swift, downward path of pressure. It would begin with an irate mayor reading the headlines who would then call the PC who would then call Chief Drum who would then call Hightower who would then call—Leland, the man at the bottom of the totem pole; the final recipient of an avalanche of fury and consternation.

"Do something," he'd be told. And that "something" would set off a chain-reaction of mostly useless, but, nevertheless, symbolic actions. Flooding robbery prone areas with Anti-Crime people and all available plainclothes cops would result in poor radio car response time. Cops would be taken away from their regular assignments and all the precinct's statistics would suffer.

Even if all this effort resulted in the capture of the Poet Bandit, the thrill of victory, Leland knew, would be short-lived. The next day, Hightower would be on his case about getting the arrest and summons activity back up. It was a no-win situation.

There was no doubt this was a pattern crime, but the question was: Should he notify the borough commander? Not a good idea. Hightower would bombard him with a bunch of questions to which he had no answers.

Leland came to a decision. He would not tell Hightower about the Poet Bandit just yet. Maybe, with a little bit of luck, the Poet Bandit would make a mistake and get caught before he made the papers and cost Leland his command.

He slid the poems across the desk to Seidel. "I want this kept low-key. From now on, no one will refer to this man as the Poet Bandit."

Seidel studied the ash at the tip of his cigar. "You're too late, Boss. Half the merchants in the precinct are calling him that."

At the door, Seidel stopped and turned toward Leland, who was still reeling from Seidel's comment that the entire community knew about the Poet Bandit. "There's something different about you, Cap, but I can't put my finger on it."

"What? Oh... how long were you a detective, sergeant?" Leland asked.

"Nineteen years."

In spite of Leland's distress over the Poet Bandit, he smiled at the confusion on Seidel's face. "I shaved off my mustache," he said.

"Yeah, that's it." An embarrassed Seidel puffed his cigar. "I knew it was something."

He turned and collided with a tall, thin black girl wearing small, wire-rimmed glasses. "Hi, Captain." She came in rubbing her shoulder. "Ronnie Newbert, your Community Affairs Officer. You wanted to see me?"

"Yes, come in."

She was another important key member of his staff whom he hadn't found the time to talk to. As the one responsible for maintaining liaison with the people who lived and worked in the precinct, the community affairs officer was a valuable resource to a precinct commander. Leland was scheduled to go to his first Community Board meeting within the hour. He would have preferred to have a little more time to talk to her, but he was quickly learning that time was a luxury a precinct commander didn't have.

He motioned the officer into a chair. "How long have you been the community affairs officer?"

Newbert pushed her glasses back on her nose. The thick-lenses gave her a wide-eyed studious look. "Three years."

"You like the job?"

"I sure do. People are my line of work. I'm in the sociology graduate program at NYU. Besides," she added with a smile, "this job gives me some great topics for term papers."

Leland nodded, pleased with Newbert's answer. Too often cops took jobs like community affairs just to get out of patrol. But this position was too valuable to waste on someone like that.

"Ronnie, we're going to a Community Board meeting in a few minutes. Give me a rundown on who'll be there."

"Heidi Vancamp is the president of the Community Board. She can be a pain in the butt sometimes, but generally we get along with her." Newbert rolled her eyes. "I guess you heard about the Reverend Munyika?"

"He's already picketed the station house twice since I've been here."

"Let me give you a little background. The Reverend Kawasi Munyika aka Leonard Smalls, was a two-bit gang-banger from the DeWitt Clinton projects in the south Bronx. In prison he found religion, or so he claimed, and when he came out he morphed into the Reverend Kawasi Munyika. As you may discern from my tone, Captain, I am no fan of Leonard Smalls aka the Reverend Kawasi Munyika."

"Duly noted. Does he go to the Board meetings?"

"Only if he has an axe to grind. Unfortunately, he'd been pretty quiet lately."

"Why unfortunately?"

"Because publicity is like oxygen to him, Captain, and right now he's sucking air. He hasn't been in the headlines for almost three months. I'll bet he's probably scouring the papers as we speak, looking for some dumb issue to jump on."

"How big is his following?"

"Not big, but very militant and very vocal. If he gets on someone's case, he's bad news."

"Anyone else I need to know about?"

"Yeah, Vera Roland, the president of the Seaman Street Block Association. Let me tell you, Captain, she is *shrill*. Always carping about drugs on Seaman Street. You're gonna hear from her tonight sure as the sun will rise tomorrow."

"Are there drugs on Seaman Street?"

"Are there Chinamen in Chinatown?" Newbert blurted out. "Oh, I'm sorry, Cap. I forgot you just got here. Seaman Street is the worst drug block in the precinct."

"So what did Captain Sperling tell her?"

"The usual. Narcotics has been apprised of the condition."

"And are they?"

"Oh, yeah, but you know how it is. They come when they can, but there's always other priorities."

"Anyone else?"

"The usual suspects. You'll get to know them after a few meetings. They always have the same complaints—double-parking, vandalism, kids running wild. They're loud, but they're harmless."

Leland looked at his watch. It was time to go. "Okay, Ronnie," he said, trying to ignore the butterflies in his stomach. "Let's go meet the community."

~~

When he and Police Officer Newbert walked through the doors of the junior high school auditorium, there were more than two dozen people seated or milling around the foot of the stage. "This about the usual number?" Leland asked his community affairs officer.

"Yeah, we seldom get many more than this."

A dais had been set up on the stage with name cards for each agency representative. He saw that he was to be seated between the Fire Department and the Sanitation Department.

A woman with short-cropped salt-and-pepper hair and wearing a white blouse and dark gray slacks strode up to them purposefully. Leland judged the woman to be in her mid-sixties, but with her thin, trim body she looked much younger. She looked the type that ran ten miles every morning before breakfast.

She fixed him with piercing, inquisitive gray eyes. "Captain Leland, I presume?"

Newbert stepped forward. "Captain, I'd like you to meet Heidi Vancamp."

The woman's handshake was firm. "Welcome to the precinct, Captain. I hope we have a long and fruitful association."

"So do I." To himself, he thought: but not *too* long.

Newbert introduced Leland to several others whose names he promptly forgot. In time, he was certain, he would come to know them all.

Five minutes later the meeting was called to order. While routine business was being discussed, Leland took the opportunity to study the audience. He saw Gloria Perez sitting in the third row and impulsively straightened his tie.

He was dismayed at the small number of people in the audience. He knew people were quick to complain. Since he'd been assigned to the precinct, he'd personally fielded over a dozen complaining phone calls a day. Surely this small group couldn't have made all those calls. Why wasn't the rest of the community here? Of course he knew the answer: Apathy. Most couldn't be bothered attending meetings like this. And that made him wonder: What kind of people *did* attend these meetings? Chronic complainers or concerned citizens? He fervently hoped the latter. Apathy, he knew, created a power vacuum in the community and someone like the Reverend Munyika was only too happy to fill it.

As if on cue, Munyika appeared at the back of the auditorium. An entourage usually surrounded him, but tonight he was alone. He took a seat in the last row as Mrs. Vancamp announced that it was time for questions and answers. Most of the audience's questions were not police-related, but they insisted on directing those questions to him. Newbert, a veteran of these meetings, knew that the other representatives to whom the question should have been addressed were only too glad to let the police department handle it. When the questions started, Newbert took a seat directly behind Leland. If it wasn't a police-related question, she'd lean forward and whisper, "That's for Sanitation" or "Give it to Water," and Leland, following Newbert's instructions, passed it on. With her able assistance and prompting, he fielded the police-related questions with little difficulty. Most of the topics were predictable. Street narcotics, vandalism, and auto thefts were the main concerns of the speakers.

As he fielded each question, he began to relax. This was what he was good at: Thinking on his feet, talking to people, and solving problems. But just when he started to feel comfortable, just when he began to believe that these meetings were not the dreaded inquisition that so many of his colleagues had described them, a well-dressed elderly woman stepped up to the microphone.

"My name is Eleanor Fielding," she said in a small quavering voice. "I live on the Hill and I have a question for Captain Leland."

Leland leaned into the microphone. "Yes, Ma'am? What can I do for you?" he asked confidently.

"Captain, what are you doing about the Poet Bandit?"

Leland felt as though he'd been punched in the stomach. The last thing he wanted to hear mentioned in a forum like this was the Poet Bandit.

"Well... ah... Mrs. Fielding," he stuttered, "we're doing everything we can regarding these robberies. All our radio cars and foot patrol officers have been apprised of his MO, and they've been instructed to give the Hill—I mean the northern end of the precinct special attention."

Leland heard Newbert groan and knew he'd said something wrong, but he didn't know what.

A rail-thin black woman, sitting in an aisle seat next to the microphone, jumped up.

"That's Vera Roland," Newbert whispered. "Fasten your seatbelt. It's gonna be a bumpy ride."

"*Captain*," she shouted—or more precisely shrieked, "the Hill don't need no special attention. They already got more police than they need. If you're gonna give any place special attention, it oughta be the Valley. We—"

"Oh, come off it," a well-dressed man seated at the other side of the auditorium, shouted. "The Valley gets plenty of attention."

As Heidi Vancamp futilely banged her gavel to restore order, the entire audience jumped to its feet shouting accusations and pointing fingers at each other. "*Please!*" she bawled into the microphone. "Let us have order. Everyone will get a turn. Nothing will be accomplished by shouting."

When order had been restored, she said quietly, "I believe what Captain Leland meant was that his officers have been given special instructions. No additional officers have been assigned to the Hill. Is that not correct, Captain Leland?"

She was smiling, but the look in her eye said she wanted to strangle him for upsetting her meeting. Leland, baffled by the commotion he'd caused, nodded in acquiescence.

"I ain't finished yet," Vera Roland shrieked.

Vancamp nodded pleasantly. "What did you wish to add, Mrs. Roland?"

Roland pointed a finger at Leland. "I want to know what he's gonna do about the drug problem on Seaman Street."

A few groans went up from the audience. Roland turned on them. "Easy for you to sit there all complacent, but you don't have to live on no street where drugs are sold out in the open in front of our children."

Leland wasn't enjoying being pilloried by the shrill Vera Roland, but he was grateful that her outburst had shifted the group's attention away from the Poet Bandit.

"Mrs. Roland," he said in a quiet, reassuring tone, "even though I'm new to the precinct, I'm aware of the problem on Seaman Street. The Narcotics Division has been notified of the condition and—"

"Oh, come on. That's the same damn tired story Sperling gave me. And now he's gone. I'm gonna tell you one thing. You don't do somethin' about Seaman Street, *you* gonna be gone, too!"

Before Leland could respond to her blatant threat, Vera Roland turned and marched out of the auditorium, followed by a dozen people. Leland looked toward the back of the auditorium to see what Munyika's reaction was to all this, but he was gone.

It seemed like hours to the beleaguered Leland, but the meeting ended a few minutes later. Leland, wishing for something stronger, poured himself a much-needed cup of lukewarm coffee with a sweaty hand while Newbert quietly explained what had happened.

"You see, Cap, when you say something like 'special attention,' they think you're talking about more cops. And that's a touchy issue in this precinct. Some of these people go out in the street and *count* radio cars to make sure they're getting their fair share." She looked at Leland over her wire-rimmed glasses. "I wouldn't use the term 'special attention' anymore."

"Thanks," Leland said dryly, "I'll try to remember that."

Gloria Perez, flashing an amused grin, walked up as Newbert left to speak to the head of the PTA. "Well, that was quite a baptism of fire."

Leland grinned weakly. "Wounded, but not mortally. I'm gonna have to work on deleting certain words from my vocabulary."

"It would be a good idea to lose 'special attention.'"

"I seem to be the only one around here who doesn't know the emotional impact of that term."

Her eyes twinkled. "How could you? You're from One Police Plaza."

"You make it sound as if I've been living on another planet," he said, irritated by the mocking tone in her voice.

"Captain, don't be so touchy. The truth is, when it comes to a place like the Bronx, One Police Plaza might as well be another planet." She studied him with her beautiful dark eyes. "There's something you have to realize about the 55th precinct. The people who live here are afraid. Afraid the police won't protect them or afraid the police will strip their neighborhoods to add police coverage to others. That's why a term like 'special attention' has such an emotional impact. To the people in the 55th precinct, police coverage *is* literally a life and death issue."

Leland studied the attractive woman and tried to figure out what her game was. Obviously, she was knowledgeable about how the police and the neighborhood interacted. From her reputation he expected her to be harassing him about something his cops did, or didn't do. Instead, she was offering him advice which, even in his anger and embarrassment, he had to admit was sound. "I'll try to remember that," he said.

She tossed her head, gracefully sweeping her long black hair off her shoulders. "You certainly have your hands full with the Poet Bandit and the IAB investigating the Joy Lounge."

"How do you know about that?" he asked sharply. The IAB investigation was supposed to be confidential.

She shrugged, evidently enjoying his discomfort. "I hear. I see."

He studied her face to see if there was some veiled threat implied, but all he saw was her dazzling smile.

An elderly woman tapped him on the shoulder. "Captain, could I talk to you about a big problem?"

"Sure, in a moment. I—" He turned back to Gloria, but she was already walking toward Heidi Vancamp. He turned back to the woman, surprised that he felt irritated with her for interrupting his conversation. He shook off the irritation. "Yes," he said pleasantly. "How may I help you?"

Delighted to have him all to herself, she took his arm and led him away from the others. "It's about my neighbor," she began, "and her undisciplined dog..."

Leland didn't get home until after eleven. He made himself a double martini, flopped down on the couch, and switched on CNN. He stared at the screen, but he wasn't listening to the earnest anchor who was babbling about a snowstorm somewhere in the Midwest.

He was thinking about today. It had been a tough day, but then again, every day had been a tough day since he'd come to the Five-five. But what bothered him most about today was the unexpected appearance of Munyika at the Community Board meeting. He'd come alone and so quietly that not even Ronnie Newbert had noticed him. He'd sat in the back of the auditorium, studying him. Why? What was he thinking? What was he planning? Did he have anything to do with Mrs. Roland's outburst?

Trying to answer those questions kept Leland awake most of the night.

Chapter Twelve

It was December fourteenth. With Christmas less than two weeks away, the dreaded holiday season was underway with a vengeance. Gloominess descended on Leland like a heavy shroud. He was supposed to be in St. Thomas during this asinine lets-all-laugh-and-be-merry time, but his assignment to the Five-five had, of course, changed all that. To give himself some measure of comfort, he'd promised himself he would not attend any of the dozen-plus Christmas party invitations he usually received.

But that was easier said than done and even that promise had to be broken. He'd received three invitations for this week alone. The first was an invitation to Chief Drum's annual Christmas Party, which was in reality a command performance that one ignored at one's own peril. Then there was the handwritten invitation from Heidi Vancamp inviting him to a "small Christmas cocktail party" at her apartment. He couldn't very well turn down an invitation from the president of the Community Board.

Then, Lieutenant Barry invited him to the precinct Christmas party that was going to be held in less than an hour at the Paddy Corr's. Of the three invitations, this was the one he dreaded the most. His cops still barely talked to him and his appearance was sure to put a damper on what was supposed to be a festive occasion. On the other hand, he was the precinct CO. How could he not go?

And if all that weren't enough to put him in a foul mood, he'd been reading the department's Special Orders, which recorded the transfer and promotion of members of the department. To the uninitiated, these pages of transfers meant little. But to a politically astute OPP-hand like himself, these names and assignments chronicled the rise and fall of careers and revealed the shifting sands of power within the department.

December was a traditional time for promotions and Leland glumly read the names of captains being promoted to deputy inspectors, and deputy inspectors being promoted to full inspectors, and full inspectors being promoted to deputy chiefs. Of the names he recognized, a handful deserved the promotion. But what galled him was that far too many didn't.

He threw the orders on the desk in disgust and went to look out his office window. It was raining and the tenement across the street shimmered in the thin veil of water cascading over the windowpanes. A month ago, it would have been inconceivable that he would become the commanding officer of the Five-five precinct. A month ago he'd hoped—perhaps dreamed was a better word—that maybe, just maybe, Drum would slip his name onto a promotion list. Instead, here he was the commanding officer of the Five-five. *Camp Fuckup. Fort Frenzy.*

His game plan called for getting promoted next December, but now, for the first time since he'd formulated his plan to become the police commissioner, he began to wonder if he'd meet that timetable. His performance in the Five-five so far was appalling. If he couldn't turn this precinct around, if he couldn't get the cops to do their jobs, then there was no chance of a promotion next year either. There was, however, a very good chance of getting derailed and becoming, like Apple Cheeks, a captain for life.

He picked up the Orders, intending to toss them in the file basket when he saw a name he recognized. *Effective 0001 hours this date, Inspector Nathan Berne is transferred from the Chief of Detectives Office to Public Morals Division as the commanding officer.*

He sat down and reread it again. Since Hector Torres had been attacked in the Joy Lounge, he'd been trying to get Public Morals to target the Joy for special attention, but the CO, who was about to get promoted to deputy chief, told Leland he couldn't afford the manpower. What he really meant was that he had no intention of jeopardizing his promotion by aiding and abetting some lunatic precinct captain's crusade against a nondescript dirt-bag bar in the Bronx.

But now, Nat Berne was the new CO and Leland was the one responsible for him making captain. Seven years earlier, Berne had complained to Leland about the voluminous material he had to read and memorize for the captain's exam. Leland let him borrow his own eight-inch thick stack of flashcards, which highlighted the salient points that Leland had painstakingly culled from the more than thirty law books, department manuals, and tomes on management and supervision that appeared on the captain's test bibliography. When Berne passed the test, he bought Leland an expensive bottle of single-malt scotch and effusively credited Leland's flashcards for helping him come out number five on the list. *It was payback time.*

Leland dialed the Public Morals number and a moment later he had Berne on the line. "Nat, congratulations on your promotion."

"Thanks, Richard. Hey, I'll never forget what you did for me, buddy."

"I'm glad you remembered. It saves me the trouble of trying to think of a tactful way of bringing it up. I need a favor."

There was a moment of silence on the other end of the line. "Richard, I just got here. I don't even know my own telephone number yet. How about giving me a couple of weeks to settle in, then—"

"Can't wait that long, Nat. I need this favor yesterday."

Berne sighed on the other end of the line. "What do you need?"

"There's this bar in my precinct called the Joy Lounge..."

After he hung up, Leland stared at the telephone, astonished at his uncharacteristic behavior. In his tenure at One Police Plaza, he'd worked hard to master the fine art of finessing people into doing what he wanted. Subtlety and time were the main tools. A meeting here, a lunch there, perhaps a couple of drinks after work, and soon he had what he wanted. Now, he could hardly believe the way he's coerced Berne into agreeing to help. At OPP such a crass approach would have been considered bad form. Idly, he wondered if he'd lost his carefully nurtured diplomatic touch. Then it occurred to him: He was in patrol now, where things had to be done yesterday. There simply wasn't time for the long, drawn-out dance of headquarters diplomacy.

He looked at his watch and frowned. It was time to go to a Christmas party.

~~

For as long as anyone could remember, the Five-five precinct Christmas party had been held at Paddy Corr's. Once a year—because no one else ever rented the room—Paddy threw open the windows of his upstairs banquet room to ventilate the smoke and stale-beer air of last year. In keeping with the spirit of the season, he made a half-hearted attempt to clean the faded carpet and grudgingly change the threadbare tablecloths. But the cops knew they couldn't trust Paddy to do the right thing and so every year the Christmas party committee, fortified with pitchers of beer, descended on the room and managed to tape, tack, glue, and nail enough streamers, bells, reindeer, and Santa Clauses to magically transform the ugly duckling room into a cheerful and brightly-decorated winter wonderland.

The music, provided by a budding DJ who was a cop's son, was always too loud. But no one complained. By default Charlie Reece, the most rotund cop in the precinct, got to play Santa and distribute gifts, which had been surreptitiously slipped into his bulging bag by parents. With plenty of hotdogs, hamburgers, chips, and soda for the kids and booze and wine for the adults, it made for a good party and every cop in the precinct, including those who were single or Jewish, made every effort to attend. Neighboring precincts helped out by providing overlapping coverage so that any Five-five cop who wanted to attend could.

By the time Leland arrived, the party was in full swing. Reece had already given out his bag of goodies and clusters of children, ankle-deep in torn, colorful wrappings, were engrossed in assembling and disassembling their new toys and games. Most of the cops lined up three-deep at the bar to discuss the job while wives and girlfriends, weary of the non-stop talk about the "job," sat at tables and discussed more important things like children and the latest sure-fire diet.

When Leland came into the room, he almost expected a replay of those scenes in old western movies where everything comes to a halt when the sheriff comes through the folding doors. It was worse: No one paid the slightest bit of attention to him. Once again, he had second thoughts about coming. His flurry of memos, the command disciplines, the Joy Lounge, as well as his newness to the command had not made him a hit with the cops. On the other hand, he knew that the longer he remained aloof from them the harder it would be to establish rapport later. He reminded himself that he didn't come here to enjoy himself, he'd come hoping to chip away at the wall of hostility he'd been experiencing since the first day he turned out a platoon.

He stepped up to the bar feeling self-conscious and out of place. "Could I have a beer?" he shouted over the ear-shattering music.

Paddy Corr, alone behind the bar, darted back and forth like a crazed leprechaun as he tried to keep the glasses full. Given this group it was a Herculean task and he should have had help. But Paddy always insisted on personally tending bar at these Christmas parties. He said it was because he liked to personally serve the Five-five cops and meet their families. But there was another reason as well: The pragmatic old man was afraid his regular bartender would give the place away to this horde of beer-guzzling cops.

He passed Leland a beer and stuck his hand out. "You must be Captain Leland."

Leland shook the little man's wet, sticky hand. "Yes, I am."

"You've a fine bunch here, Captain," he said with a thick brogue. "A fine bunch."

Leland suspected Paddy's definition of "fine bunch" was different from his, but he had no intention of pursuing the matter further.

Sergeant Seidel was sitting on a stool next to Leland. With a beer in one hand and a cigar in the other, he was regaling his enthralled and attentive audience of young Anti-Crime cops with war stories about when he was a detective. He turned to Leland. "Cap, great party, huh? Times like this I almost wish I was Catholic. He pronounced it *kat-lick*."

"So does your rabbi," Gene Quigley muttered into his bottle.

Seidel jammed the cigar into his mouth. "What's that supposed to mean?" he asked through clenched teeth.

Quigley, his courage bolstered by four beers, said, "Look at you, Sarge. You drink, you cuss, you like the Clancy Brothers for chrissake. A good Jew don't do those things."

"Look who's talking, you little turd. The Irish are supposed to be tall, handsome, and witty. All the things you ain't."

While the others made fun of a grinning Quigley, Seidel said to Leland. "I was just instructing my people here on the resourcefulness of the criminal mind. Years ago, when I was a second-grader in midtown we got a rash of thefts from Korvette's."

"What's a Korvette's?" Paul Carrington asked.

Seidel took the cigar out of his mouth and muttered to Leland out of the corner of his mouth, "I'm working with friggin' babies here. Can you believe these guys are too young to remember E.J. Korvette? Paulie," he pinched the young cop's cheek and said in slow, measured tones, "Korvette's was a department store. Like Kmart? So anyway, we're getting our jocks knocked off by some perp stealing handbags out of the ladies' room."

"A purse snatcher in the ladies' room?" Quigley asked, wide-eyes. "Were those broads blind or what?"

"No, no. Here's the MO. A woman goes into the jake to take a whiz or whatever. Where's she gonna put her handbag?"

"How should I know?" Quigley said.

"Quigley," Seidel said patiently. "I know it's hard, but try to use the little imagination you got. You're a woman. You gotta take a whiz. You got this humungous bag with you. What are you gonna do with it?"

Quigley screwed up his face in concentration. "Put it on my lap?"

"Quigley, think about that for a second."

"Okay. On the floor."

"You're gonna put your expensive Gucci leather bag on that filthy floor?"

"I don't own an expensive Gucci leather bag," Quigley said in exasperation.

"How about the hook on the back of the door, numb nuts?"

"How should I know they got hooks on the back of the door?"

"They always got hooks on the back of doors in ladies' rooms."

Quigley smirked. "How come you know that, Sarge? You hang out there or what?"

Seidel waited for the laughter to die down and continued. "Here's the deal. While she's tending to business, the perp reaches over the top of the door and snatches the bag."

"Great MO," Carrington said. "So what'd you do, Sarge?"

"I told the manager to take the hooks off the door."

"Is that how you made first grade?" Quigley asked.

Seidel responded with a blast of smoke into the smirking cop's face. "It solved the problem, dickhead. At least for a while. Two weeks later, I get a call from the manager. They're stealing handbags out of the ladies' room again. Get this. He tells me the perps steal hooks from the hardware department and screw them back on the doors in the ladies' room." Seidel tapped the side of his head. "The criminal mind. Never underestimate it."

"So what'd you do?" Carrington asked.

"The dopey manager thinks he's Dick Tracy—"

Quigley poked Carrington. "Hey, Paulie, you know who Dick Tracy is?"

"Of course I do. Warren Beatty. I saw the movie on cable."

Seidel, ignoring the both of them, continued. "The manager tells me his store dicks are staking out the ladies' room. I tell him forget the ladies' room, stake out the hardware department. Three days later they nab five Colombian women with rap sheets as long as this bar. Case closed."

"Amazing," Quigley said in awed tones. "I want to be just like you when I grow up."

Seidel thumped the bar. "Hey, Paddy, how about another round over here, but skip Quigley. He gets nasty when he drinks."

While Leland was listening to Seidel, he was surreptitiously people watching. The cops looked very different out of uniform. Perhaps because out of uniform they didn't have to act like cops. A smiling Charlie Reece was showing his son how to operate a video game. The proud, happy father was a very different man from the intractable PBA delegate who'd sat in his office three times in the past week vehemently protesting the blizzard of command disciplines.

Out on the dance floor an attractive auburn-haired young woman—was it Peggy Garrigan? he wasn't sure of the name—was surrounded by a gaggle of young teenage girls intent on learning the intricate steps of a line dance. Even the banter between Seidel and his cops spoke volumes. Only men who truly liked and respected each other could talk to each other that way.

In this comfortable oasis, away from the pressures of the job, this roomful of police officers and their families could forget death, the Joy Lounge, IAB, family fights, and civilian complaints. For a brief moment they could be just husbands, wives, boyfriends, and girlfriends.

Friends.

Leland felt a sudden surge of loneliness. Christmas was a season of family, a season of togetherness. When his mother died five years earlier, it took the will to live out of his father and he, too, was gone within the year. Leland had no brothers or sisters—just a handful of relatives that he barely knew scattered across the country. Marilyn had been his only family. They'd planned a Norman Rockwell-like family life—a house on Long Island, kids, and a dog. Leland was all for it, but he insisted on holding off on their plans until after the captain's exam. In the end, none of it came to pass. The divorce was finalized one week before the exam.

Leland cursed Charlie Drum for ruining his vacation and he cursed Charlie Drum for putting him here in this godforsaken precinct. Suddenly he had an overwhelming need to get out of there. He didn't care what they would say about him later. He had to get away. As he turned to leave, he bumped into a woman who sloshed wine across his sleeve.

"Oops, sorry—" A perky, dark-haired woman stepped back. "I think I spilled my wine on you."

Leland wiped his sleeve with a handkerchief. "That's OK. It was my fault."

She cocked her head and pointed a finger at him. "You're Captain Leland."

"Guilty."

"Well, Captain, I have a complaint."

From the brightness in her eyes it was clear this wasn't her first glass of wine. Leland braced himself. Apparently, this attractive young woman, who had summoned up the courage with the aid of a couple of glasses of wine, was about to tell him what they all wanted to tell him. He smiled grimly, waiting for the attack. "What's your complaint?"

"You're working my husband too hard. He's always making arrests. He's never home. It's not fair. Why can't other people make arrests? You should—"

A crying baby across the room stopped her in mid-sentence. "Oops, gotta go. My baby calls." As she turned away, she said, "Captain, I'm a little tipsy. Forgive me. But I mean it. Every word." Leland heard the desperation in her tone. "He shouldn't have to spend so much time away from me and the baby." Before he could ask her name she was gone.

Jack Barry was sitting at a table with his wife and five teenage daughters, all of whom looked like carbon copies of their father. He saw Leland wandering toward the door, looking like a lost soul. "Excuse me," he said to his wife. "I gotta rescue the captain."

Lieutenant Barry slipped up behind Leland and took his arm. "Hey, Cap, let me introduce you to everyone."

Reluctantly, Leland turned away from the door just fifteen feet away. So near and yet so far. "Sure," he said, forcing a grin. "Let's do it."

For the next half hour, Leland followed Barry from table to table making polite conversation with police officers and their families. Except for Billy Lafferty—who made a point of getting up and going to the men's room when Leland approached—everyone was cordial. Still, Leland could sense a certain tension. Clearly he was putting a damper on the festivities. He saw the veiled hostility in their eyes—even in the eyes of wives and girlfriends—and wondered at how many breakfasts and dinners he'd been the main topic of conversation.

"Jack, I gotta go," he said to Barry, who was clearly embarrassed by the way things were turning out. "I have a few things to clear up at the precinct."

Barry walked him to the door. "Captain"—he hesitated, trying to find the right words—"what just happened... it's nothing personal. It's just that the Five-five is a shithouse precinct and working in a shithouse brings people together. They're a tight bunch."

"The siege mentality?" Leland asked, surprised at the bitterness in his voice. "The 'us against them' syndrome?"

"It's more than that, Cap. Last year I took my family on vacation to a small island off the coast of Maine. We had a lousy time. The people were surly, almost hostile. I didn't understand it. On the way off the island, a ferry deckhand explained it to me. He said the islanders were a close-knit group. They're born, raised, and die on that island. They know everything there is to know about everyone who lives on that island. They're suspicious of outsiders. It's not that they don't like them, it's that they don't know them. The Five-five is like an island, Cap. They just don't know you yet."

"Thanks, Jack. Go back to your family." He still wasn't sure Barry had what it took to be his Operations Coordinator, but there was no doubt he was a decent man. Then he remembered the woman who spilled wine on him. She was on the dance floor gently rocking her baby to the rhythm of the music and looking rather sad. "Jack, who is that woman?"

Barry turned toward the dance floor. "The one with the baby? That's Carol Mazzeo. Eddie Mazzeo's wife."

Back in his office Leland thought about what Barry had said and was struck by the aptness of the analogy. Maybe the cops in the Five-five did think of themselves as islanders; drawn together by mutual interests and suspicious of outsiders. Bleakly, he wondered if he could ever become one of them. Bleakly, he wondered if he even wanted to become one of them.

~~

It was almost two-thirty in the afternoon the day after the precinct Christmas party and Peggy Garrigan and Eddie Mazzeo were enjoying a relatively quiet tour. Mazzeo was especially grateful for the lack of activity. He'd awakened this morning with a pounding head and the throbbing headache had stayed with him despite the copious amounts of coffee he'd been drinking all day.

Their regular sector was in the Bulge, but with a steady stream of cops being summoned to IAB every day, everyone had been shifted around and they'd been assigned to Sector Adam on the Hill.

It had been a while since the Joy Lounge incident, but Peggy was still angry with Mazzeo. That night, when he said he was going to Corr's with the guys, she'd vowed never to speak to him again. But the next day, when she'd found out what had happened, her smoldering anger and hurt quickly dissipated. But not for long. When she realized what an incredibly stupid thing he and the others had done she was furious with him all over again.

"Eddie, whose idea was it to go back to the Joy?"

Mazzeo rubbed his temples. "Peggy, I'm in no mood to talk about it. Okay?"

"I know you're not dumb enough to come up with such a hare-brained idea, but you're macho enough to go along with it."

"Is that supposed to be a compliment?" he asked, trying to break her antagonistic mood.

"No," she snapped. "Just tell me whose idea it was."

Mazzeo stopped for a light. "Peggy," he said quietly, looking straight ahead, "don't ask me any more questions. The less you know, the better. The subject is closed."

The radio dispatcher interrupted the uneasy silence. *"Sector Adam respond to 2315 Morris Avenue, apartment 17F, report of unconscious child."*

Mazzeo stomped on the accelerator.

Any call involving a child always made the stomach tighten and the adrenaline flow. Cops got used to a lot of things, but a child in trouble wasn't one of them. And it was worse when a cop has a young child of his own. As they sped to the location in tense silence, both Peggy and Eddie Mazzeo were thinking of his little boy.

Morris Avenue was *the* block on the Hill and 2315 was *the* address. The upscale 18-story building, perched atop the highest elevation in the precinct, offered a commanding view of the entire neighborhood below. Real estate agents boasted that from the tenth floor and up, it was possible to see lower Manhattan's famed skyline on a clear day. What they failed to mention was that there hadn't been a clear day in New York City since 1948.

Mazzeo was surprised to see an ambulance pull in right behind them. It was not uncommon to wait for a half an hour or more for a bus to show up.

"How'd you get here so fast?" Mazzeo asked the paramedics.

"Luck," a diminutive black female paramedic said as the four of them crowded into the elevator. "Just happen to be passing."

Cops and paramedics usually took these opportunities to engage in good natured banter or just trade war stories, but their minds were on a child waiting for them in an apartment upstairs and they rode the elevator to the 17th floor in strained silence.

A thirty-something, well-dressed woman, attractive in a severe sort of way, opened the door. "She's in here," she said, leading them into a small, but cheerful, bedroom whose walls were decorated with Disney character cutouts.

A little girl clad only in diapers was lying on the floor. She wasn't moving. As the paramedics began their resuscitative and diagnostic procedures, the mother walked out of the room. Peggy followed, slipping an Aided Card onto her clipboard. "Mrs.—?"

"Bellows. Cynthia Bellows."

"Mrs. Bellows, I'll need some information for my report. What's the child's name?"

"Molly."

"That's a nice name."

The woman lit a cigarette and blew a line of smoke toward a picture window that faced south. Manhattan was out there somewhere, but a thick, yellow haze obscured it.

"Can you tell me what happened?" Peggy asked.

"I put her in for her afternoon nap at two-fifteen. About ten minutes later I heard this thump. I rushed in and she was lying there on the floor just as you saw her."

Peggy looked up from her clipboard. "You left her there? You didn't try to pick her up or—"

"I didn't know what to do," the woman snapped. "I seem to remember you're not supposed to move anyone who's fallen. If there's a neck injury, can't you cause more damage?"

"Yeah, that's true," Peggy said, trying to keep her mounting anger in check. "Most mothers wouldn't have thought of that."

The woman gave Peggy a sharp look, but said nothing.

"How old is Molly?"

"Seventeen months. What will you do with her?"

"As soon as the paramedics stabilize her, she'll be taken to the hospital." On impulse, Peggy said, "Has Molly ever been to a hospital?"

"Once. When she was first learning to walk, she stumbled in the bathroom and struck her head on the tub."

"Oh, wow. Was she hurt seriously?"

"I think she got five or six stitches."

The paramedics wheeled the child out on a gurney and Peggy saw a large, purplish bruise on the child's forehead. She was conscious, but she stared at the ceiling with flat, dazed eyes.

"How is she?" the mother asked.

"She's regained consciousness and she's responding," the female paramedic answered. "But we won't know the extent of her injuries until we can get her to the hospital."

The other paramedic, who'd gone to ring for the elevator, shouted from the hallway, "It's here. Let's go."

Mrs. Bellows sat down and crushed her cigarette in an ashtray.

Peggy stopped at the door. "Aren't you going to the hospital with your daughter?"

"What? Oh, yes, of course." She jumped up. "Let me get my purse."

On the ride down in the crowded elevator, Peggy squeezed into the back corner and studied the woman. Clearly, Mrs. Bellows had money. Under her cashmere wrap, she was wearing a silk blouse and matching cashmere skirt. There was no wedding ring, but on her right hand was a diamond that had to be several carats. Self-consciously, she glanced down at her own chipped nails, wishing she could afford a weekly manicure. She didn't recognize the woman's perfume, but it certainly smelled expensive.

At the hospital, Peggy and Mazzeo gathered the remaining information they needed for their report and left. As they pulled away from the curb, Peggy said, "Eddie, what'd you think of all that?"

"I'm glad the kid wasn't hurt badly." He added with a grin, "And it's a nice change of pace going to an aided case where you don't have to worry about roaches crawling up your leg."

"What about the mother? Didn't she seem a little… detached? Cold?"

"She's probably in shock. I'd be a wreck if something like that happened to little Eddie. Why? What are you thinking?"

"Child abuse."

"Come on. Based on what?"

"Molly was injured before. Her mother said she hit her head on a tub."

"Kids are always doing stuff like that."

"Eddie, she couldn't even remember how many stitches her child got. What kind of mother is that?"

"You're not a mother. You don't understand."

Peggy stung by his words, lashed out. "And you're such an expert!"

"Hey, don't get yourself in an uproar."

"What about the bump on the kid's head?"

"She fell out of the crib. What the hell do you expect? Peggy, look at the mother. She's educated and she's got bucks. People like that don't abuse their kids."

"Eddie, you're such an incredible jerk. What the hell does money have to do with child abuse?"

"All right, so I'm no psychologist. But I'm telling you, you're off base."

"Head back to the house, Eddie. I'm gonna call this into the State Central Registry."

"Peggy, don't be stupid. People like Bellows have a lot of weight. You throw a stone at her, she'll drop a whole friggin' building on you."

"I can't believe you're talking like this, Eddie. Maybe she's not abusing the kid. God I hope not. But I have a bad feeling about this and I want the experts to decide. If I'm wrong, I'm wrong."

"I'm telling you, I know women like Bellows. When she finds out what you did, she'll drop a letter on you. You want to go to the Bureau? You don't need that kind of grief."

Peggy glared at him. "You don't either, but you went back to the Joy Lounge with the others."

Mazzeo pulled into the curb in front of the station house, shut off the engine, and rubbed his temples. "Peggy, for the last time, I stopped at Corr's. That's all. And that's the last time I'm gonna talk about this."

Chapter Thirteen

Sergeant Gus Labonte stood before the outgoing platoon and tugged at his seventeen-and-a-half-inch collar. Even though it was twenty-eight degrees outside, he was sweating profusely because he always sweated profusely.

He glowered at the men and women in the ranks. "All right, listen up. The captain wants to say a few words to you in front of the desk. We're gonna march out there in a neat, orderly formation. I don't want a repeat of the fiasco that Sergeant Engle had. Do I make myself clear?"

Lafferty piped up. "Hey, Sarge, it ain't our fault Engle don't know his left from his right. What if you do the same thing?"

Labonte peered over his reading glasses at the wisecracking cop. "Lafferty," he said, wheezing softly. "It don't matter if I say turn *inside out*, you will execute in the proper direction. And God have mercy on the puke who tries to make me look bad. Do I make myself clear?"

Forty heads bobbed up and down in unison.

Labonte had been a Marine drill instructor before he came on the job. In those days, he was tall, lean, and mean. He was still tall and mean, but at three hundred pounds he was no longer lean, and every man and woman in the room knew that "Lard-ass" Labonte always made good on a threat.

Leland stood behind the desk and nodded approvingly as the platoon came smartly out of the muster room. At least Sergeant Labonte knew how to post a platoon. Then he cringed when the sergeant yelled, "Right face." But to his surprise, the entire platoon turned left to face the desk.

Leland cleared his throat. "I want to talk to you about summons activity."

The groans from the back of the ranks told him why the Five-five had the lowest summons activity in the city. He scanned the police officers in the ranks. Finally, he was beginning to recognize some faces—Reece,

Lafferty, Garrigan, Mazzeo, Elliot and his partner, Oliver. He paused to collect his thoughts. Talking about summons activity was a ticklish subject and he didn't want to be accused of setting quotas.

"Perhaps some of you aren't aware of the many different kinds of summonses that can be issued," he began. "For instance, I drove by the Joy Lounge last night and I saw a dozen cars doubled-parked, parked in front of fire hydrants, and in bus stops. All clear violations."

At the mention of the Joy, the fidgeting stopped and forty pairs of eyes locked on him. Finally, he had their attention. "Then, I saw this man parked in front of the Joy and the music coming from his radio was extremely loud. Officer Garrigan, what would you do about that?"

Peggy jumped at the sound of her name. She didn't think he knew who she was. "I'd tell him to lower it, Captain."

"What if he didn't?"

She wanted to say she'd make the sonofabitch lower it, but she couldn't say that to the captain. She shrugged helplessly. "I don't know, Captain."

"Under *Patrol Guide* 116-28 you can issue the owner a summons for noxious noise. And while you're at it, you should check to see that the car is properly registered and inspected."

Several eyes widened and there were a few nudges.

"So," Leland continued, "there are plenty of violations out there. I saw a couple of dozen within a half block of the Joy Lounge myself." He scanned the faces in the ranks and saw a few smiles that weren't there before. "Okay, Sergeant, post the platoon and come back and see me."

Labonte hitched up his gun belt, shouted, "Right face," and marched the platoon out the door. A moment later he was in Leland's office.

"Sergeant Labonte, are you aware of the provisions of PG 109-12 regarding tax stamps for jukeboxes?"

Labonte ran a beefy hand over his mouth. "Uh, actually, Cap—"

"It says every jukebox must have a current tax stamp."

"Oh, yeah, that. I knew that," Labonte lied.

"Good. How about the Joy Lounge? Do they have a current tax stamp?"

It finally dawned on the sergeant what Leland was driving at. "I'll go check that out right now."

"That's a very good idea." Leland said, making it sound as thought it was the sergeant's idea all along.

Leland walked the big sergeant to the door. "By the way," he said quietly. "You might see some sector cars out of their assigned areas tonight. Especially around the Joy Lounge. I wouldn't worry about it."

"Sure, Cap. Whatever you say."

~~

An hour after the platoon turned out, Leland heard loud, angry voices and came out of his office to investigate. Gloria Perez was standing in front of the desk engaged in a heated discussion with Sergeant Labonte. Police Officers Oliver and Elliot stood to the side holding a manacled prisoner between them.

"What's the problem?" Leland asked.

Gloria started to speak, but he cut her off. "Sarge, why don't you tell me what's going on?"

"A store security guard caught this guy shoplifting and they called us. When Elliot and Oliver tried to put the cuffs on him, he threw a punch at Elliot. We're booking him for assault and petit larceny."

"So what's the problem?"

Gloria, irritated at the way Leland cut her off, said, "The problem is that Tony is on probation. I just got him a job last week and he's been doing fine."

"Doing fine? He got caught shoplifting and he assaulted a police officer."

"Twenty bucks worth of CDs. Big deal. I can ask his probation officer to overlook that, but if he's arrested for assault, he'll go back to prison."

Leland looked at Elliot's face. There was an ugly welt under his right eye. "Is that where he hit you?"

Elliot nodded silently. His face was a mask of neutrality, but Leland knew he, and every other cop in earshot, was waiting to see if this asshole commanding officer was going to cut his prisoner loose.

"Book him for assault and petit larceny," Leland said.

"Captain," Gloria said in exasperation. "Putting everyone behind bars isn't the answer."

"Neither is punching a police officer, Miss Perez."

"Look, if he stays out of prison he can work. What if he apologizes to the officer?"

Leland looked into those velvet eyes that were burning with frustration. From the first moment he'd met her, he knew he was going to have trouble with her. He just didn't think it would be this soon.

"Miss Perez, I do not dispense frontier justice nor do I have the authority to suspend the Penal Law of New York State. If you want to plead for this man, I suggest you do it before a judge."

"Law and order," she said, her voice quivering with fury. "The motto of a real progressive police department." Without another word she turned and walked out of the station house.

Leland watched her go with a feeling of melancholy he couldn't explain.

~~

"You know what Labonte's problem is?" Lafferty asked.

"No, but I'm sure you're gonna to tell me," Reece said, turning the radio car onto a side street.

"He's got a psychological thorn stuck in his paw. That's what makes him such a sonofabitch."

Reece glanced at his partner. "You know, Billy, you got a touch of the poet in you."

"Up yours."

"Sector George, respond to 495 Tilton Street. Meet the super out front."

Lafferty keyed the mic. "Sector George, ten-four." Then he returned to the other topic that he'd been obsessing about since the beginning of the tour. "How many guys IAB interrogate so far?"

"Twenty," Reece answered as he made a U-turn.

"How many you figure they'll talk to?"

"Everyone who was working that night. We're the usual suspects."

Lafferty shook his head. "Those IAB scumbags give me the creeps." Then, in a more positive vein he added, "But they got shit, right, Charlie? Thanks to your pantyhose, the assholes in the bar can't ID us."

Charlie Reece made a left into Tilton Street. "Don't sell IAB short. All they gotta do is turn one of us."

"Who'd incriminate himself?"

Reece gave his partner a sideways glance. Lafferty was a street-wise cop, but when it came to department politics he was as naive as a tourist taking a midnight stroll through Central Park. In his six years as a PBA delegate, Reece had seen enough to know that IAB had ways to get what it wanted. "Immunity, Billy," he said. "Offer a cop immunity and he'll spin like a top."

Lafferty bit his lip and thought about Reece's comment in silence until they pulled up in front of 495 Tilton.

For years the residents of Tilton Street, located at the fringe of the Valley, had valiantly fought to maintain their status as a respectable block. But in spite of their best efforts, the block had become infected by the creeping blight that created ghettos. Slowly and inexorably it made its way from tenement to tenement and block to block the way a jungle reclaims the land. Three abandoned cars and a street littered with debris were mute testimony to that lost battle.

The super, an old black man with yellowed, rheumy eyes, was anxiously waiting for them on the stoop.

Lafferty got out of the radio car. "Whaddaya got, pal?"

The super hopped from one foot to the other as though he had to go badly. "Apartment Five C. You gotta see this."

"What's the problem?"

"Officer, you gotta come see for yourself."

Before Lafferty could say anything else, the old man, with an agility belying his age, ran inside and hit the stairs two at a time.

By the time they got to the top floor, Reece's chest was heaving from the exertion of climbing five flights. He grabbed the banister to steady himself. "Why," he wheezed, "is it *always* the top floor?"

A skinny Lafferty, who wasn't even breathing heavily, brushed past him. "Lose some weight, Jumbo." He poked his partner with his nightstick. " I'm telling you right here and now, fucko, you take a heart attack, I'm not giving you mouth to mouth."

To the super Lafferty said, "What's your name, pal?"

"Walter."

Lafferty rested his hand on the wall, but quickly pulled it away when he saw a roach the size of a VW Beetle lumbering toward him. "Walter, before we go any further, tell us what we're getting into."

The super looked at the two cops wide-eyed. "Apartment five, Mrs. Kibby. You gotta see for yourself." The super pointed at a paint-chipped steel door. Like most apartment doors in the Valley this one bore the scars of previous break-ins.

Reece's heartbeat had almost returned to normal, but he was cranky after the long climb. "Hey, pal," he said in a raspy voice, "I ain't gonna play *Twenty Questions* with you. Tell us what's going on."

Lafferty chuckled. "Hey, Charlie, did you ever notice that when you're out of breath you sound just like Marlon Brando in the *Godfather*?"

"Up yours. What's the fucking problem?" he asked the super, sounding exactly like Marlon Brando.

The super's watery eyes glistened in the dim hallway light. "Balloons," he whispered, pushing open the door to apartment five. "Balloons."

From the hallway, Reece and Lafferty peered into the dimly lit apartment and stared in disbelief. The floor from the foyer to the living room was completely covered with water-filled balloons. Gingerly, Reece kicked one of the balloons and it careened into another, setting up a chain reaction of wobbling balloons.

Shuffling to avoid bursting a balloon, the two cops made their way into the living room. Mrs. Kibby, a heavyset woman with her gray hair in a tight bun, sat in a chair looking out the window. Balloons were everywhere. On the table, the couch—there was even one perched precariously on a lampshade.

Reece pushed his hat to the back of his head. "Mrs. Kibby, I'm officer Reece. Are you okay?"

There was no reaction from the woman, who continued to stare out the window.

Lafferty shuffled up behind Reece. "Hey, Charlie," he whispered, making a stabbing motion with his right hand. "Watch your ass. This reminds me of the movie *Psycho*."

The super tugged on Lafferty's sleeve. "Officer, lemme show you. There's more."

He led the two cops into the bedroom. There were balloons everywhere—on the bed, in dresser drawers, and on the floor of the closet.

"What's the deal?" Lafferty said to the super. "The old lady get off on dropping water balloons on people's heads or what?"

The super blinked his rheumy eyes. "Ain't no water in them balloons. That's piss."

"*Jesus H. Christ*!" Lafferty jumped back, lost his balance, and stomped on a balloon. It burst, splattering urine onto his shoe and pants leg. He hopped in the air. "Sonofa*bitch*!"

Reece grabbed his partner in a bear hug. *"For chrissake will you stand still?"*

Lafferty's pinched face grew still tighter. "I got *piss* in my shoe," he said through clenched teeth, "and you want I should stand still?"

"You keep hopping around like that and we'll all have piss in our shoes.

Lafferty soberly regarded the balloons surrounding them. "Charlie, how much do you think one of these things weighs?"

Reece warily nudged a balloon with the toe of his shoe. "How the hell should I know? Why?"

"Because liquid weighs a lot and this is an old building. If this floor collapses, it'll start a chain reaction and we'll all end up in the basement either crushed to death or drowned in a sea of piss. I'm getting the fuck out of here."

Reece grabbed his sleeve. "No, you're not. Get on the horn and call for Labonte. I'll talk to the old lady."

As though he were traversing a minefield, Reece carefully shuffled through a gently bobbing sea of balloons and went back to the living room. Mrs. Kibby was still sitting at the window. He stopped ten feet from the woman and stepped behind a couch. Psychos, or EDPs—emotionally disturbed persons, as the department euphemistically called them—were notoriously unpredictable. Adrenaline, fueled by a nervous system gone awry, made EDPs fearless, impervious to pain, and possessing superhuman strength—a deadly combination that had sent more than one unwary cop to the hospital. And Reece, through personal experience, had come to learn that size, weight, or age had little bearing on an EDPs danger potential.

"Mrs. Kibby, I'm Officer Reece. Can you tell me why you've collected all these balloons?"

She turned away from the window and squinted at him as her eyes refocused from the bright light outside to the apartment's dim interior. "I have to save my life forces," she said softly.

"Ah, I see. Where exactly do these... life forces come from?"

"From inside me." Tears welled up in her eyes. "I do my best to hold the life forces in, but then the pain gets so bad that I have to let them out."

"Mrs. Kibby," Reece said gently. "It's okay to urinate. Everyone does."

She gave him the kind of patronizing smile that one gives to someone who doesn't understand important principles. "You can't fool me, young man. It's my life forces in those balloons. That's why I save them." She brushed away a wispy strand of gray hair from her eyes. "I've been trying to think of some way to return the life forces to my body."

"And you haven't thought of a way yet, have you?"

She shook her head sadly.

"Thank Christ," he muttered, considering the possibilities.

Lafferty shuffled back into the room. "The sergeant's on the way."

"Call for a bus," Reece said quietly. "We got an EDP."

Lafferty, looking like Charlie Chaplin, shuffled back to the kitchen and Reece continued his questioning. "How long have you been saving these... life forces, Mrs. Kibby?"

"Almost a year."

Reece's eyes dropped to the balloons surrounding him. "A *year* of..."

"I've run out of room. I haven't been able to sleep in my bed for three days. I asked Walter if I could store some balloons in the cellar, but he said there wasn't any room."

"Mrs. Kibby, where did you get the idea that the stuff in the balloons is your life forces?"

"A voice. It was just a year ago that a voice told me I was losing my life forces every time I went to the bathroom. Since then I've done my best to hold them inside me." Her melancholy eyes swept the apartment. "What am I going to do?"

Reece took his hat off. He was going to put it down, but every surface was taken up by a balloon. He put the hat back on his head. "Mrs. Kibby," he said cheerfully, "you're lucky I'm here."

She squinted at him suspiciously. "Why is that?"

"Because I know all about life forcess. I had a case like this just last week and I got a chance to talk to a bunch of scientists about it. First of all, I can report to you that you're not losing your life forces."

She shook her head adamantly. "Oh, yes I am."

"Oh, no you're not. And I can prove it. You say you've been losing your life forces for a year. Right? Well, if that's true, you'd be dead. Think about it. *No* one can live without life forces for a whole *year*!"

Uncertainty crept into her voice. "Well, I don't know..."

Reece heard Sergeant Labonte coming up the stairs. More specifically, he heard the sergeant's lumbering footsteps and heavy wheezing.

Reece gave her his best used car salesman grin. "Hey, would I lie to you? And I got more good news. I know a place where you can get yourself checked out. You know, to make sure your life forces aren't leaking out or anything."

Her hand fluttered to the collar of her frayed housedress and her facial expression was a mixture of hope and skepticism. "Oh, I wouldn't know how to get there. I seldom leave the apartment anymore."

"No problem. I got a bus... I mean an ambulance coming. They'll take you to see those scientists I was telling you about." He saw that she was still hesitant. "Jeez," he added, "it must have been tough for you this past year. All alone, worrying about something like this."

Tears glistened in her eyes. "Since Harry died six years ago, I've been all alone in the world."

"Harry? That your husband?"

"My cat."

"I see. I'm sorry." Reece heard wheezing and labored breathing behind him and turned slowly. The sergeant's round, florid-faced was drenched in sweat. "Sarge, is Mrs. Kibby's transportation here?"

The fatigued sergeant, unable to speak, could only nod.

Reece turned back to the woman. The moment of truth was here. Up until now he'd remained safely out of range, but now that he'd gotten her confidence he couldn't afford to blow it by remaining behind a sofa. EDPs might be nuts, but they were acute observers. If she sensed he was afraid of her, the rapport he'd so carefully established would be shattered and she might go ballistic. He didn't relish the idea of wrestling on a bed of piss balloons with a sixty-something psycho.

Shuffling through the balloons, he came around the sofa and moved toward her. Out of the corner of his eye he saw Lafferty and the sergeant move into a position where they could help him if necessary. As he moved closer he watched her eyes carefully. The eyes were the key. Shiftiness, inability to maintain eye contact, or a wide-eyed look of fear were all indications that the short-circuited brain behind an enigmatic face was going to snap. But all he saw in her eyes was bewilderment and sadness.

He offered his hand. "Come on, Mrs. Kibby, I'll help you downstairs."

Gently, she put her hand in his. "Thank you, officer," she said, in a child-like voice. "You're very kind."

As they shuffled toward the door, Sergeant Labonte, who now had enough air in his over-taxed lungs to speak in a strangled rasp, whispered to Reece, "I took Donati off a foot post. He's downstairs with the bus. He'll accompany Mrs. Kibby. You get back up here. You and Lafferty have a few things to do."

Reece swore to himself. He wanted to tell the fat-assed bucket of lard that after the great job he'd done with Mrs. Kibby, he shouldn't have to climb five flights *again*. But not wanting to upset the old woman, he said in an amiable tone, "Sure, Sarge, I'll be right back."

When Reece and the woman were out of hearing, Labonte pushed his hat to the back of his head and surveyed the balloon-filled apartment. "Piss!" he said. "What the hell are we gonna do with all this piss?"

By the time Reece, wheezing almost as badly as Labonte, stumbled through the door of the apartment for the second time, Sergeant Labonte had come to a decision.

"Throw 'em out the fuckin' window," he announced to a startled Reece and Lafferty. "You," he pointed at the super, "get a hose out to the front of the building. As the balloons come down hose everything into the street."

Lafferty's face pursed at the thought of handling hundreds, maybe *thousands*, of piss balloons. "Sarge," he said. "We can't throw this stuff out the window. We're liable to start a fucking cholera epidemic or something."

Labonte wiped his brow with a damp handkerchief and put his hat back on. "Considering this neighborhood, a cholera epidemic would be an improvement." At the door he yelled over his shoulder. "And don't milk this. I don't wanna hear you guys putting in for overtime."

After the sergeant left, an enraged Lafferty, forgetting for a moment where he was, spun around. He tripped on a balloon and fell forward with a strangled scream. Fortunately, none of the balloons broke under his light weight. Snarling, he scrambled to his feet. "That mother-*fucker*! He wants them thrown out the window. I'll throw them out the window." He grabbed the nearest balloon and shuffled toward the open window. "Right on his fat fucking head."

Reece, looking like a heavyweight version of Charlie Chaplin, quickly shuffled after him. "Don't do anything stupid, Billy. You pop Labonte with a piss balloon he'll rip your spleen out."

Lafferty, holding a balloon out the window, stopped. "Maybe you're right. Who's driving Lard-ass?"

"Perkins."

"Another useless scumbag." Lafferty let go of the balloon.

Reece lunged for the window. "You *asshole*!" He looked down, expecting to see Sergeant Labonte standing at ground zero. But there was only his radio car. The balloon wobbled toward the car parked below. Reece could see Perkins behind the wheel, reading a *Playboy* magazine. The balloon splattered across the windshield, spraying Mrs. Kibby's life forces across the hood. The sergeant's startled driver jumped out and looked up. He started to say something, but dove for the safety of the car when he saw another incoming. This one glanced off the roof and splattered on the sidewalk.

"No points," Reece shouted gleefully. The balloon's gotta burst on the car or—" He stopped when he saw Sergeant Labonte step out from the building and shake his fist up at them.

Lafferty shrugged helplessly. "There's a real wind shear up here," he yelled at the animated sergeant below.

Labonte tried to hitch his gun belt above his enormous stomach, but it simply slid back to where it always was—just above his crotch. *"Don't let another balloon go until I'm out of the block,"* he bellowed. "Is that clear?"

Lafferty nodded, but out of the side of his mouth he whispered to Reece, "What's the worst he can do to me? It'd be worth a few days off to bounce a piss balloon off his fat head."

"Don't do it, Billy. He could have you locked up for assault."

Lafferty pulled the balloon closer to him, "I never thought of that."

As the sergeant was getting into his car, he looked up at them and smiled. The two cops groaned. Labonte *never* smiled. "I forgot to tell you, Lafferty," he shouted. "A telephone message came in for you. You're to report to IAB Monday morning at 0800 hours."

Lafferty snapped his head back, whacking it on the window. "Sonofa-*bitch*!" he yelled, backing into the room rubbing his head.

The two partners looked at each other for a long while in silence. Then, Lafferty, with more trepidation than bravado in his voice, said, "I guess it's my turn in the barrel. What do I gotta do, partner?"

"Just show up," Reece said somberly. "I'll notify the PBA office to provide a lawyer."

"IAB," Lafferty mused. "Those scumbags give me the creeps."

"Yeah, and they're playing games, too."

Lafferty stopped rubbing his head. "Whadda ya mean?"

"Today's Friday. They're giving you the weekend to think about it."

Lafferty rubbed the knot on the back of his head. "Those dirty bastards."

Reece handed Lafferty his hat. "Just watch your big mouth when you get there, you little hump. You get very sarcastic when you're scared."

~~

Peggy Garrigan slammed down the telephone in the complaint room. "I don't *believe* these people."

Mazzeo, who'd just completed a traffic accident report, looked up. "What'd they say?"

"The case has been assigned to the borough Sex Crimes Squad. They did some preliminary investigation, but they're all backed up, yada, yada. The bottom line is they haven't done a damn thing."

"They probably are backed up. We're all backed up."

Peggy glared at him. "I called this case in yesterday. They should have started an investigation immediately."

Mazzeo dropped the report on the clerk's desk. "You're dreaming."

Peggy ran her fingers through her short hair. Something she always did when she was exasperated. "Eddie, how can you be so complacent? We're talking about a little girl's life."

"No, *you're* talking about a little girl's life."

"What's that supposed to mean?"

"I think you're wrong. I don't think there's any child abuse there."

"I don't know for sure either. All I ask is that they investigate it."

Mazzeo stood up. "Come on, we gotta get back on patrol."

He saw the look on her face and said, "Don't worry, they'll get to it."

"When Molly's dead?" Peggy replied bitterly.

Chapter Fourteen

At the sound of the door chime, Saul Weinberg looked up from polishing his glass cases and sighed with relief. It was almost 10:30 in the morning and he had yet to make a sale. He was a superstitious man, especially when it came to business. After forty years in the jewelry trade he was convinced that if he didn't have a paying customer by eleven o'clock, the rest of the day would be a total loss. This year, seasonal sales were off and with Christmas just a week away, he needed all the business he could get.

He smiled at the prosperous man with the nattily trimmed beard. "May I help you, sir?" he asked.

Without saying a word, the man handed him a piece of paper. The jeweler's smile froze and then melted into fear as he read the note. He looked up into the man's dark, hypnotic eyes imploringly. He was about to protest that he wasn't worth robbing, that he hadn't even made a sale today. But then the man put his hand in his pocket and Weinberg was sure he had a gun. The jeweler paled and with a shaky hand hit the "no sale" key. The register drawer sprung open.

~~

Seidel stuck his head in the door, waving a piece of paper in a clear plastic wrapper. "Number four, Cap. The Poet Bandit has struck again."

Leland cradled his head in his hands and read the poem.

Dogs that bark at waning moons
Tear the night with haunting tunes
Smooth as silk or coarse as wool
The moon exerts tremendous pull

He reread it again. "Has your psychiatrist friend seen this?"

"I read it to him over the phone. He thinks the Poet Bandit's really nuts. Actually, he used the word psychotic and a couple of other technical words."

Leland rubbed his throbbing temples. "Sarge, I asked you not to use the term 'Poet Bandit.'"

Seidel took the paper back from Leland. "I swear to God, Cap. I don't use that term around anyone but you."

Seidel disappeared in a cloud of smoke, leaving Leland to wonder if the Poet Bandit was going to be the one to torpedo his career. Well, if he was, he'd have to get in line.

~~

It was after seven by the time Leland left the precinct for Heidi Vancamp's Christmas party. He was not looking forward to a night of forced good cheer, but he told himself it was a good opportunity to meet the people on the Hill. Still, as he rode the mirrored elevator to Vancamp's ninth floor apartment, he wondered if that was the real reason or was it because Heidi had said Gloria Perez would be there.

He rang the bell and Heidi, wearing an ankle-length red dress that accentuated her trim figure, stuck her hand out. "Captain Leland, I'm so glad you could make it. Come in. Let me introduce you my other guests."

The twenty-odd people hardly filled the large, ornately furnished living room, which was accented with Oriental paintings and eighteenth century objets d'art. Leland, who'd eaten nothing since an early morning bagel, eyed a table covered with attractively displayed platters of shrimp, cheese and hors d'oeuvres. He started inching toward the table, but Heidi took his arm and steered him toward her guests.

The first one she introduced him to was Paula Wheatley. The gaunt woman, whose facial skin was pulled back so tightly that she was incapable of smiling, was mute testimony to the hazards of dealing with a discount plastic surgeon. Heidi quickly introduced him to a dozen others. Leland, futilely trying to remember names, nodded and wondered which ones were the movers and shakers in his precinct. But it was impossible to tell. Heidi's introductions—names only, no titles—offered no clue.

In the next half hour, he was buttonholed by a succession of people who insisted on expressing their opinions on everything from free condoms to crowded prisons. A retired Wall Street lawyer asked Leland's opinion on capital punishment. As Leland was about to answer, he was suddenly aware that others nearby stopped talking to hear his answer and it reminded him that he hadn't been invited because he was Richard Leland; he'd been invited because he was the commanding officer of the precinct and anything he said could be interpreted as the policy of the police department.

In the past, he always enjoyed discussing controversial issues, but now he found himself monitoring what he said, offering tepid, safe responses that bore little resemblance to what he truly believed.

His rumbling stomach reminded him that he still hadn't eaten. He started edging toward the food, but a gloomy man who seemed to be there against his will, stood between him and the food. Leland stuck his hand out. "Richard Leland, I'm the new precinct captain."

The man returned a limp handshake. "Kurt Vancamp. Heidi's husband."

There was a long, awkward pause as Leland tried to imagine why the ebullient Heidi had married this funereal man. "You must be very proud of your wife," he said finally. "She's done a lot for the community."

Vancamp shrugged. "She'd have been better off running for congress instead of wasting her time trying to bail out this sinking ship."

"You think the Bronx is a sinking ship?"

Vancamp fixed Leland with a baleful eye. "Unless you have a better metaphor for the disaster that is the Bronx."

"If you feel that way, why are you living here?"

Vancamp nodded toward his wife, who was smoothly moving from one group to another. From the smile on her face she was clearly enjoying herself. "If it was up to me, we'd be living in a condo in Manhattan, but that'll have to wait until Heidi realizes she's not Joan of Arc."

Like a specter, Paula Wheatley, the poster woman for bad plastic surgery, materialized from the crowd and seized Leland's arm with a claw-like hand. "Captain Leland, as the president of our little group here on the Hill, I want to welcome you to the community."

"What group is that, Mrs. Wheatley?"

"Community United Together."

CUT. Leland remembered the description Barry had given him his first day in the precinct regarding CUT's goal: *Keep the riffraff in Death Valley and off the Hill.*

"Your predecessor, Captain Sperling, was such a nice man," she gushed. "Did you know him?"

"No, I didn't."

"Such a nice man," she repeated in a tone that sounded like the beginning of a Brutus-is-an-honorable-man speech. "But he did not make decisions easily." She stared at him with eyes that seemed incapable of blinking.

Translation: She didn't like his decisions.

"We have so many problems in this precinct, as I'm sure you know, Captain."

Leland nodded in agreement. He knew only too well the problems in the Five-five precinct.

She squeezed Leland's arm and her talons dug into his flesh. "There's that dreadful man, Reverend Munyika," she said, nodding toward the door.

Leland was surprised to see Munyika here. For a brief, paranoid moment he thought there might be some kind of an alliance between him and Heidi, but he quickly dismissed that unworthy thought. Heidi Vancamp cared too much about the community to get mixed up with an agitator like Munyika.

"What are you going to do about him?" Mrs. Wheatley whispered as the talons dug deeper into his arm.

"I'm trying to establish a working rapport with him." Leland watched Munyika work the crowd. Whatever else he was, he had charisma. A steady stream of bankers, lawyers, and business executives literally tripped over each other to shake his hand.

"Well, you certainly could stop him from stirring up those *people* into a frenzy every time he drags some bogus cause out of the gutter."

Leland tried to keep a straight face. "Mrs. Wheatley, the Reverend Munyika and his *people* are protected by the First Amendment. They have a right to free speech." In spite of his personal dislike—and fear—of the dangerous Kawasi Munyika, he took perverse pleasure in waving the Constitution in the face of people like her. As far as the Mrs. Wheatleys of the world were concerned, the Constitution was written for *them*, not for *those* people.

She tried for a smile, but the best she could manage was a stiff-faced grimace. "Really, Captain, don't you think there's a limit to free speech?"

"That's for the Supreme Court to decide. I just enforce the law."

Leland saw her left eyebrow arch in displeasure and wondered what she would have to say to his successor about the "nice Captain Leland."

She moved on to discussing the pros and cons of alternate side of the street parking and Leland desperately looked around the room for a means of escape. He'd made his appearance. He'd met the Hill community. Now it was time to get the hell out of there.

Then he saw Gloria come in. She was wearing a short black dress with a bias cut that caressed her thin, lithe body. He continued to nod and make appropriate grunts to Mrs. Wheatley's non-stop monologue, and all thoughts of leaving the party vanished from his mind.

He finally escaped from the tedious Mrs. Wheatley, only to be captured by an animated old man who was convinced the solution to crime in New York City was to arm the cab drivers. As he slipped away from the old man and slugged down a glass of warm white wine that someone had stuck in his hand, the Rev. Munyika's mellifluous voice boomed across the room. "Isn't that right, Captain?"

Leland turned and feigned surprise at seeing him. "Reverend Munyika, good to see you. I'm sorry, isn't what right?"

Munyika's smile was full of contempt. "I have just been telling these good people that police brutality and corruption are on the rise. Isn't that right?"

Every eye in the room turned toward Leland and all conversation stopped. Leland knew there was no way he could win a verbal sparring match with someone as outrageous as Munyika and he suddenly wished he was still in conversation with Mrs. Wheatley.

"I think you know better than that, Rev. Munyika," he responded with a game smile. "Since the Knapp Commission, the police department has created numerous policies to deal with police brutality and corruption."

Munyika's booming laughter filled the room. "Ah, the police department's party line. How often have I heard that?"

"Corruption is not just a police issue, Rev. Munyika." Gloria stepped through the group and stood in front of Munyika. "Read the headlines. It's in politics—even the clergy," she added with a disingenuous smile.

Munyika's smile remained frozen on his face, but his eyes flashed in anger. "And we must fight it wherever we find it. Isn't that right, Ms. Perez?"

"That's absolutely right, Reverend Munyika."

There was a hushed moment as the guests held their collective breaths waiting to see what would happen next. But Munyika blinked first and turned away, and the resumption of a dozen interrupted conversations broke the tense silence.

Leland tried to maneuver his way toward Gloria, but a succession of people with problems, which apparently only he could solve, kept buttonholing him. Finally, he got close to her. Since he'd seen her come through the door, he'd been planning what he would say. First he would apologize for his curt behavior yesterday. Then he would explain that he didn't have the power to dismiss an assault charge. He was certain she would understand. Then he would thank her for coming to his aid with Munyika.

"Good evening, Ms. Perez."

"Captain Leland, I'm surprised you found time to break away from your crime-fighting duties to spend time at a boring Christmas party."

"Ms. Perez"—he heard himself say in a rude tone—"it's part of my job to attend boring parties and talk to boring people." *Damn it! Why did she always make him say things he had no intention of saying?*

Instead of snapping back at him as he thought she would, she tapped his glass and said. "I thought police officers weren't supposed to drink alcohol on duty."

Exasperated by her needling tone, he snapped, "This doesn't qualify as alcohol. It's swill."

She laughed, a beautiful, lilting laugh that made him swallow hard. "You're right, Captain. It is swill." She leaned close to him and he could smell her perfume. " Heidi is a wonderful woman, but she knows nothing about wine."

That broke the tension between them and for the next ten minutes they managed to have a pleasant conversation without any real or imagined digs.

Leland held up his empty glass. "I could use another glass of swill. How about you?"

As he was heading for the makeshift bar in the dining room with their empty glasses, a well-dress, distinguished middle-aged black man intercepted him. The face was familiar, but Leland couldn't place him. "You must be Captain Leland," the man said with an engaging grin. "I'm Thaddeus Archer."

"Of course. Senator Archer. Good to meet you." Leland smiled pleasantly, but inwardly he was appalled with himself for not recognizing the high-profile State Senator whose district included the Five-five precinct. Archer, an outspoken critic of city government—especially the police department, was not someone you wanted for an enemy. Even Charlie Drum was afraid of him.

"So how are you getting along in your new assignment, Captain?"

"There's a lot to learn, Senator. But I'm working on it."

Archer took Leland's arm. "Do you have a moment? There's something I'd like to talk to you about."

Leland looked longingly over his shoulder at Gloria, who'd been cornered by Mrs. Wheatley. He would rather have gone back to rescue Gloria, but he couldn't ignore the influential Thaddeus Archer. He put the two empty glasses down on a nearby sideboard. "Sure, Senator," he said with an easy smile. "I have all the time you need."

Archer led him to a quiet spot in front of a large picture window away from the rest of the people in the room. "Look at that," he said, pointing at a commanding view that swept west over the rooftops of tenements. In the distance, the twinkling green lights of the New Jersey Palisades flickered. In the inky darkness below, the street lights sparkled like diamonds. "It's a beautiful sight at night isn't it?"

Leland nodded. It was spectacular.

"Too bad the view is only beautiful at night." Archer turned away from the window. "You and I know what the Bronx looks like in the daylight, don't we, Captain Leland? We see it for what it really is: a broken, shabby place."

Leland was about to disagree, but then he realized that Archer was giving a political speech and the question was rhetorical.

Archer continued. "But I believe we can restore the Bronx to its former greatness. With people like you, Heidi Vancamp, and me, we can make this a place that we can all be proud of."

"I believe we can, " Leland said, wondering where this conversation was going.

Archer stroked his pencil-thin mustache and turned back to the view. "So much to do with so few resources. You know, Captain, every year at budget time we legislators agonize over how best to use the meager funds we have at our disposal. How to get the best bang for the buck as it were."

Leland recognized the line. Archer had used it in his last reelection bid.

He turned his charismatic smile on Leland. "Oh, I know a lot of folks think we legislators are irresponsible and just trying to line our own pockets. And frankly, that charge is all too often true of some of my colleagues. But I can assure you it isn't true of me. I have nothing but the highest regard and affection for my constituents here in the Bronx. I tell you this because I'm confident you feel the same way." He looked at Leland appraisingly. "I have many friends in police headquarters and they have only good things to say about you."

"Thank you, Senator," Leland responded, wondering who those friends were, if indeed, he had any.

Archer waved a hand in dismissal. "I don't say this to flatter you. I say this because I think you and I are of one mind. We both want to do the most with the limited resources we have at our disposal."

"And that's what I've been trying to do, Senator."

Archer nodded sympathetically. "With, perhaps, one minor exception."

Leland stiffened. Had he screwed up already? "What exception is that?" he asked with a tight smile.

"This Joy Lounge thing. I hear the bar is being harassed daily by your police officers."

"Harassed? Senator, a police officer was seriously injured trying to break up a fight in that bar. He—"

"Yes, of course, of course," Archer said soothingly. "That was a dreadful, despicable act and the ones responsible should be brought to justice. But I wonder if all this special attention by your police is a wise use of your precious resources."

Leland looked into the smiling, urbane face of Senator Archer and a disturbing thought suddenly occurred to him: Could the senator be the mysterious owner of the Joy Lounge? Then he remembered his own promise uttered in anger and sincerity in the emergency room the night Hector Torres was beaten—he would shut down the Joy. If Archer owned the bar, then what had seemed like a simple, honest statement at the time had now taken on a whole new meaning. When he'd made that promise, he never dreamed he might have to bump heads with someone as powerful as Senator Archer. "What would you suggest I do, Senator?"

"Far be in for me to tell you how to run your precinct, Captain. But I suspect you have to practice, as we do in the State legislature, some form of financial and resource triage. Fix what can be fixed and abandon what's hopeless. There's no question that the Joy Lounge *is* a terrible place, but it seems to me that there are so many more important things in this community that need police attention."

Leland struggled to contain his anger. He wanted to tell the senator to go to hell, but all that would accomplish would be to grease the skids on his own career. "I'll take another look at the situation," he said blandly.

Archer slapped Leland's shoulder. "I'm glad we see eye to eye on this unfortunate issue. My friends in headquarters were right. You are a bright, rising star." He glanced at his watch. "I've got to be going. I have a flight to Albany in less than an hour."

When Leland returned to Gloria with two refills, she waved a full glass in his face. "A girl could die of thirst waiting for you."

"I'm sorry. I met Senator Archer and—"

"I know. I saw you two huddled over by the window. Do you want to tell me what it was about?"

"No," he said with more vehemence than he intended.

"Don't mind me," she said, taking no notice of his tone. "I'm a professional Yenta. I like to know what's going on."

He put his glass down. The wine was lousy. He was feeling guilty about not standing up to Archer, and the room was becoming claustrophobically stuffy. "I could use a real drink," he blurted out. "How about you?"

To his immense surprise, she put her glass down and said, "You talked me into it."

When they got out on the street, they both pulled up their collars to ward off the icy wind blowing up the hill. "I don't know this neighborhood all that well," he said. "Can you suggest a place?"

"Well there's always the Joy Lounge."

"Why do you mention the Joy?" he asked with some alarm. Had she overheard his conversation with Archer?

"Just kidding." She studied his face in the dim streetlight. "Why do you think there's a hidden meaning in everything I say?"

"I guess because I always think there is."

"My, aren't we paranoid. There isn't a decent bar in the neighborhood except for Paddy Corr's and I'm sure you don't want to go there."

"No, I don't." The last thing he wanted to do was go for a drink in a cop bar.

She took his arm. "Come on. I just thought of a good spot."

They got into his car and drove a few blocks. Then she said, "There's a parking spot. Grab it."

Leland turned off the engine and looked around. They were still on the Hill and there wasn't a bar or restaurant in sight. "Where is it?"

"There." She pointed to a modern hi-rise across the street. "It's where I live."

"But—"

"I don't have a liquor license, but I do have booze and ice and glasses. Is there a problem?"

A pleased Leland shook his head. There was no problem at all.

~~

While she mixed the drinks in the kitchen, he sat in the small, modestly furnished living room. The apartment was reasonably large by New York City standards and the fact that it was located on the Hill meant it had to cost plenty. His own apartment in Queens, a third the size, cost him a good chunk of his take home pay. He wondered how she could afford it and it suddenly occurred to him that she might have a very wealthy boyfriend. He ran his hand across a threadbare sofa arm. The furniture was stodgy and nondescript. He was disappointed in her lack of imagination and flair. From the way she dressed, he'd assumed she had better taste.

There were several photos on the shelf behind the TV. One showed her standing between an attractive woman, who looked like an older version of Gloria, and a handsome man with silver-gray hair. They were linking arms and smiling directly at the camera.

Gloria came in and handed him his martini on the rocks. As if reading his mind, she said, "That's my mom and dad. He pays the rent. It was a concession I had to make. He refused to let me live in the Valley."

She kicked off her shoes and tucked her long, tanned legs under her. "What do you think of my decorating skills?" she patted the old couch. "Pretty tacky, huh?"

"No, I think it's very nice," he said with what he hoped was a sincere tone.

"You're a terrible liar, but thank you. I rented the apartment fully furnished from an elderly gentlemen who moved to Florida. It's a great apartment, but the furniture really is awful."

"It is. I thought you'd raided the Salvation Army."

She held up her glass to him in salute. "Ah, a sense of humor under that serious demeanor."

"Of course I have a sense of humor," he said defensively.

"Could have fooled me."

"Why do I get the feeling that you're always making fun of me?"

"You're so easy. I'm sorry. I guess it's because you're always so grave, as though you're on *Face the Nation* all the time."

He wasn't aware that he came across that way. "I guess it's because I feel as though I'm under constant scrutiny. Even at the party tonight, there's no such thing as small talk. An off-hand remark tonight could come back to haunt me tomorrow. I found myself choosing my words carefully and I don't like that. I like free-wheeling discussions and arguments, but I'm the CO of the precinct and I have to watch what I say."

She cocked her head in a way that he found charming. "Could you be exaggerating your importance just a tad?"

"You were at the Community Board meeting. All I said was 'special attention' and all hell broke loose."

She jiggled the cubes in her glass. "Point for you."

"Point? Do you view everything as a competition?"

It was her turn for reflection. "Yeah, I guess I do."

"Why?"

I suppose it's the way I was brought up. Both my mother and father are attorneys. They're wonderful people but when they're in the courtroom they are aggressive, competitive, and demanding. I guess some of that has rubbed off on me."

"Where do they live?"

"Westchester."

"You don't get along with them?"

"I adore them," she said sincerely. "They're my role models."

"So what are you doing in the Bronx?"

"After law school I was offered a couple of very lucrative jobs, but I turned them down."

"You wanted to be a social worker instead."

"Now who's making fun?"

"Point for you."

"In spite of what you think, I'm not a bleeding-heart liberal. I have every intention of becoming a very successful lawyer and making lots of money. But right now I think I owe society something and that's why I'm here. I've been working here for a year and I intend to give it another year, then I'm outta here."

He studied the beautiful, enigmatic woman sitting on the couch with confusion. She didn't fit the stereotype that he'd conjured up for her. "Do you think you can really change things?" he asked.

She laughed out loud. "Captain, I have no illusions about what I'm doing. Sometimes the things I do help people, sometimes they don't. I get lots of kids jobs. A few of them end up stealing from their employers or getting re-arrested, but some of them actually use the opportunity to make a life for themselves."

"I'm sorry I got a little testy yesterday about the arrest."

"I got a little hot under the collar myself. I told you we were on different sides of the fence."

"I guess we are," he said, regretting that it had to be that way.

"You know, it really would be best for everyone if Tony stayed out of prison. He had a job. Now the city is paying for his room and board."

"He shouldn't have punched that police officer."

"Of course not, but men like Tony see violence as the only way to deal with a problem."

"I don't buy that."

"How could you? You're not a liberal."

He decided not to take that as a barb. "What kind of law are you going to practice when you spring yourself from here?" he asked, changing the subject.

"Criminal law. I'm going to get rich defending people wrongly accused of crimes."

Leland, who had a cop's ingrained dislike of defense attorneys, said, "What if they're guilty?"

She sighed. "Ah, the dilemma of all lawyers."

"What's the dilemma? The Constitution says everyone has a right to counsel and it doesn't hurt if the defendant has a lot of money."

"I've always had trouble with that. I'll defend anyone—pro bono if necessary. But I have to believe he's innocent."

"What about the defendant's right to counsel?"

"God knows there are plenty of lawyers. Let him find someone who is a little more ethically flexible than I am." She saw the perplexed look on his face and said, "I kinda screw up your image of a liberal-lawyer-social worker, don't I?"

"Yes, you do."

She took his empty glass and without asking him if he wanted another went back to the kitchen. When she returned, she resumed her place on the couch. "Enough about me," she said. "You don't look like a cop. Why'd you become one?"

"What should a cop look like? If I were hypersensitive I might conclude that question smacks of prejudice, as though there is one single 'cop-type.'"

She waved her glass in surrender. "Well played, Captain. Another point for you."

Her question rankled him, but he found it impossible to stay angry in the face of her radiant smile. "I wanted a job where I could help people," he said quietly. "A job where I could so something meaningful; a job where my success was strictly up to me; a job where I could go to the top using just my skills and talents; and most of all a job where politics didn't matter."

"Oh, my God, and you picked the police department?" she asked incredulously.

He grinned sheepishly. "I had no idea what I was getting into."

"That's so funny."

"Not from where I'm sitting."

She fingered the single strand of pearls around her neck. "Why is politics a problem?"

"When I was growing up I saw what office politics did to my dad. He worked for a large paper company. He was a smart, competent, honest man. Too honest, as it turned out. When he saw something wrong he spoke out, regardless of the consequences."

"What happened to him?"

Leland grunted bitterly. "He never got past mid-level manager." Leland shook his glass and watched the ice cubes bob up and down. "Anyway, I swore I'd never work in a place where politics could hamper my career."

She regarded him with genuine sympathy. "You poor man. Except for Congress, I can't think of an organization that is more political."

"So I've learned," he said, thinking of Charlie Drum, Lucian Hightower, and Senator Archer. "Bottom line is my father was wrong. There's nothing to be gained by risking your career. I recognize there's politics in the police department and I've learned how to use politics to my advantage."

He stared into his half-finished drink, stunned at what he'd just said. He'd never told anyone these things before. Knowledge was power. And power could destroy. And now he'd made himself vulnerable. *What the hell was the matter with him?*

He put his drink down and stood up. "It's getting late. I'd better be going." The truth was he didn't want to leave. He hadn't felt this relaxed or this comfortable for a very long time. He was attracted to Gloria and that disturbed him. He reminded himself that he had only one important job to do and that was to survive the Five-five. The last thing he needed was an intelligent, beautiful woman distracting him from that, especially one from the enemy camp.

At the door she looked at him with an inscrutable smile that both charmed and irritated him. "Can a liberal-lawyer-social worker offer a piece of advice?"

"Sure."

"Don't try to be all things to all people, Captain. I suspect you're a good man and a competent one. Don't get in your own way."

"What's that supposed to mean?"
She shrugged. "I'll let you answer that one."

Chapter Fifteen

Elliot and Oliver came out of a tenement where they'd just taken a burglary report and looked up at the sky. Earlier in the day a few snow flurries had come down and the sky, an angry roil of gray and black clouds, promised more.

"I think we're gonna have a white Christmas," Oliver said.

"It's what my kids have been praying for." Elliot tossed the key to Oliver. "It's your turn to drive."

Back in the radio car, Elliot keyed the mic. "Sector Adam back in service from that past burglary at 374 Duval. Resuming patrol."

He glanced up at the old tenement. "That's the third TV they got from that dude in seven months. You'd think he'd stop buying TVs. If that was me, I'd—" He stopped talking when he saw Oliver studying something in the rearview mirror. "What's up?"

"Don't turn around. There's a car following us. A tan Taurus."

"IAB?"

"Could be. I noticed it when we were on our way to the job."

Elliot twisted the rearview mirror so he could see the car. "A couple of guys on the late tour said they thought they saw unmarked cars following them," he said uneasily.

Oliver slammed his hands on the steering wheel. "Godamn that Lafferty for talking us into going back to the Joy."

"Shut up," an alarmed Elliot whispered. "The car could be bugged."

Oliver chuckled in spite of his uneasiness. "Jimmy, you are one dumb sonofabitch, you know that? If the car's bugged, don't you think the microphones can pick up whispering? I don't know how you're ever gonna pass that sergeant's exam."

"Just don't mention the Joy Lounge out loud, that's all," Elliot whispered.

Oliver jammed his foot on the accelerator and the car leaped forward. Elliot grabbed the dashboard. "What the hell are you doing?"

"I'm gonna double back and see who's in that car."

"Are you crazy? If it's IAB, you don't want to mess with them."

"Fuck 'em. No one follows me in my sector."

Oliver sped around the next corner and made a series of rights until he was back on Duval. He sped down the street and stopped at the corner. At the next intersection the Taurus was stopped and two heads in the front seat were swiveling from side to side.

Oliver roared up behind them, hit the lights and siren, and motioned the car to the curb.

Elliot folded his arms. "I ain't getting out. You want to have a pissing contest with IAB, go do it yourself."

"You're still my partner, Jimmy. You ain't no sergeant yet. What if those two just did a liquor store? You want me to take them on myself?"

Elliot muttered an oath and yanked the door open.

Oliver came up to the driver, a beefy, red-faced white man in his early thirties. He had cop written all over him. "License and registration," Oliver said.

"What'd I do?" the man asked.

"Sir," Oliver said more pointedly. "Please just give me your license and registration."

Elliot moved up to the other side of the vehicle and flashed his light into the back seat. He was looking for some sign that it was a police vehicle, but he saw nothing. The passenger, a thin white man in his early forties, glared at him. Elliot smiled back.

Oliver peered into the car. "You guys cops?"

The driver stared straight ahead. "No."

Just then, the passenger shifted in his seat. His jacket fell open and Oliver saw a holstered gun. "*Gun!*" he shouted, yanking out his own gun.

Before the two in the car could react, both Elliot and Oliver had their guns drawn and pointed at them.

Oliver yanked the door open. "Out!" he yelled at the driver. "Keep your hands where I can see them."

"Wait a minute—" The driver began to protest, but Oliver pulled him out of the car and shoved him to the ground. At the same time, Elliot dragged the passenger out and made him spread eagle on the ground.

"For chrissake we're cops," the passenger muttered into the sidewalk.

"Bullshit," Oliver said. "Too late to change your story now, pal."

Oliver knew they were cops as soon as he saw them. He also knew they were from IAB and he was incensed that not only were they following him, but they had the balls to lie to him, too.

With both men spread-eagled on the ground, Oliver searched them and came up with their guns and shields. The IDs said the driver was a cop and the passenger a lieutenant.

The lieutenant said, "All right, fun's over. Take the cuffs off."

Elliot and Oliver looked at each other. The right thing was to take the cuffs off, but at the moment, neither of them felt like doing the right thing. "I think you two are cop impersonators," Oliver said. "Jimmy, call the sergeant."

"For chrissake," the lieutenant said through clenched teeth. "Look at our ID cards. We're cops."

Oliver looked at the photo and down at the lieutenant. "It sort of looks like you," he said, trying not to smile, "but sometimes it's hard to tell you white guys apart."

~~

When Sgt. Labonte arrived, the two IAB cops were still handcuffed and on the ground.

Labonte pushed his huge bulk out of the car. "Whadda you got?"

"I think we got two cop impersonators."

"*I'm Lieutenant Fowler from Internal Affairs,*" the lieutenant shouted from the ground. "Get these goddamn handcuffs off me. I'm freezing my ass off."

At the mention of IAB, Labonte paled. He looked from Elliot to Oliver. "Are these guys cops?"

"First they said they weren't. Now they say they are," Oliver said. "I don't know what to believe, Sarge."

"Do they have ID?"

"*Yes, we have ID!*" the lieutenant shouted. "Just look at it, for chrissake."

Labonte studied the two ID cards and got down on his hands and knees to compare it against their faces. He looked up at Elliot and Oliver. "They're cops, you idiots. Get the cuffs off. But first, help me up."

~~

Back at the station house the incident quickly escalated as reinforcements for both sides arrived. PBA delegate Charlie Reece came in from home and advised Elliot and Oliver not to make a statement until they had an opportunity to speak to a PBA lawyer. An SBA union official came up from Manhattan and advised Sgt. Labonte to do the same. Then an irate IAB inspector showed up and insisted on conducting a full-scale investigation. But it wasn't much of an investigation because the only ones who would talk to him were his two IAB cops.

For the next hour, there was a great deal of finger-pointing and high-decibel accusations hurled from both sides. Finally, Leland, who was already late for Chief Drum's Christmas party, broke the standoff. He took the IAB inspector into his office and closed the door.

"I'm going to bring those two cops up on charges," the red-faced inspector said. "They knew damn well they were cops."

"Inspector, you're men were wrong," Leland said. "How many cop-on-cop shootings have we had in the past few years? You know, and I know, what the department policy is: it's incumbent on police officers in civilian clothes to identify themselves to uniformed officers and IAB doesn't get a pass on that. My God, someone could have gotten shot out there."

The inspector looked away from Leland's accusing glare. "All right. Maybe my people didn't handled the situation as well as they could have. What do you say, we just drop the whole thing."

It took all of Leland's powers of persuasion to convince Reece, and the two union delegates that it was in everyone's best interest to drop the whole matter.

∽∽

Elliot and Oliver got a standing ovation when they came into the locker room at the end of the tour. Lafferty banged his nightstick against the side of the locker. "Way to go, guys. You bagged two IAB scumbags."

A grinning Oliver accepted high-fives from everyone, but Elliot went quietly to his locker. Farlier, in the heat of anger, it had seemed like a good idea, but now that he had time to reflect he realized they could have gotten into some serious trouble.

Oliver sat down next to his partner and slapped him on the back. "What's up, pard?"

"I could have blown my chance of getting promoted."

"Big deal. So you'd stay a cop. You ain't never gonna have this much fun as a sergeant."

Elliot cradled his head in his hands. "George, just shut up. Okay? Just shut the hell up."

~~

Paxton's Ale House was only a stone's throw from police headquarters. The restaurant's décor, featuring the standard English Pub brass and stained-glass motif, was the watering hole of choice for headquarters retirement and promotion parties. Tonight, just five days before Christmas, more than fifty cops, bosses, and civilians crowded into the back room for the Chief of Department's annual Christmas party.

Headquarters parties were not like most parties. People came to these events for a variety of reasons, the least of which was to have a good time. Mostly they came because they had to, or because it would be a mistake to pass up the opportunity to cultivate a "hook," or simply because they wanted to keep tabs on their enemies. As a consequence, you were more likely to run into someone who wanted to stab you in the back than pat you on the back.

The IAB-Elliott and Oliver flap had made Leland two hours late for the party. He was exhausted from averaging fifteen hours a day in the precinct and four hours of sleep a night. What he wanted to do most was go home and flop into bed, but instead he'd come to Charlie Drum's party because it was important that he get face-time with the Chief. He'd been out of OPP for only three weeks, but he knew that out of sight, out of mind was never truer than in the culture of One Police Plaza.

A waitress directed him to a back room where the party was in full swing. At the Five-five-precinct Christmas party, Leland had been the highest-ranking member of the department, but here, with a top-heavy contingent of deputy chiefs, assistant chiefs, deputy commissioners, and prominent politicians, he was one of the lowest ranking members. Leland knew all of them by sight and most of them personally.

Despite the large crowd, the noise level was surprisingly low because Charlie Drum's parties were, by default, anemic affairs. The sight of the ever-watchful, ex-alcoholic Charlie Drum prowling through clumps of men looking for the man who had that one drink too many made the attendees as wary as a herd of wildebeests invited to a picnic by a hungry pride of lions. His vigilant and relentless omnipresence subdued even the most ardent party animal.

The proper protocol was for Leland to seek out Chief Drum and pay his respects, but the Chief was engaged in conversation with the president of the City Council and Leland took the opportunity to head straight for the bar. Just as the bartender handed him a martini, a voice behind him whispered, "Three weeks on patrol and already an alcoholic."

Leland turned toward a grinning Lieutenant Tim Frazer. "Timmy, how're you doing?"

"Good, Richard. How are they treating you out in the provinces?"

"Don't ask."

"That bad, huh?" Frazer lowered his voice. "How's the investigation going?"

"The vultures are circling. IAB's been in and out of the precinct picking up roll calls and checking records. Some of the cops said they've seen Internal Affairs people following them to jobs."

"You know cops. They're all paranoid."

"Not this time. Just before I came here I had to stop two of my cops from arresting an IAB surveillance team."

"Wow. Things gotta be tense up there."

"The precinct is a madhouse. Timmy, you wouldn't believe the collection of screwballs I have."

"Sounds like you could use a drink." Frazer signaled the bartender.

It took two martinis for Frazer to fill Leland in on the latest headquarters' gossip and Leland to describe the trials and tribulations of being the precinct commander of the infamous Five-five.

Frazer looked at his watch. "Hey, I gotta split. I've paid my respects and it's time to get out of here." As he swept his money up off the bar, he said, "Richard, don't be a stranger. Stop up and see us."

"I will. As soon as I get a spare minute."

He watched Frazer pick his way through the crowd. There was something different about Timmy Frazer, but he couldn't quite put his finger on it. Maybe it was the condescending tone he used when he talked about precinct cops or maybe it was the way his eyes glazed over when Leland tried to tell him how hard it was running a precinct without enough manpower, limited resources, and constant interference from OPP and the borough office.

Whatever it was, there had been a striking change in the three short weeks since Leland had gone to the Five-five. Then, as he speared the olive in his martini, it suddenly occurred to him what the change was: *Their roles had become reversed.* Leland had been Frazier's mentor, now he, Richard Leland, was on the outside looking in. *Three weeks!* Leland thought incredulously. Could it have taken just taken three weeks to lose everything he'd worked for?

A grumbling stomach reminded him that he hadn't eaten since early this morning. He slowly made his way through the crowd toward the food table, saying hello to people he knew and trading tired quips about being back in the "real world." He arrived at the food table too late. Everything had been picked clean and all that was left were a couple of slices of cheese and a few unidentifiable pieces of rolled-up luncheon meat.

Johnny Wallace came alongside Leland. "Hey, Boss. How're you doing?"

"Hey, Johnny. Where'd all the food go?"

"You're too late, Boss," the chubby sergeant said out of the side of his mouth. "The free-loading hyenas had the table picked clean before the head melted on my first beer."

Leland looked at his empty glass. "Well, if I can't get anything to eat, I might as well get another drink."

"*Ten cuidado*," Wallace whispered, shaking his own half-empty glass. "The Great God Drum sees all and knows all."

It had been rumored that Drum counted how many drinks his people took at these parties. But Leland didn't believe it. "That's just office scuttlebutt," he said.

"No, it ain't. At the last party, Drum told me *exactly* how many beers I had." The sergeant shook his head. "Jesus, I hate reformed drunks. They say Drum was an all right guy when he was a boozer. But look at him now." Wallace cast a baleful look toward the Chief, who was still in animated conversation with the City Council president. "Maybe the sonofabitch will start drinking again and loosen up." He leaned forward and whispered, "Anyway, screw him. For every beer I have here, I go to the bar outside and have two more."

"You always were a resourceful man, Johnny."

In spite of Wallace's forced joviality, Leland saw sadness in the sergeant's eyes. "How's your wife doing?" he asked.

The forced smile vanished. "We're taking it one day at a time."

"Johnny, if there's anything I can do, just ask. Hell, I'll even take a shot at babysitting."

"Thanks, boss. My folks have been watching the kids. It gives me a chance to spend time with Eleanor."

There was an awkward pause. Leland saw that Drum had finished his conversation with the City Council president. He shook the sergeant's hand. "I gotta say 'hail' to the Chief. You take care. And remember, if there's anything I can do you've got my number."

"I appreciate that, Boss."

As Leland made his way through the crowd, he remembered what Wallace had told him about Drum counting drinks. It was absurd. Not even Charlie Drum would stoop to that. *Or would he?* He handed his half-finished martini to a passing waiter.

Chief Charles Drum, holding a glass of ginger ale in front of him like a badge of honor, fixed his predatory eyes on Leland as he approached. "Richard, glad you could make it."

"Sorry I'm late, Chief. I got tied up at the precinct."

"Business before pleasure."

"I saw you talking to the City Council president and I didn't want to interrupt."

"You should have. That sorry sonofabitch is one poor excuse for a politician. He'll be out on his ass after the next election. So, Richard, how are things going in the Five-five?"

"Good, sir," Leland answered, knowing full well that Drum knew exactly how things were going in the Five-five. "There's a lot to learn."

There was a burst of laughter from across the room and Drum's head, swiveling like a gun turret, spun to see who was having so much fun at his party. "And how are you getting along with Chief Hightower?"

Leland was certain that Drum knew all about that too. "Chief Hightower has very high standards and I'm doing my best to comply with them." Even though Drum and Hightower were avowed enemies, it would have been poor form for a captain to bad-mouth one chief to another.

Leland watched Drum's eyes scan the room and could almost hear the chief tallying up the drinks in his head. "Richard, just because you're in the Bronx, there's no reason to go native."

"Sir?"

"That PR broad. The community activist? What's her name?"

"Gloria Perez? She's not Puerto Rican, she's Venezuelan. She—" He stopped. Why was he explaining her ethnic origin to Charlie Drum?

"Appearances are important, Richard. You don't want to be seen getting too close to a Puerto Rican—Venezuelan, whatever. You get my drift?"

Leland was too stunned to answer. He didn't know what surprised him the most, hearing this not-so-subtle racism from the man who only months earlier had issued his Code Words for Racial Slurs memo or that he knew who Gloria Perez was.

Drum's eyes narrowed and Leland turned to see what Drum was looking at. Johnny Wallace was standing in the middle of a group telling a joke.

"Wallace thinks he has me fooled," Drum said quietly. "But I know that drunk is going outside for more drinks."

Leland was shocked by Drum's characterization of Wallace as a drunk. "Chief, Wallace likes a drink, but he's no alcoholic."

Drum glared at him. "You have a lot to learn, Richard." He looked at Wallace. "If I see him take one more drink, he'll find himself working a late tour in a Staten Island precinct this Christmas Eve."

Abruptly changing his mood, he slapped Leland on the shoulder. "Well," he said expansively, "it's been good seeing you, Richard. I see the First Dep has arrived. I'd better say hello to him while he's still sober."

He left Leland standing alone in the middle of the room wondering what to do about Johnny Wallace. *Was this a test?* He wouldn't put it past the devious Drum. If Leland told Wallace that he was being watched and Drum found out about it, he'd judge it an act of disloyalty. On the other hand, if he didn't warn the hapless sergeant, there was no doubt that Drum would follow through on his threat to dump Wallace back to a precinct.

Captain Roger Wolfe slapped Leland on the back. "So," he asked with an alligator smile, "how is it in the trenches, Richard?"

Leland had spotted Wolfe earlier and was determined to avoid him, but the captain had boxed him between a table and the wall. "Busy," Leland answered. "Real busy, Roger."

"Not too busy, I trust, to get your accident-prone location report in on time."

"That one of your projects, Roger?"

"Yes, and I must say the timely response of your colleagues in the trenches has been less than admirable. Eighty-six percent of the reports were late last month."

"I hate to burst your bubble, Roger," Leland snapped, "but a precinct CO has a whole lot more important things to do than collect accident data."

Wolfe, the quintessential headquarters bureaucrat, blinked as though he'd been slapped in the face. The captain's job security depended on the dozens of useless and time-consuming projects he dreamed up every year. The accident-prone-locations project was just the latest of Wolfe's brainchildren. So far this year, he'd spawned idiotic projects that required precinct commanders to compile lengthy statistics on bicycle accidents between the hours of dusk and dawn, burglary victims over sixty-five, and summonses issued to double-parked cars on Saturday nights.

All day long, Wolfe's computer churned out impenetrable data based on the precincts reports, but it didn't matter to Drum, who usually ignored Wolfe's arcane findings anyway. He was interested only in a precinct commander's reporting compliance.

"I'm disappointed in you," Wolfe said. "Of all people, I thought you would recognize the value of these reports. It's my belief that precinct COs sit on a lodestone of statistical information which can be useful to them. They just don't know how to mine it. I do it for them and I think a little extra time preparing a report is a small price to pay for such important information."

Grudgingly, Leland had to admire the way Wolfe had created a career out of nothing. Still, he wanted to tell the pompous captain that the results of his projects seldom got back to the precinct level, and those that did were useless or impossible to implement. But he realized that Wolfe had Drum's ear and he wouldn't hesitate to tell the Chief that Leland, after only a short time in the "trenches," had begun to think like a precinct drone. Indeed, he regretted his earlier remark about having more important things to do.

"Tell me," he said, changing the subject, "what's going on in the Puzzle Palace since I've been gone?"

Wolfe, the consummate gossip, was known as the Matt Drudge of OPP. When he wasn't dreaming up useless projects, he roamed the halls of One Police Plaza soaking up tidbits of gossip.

The captain, now on a topic that he truly enjoyed, lowered his voice. "A bloodbath is in the making," he said solemnly. "I hear the Chief of Patrol's head is on the chopping block."

"Townsend? Who'll take his place?"

"Probably Klein from Personnel and that'll set up a domino effect in the ranks above deputy chief. Some will go up, some will remain in place, and some will go out the door," he added cryptically.

"So who's going where?"

Wolfe glanced around and whispered, "I'm not at liberty to say." Wolfe was never happier than when he knew something no one else did.

"Just tell me this," Leland persisted. "Will Hightower be moved out of the Bronx?"

"Not a chance. Drum is orchestrating this massacre and he'd love to whack Hightower, but it wouldn't be politically correct, not with Lucian being the highest ranking black in the department. Short of discovering he's a serial killer, the PC himself couldn't oust him. Drum can't get rid of him, but he'll see to it that he stays in the Bronx for a very long, long time."

That was the most depressing news Leland had heard all day. His only hope for surviving two years in the Five-five was to get away from the hypercritical Lucian Hightower. If Wolfe was correct—and given his track record, there was no reason to believe otherwise—it was going to be a long, long two years.

"What does the PC say about this?"

"That man's brain-dead. He came from Detroit a year ago and he still doesn't know where Staten Island is."

For once Leland had to agree with Wolfe's assessment. Commissioner Bruce Randall, who'd come to New York City by way of Detroit, was the weakest and most ineffectual commissioner the police department had ever seen. He'd been the search committee's compromise candidate, and from day one had been a fish out of water.

Charlie Drum, a shrewd opportunist, saw that Randall was incapable of dealing with the political realities of New York City with all its diverse and multilayered problems, and he quickly stepped in to prop up the floundering commissioner. He even recommended appointing a First Deputy Commissioner—the PC's second in command—a man who was equal to Randall's incompetence and who would leave Drum to run the department unencumbered by a meddlesome PC and First Dep.

Randall, grateful for someone to take charge and make the hard decisions, hardly noticed—or cared—that Drum was, himself, an incompetent tyrant. Together they formed the perfect symbiotic relationship: Bruce Randall was nominally the police commissioner, but Charlie Drum was the wizard behind the curtain.

Wolfe looked at his watch. "Well, I've done my penance here. I'm going home." Before he left, he made Leland promise to get December's accident reports in on time.

While Leland had been talking to Wolfe, he'd been keeping an eye on Wallace. The sergeant finished a conversation with two men, looked at his empty glass, and started for the bar. Leland glanced around the room looking for Drum, but the chief was nowhere to be seen. As Wallace passed, Leland reached out and grabbed his elbow. "Johnny, did I ever tell you the joke about the nun and the rabbi?"

Wallace's eyes lit up. "Hey, I haven't heard a good joke since Christ was a corporal. Wait. I'll get a drink and—"

Leland applied pressure to Wallace's elbow. "I want to tell you this joke *now*."

Wallace caught the urgency in Leland's voice. "What's up, Boss?"

Leland didn't know where Drum was, and he didn't dare look around. He forced himself to smile and said quietly, "Drum has been watching you. You take one more drink and you're history."

"Jesus!" Wallace nervously licked his lips. "I'd better get out of here."

"Smile, Johnny, I'm telling you a funny joke."

Wallace tried a sickly smile.

"You can do better than that."

Wallace forced a big grin. "How's that?" he said through clenched teeth.

"Much better. You can't leave now. He'll know I told you," Leland said with a wide, stupid grin on his face.

"What'll I do?" Wallace grinned back at him.

"Go to the bar and order a Coke. After a few Cokes, leave."

"A *few* Cokes! I can't drink *three* of those things."

"All right. Two."

Wallace nodded, the pasty smile frozen on his face.

"Okay," Leland said, still grinning. "I just told you the punch line. Now laugh your ass off and go get yourself a Coke."

"Boss," Wallace said through clenched teeth, "this is fucking nuts."

Suddenly the absurdity of the moment struck him and he started to chuckle. Then the chuckle turned into a guffaw and that turned into a belly laugh. Tears coursed down his cheeks. Leland, caught up by the sergeant's contagious laughter, joined in.

Wallace left for his Coke and Leland wiped a tear from his eye, feeling as though he'd been dropped into the middle of a very bad Kafka play.

After a suitable time he, too, left the party. On the way home to Flushing, he rehashed his conversations with Drum and Timmy Frazer. Something had changed. Something was different.

He was no longer one of "them." And he certainly wasn't one of the Five-five. So where did he belong?

Chapter Sixteen

  Billy Lafferty arrived at IAB headquarters on Poplar Street in Brooklyn at exactly 7:45 a.m., fifteen minutes early for his appointment. The chronically late Lafferty would have been late this morning, too, but Charlie Reece had called to harass him out of bed at the ungodly hour of five-thirty.
  Lafferty stood on the sidewalk and looked up at the old, brooding, slightly sinister building. It had once been a precinct station house, but now it unintentionally personified the mysterious and secretive work that went on behind its locked doors.
  Lafferty pushed the heavy oak door open and went inside. A lethargic man in civilian clothes looked up from the sports section of the *Daily News*. "Sign the book and wait in the next room," he said and returned to his reading.
  Lafferty wrote his name in the large sign-in book and counted five names before him. These IAB scumbags start early, he thought.
  In the waiting room, five tense uniformed police officers sat erect on metal chairs lined up against a wall. It looked like a dentist's office where root canal surgery was the special of the day. Lafferty sat down and nodded to them, but they avoided eye contact with him as though they were afraid of guilt by association.
  Lafferty blotted his clammy palms on his trouser legs and looked around the room wondering where they'd hidden the surveillance camera. The large room, painted in garish glossy blues and greens, had once been the muster room of the station house, but the only remnant of its former use was the large, elevated oak desk. All the other furniture had been stripped away.
  Two men in civilian clothes came downstairs carrying attaché cases. Engaged in quiet, animated, conversation, they hardly glanced at Lafferty and the other officers as they passed. Lafferty watched them intently and

wondered if they were working on the Five-five investigation. He made a half-hearted attempt to memorize their faces, but he forgot what they looked like before he heard the front door slam.

He rested his head against the wall and tried to clear his mind, but he was distracted by the sound of a radio playing upstairs somewhere. The radio was tuned to one of those stations that played syrupy elevator music all day. It figures, he said to himself, not knowing exactly what he meant by that.

He heard muted voices and an occasional outburst of laughter. "I didn't think these guys had a sense of humor," he muttered. The cop sitting next to him gave no indication he heard the comment.

A short, chubby man, clutching a battered leather briefcase—very much like the kind Lafferty carried when he was a kid at St. Teresa's—came through the door. His wrinkled trench coat, trailing below his knees, was flapping and his wide tie, which had been in style in the early seventies, was askew. He definitely wasn't a cop, so he had to be a lawyer. Lafferty looked at the five cops sitting alongside him and wondered which one of these poor bastards was going to be represented by this dork.

The man pulled a crumpled piece of paper out of his pocket and squinted at it. "Officer Lafferty?"

Lafferty shot to his feet. "That's me."

The lawyer peered at him through thick eyeglasses that magnified a pair of soft brown eyes. "Frank Toomey," he said offering a clammy hand. "I'll be representing you at this hearing." He took Lafferty by the arm and led him to the other side of the room.

The disheveled attorney was perspiring profusely. Lafferty eyed a bead of sweat rolling off the end of the lawyer's bulbous nose with alarm. "*You're* representing *me*? You're more nervous than I am, for chrissake."

"It's nothing," the lawyer said, wiping his face with a damp handkerchief. "It's warm outside, that's all."

"*Warm*? It's gotta be twenty-eight out there. You related to Gus Labonte?"

"Who?"

"Never mind."

"Okay. Whatever. I sweat all the time. It doesn't mean anything."

Lafferty made a mental note to kick Charlie Reece in the balls for inflicting this loser on him. "So, Mr. Tumor—"

"Toomey."

"Whatever. You got any experience with these IAB hearings?"

"Oh, yes. You?"

"None. I go to CCRB all the time, but I've never been here."

"This is nothing like the Civilian Complaint Review Board, I can tell you." Toomey waved his damp handkerchief. "But I wouldn't sweat it."

Lafferty chuckled nervously, watching a new bead of sweat form on the lawyer's upper lip. "Easy for you to say."

Toomey loosened his tie and grunted.

Lafferty tugged at his collar. This guy was making *him* warm. "Are you okay?" he asked the sweating lawyer. "You look like you're gonna take a heart attack, for chrissake."

"No, I'm fine. This always happens. I—"

"Police officer Lafferty?" A man in civilian clothes was standing at the foot of the stairs.

"Yeah, that's me."

"Let's go. We're ready for you."

Toomey grabbed Lafferty's sleeve. "A few ground rules," he whispered. "Answer the question, but don't volunteer information. This isn't a court of law, so the normal rules of evidence don't apply. You can take the fifth amendment if you want, but they'll probably suspend you."

"Why would I take the fifth?"

"I'm just telling you, that's all. Oh, and one more thing. I'll try to put my arm over the back of your chair. If they ask you a question that I think is loaded or dangerous, I'll squeeze your shoulder or something."

Lafferty didn't relish having Toomey's sweaty hands all over his uniform, but he nodded and said, "Okay. Let's get this over with."

The first thing Lafferty noticed when he walked into the interrogation room was a tape recorder sitting on a metal table. "Is this SOP?" he whispered out of the side of his mouth.

The lawyer nodded and dropped into a metal folding chair. The next thing Lafferty noticed were the sparse furnishings—a long metal table and five folding chairs; two on one side and three on the other. The walls were bare, but Lafferty could see that there had been pictures at one time because the paint where the pictures had been was a different shade. There were heavy-duty metal screens covering every window. Lafferty wondered if it was to keep people in or out.

Three men came into the room. The man who had summoned them from downstairs spoke first. "I'm Sergeant Walsh. I'll be conducting the interview." He introduced the others, a lieutenant and a captain. Walsh looked at Toomey. "Counselor, are you ready?"

Toomey tugged at his damp collar. "We're ready."

The lieutenant sat next to Walsh across the table from Lafferty and Toomey. The captain, who hadn't said a word, pulled his chair to the side so that it was just barely in Lafferty's peripheral vision.

Walsh pressed the start button and Lafferty stared hypnotically at the slowly turning reel as the sergeant, in a monotone voice, put a voice heading on the tape.

Lafferty jerked his head up from the tape recorder when the sergeant said, "Officer Lafferty, I wish to advise you that you are being questioned as part of an official investigation by the Police Department. You will be asked questions specifically directed and narrowly related to the performance of your duties."

Lafferty's eyes went back to the turning reel and he only half-listened as the sergeant droned on about his rights and privileges guaranteed by the Constitution and the laws of the state of New York.

It wasn't until the sergeant said: "You have the right not to be compelled to incriminate yourself" that Lafferty began to feel really uneasy. He'd given the Miranda Warnings to hundreds of prisoners, but it was weird hearing someone recite those rights to him.

The preliminaries finished, the questioning began. "Officer Lafferty, how long have you been in the police department?"

For a moment, Lafferty's mind went blank. Then he said quickly, "Eight years."

"And how long have you been assigned to the Five-five precinct?"

"Four years." He wiped his sweating hands on his thighs.

"Were you working the night of December sixth?"

"Yeah, a four-to-twelve. Hey, you guys know that. Why are you—" He stopped when he felt Toomey's finger poking his back.

Sgt. Walsh smiled. "Officer, we have to ask these questions to establish background."

"Yeah. Whatever." The poking ceased.

"Who were you working with that night?"

"Charlie Reece."

"Did there come a time that night when you and officer Reece responded to a Ten-thirteen at the Joy Lounge?"

"Yeah."

"What other police officers were there?"

He waited for a poke. When none was forthcoming, he said, "I don't know. Things were pretty hectic."

"I'm sure it was, but you had to notice someone else there."

"Nope." Toomey poked him, but he ignored it. "Like I said, things were really hectic."

The lieutenant, speaking for the first time, pointed at the ribbons over Lafferty's shield. "I see you're an experienced police officer. I'm sure you have very good powers of observation. How can you say you don't remember who was there? These are the men and women you work with everyday."

Lafferty, bridling at the lieutenant's sarcastic tone, snapped, "Bottles were coming off the roof, *Lieutenant*. People were spitting in my face and throwing shit at me." Lafferty ignored Toomey's finger, which was drumming a frantic tattoo on his back. "I didn't have time to conduct a roll call. If you guys—"

"Excuse me," Toomey interrupted. "May my client and I have a short recess?"

Walsh looked at his watch. "The time is 0814 hours," he said, shutting off the recorder. "Counselor, you can use this room. When you're ready, we'll be outside."

Toomey wiped his forehead while the three men filed out of the room. After the door closed, he said, "Officer Lafferty, I advise you to answer the questions. Being argumentative and evasive is counter-productive."

Lafferty mumbled something.

Toomey leaned forward. "What?"

Lafferty put his hand to his mouth and mumbled again.

"I'm sorry, I still didn't get that."

"I said"—Lafferty voice dropped to a mere whisper—"the room is bugged."

Toomey's large, puzzled eyes fixed on Lafferty. "Bugged?" he repeated. "Officer, this is New York City, not Damascus. I can assure you the room isn't bugged."

"I don't trust these mothers," Lafferty whispered.

"That's neither here nor there," the exasperated attorney said. "The point is—" Toomey realized he, too, was whispering and resumed in a normal voice. "The point is you should answer the questions truthfully and in a straightforward manner."

Lafferty dropped to a crouch and ran his fingers under the table.

"What are you doing?" an alarmed Toomey asked.

"I'm looking for a microphone."

"There *is* no microphone. That would be a gross violation of client-attorney confidentiality."

Lafferty gave up his cursory search. "Fuck it," he said. "They could hide a microphone anywhere."

"Why don't you want to answer that question?" Toomey asked, trying to distract Lafferty from his paranoia.

"Hey, I'm not going to hand up the guys I work with. These scumbags are such hotshots, let *them* figure out who was there and who wasn't."

Toomey wiped his brow with a handkerchief that was now fairly dripping with perspiration. "Officer Lafferty," he said in frustration, "I'm here to represent you. You can, of course, take my advice or ignore it. But I have to tell you that if you persist in this evasive and argumentative behavior, you risk getting suspended."

Lafferty thought about that for a moment. "Okay, maybe you're right. Call the humps back in here and let's get this over with."

A relieved Toomey said, "Remember," he said quietly, "If I poke you, be careful."

The three IAB supervisors came back into the office, but before they resumed, the captain made a point of separating Toomey's and Lafferty's chairs. A wide-eyed Lafferty looked at Toomey and mouthed the word "*bug*."

Walsh pressed the record button and looked at his watch. "The time is now 0820 hours. The interview is resuming."

Walsh repeated the question he'd asked before the recess. "Officer, who else responded to the Ten-thirteen?"

Reluctantly, Lafferty told him who was there and recounted his actions at the incident.

"What time did you sign out that night?" Walsh asked.

"Around one-forty."

Walsh shuffled through some papers and said, "The sign-out book indicates you signed out at 0148 hours."

"Well if you know that, why the hell are you asking me?"

Attorney Toomey, loudly clearing his throat, sounded like he'd swallowed a goat.

Lafferty glanced at his attorney, half expecting to see him having the big one right there. Instead, Toomey glared at him with big soft brown eyes as he rubbed his glasses furiously with a sweat-soaked handkerchief.

"I want to make sure we have the times right," Walsh explained.

"Whatever. If it says I signed out at 0148 then that's what I did."

"Did you go straight home?"

"No."

"Where did you go?"

Lafferty glanced at Toomey for guidance and saw the captain, who was sitting behind and to the right of the attorney, staring at him intently. Lafferty's focus shifted to the attorney's face and he saw Toomey nod imperceptibly.

"A bar in the precinct," Lafferty answered.

"Paddy Corr's?"

"Yeah." It suddenly occurred to Lafferty that they already knew the answers to these questions. They were looking to catch him in a lie.

"Who else was there?"

Lafferty saw a chance to break balls. "There was a guy from Con Ed. I don't know his name. Then there's this drunk, Stanley. He's always there."

Walsh's only reaction was a good-natured smile. "I meant who was there from the precinct?"

Disappointed that he didn't get more of a rise out of the sergeant, Lafferty reluctantly recited a list of names.

"What time did you leave the bar?"

"I don't remember."

The lieutenant scribbled a note and passed it to Walsh.

The sergeant glanced at it and slipped it under his other notes. "Was it five minutes? An hour? Till closing?"

"I don't know. Maybe an hour or so. I can't be sure."

"Did you go straight home?"

"Yeah."

"Where do you live?"

"New City."

"How long does it usually take you to get home?"

"I don't know. Maybe forty minutes."

"So you arrived home at approximately 3 a.m.?"

"I guess—"

"More like three-thirty," Toomey interjected.

Walsh looked at him quizzically and rechecked his own notes. "You're right, counselor. It would be around three-thirty."

"Good thing someone around here can add," Lafferty muttered. He wasn't sure if the sergeant had made an honest mistake or if he was trying to be cute. But he was beginning to think that maybe his disheveled, soggy lawyer wasn't such a dork after all.

"So you got home around three-thirty. Did anyone see you arrive at that time?"

"What kind of neighborhood you think I live in? *Nobody's* up in New City at that hour."

"I thought maybe your wife might have been up watching TV."

"Nah, she's in the crib by ten."

Walsh's affable grim vanished and he fixed Lafferty with eyes that had suddenly gone hard. "Officer, did you take part in the assault of patrons at the Joy Lounge that night?"

The abruptness of the question startled Lafferty and his mouth went dry. "Why would I do a thing like that?" he blurted out.

Walsh stared quietly at Lafferty. The only sound, which had suddenly become very loud, was the whirring of the tape recorder's motor. "You didn't answer my question," the sergeant said, finally breaking the silence.

"No, I didn't assault anyone," Lafferty snapped.

"Do you know who did?" the sergeant persisted.

"No, I don't."

"Officer Lafferty, is there anything you'd like to add?"

There was plenty he wanted to add. He wanted to say that the skells in the Joy Lounge deserved a good beating. He wanted to say that IAB scumbags should stop harassing cops. He wanted to say that IAB hard-ons should quit hiding behind desks and tape recorders and get out into the street and start acting like real cops. That's what he wanted to say, but instead, he shook his head and said, "Nope. I got nothing to add."

Walsh consulted his notes and looked up. "We'll take a short recess. Would you guys like some coffee?"

Toomey said yes. Lafferty said no.

Sgt. Walsh brought a Styrofoam cup of coffee for Toomey and left the room. An ever-suspicious Lafferty waited until his lawyer put the cup to his lips and said, "It's probably laced with some kind of drug."

Toomey jerked the cup away from him spilling coffee on his seventies tie. "Jeez, why do you say that?"

"I told you, I don't trust these mothers."

Toomey put the cup down and Lafferty noted with perverse satisfaction that he didn't touch it again.

Now that the interrogation was almost over, Lafferty was feeling a whole lot more relaxed. He shrugged his shoulders and rubbed the back of his neck, which had become stiff with tension. "That wasn't so bad, counselor. By the way, nice move catching him on the time. You made him look like a real schmuck."

A weary Toomey regarded Lafferty through his thick glasses. "I assure you that wasn't my intention."

"Fuck'em. These guys need a good zinger up the old wazoo once in awhile." He looked at his watch. "Hey, what do you figure, a few more minutes here?"

Toomey took off his glasses and wiped them with his sopping handkerchief. "I think a little longer than that," he said, putting on his sweat-streaked glasses.

Five minutes later, Sgt. Walsh and the others returned. "Okay," the sergeant said, "We have a few more questions. Let's get started."

As the sergeant pressed the record button, Lafferty glanced down at the handful of yellow legal pad pages in front of Walsh. Every page was filled with questions written out in a small neat hand.

Lafferty rubbed the back of his stiff neck.

∾∾

At the same time Lafferty was answering IAB's questions for the fourth and fifth time, Peggy Garrigan was picking up at a phone in the station house clerical office. It had been a week since she'd made her complaint about Mrs. Norville, but so far she'd heard nothing from the Special Victims Squad or the State's Child Welfare Agency. It didn't surprise her. The department seldom provided feedback to the cop on the street and outside agencies were even worse.

She dialed the number and heard the raspy Brooklynese voice of Tony Fazio, the detective who'd been assigned the case. "Fazio, Special Victims."

"Police officer Peggy Garrigan. I'm calling about the status of the Molly Norville case."

"Closed."

"Closed? How could you do that so fast? Didn't you—"

"Garrigan, I went to the hospital the same day you filed the complaint. I talked to the attending physician and the mother."

Peggy noticed an edge of testiness in the detective's voice. He, like most detectives, didn't appreciate being questioned by a mere street cop. "What did the doctor say?" she asked.

"That Molly's injuries were consistent with falling out of a crib."

"Knocked unconscious from a crib fall?"

"Garrigan, the magic word is consistent. Last month I had a scalded kid case. The mother said she was about to bathe her kid in the sink, the phone rings, she goes to answer it and the kid takes a header into the sink and winds up with first degree burns over sixty percent of his body. We knew the mother was lying because there were no splash burns on the kid."

"Splash burns?"

"If kid falls into hot water, he'll have splash burns on his body. If a mother lowers him into scalding water, they're won't be any. There were none. Evidence. I need evidence. That's how I make arrests. The doctor can only go by what he sees and there's no reason to doubt Mrs. Norville's story."

Peggy, irritated by the detective's patronizing tone, struggled to keep her temper in check. "Fazio, this wasn't the first time Molly has been to the hospital."

"I know. Mrs. Norville told me. I asked the doctor to review the records. She got six stitches in her forehead. Again, the doctor said—"

"The injuries were consistent with the story."

"You got it."

"What about the bruises on her arm?"

"Old. The doctor couldn't offer an opinion on them. Some kids bruise easily. I should know, I've got five of 'em."

Peggy ran her hand through her hair in frustration. "What did the mother say about all this?"

"The same thing she told you."

"She's lying."

Fazio sighed at the other end of the line. "How do you know that, Garrigan?"

"I just know."

"Woman's intuition?"

"What the hell does that mean?"

"It means we don't lock up people on intuition. How long you been on the job?"

"Two years. What's that got to do with it?"

"How many child abuse cases have you seen?"

"Just this one."

"I got twenty-six years in the job and I see dozens of child abuse cases a year. Real abuse. Kids branded with hot irons, tied up with wire, burned with cigarette butts."

"All right, Fazio. You've convinced me. You're an expert. But I was there. I saw the way the mother acted. I'm telling you—"

"Garrigan"—the detective's tone had gone from testiness to weariness—"I'm up to my eyeballs in open cases, all right? It's hard enough investigating the real ones without chasing down feminine hunches."

"Did you go to Molly's apartment?"

"Yeah. And I applied downward pressure to the crib gate and it gave way. If Mrs. Norville is guilty of anything, it's having a defective crib. I advised her to replace it."

As Peggy listened to Fazio talk, she began to doubt herself. Still, something in the back of her mind told her she was right. "Fazio, answer me one question. Do you really think Mrs. Norville is innocent?"

There was a long pause and then the detective said quietly, "I don't know, Garrigan. Could she be lying? Sure. Could she be guilty of child abuse? Perhaps. But without evidence there's nothing we can do."

"What did Child Welfare say?"

"Their investigator was there at the hospital with me. She agrees with me." When he didn't hear a response from her, he said, "Listen, Garrigan, let me give you a piece of advice. I know the kid got to you. No one likes to see a little kid get hurt. But you got a long way to go in this job. If you get personally involved with everything you see, you're not gonna make twenty."

"Thanks for the advice," Peggy said, slamming the phone down.

~~

Eddie Mazzeo slouched behind the wheel of his RMP waiting for Peggy to come out. They'd come back to the station house because she said she needed a summons book, but he knew she was on the phone harassing the poor investigating detective. Mazzeo glanced uneasily into the rearview mirror. They were supposed to be on patrol and Labonte was working today. He didn't need to have Lard-ass find them out of their sector.

Finally, Peggy came out of the station house and Mazzeo started the engine. He could tell from the look on her face that she was ticked. He waited until she got into the car and slammed the door before he spoke. "What'd he say?"

"What'd who say?" She pretended she didn't know what he was talking about.

He waved her summons book in her face. "You got twenty-four left in this one. You expecting a busy day?"

"The detective closed the case."

"All right. You wanted an investigation. You got it."

"That wasn't an investigation."

"Peggy, you can't let every little thing eat you up."

She turned and looked at him with a cold fury. "The only thing that's 'little' about this case is Molly." She cranked the window down. "Let's take a ride over to Morris."

"It's not our sector."

"Eddie, just do it. Okay?"

"No. Morris is on the other side of the precinct. We can't just go where the hell we please."

"Fine. I'll go after work."

Mazzeo slammed his hand on the steering wheel. "Goddamn it, Peggy, quit acting like a rookie. You did what you were supposed to do. Now drop it."

"I won't drop it," she said stubbornly.

"All right, do what you want. But when you get jammed up, don't come crying to me."

Before she could answer, she was interrupted by the dispatcher. *"Sector Frank, respond to 1473 Juniper, meet the owner regarding a burglary..."*

Chapter Seventeen

The owner of the Lambros Luncheonette, an exasperated rotund Greek with a thick mustache, met Garrigan and Mazzeo at the front door. "Forty years in this business!" he said smacking the side of his head. "I never see nuthin' like this *skata*."

Mazzeo squeezed past the fat man. "What happened?"

"What happened? I was robbed. That's what happened."

"Someone held you up?" Peggy asked.

"I come in to open this morning and—boom, I seen I was robbed."

"You were burglarized," Mazzeo corrected. "How much money did they get?"

"What money? Who would leave money here at night? Am I crazy?"

"So what'd they get?"

The little Greek's eyes bulged. "Come, I show you."

He led them into the tiny kitchen. "There!" He pointed at a small table cluttered with dirty dishes and empty beer bottles. "Look for yourself."

Mazzeo rolled his eyes. The Greek was a "twenty-questions" type complainant. They never gave simple, straight answers. They expected you to keep asking questions until you guessed what happened. "What am I looking at?" Mazzeo asked.

"The *malakas* ate here," the Greek answered as though it were perfectly obvious. "The *bastardes* cooked a meal and ate it right *here*." He thumped the table with his beefy hand for emphasis.

Mazzeo tried not to grin. "No kidding, they ate here?"

"I said somethin' funny?"

"How'd they get in?" Peggy asked.

"The back door."

"It's not alarmed?"

"Alarms cost money. I look like I'm made from money?"

Mazzeo pushed his hat to the back of his head. "Let me see if I got this right. A couple of burglars broke in here. They didn't take anything, they just cooked something, and… what'd they eat?"

The Greek ticked the menu off on his pudgy fingers. "Soup, soulvaki, shiskebob, rice, three beers, two coffees; and for desert, rice pudding and ouzo."

"Ouzo? You don't have a liquor license," Peggy pointed out.

The Greek shrugged. "I keep a bottle. Just for my friends. No charge. The sonsofbitches drank half of it."

Peggy leaned down and peered at one of the glasses. "Lipstick. One of them is female."

The Greek slapped the side of his head. "Why me? It's not hard enough making a living. Now I got *malakas* cooking *my* food in *my* kitchen."

"It could have been worse," Mazzeo said.

The bulging eyes narrowed. "What could be worse?"

"A couple of years ago we had a residential burglar who was driving us nuts in the precinct. His MO was to take a dump on the kitchen table before he left."

The luncheonette owner tugged at his mustache, mulling that one over. "Better that," he said after a while. "He takes a crap at least it don't cost me nothin'."

~~

When they came into the station house to drop off the report, Leland was behind the desk reading the command log. "Hey, Loo," Mazzeo said to Lieutenant Hanlon, "wait'll you get a load of this wacky sixty-one."

Leland looked up. "What do you have, Mazzeo?"

"Couple of burglars broke into Lambros Luncheonette and cooked themselves a meal, Cap."

Hanlon peered over his glasses. "What'd they take?"

"Nothing. I guess you could say they just ate and ran."

Hanlon chuckled. "Probably figured they could cook better than old man Lambros."

Leland took the sixty-one from Mazzeo and read it in stony silence.

"We need something like this once in awhile," Hanlon said to Leland. "It adds a little levity to a gloomy world. Don't you think?"

Leland looked up from the sixty-one and he wasn't smiling. "Have we ever had an MO like this before?"

"Not as far as I can remember. Why?"

Leland tossed the sixty-one on the desk. "This is just the sort of thing the newspapers love. If they get wind of this, they'll eat us alive."

Hanlon grinned. "Good pun, Cap."

"I didn't mean it as a pun, Lieutenant." Leland started back toward his office. "Any calls from the press about this matter," he yelled over his shoulder, "refer them to me."

"You got it, Boss." A perplexed Hanlon watched the CO disappear into his office wondering if Leland was completely devoid of a sense of humor or if it was just an occupational hazard of being a precinct CO.

~~

"Sector Boy... disorderly man... 219 Hendricks Street..."

The call was for a disorderly man, but when Lafferty and Reece pulled up to the location, all they saw was a middle-aged black woman holding a bloodstained handkerchief to her head.

"My husband"—the woman said even before they got out of the car—"he's acting crazy."

Lafferty stood far enough away from the woman so he wouldn't get blood splattered on him. "What's your name?"

"Wilma Henderson."

"Husband's name?"

"Calvin Henderson."

"How about that," he muttered to Reece. "A real married couple. Same last names and all. What happened?" he asked the woman.

"Since he came home from work last night he's been acting real strange."

"Why did he hit you?"

"I told him the TV was broke."

"Touchy bastard," he muttered to Reece. To the woman he said, "He do drugs?"

"No, sir."

"He been drinking?"

She pursed her lips. "Yes, but he doesn't usually drink."

Lafferty smirked. "Yeah, right. He own a gun?"

"No."

"If he don't, he's gotta be the only one in this friggin' neighborhood who doesn't," he muttered to Reece. "How about a knife?"

"No. Officer, my husband has never been in trouble before."

"Where is he now?"

"Upstairs. Apartment Five C."

Lafferty and Reece looked at each other and said simultaneously, "The top floor."

They climbed the five rickety flights with Lafferty in the lead, Reece next, followed by the woman in the rear. When they got to the fifth floor landing, she pointed to a partially opened door at the far end of the hallway. "That's my apartment."

Reece looked at his partner and they were both thinking the same thing. *A family fight.* Anything could—and often did—happen at family fights. It was the most dangerous call a cop could go on. "You ready?" Reece asked.

Lafferty nodded stoically and wrapped his nightstick's thong tightly around his hand. As they moved down the hallway, hoping to make a stealthy entrance into the apartment, the woman yelled out, "Don't hurt him, officers."

Lafferty winced. The last thing he needed was a drunken, abusive husband being warned that cops were coming to call. "I'm glad he popped her," he muttered to Reece. "I wouldn't mind cold-cocking the big-mouthed bitch myself."

When they got to the open door, Lafferty flattened himself against the wall. She'd said he didn't have a gun, but Lafferty knew that wives were not to be trusted. Once before, a wife had told him her husband didn't have a gun. After he'd wrestled the gun away from the crazed husband and showed it to her, her response had been: "Oh, *that* gun."

Reece wrapped the open door with his nightstick. "*Police!* Come on out, Calvin. We want to talk to you."

Except for James Brown shrieking on a stereo in the next apartment, there was silence in the hallway. Reece sighed. "We gotta go in. Ready?"

Lafferty nodded, kicked the door all the way open, and they both rushed in. The living room was small, but neatly furnished—except for an overturned coffee table and an upset Christmas tree. They searched the rooms and closets in the tiny apartment but didn't find Calvin. "This guy must be Houdini," Lafferty said, looking under a bed.

"Maybe he went up to the roof?" Reece offered.

They went back into the living room. Lafferty opened the window and stuck his head out. "Whoa!" He jerked his head back inside. "He's out there," he whispered.

"Out where? There's no fire escape."

"He's on the fucking ledge."

"That's ridiculous. It's only twelve inches wide."

"You tell him that."

Cautiously, Reece stuck his head out the window. Calvin Henderson had walked along a twelve-inch ledge to the end of the building, a distance of fifteen feet. His back was toward the window and he didn't see Reece watching him. The cop ducked back in and ran toward the kitchen. "I'll call for Emergency Service, you keep an eye on him."

"What for? He ain't goin' nowhere but down."

While Reece was calling Emergency Service, Lafferty stuck his head out the window again. Henderson turned at that moment and fixed his watery, blood-shot eyes on Lafferty.

"Hey," Lafferty said casually. "How're you doin', pal?"

"I ain't doin' good." The voice was slurred. Calvin Henderson was drunk as a skunk.

"So what are you doin' out here?"

"I'm gonna kill myself."

Lafferty knew that wasn't true. At least not at this moment. If he really wanted to kill himself, he'd already have done a swan dive off the roof and Emergency Service would be scrapping him off the sidewalk with snow shovels. Lafferty's experience was that real suicides jumped without fanfare or the need for an audience.

"Hey, Calvin. So you popped your old lady. Big deal. Come in and we'll talk about it."

"Thirty years of marriage and I never laid a hand on that woman. I'm so ashamed."

Thirty years? Lafferty didn't know anyone who'd stayed married more than five years, let alone thirty. "Hey, it happens," Lafferty said. "It's not the end of the world. Neither is a broken TV."

"I ain't out here because of no damn broken TV."

"So what's the problem?"

Henderson turned away and Lafferty thought he was going to go. But Calvin turned back and there were tears in his eyes. "I... lost my job."

"Oh, well. OK. That's more serious than a busted TV. But you can get another job."

"Where? I'm fifty-nine years old. I've been a maintenance man with the same company for over thirty-six years. Ain't no one gonna hire me."

Lafferty was becoming more and more impressed with Calvin Henderson. He'd never met anyone who had held the same job for thirty-six years either. "Why'd they can you?" he asked.

"They call it downsizing. Said they didn't need me no more. Thirty-six years all gone for nuthin'. How can that be?"

The wisecracking Lafferty had no answer.

Reece tugged at his sleeve. "Excuse me, Calvin," Lafferty said. "Don't—" he almost said, "Don't go away," but he caught himself. "I'll be right back."

"Where's Emergency Service?" he asked Reece.

"They're on the way. But they'll be a while. All the trucks are tied up at a fire in Pelham."

"All right. I'll try to keep him talking."

Lafferty repositioned himself so that he was sitting on the windowsill with half his body outside. It wasn't very comfortable, but at least he could see Calvin without getting a stiff neck.

A small crowd was beginning to gather in the street below and apartment windows across the street were filled with curious neighbors. Three men had come out on one of the fire escapes with a cooler of beer as though they were about to watch a sporting event.

"Hey, Calvin," Lafferty said. "Why don't you come in. It's cold out. We can talk better inside."

Henderson shook his head violently. The motion upset his alcohol-affected equilibrium and he swayed away from the wall. A chorus of groans went up from the spectators. A voice from the beer cooler crowd shouted, *"Go for it, baby. Jump."*

For one brief, impetuous moment, Lafferty considered firing a bullet into the window over their heads just to get them to shut up. But that was too crazy even for him. Instead, he yelled, "Shut the fuck up you morons before I come over there and stick that cooler up your ass."

One of the men stood, dropped his pants, and mooned Lafferty.

"I'll remember that ass, asshole," Lafferty shouted above the laughter.

"Those boys are right," Calvin said morosely. "I'm better off dead. At least there's insurance."

"That's the booze talking, Cal. I can tell you're a good guy, a working man. You got any kids?"

"A son. He's a major in the Marine Corps."

Lafferty heard the pride in Calvin's tone. "A major? Well, goddamn, what would he think about this, Cal? Suicide is the loser's way out."

"Stop talking like that," Reece hissed from inside the room. "You'll make him jump."

"Leave me alone," Lafferty muttered out of the side of his mouth. "I know what I'm doin'." All the time he'd been talking to Calvin, he'd been watching the man's eyes. So far he hadn't seen that thousand yard stare of the psycho. What he did see was fear. And that was encouraging. A man who is afraid doesn't want to die. Lafferty extended his hand. "Come on in, Cal. You owe it to your wife and son."

Calvin started to cry and that concerned Lafferty. A man blinded by tears had no business standing on a twelve-inch ledge fifty feet above the street. "It's okay, Cal. Just come back in. Will you do that? For your wife? For your son?"

After a look silence, Calvin wiped his eyes and said softly, "Okay..." Calvin's chest was heaving uncontrollably. Lafferty didn't like that either. People who hyperventilated passed out.

Lafferty offered encouragement. "Don't look down. Don't think about anything. Just take real small steps."

As Calvin started to turn around on the narrow ledge, he lost his balance. Only his flailing arms prevented him from toppling off the ledge. A roar went up from the crowd, which had now multiplied to more than a hundred. Someone from the street yelled: *"Jump!"* Several others took up the taunt. A furious Lafferty looked down at the crowd to see who was doing it, but all he could see was a sea of faces—some horrified, some grinning—looking up at him.

Now that Calvin had decided not to commit suicide, the reality of where he was hit him and he was suddenly paralyzed by fear. "I... can't turn around," he said breathlessly.

"You don't have to turn around," Lafferty explained. "Just back up. Real slow."

"I... can't... My legs won't work."

Lafferty saw Calvin's legs buckle and was afraid the man was going to pass out. He ducked into the room. "Where the hell is Emergency Service?" he shouted at Reece.

"I made another call. They're on the way."

"So's Christmas. He wants back in, Charlie, but he can't move."

"He'll have to hold on until help gets here."

"He can't hold on. He's scared shitless and some of those mothers out there are telling him to jump. We gotta do something."

"What can we do? We have no ropes, no equipment—" He stopped talking when he saw Lafferty unbuckling his gun belt. "What are you doing?"

"I'm going out after him."

"The hell you are. You'll both go off the ledge."

"We'll take it nice and easy."

"Billy, wait for the trucks."

"He can't wait that long." He poked Reece's fat belly and chuckled nervously. "Normally, I'd flip you to see who goes out, but your fat ass won't fit through the window."

Reece smacked his hand away. "Billy, you're not going out there."

Lafferty flashed a weasel grin. "Are you saying that as my partner or my PBA delegate?"

"*I'm saying that as the only sane person in this fucking room!*" Reece bellowed.

Lafferty tossed his gun belt on the couch. "Rip the window shades and drapes down. I want everything out of the way. We may have to come back in here in a hurry."

Before Reece could protest further, Lafferty was out the window. His appearance brought jeers and whistles from the crowd. He'd have given them the finger if he could have pried his trembling hands away from the brick wall. Reminding himself not to look down, he used the bricks as handholds and stood up very slowly. "I'm gonna help you back in, Calvin. We're gonna do it nice and slow. No quick movements. Okay?"

Calvin nodded vigorously, too terrified to speak.

Slowly, Lafferty slid his feet along the ledge, which, to the petrified cop appeared to be no more than four-inches wide. With every step he heard a chorus of *oohs* and *aahs* from the spectators below. After what seemed like an eternity, he reached Calvin. Slowly, so as not to pull himself off balance, he reached out and gripped the man's belt. It was only then that he allowed himself to take a breath. *So far, so good.* Now all they had to do was move backward nice and slow. A piece of cake. "Okay, Calvin, I got you. Let's go."

Calvin didn't move. He looked over his shoulder at Lafferty imploringly. "I can't move, officer."

"Goddamnit," Lafferty hissed. "I ain't gonna stay out here all day. Now move your ass before I change my mind and leave you out here." He tugged at the belt and Calvin took a tentative step.

Slowly the two men shuffled along the ledge backward. A teenager on a roof across the street shouted, "Yo, old-timer, why don't you jump and take that cop with you?"

The blood was pounding so loud in Lafferty's ears that he never heard the taunt. Now they were five feet from the open window where Reece was waiting for them. Ignoring his own warning to Calvin, Lafferty glanced down and was almost overcome with a wave of vertigo. But before he looked away, he saw three Emergency trucks below and a handful of cops scrambling to set up a net.

"Five feet," Reece whispered to his partner. "Five feet and you're in, buddy."

Lafferty heard pounding feet and voices coming from inside the apartment. The Emergency cops had arrived. He turned his head and saw an ES sergeant watching him from the window. "How you doing, officer?" he asked calmly.

"Okay, Sarge."

"If you want to stop right there, my men are on the roof getting ropes ready. They'll come down and get you."

"No, that's okay, Sarge." Lafferty didn't want to stay out there a second longer than he had to. "We're coming in."

The sergeant climbed out the window. He was wearing a harness with a rope that was attached to something inside the apartment. At that moment, Lafferty would have given his pension to be wearing that harness.

The sergeant inched forward and took hold of Lafferty's belt, and the three men, held together by flimsy handholds on belts, shuffled backward toward the opened window and safety.

Finally, they were there. Hands reached out and pulled Lafferty and Calvin inside. The tiny room was swarming with ES cops carrying harnesses, ropes, and poles over their shoulders. A half dozen radios squawked unheeded messages.

An ashen-faced Reece couldn't stop slapping Lafferty on the back. "You sonofabitch..." he kept saying over and over. "You crazy sonofabitch..."

The ES sergeant climbed through the window. "Okay, officer," he said to Lafferty. "You can let go of him now."

Lafferty glanced at his hand. He was still holding on to Calvin's belt in a death grip. He looked around at the sea of relieved, smiling faces. "Hey, Sarge," he said out of the side of his mouth. "I can't."

"You can't what?"

"I can't let go."

"Why not?"

"My fucking hand's locked."

Two amused ES cops cut the loops on Calvin's pants, leaving the belt clutched in Lafferty's hand. Calvin turned and hugged Lafferty. "Thank you, officer. Thank you..."

Uncomfortable with the show of affection, Lafferty patted Calvin's back with his free hand. "Yeah, no problem, Cal. You take care of yourself, buddy."

Calvin was led away to a waiting ambulance.

Lafferty held up his hand, still clutching the belt. "Now what?"

"Gotta take you to the hospital," the ES sergeant said grimly.

"What for?"

"So they can remove the belt surgically."

"No fucking way are they gonna—" Lafferty's pinched face broke out into a toothy grin when he saw the grinning faces around him.

~~

As Reece drove them back to the station house, Lafferty's hand finally unlocked and the belt dropped from his grasp. "Man, do I need a drink." He stretched his cramped fingers. "You can buy me a beer when the tour is over."

"Go fuck yourself," Reece snapped. "Do you realize it's *four days before Christmas*? I could have been drinking a beer at your wake you dopey asshole."

"Hey, I knew what I was doing."

"Billy, you *never* know what you're doing."

"Thanks, pard."

"Let me ask you something. You're always ranting about niggers. Why'd you risk your life for him?"

"Cal? He's no nigger. Munyika is a nigger. The skells at the Joy are niggers. Calvin is a black man. There's a difference. He works and he's married all those years."

Reece shook his head in exasperation. "You're strange, Billy. You know that? You're really strange."

"Yeah, that's what my two ex-wives said, too."

They rode in silence for a while, then out of the corner of his eye Reece saw Lafferty shiver. "You all right?"

"Yeah, yeah. I'm fine." Lafferty was quiet for a while. Then he said, "Charlie, all the time I was holding on to Cal out there, I figured I could always let go if he jumped." He looked at his partner with genuine fear in his eyes. "I wouldn't have been able to let go." He looked down and his hands were shaking uncontrollably.

Reece looked away. "When the tour's over I'll buy you a beer, you hump."

Chapter Eighteen

The Christmas Eve day tour came to a quiet end and everyone breathed a sigh of relief. The last thing anyone wanted was to make an arrest and spend Christmas Day in court arraigning a prisoner.

Peggy Garrigan wished Eddie and the others a Merry Christmas and went to her car. Now, sitting behind the wheel, she wondered, once again, if what she was about to do was the right thing.

She was going to her father's tomorrow. She should go home and do something about the pile of unwrapped presents that she'd bought for her father, her two sisters, her two brothers-in-law, and her assorted nieces and nephews. So why was she sitting in her car on Christmas Eve contemplating something that was probably going to get her in a whole lot of trouble?

Once again, she reviewed the pros and cons. The cons came first. It wasn't her job to investigate a possible child abuse case. Hadn't the experts determined that there was nothing to investigate and closed the case? Who was she, a mere precinct police officer, to question their judgment?

Then the pros chimed in. Well, hell, why shouldn't she question their judgment? Wasn't she the one who had interviewed Mrs. Norville? Wasn't she the one who'd sensed that something wasn't quite right in the Norville household; something she couldn't write down on a complaint report? Her father had always told her to trust her instincts and she was going to do just that. She dismissed further doubts from her mind and started the car.

She parked across the street from 2315 Morris Avenue and stared up at the neat rows of apartment windows. There had to be at least seventy apartments. Surely, someone in one of those apartments had to have seen or heard something. A discomforting thought suddenly shook her resolve: *If there was something to see or hear.*

Looking at the massive building made her realize what a daunting task she had before her. She certainly didn't have the authority to do what she was about to do. If the department got wind of what she was up to, she'd face serious disciplinary consequences. Maybe even the loss of her job. She dismissed these negative thoughts from her mind, took a deep breath and opened the car door.

The interior of the apartment building was immaculate, light years away from the stinking, squalid tenement hallways in the Valley. The highly polished marble floor gleamed in the well-lighted vestibule. There were even fresh poinsettias in a large round centerpiece by the elevator bank. A six-foot Christmas tree twinkled in the lobby. Everything about the building spelled money and class. Once again, doubts welled up in her. Maybe Eddie was right. Maybe rich people didn't abuse their kids. No, that wasn't true. Money, she knew, had nothing to do with child abuse.

She looked down the corridor at the double rows of apartment doors, wondering where to start. "What the hell," she muttered, and rang the nearest bell. There was no one home in apartment 1A or IB. She thought she heard a floor creak behind the door of apartment 1C and had the uncomfortable feeling that someone was watching her through the peephole, but no one answered the bell.

The occupant of 1D, an elderly woman in her seventies, opened the door, but only after she made Peggy hold her ID up in front of the peephole. Even so, she studied Peggy suspiciously from behind a three-inch opening in the chain-locked door. "Yes, what do you want?"

Peggy gave her a big smile, which she hoped hid her nervousness. "I'm Police Officer Peggy Garrigan. We're conducting a survey of children in the precinct."

"Why?"

"To assess their needs in terms of what the police department can do for them."

The woman nodded curtly. "Well, I like that. From what I can see of young people today, they need all the police supervision they can get."

"Oh, I don't mean in a punitive way, Mrs.—"

The woman studied Peggy with small, squinty eyes, trying to decide if she wanted to give her name to a perfect stranger. "Hotchkiss," she finally answered.

"Mrs. Hotchkiss, are there any children living on this floor?"

"No. Not many in the building, matter of fact. "There's a family on the tenth floor, and a couple more on the sixteenth or seventeenth. Can't remember which."

"Thanks for the information."

Mrs. Hotchkiss nodded curtly and slammed the door.

Peggy heard the old woman reworking the locks and bolts as she headed down the hallway toward the elevator. If there were only a few families in the building with children, it made sense to start with them. New York City apartment dwellers were notorious for not knowing their neighbors, but having children might give them something in common.

After four tries, she found the woman on the 10th floor who had a child. Mrs. Banks, a woman in her early forties, studied Peggy's ID carefully. "Yes, what's this about?"

Peggy gave her the same spiel she'd given the lady on the first floor. "How old is your child?" she asked.

"My son is ten."

Peggy hid her disappointment. It wasn't likely that a woman with a ten-year-old boy would have much in common with the mother of a seventeen-month-old girl. Peggy broke the ice by asking some general questions about the woman's concerns for children's safety. Then she moved on to some carefully guarded questions about child abuse. Mrs. Banks stated emphatically that she'd never personally seen an incident of child abuse in her life. Finally, after small talk about what the police department hoped to do for the children of the neighborhood, Peggy said, "I understand there are children on the sixteenth or—"

"Seventeen. Cynthia Norville and another woman. I can't remember her name. She has a little boy around the same age as Cynthia's daughter. I've seen them together in the playground occasionally."

Peggy got off the elevator on seventeen. She glanced down the hallway at Norville's apartment door and prayed the woman wouldn't make an appearance. She doubted Mrs. Norville would recognize her out of uniform, but, still... She worked her way down the hallway, ringing the bells of all the apartments on the same side of the building as Norville's. Just as it was on the first floor, some people weren't home and those that were had nothing significant to offer.

She came to Apartment 17D, the apartment next to Norville's, and rang the bell. An attractive young woman with short frosted hair and a loose fitting sweatshirt opened the door. She examined Peggy's credentials. "Wow, am I under arrest or what?"

"No, nothing like that. I'm conducting a survey, Mrs.—"

"Helen Jurek. Come on in. Conducting a survey on Christmas Eve? That's dedication. Would you like something? Coffee? Soda?"

"No, thanks."

The woman swept a Power Ranger off the couch and tossed it on a pile of toys on the floor. "Sit down. You'll have to excuse the mess. Robert is a one-man wrecking crew."

Peggy took in the apartment at a glance. It had a similar layout to Norville's, but without the invisible million-dollar view of the Manhattan skyline and the expensive furnishings. There was something comfortable about this apartment that she hadn't experienced in Norville's. She decided it was the easy casualness. There was a stack of newspapers and magazines on the coffee table. Apparently the little boy had been playing with blocks, which were now strewn across the living room carpet.

She didn't recall seeing toys in Norville's living room. In fact there had been absolutely no clue that a small child lived there. Then she saw the Christmas tree and tears welled up in her eyes. Underneath the tree were dozens of gaily-wrapped presents She suddenly knew what was wrong in the Norville apartment: There had not been one present under Mrs. Norville's small Christmas tree.

Peggy nodded at the blocks. "Is he going to be an engineer?"

"For today anyway. Right now he's sleeping. Thank God."

"I imagine they're a handful at that age."

Helen Jurek ran her fingers through her hair. "Oh, God, yes. I'm dreading the 'terrible twos.' I'll probably wind up in a nut house. She fluffed up a throw pillow. So, what kind of survey are you doing?"

"We're asking parents to tell us what they perceive as community problems that might concern their children which, hopefully, the police department will be able to address."

"I don't think there's much you can do for Robert. He's only sixteen months."

"Do you take Robert to the playground?"

"Whenever I can."

"Have you ever had a problem with strange men loitering in the area?" This morning ,Peggy had reviewed the complaint report index and knew that a flasher had been arrested in the neighborhood playground less than a week ago.

The woman frowned. "Not personally, but I heard a man was recently arrested for exposing himself. That really disturbed me."

"That's one of the quality-of-life issues we want to target." Peggy saw that she'd struck a responsive chord in the young mother. "Is there anyone else in the building who uses the playground?"

"My next door neighbor, Cynthia Norville."

"How old is her child?"

"Molly's a month older than Robert."

"How wonderful. I guess you four go to the playground all the time."

Jurek looked away. "Not really. Sometimes we meet there by chance."

Peggy noticed a subtle change in the woman. The happy, easygoing smile was gone. She'd become more guarded. Peggy picked up a photo of a baby from the coffee table. The chubby, smiling face was half-hidden by a wooly hat pulled down over his ears. "This must be Robert."

The woman beamed. "Yes."

"He's beautiful."

"Thank you," she gushed. Like all new mothers, she'd been hearing compliments about her baby since his birth, but she never tired of hearing them.

Peggy continued to stare at the photo. "At this age children are so... fragile, aren't they?" The woman nodded thoughtfully.

Peggy went on. "They rely on parents and adults to take care of them, to protect them from harm."

"Who'd want to harm a little child?" Helen Jurek glanced down the hall toward her baby's bedroom.

Peggy let that question hang in the air for a moment and then said, "Unfortunately, some people do, Mrs. Jurek."

A stricken look flashed in the young mother's eyes and she flicked an imaginary speck of dust from the back of the couch. "I guess in your line of work you see some terrible things."

"Yes. But you get used to it. Except for the children. You never get used to seeing kids hurt. Sometimes adults bring on their own problems, but never little kids. They're always victims." She carefully watched Helen Jurek's face. "You know what's so tragic about child abuse? So many times, adults know what's going on, but they don't speak up."

"I guess... I would guess they might be afraid of being wrong," Mrs. Jurek replied softly.

"Yeah, I suppose. But what if they're right?" She saw she had Mrs. Jurek's undivided attention. "One of the issues we're concerned about is child abuse, whether it's in the playground, the school, or the home. Mrs. Jurek, have you ever seen an instance of child abuse?"

"No." The answer came too quickly.

"Have you ever suspected that child abuse might be occurring?"

"No." This time her answer was slower in coming. Mrs. Jurek looked at her watch and stood up. "I'm sorry, Officer, but Robert will be waking up soon, and my husband will be coming home. I have to get dinner started—"

"I understand." Peggy rose from the couch and handed the woman a piece of paper with her name and home telephone number on it.

The stricken woman looked at it as though she'd suddenly been given a ticket in her own living room. "Why are you giving me this?"

"Just in case you remember anything or hear anything." She put her hand out. "Mrs. Jurek, thanks for your time."

Outside in the hall, Peggy leaned up against the wall and exhaled slowly. Interviewing someone without being able to reveal the real reason for the interview was exhausting and the effort expended in delicately skirting the issue had drained her both physically and mentally. What she wanted to do right now was to go home, take a hot bath, and wrap those presents. But there were four more apartments to visit.

By 8 p.m., she'd visited the last of the apartments on the seventeenth floor. She'd used the same story, slowing leading up to the issue of child abuse. Mrs. Norville's neighbors were suitably shocked at the idea of anyone abusing a child and they were just as adamant in stating that they'd never personally witnessed a case of child abuse.

Peggy was convinced that of all the people she'd spoken to, at least one of them was lying: Helen Jurek. All the time she'd been talking to her, the young mother had been unconsciously clutching a teddy bear protectively to her breast.

~~

Leland finished reviewing a stack of complaint reports and looked up at the clock with bleary, blood-shot eyes. Nine o'clock. *Christmas Eve.* Even though he'd been in the station house since seven this morning, he'd been toying with the idea of working through the night. Anything was preferable to going home to a lonely, dreary apartment. But there would be talk. *I hear he worked Christmas Eve and Christmas Day... Doesn't he have a life...? What's with Captain Scrooge...?*

Leland glanced at his wall calendar. A woman in a thong bikini was walking along a white sandy beach on St. Thomas surrounded by shimmering cobalt water under a cerulean sky. "That's where I should be," he muttered and turned off the light in his office.

Marv Seidel, looking out of place in a uniformed shirt that was so tight he couldn't button the collar, was filling in as desk officer. Most of the Jewish cops volunteered to work Christmas Eve so the Christians could be at home with their families.

"Gonna call it a night, huh, Cap?"

"Yeah." Leland scratched his signature in the command log. "Have a quiet night, Sarge."

"I'll do my best. You have a merry Christmas."

"Thanks."

As Leland went through the doors, Seidel said to a cop nearby, "Looking at that poor sonofabitch, I'm glad Christmas don't mean shit to me."

~~

Leland brought in Chinese food—wonton soup, an egg roll, shrimp with lobster sauce and, as a present to himself, a forty-dollar bottle of Chablis that the clerk swore would go well with Chinese food. Steve and Pam Janssen had insisted that Leland come to dinner tonight *and* tomorrow, but he'd begged off, saying he had to work. The way he was feeling, he knew he'd only put a damper on the holiday and he didn't want to ruin it for them. It was best that he spend tonight and tomorrow alone.

For as long as he could remember, it had been a tradition in his family to watch the movie, *A Christmas Carol* on Christmas Eve. But not just any version—it had to be the one with Alastair Sim. The first year they were married, Marilyn had given him the DVD as a Christmas present.

Old traditions die hard. He slipped the disc into the DVD player and watched the three ghosts scare the crap out of Scrooge while he ate Chinese food out of the carton. By eleven o'clock, he was sound asleep on the couch surrounded by empty cartons of shrimp with lobster sauce and a half-finished bottle of Chablis that didn't go all that well with Chinese food after all.

~~

In other homes across the city and suburbs, people celebrated Christmas in their own way. In Westchester, Gloria Perez had dinner with her parents in a dining room suffused in the soft glow of a dozen candles. In her apartment in Jackson Heights, Peggy Garrigan wrapped presents and swilled a bottle of cheap champagne, alternately smiling as she thought about her nieces and nephews opening their presents, and crying as she thought about Eddie Mazzeo sitting in front of the fireplace with his wife and new baby. In New City, Billy Lafferty sat in front of the TV with a can of beer and a bowl of popcorn watching a hockey game on ESPN. His wife had gone to bed at ten. The childless Olivers celebrated Christmas Eve with the Elliots and their three children. The two partners made it through dinner without one argument or mention of the upcoming sergeant's exam. In his garage, Charlie Reece, surrounded by bicycle parts, cursed and muttered as he tried to decipher assembly instructions written by a Japanese manual-writer for whom English was a distant second language. And back in the Five-five station house, Marv Seidel adjudicated the only job of this Christmas Eve—an altercation between a man and a woman that centered on whether grits was an appropriate stuffing for a turkey.

Seidel ruled it was not.

And at the stroke of midnight, Christmas came.

Chapter Nineteen

Christmas and New Year's Day came and went and neither was quite as onerous as Leland had imagined they might be. To keep himself busy during the week between Christmas and New Year's, he'd worked long hours reviewing records, riding with cops, talking to store owners and residents, and, in general, getting to know the precinct and the community.

He was pleasantly surprised by the tenor of the feedback. Almost everyone he spoke to thought the Five-five cops were doing a great job. The few complaints voiced had more to do with department policies and manpower shortages than any shortcomings of the cops in the precinct.

Besides Christmas Day, the most difficult part of the week had been the New Year's Eve detail in Times Square. It was inevitable he would have to work it. Every year, thousands of cops were assigned to Times Square and almost every precinct captain was tapped to help supervise the massive detail.

The good news was that he wasn't assigned to Chief Hightower's sector. The bad news was that he was compelled to spend the cold, frigid night watching thousands of delirious revelers ring in the New Year. Nevertheless, the crowd behaved, and the few drunken teenagers who'd managed to sneak into the cordoned-off area were quickly carted away to sleep it off in a station house. All things being equal, it had been a surprisingly pleasant night—until Charlie Drum appeared.

Leland had gone into a restaurant for a cup of coffee. Just as he was leaving, a black Oldsmobile screeched to a stop in front of the restaurant. An outraged Drum bolted out of the car and cornered the unfortunate deputy inspector who was responsible for the sector on Broadway between 44th to 45th streets. Leland stepped back into the doorway to watch.

The object of Drum's fury was *barriers*.

"*What the hell are those barriers doing in the street? Why aren't they on the sidewalks?*" Drum bellowed at the hapless deputy inspector in front of a crowd of startled revelers.

It didn't seem to matter to Drum that *all* the barriers in the Times Square area had been placed in the street and that, in fact, placing the barriers in the street had been the department's SOP for New Year's Eve crowd control since Fiorello LaGuardia was mayor.

The terrified deputy inspector wisely chose not to point out that obvious fact. Instead, he said, "Would you prefer them on the sidewalk, Chief?"

For an instant, Leland considered getting involved, but then he thought better of it. When Drum was like this, it was best to do what the deputy inspector was doing— humor him.

Drum thumped the deputy inspector's chest with his index finger. "I would have preferred them on the sidewalk *before* I got here," he growled. "Get them where they belong forthwith."

The deputy inspector, his two lieutenants, four sergeants, and twelve cops scrambled to reposition the barriers. Fortunately, the good-natured crowd cooperated and, except for a few bugle blasts and catcalls in Drum's direction, the Great Barrier Repositioning went smoothly.

Drum stood in the middle of Broadway with his arms folded and watched until every barrier was in its proper place. Then he hopped back into his car and sped off into the night, no doubt on another critical mission.

To everyone's relief, Drum didn't come back for the rest of the night and the New Year's detail was dismissed at four. Leland made it home just as the sun was beginning to brighten the eastern sky. Too pumped to sleep, he made himself a martini and tried unsuccessfully to get interested in one of the *Jaws* movies on cable. But by six he was sound asleep on the couch, still in his uniform.

~~

At ten o'clock on the morning on January second, Richard Leland was at his desk feeling surprisingly upbeat and renewed. The dreaded holiday season was finally over and it was a brand new year.

He'd always liked the beginning of a new year. It was a time of renewal. A time to start over. There was something intriguing about opening his iPhone's almost clean calendar and wondering what that calendar would look like at the end of the year. There was even a fresh start with the complaint reports, accidents, department memos, bulleting, and special orders. At the beginning of each new year, they all started at number one again.

Leland read the complaint index. They were up to forty already, and he felt a certain proprietorship with these new numbers. The thousands of complaints from last year belonged to his predecessor, Captain Sperling. From now on, these numbers were his and he was going to do everything in his power to see that they were fewer than the previous year. For the first time, he felt as though the Five-five was his command. And he felt surprisingly good about that.

Lt. Hanlon stuck his head in the door. "Cap, I have a woman on the phone. I asked her what her problem was, but she wouldn't tell me. She'll only talk to the commanding officer."

His first week in the precinct, Leland had insisted on personally speaking to everyone who wanted to talk to the commanding officer. But after hours of listening to assorted crackpots and lunatics while his work piled up, he'd issued instructions that his supervisors should filter out the chronic complainers. "Okay, put her through. What's her name?"

"Cynthia Norville."

Leland had finally learned the names of all the important movers and shakers in the precinct, but this name didn't ring a bell. He picked up the telephone. "This is Captain Leland. May I help you?"

"I certainly hope so."

The voice was cultured, but there was a hard edge of anger in it. "What seems to be the problem?" he asked as cheerfully as he could.

"One of your police officers, a Peggy Garrigan, was in my building asking questions about me."

Leland was puzzled. He thought Garrigan was assigned to a sector car. He pulled out a precinct roster and ran his finger down the list of names. He was right. She was assigned to sector John. "What kind of questions was she asking?"

"Questions having to do with the alleged abuse of my own child."

"I'm afraid this is all new to me, Mrs. Norville. If you can give me some particulars—times and dates—I'll be glad to look into the matter."

"A couple of weeks ago, my daughter hurt herself falling out of her crib. Officer Garrigan and a male police officer came. Molly was taken to the hospital for observation. Thank God she was all right. But Officer Garrigan, who took the report, was extremely rude. I was thinking of making a civilian complaint then, but I was so distraught about my daughter that I couldn't think of anything else. Then a couple of days later, I received a call from a woman at Children's Services inquiring about Molly. It was clear from her line of questioning that she'd received a complaint of child abuse. I demanded to know who made the allegation, but she wouldn't tell me. I suspected Officer Garrigan was behind it, but I couldn't prove it. Then just yesterday I overheard two of my neighbors mention that an Officer Garrigan had been to see them and asking a lot of questions about child abuse."

"Mrs. Norville, was your name mentioned specifically?"

"No, but it's quite obvious she was investigating me. Captain, that woman is harassing me and I want it stopped immediately."

"I understand. I'll look into this and get right back to you."

"I'll await your call. Let me warn you, Captain. If I don't receive a satisfactory explanation, I intend to seek legal redress. Do I make myself clear?"

He was about to say, "Perfectly," but she'd already slammed the telephone down.

He dialed the desk officer's extension. "Lt. Hanlon, what's Garrigan doing now?"

"She's in sector John. She just came off a job, Cap."

"Get her in here *forthwith*."

~~

A meek Peggy Garrigan finished her story and sat quietly facing her red-faced commanding officer.

"Officer Garrigan," Leland said in a voice constricted with suppressed anger, "there are department procedures for dealing with these situations. After you notified Special Victims and Children's Services, you were out of it. You did your job. You should have let them do theirs."

"But they didn't do their job, Captain. A couple of phone calls is not an investigation."

"That is not your concern. If you want to be a social worker, you should have gotten a job at Human Resources." He regretted the childish remark as soon as he said it. He carefully straightened the edges of a pile of reports awaiting his signature. "Officer Garrigan," he said in a more reasonable tone, "You had no authority to go into that building and conduct a, a—"

"An investigation?" Peggy offered in a small, but firm, voice.

Leland glared at the spunky little police officer. "'Witch hunt' is the phrase that comes to mind."

Peggy blinked. "Captain, I never mentioned Mrs. Norville by name. I wouldn't be that dumb."

"Well it would appear that your efforts were somewhat more transparent than you thought."

Peggy bit her lip. "What's gonna happen now, Cap?"

"That's up to Mrs. Norville. I'm going to call her back and tell her the truth."

"Am I gonna get a civilian complaint?"

"If you're lucky. She mentioned an attorney."

Peggy paled. "Oh, wow."

"Exactly. And the department won't defend you. You were working outside the scope of your authority." He saw the stunned look on her face and decided a little dose of fear might prevent a similar incident in the future. "Do you have any idea what a lawyer will cost you?"

She stared at the floor. "A lot?"

"More than a lot. The next time you want to overstep the bounds of your authority, you think about that."

Peggy's eyes misted. Eddie had warned her. Hell, she knew herself she shouldn't have gotten involved. Maybe she'd been wrong about the way she'd gone about it, but none of this would have happened if the system worked the way it was supposed to. In her short time as a cop, she was beginning to learn what most cops all learned eventually by bitter experience: The "system" didn't always work.

She blinked back tears of frustration. "Captain, I just wanted to help that little girl. In my heart, I know that she's a victim of child abuse and you know as well as I do that the abuse doesn't stop. It just gets worse."

Now that Leland's anger had subsided, he'd become ambivalent about what to do with Garrigan. There was no question she'd been wrong in going back to that apartment building to conduct her own investigation, but it showed she cared about the people she served. The department was forever decrying the lack of commitment on the part of police officers. Now, here was a police officer who showed commitment. Granted, she'd made a mistake, but it was a mistake of the heart, not the head.

Before he'd called Garrigan into his office, he'd made up his mind to give her command discipline and insist that Mrs. Norville file a civilian complaint. He comforted himself with the thought that it was the "correct" thing to do according to department policy. But deep down, he also realized it was the "correct" thing to do in terms of protecting his own career.

He studied the attractive young police officer sitting before him. Clearly she was sorry for overstepping her authority, but the fire of conviction burned in her eyes; the kind of conviction that made for a good cop. If he made the wrong decision now, he might extinguish that fervor forever.

"Officer Garrigan, I'm not going to take any action for the moment," he said abruptly. "I'll decide after I speak to Mrs. Norville. In the meantime, you will not return to that building and you will not attempt to conduct your own investigation. Is that understood?"

Peggy stared at the floor and nodded.

After she'd gone, Leland dialed Mrs. Norville's number. When he finished telling her the story, she said, "Well, what are you going to do about it?"

"Officer Garrigan has been instructed in proper department procedures. I can assure you, Mrs. Norville, this will not happen again."

"That's it?" she said incredulously. "A little slap on the wrist? That meddling girl has ruined my reputation."

"I don't think it's as bad as all that. Your name was never mentioned and—"

"Don't tell me what's bad. I want that girl transferred."

Leland tapped a pencil on the desk. "Mrs. Norville, don't you think that's a little drastic?"

"I want her transferred," she repeated in a tone that said she was used to getting her way.

Leland knew he was stepping onto a slippery slope. Up until now, the problem was all Garrigan's. All he had to do was act as a responsible commanding officer and soothe Mrs. Norville's ruffled feathers. But he felt himself getting angry, a sure sign that he was getting personally involved, and that was something he vowed he would never do.

"I want her transferred," Norville repeated.

"That," he said evenly, "is *my* prerogative, not *yours*."

There was a silence. Then she said, "We'll see about that."

After she hung up, Leland sat at his desk for a long time pondering his actions. He knew the path to deputy inspector was sown with land mines of various sorts. Some were impossible to recognize, some were impossible to avoid, but others, like a Norville-Garrigan situation, were easily sidestepped. He idly drummed a pencil on the desk and wondered why he'd chosen to step on this particular land mine.

Lt. Hanlon came in. "Cap, the building dedication is in less than an hour."

Leland looked up. He'd forgotten all about it. "Very well," he said. "Get me a car."

~~

The dedication of any new building is a magnet for politicians who are always on the lookout for sound bites and photo ops, and the dedication of the new Warren Street Library was no exception. It made no difference that the planning and funding of the project had been started more than a decade earlier by politicians who were no longer in office. The current crop of politicians couldn't pass up the opportunity to take credit for the accomplishment, make a speech, and get their pictures in the papers.

The makeshift plywood dais groaned under the weight of an assortment of major and minor political figures. It was easy to tell who was who. The major ones—the mayor, the Bronx Borough President, and Senator Thaddeus Archer—stood in a group chatting, while the minor league officials—people at the precinct and district levels—stood apart, cautiously watching, hoping for a nod of recognition from the big wigs.

Leland, who'd been ordered by Hightower to personally supervise the police detail, studied the urbane Senator Archer carefully. Last week, he'd asked Marv Seidel to conduct an informal investigation of the senator using his many contacts both in and outside the department. He wasn't too surprised when the ever-resourceful Anti-Crime sergeant had been unable to confirm what Leland suspected: That Senator Archer had a financial interest in the Joy Lounge. If Archer was the owner, he'd be too smart to leave a paper trail. He would have taken a page from the organized crime handbook and used a "front man." And that front man, Leland believed, was Alvin Tatum.

In spite of his wariness of the powerful senator, Leland hadn't heeded Archer's advice and had continued to step up police enforcement in and around the Joy Lounge. Public Morals had made several arrests, and the sector cops had been so successful in handing out parking tickets that they were now complaining that it was almost impossible to find parking violations within three-square blocks of the Joy. The precinct was amassing a persuasive case for shutting down the bar, and soon Leland planned to present his case to the State Liquor Authority.

Looking at the smiling senator with his arm around the mayor, Leland knew it wasn't a question of *if* he would hear from the senator again, but *when.*

The dedication ceremony got under way with all the pomp and circumstance that attended such events. As usual, the speeches were long on words and short on substance. Finally, to Leland's relief—and everyone else who was sitting on the uncomfortable folding chairs on this cold January day—the mayor cut the ribbon at the front door and the dedication was over.

As Leland expected, Archer sought him out. As he watched Sgt. Engle prepare to dismiss the detail, Senator Archer approached. "Captain Leland, good to see you again."

"And you, Senator."

Archer adjusted the sleeve of a well-tailored blue pinstriped suit that complemented his trim, athletic body. He gazed up at the new building. "A library. What a wonderful gift for the community." His gaze shifted to the three rows of police officers and his face assumed a pained expression. "It really troubles me that so many police officers are assembled here to handle something as mundane as a building dedication."

Leland knew what was coming, but he wouldn't bite. "Any time the mayor and such distinguished guests as yourself converge in one spot," he responded, "it's only prudent to have enough police officers to handle any and all contingencies."

Archer turned his gaze on Leland. He was still smiling, but Leland noticed an almost imperceptible hardening in the eyes. "I understand you're still wasting the valuable time of your police officers by harassing the Joy Lounge."

"Harass? I wouldn't describe it in those terms, Senator."

"What word would you use?"

"Enforcement. And it's working. I'm having a lot less trouble from that bar."

Archer frowned. "I must say, Captain, I totally disagree with your tactics."

"I know, Senator. You made your views perfectly clear the last time we met."

"And I had the distinct impression that you agreed with me."

"I'm sorry if I gave you that impression."

Archer, the quintessential politician, was not about to let someone like Leland, a lowly police captain, ruffle his calm demeanor. "Tell me, Captain, what do you expect to do with the Joy Lounge?"

Leland returned the even gaze. "I expect to shut it down."

"Do you think that's wise?"

"I don't understand."

Archer smiled and waved to the occasional constituent passing by as he spoke. "It's been my experience that establishments like the Joy Lounge often have friends in high places." Then he turned his full attention on Leland. "These friends could destroy your career," he added, coming as close to a threat as he dared.

"I don't think so, Senator." Leland met the senator's level gaze. "Friends in high places can't afford bad publicity and I wouldn't be the only one to get hurt." That was as close as *he* was prepared to come to a threat. Even if that threat was a bluff.

Archer studied him with an icy smile. "I'm surprised at you, Captain Leland. For someone with your headquarters background you're terribly naïve."

"Realistic is the word I would use. I'm going to close that bar down and, if I go down in the process, I won't go alone."

Archer was the first to look away. He glanced at his watch. "I must be going. You take care, Captain," he said, managing to make it sound like a threat.

Leland felt ambivalent as he watched the senator walk away. He was deeply concerned about what Archer could do to his career, but at the same time, he felt a certain elation. In spite of his apprehension, he'd enjoyed sparring with the senator.

Sgt. Engle came up to him and said, "The detail has been dismissed, Captain."

Leland looked around. The crowds had dispersed and the workers were loading the last of the folding chairs onto a flatbed truck. "Okay," he said to the sergeant. "Let's get back to real police work."

～～

Since they'd been dismissed from the detail, Lafferty had been complaining nonstop. "They didn't need us to watch a bunch of windbag politicians talk about a new library," he repeated for the third time in fifteen minutes.

"What's the difference?" the long-suffering Reece said. "You get paid whether you work a detail or a sector."

"I'm a cop, Charlie, not some goddamn square badge security guard. Do they think someone's gonna assassinate the mayor for cutting the ribbon on a new library?"

"Billy, give it a rest."

"Twenty cops! There were twenty cops to watch them open a fucking library. Don't you think that's a little overkill?"

Before Reece could respond, he was interrupted by a call from Central. *"Sector Charlie, report of a past robbery in a drug store 2978 152nd Street."*

"Thank you, Jesus," Reece muttered and stepped on the gas. He didn't use his siren or lights. Even though the robbery had already occurred, the perp might still be in the area. Roaring up to the scene in a police car with flashing lights and siren was not the stealthiest way to catch a thief.

As the car glided down 152nd Street, the two cops carefully scrutinized everyone on the sidewalk. Sometimes a hard, stony stare was enough to spook a perp into bolting. But the few men standing in front of a storefront taxi service simply returned the hard stares.

The drug store clerk, a woman in her late forties, was still trembling as she pointed to the note on the counter. "He never said a word," she said breathlessly. "He just handed me that piece of paper. I thought it was a prescription."

Reece read the note. *"Give me everything in the cash register'* Did you?"

"Damn right I did."

"He say anything?"

"Not a word. He just started at me with those black, scary eyes."

"He have a gun?"

"Yes, he kept it in his pocket."

"Did you see it?"

"No, but he had a gun in his pocket. I'm sure of it."

Lafferty used the end of a ballpoint pen to turn the note over. "I'll be godammed," he said with a big grin. "It's the Poet Bandit."

~~

Stars that shine crystal clear
Counterpoint all human tears
Ring a bell, bow a head
My soul is heavy, my heart is lead

Leland tossed the poem back to Seidel. "So what's this one mean?"

"Guidron says the guy's getting more dangerous and may hurt someone next time around."

Leland, recalling the psychiatrist's earlier interpretations, ticked off the perp's characteristics on his fingers. "He's a ghetto resident, potentially violent, may be suicidal or homicidal, psychotic, and depressed. Did I miss anything?"

"Nope." Seidel jammed his stubby cigar into the side of his mouth. "What I don't get is how someone so screwed up can keep getting away with these robberies."

"What's Guidron's prognosis?"

"He thinks the guy's on the verge of snapping."

"What'll happen then?"

Seidel shrugged. "Someone's gonna get hurt. So far all the victims have complied with his directions, but Guidron thinks the first one to resist is gonna be history."

"Sarge, you've got to catch this guy," Leland said, alarmed by this sudden turn of events.

Seidel looked at Leland in exasperation. "What do you think I've been trying to do?"

"I'm not blaming you. But it's clear we need more help."

"Sounds good to me. Where do you figure I get it?"

"The public."

Seidel eyes narrowed. "I thought you wanted to keep this a secret?"

"I did. But if this guy's about to hurt someone, it's more important we get him."

"What've you got in mind?"

"Your friend at the *Bronx Tribune*. Give her the story, the composite drawing, the works. If she makes it a big story, the whole neighborhood will have some idea of what he looks like. Maybe we'll get a tip."

"The *Bronx Trib* is a local paper. What if the *Daily News* or the *Post* latches on to the story?"

Leland had already thought of that. He wasn't pleased at the prospect of the Poet Bandit story going citywide, but that was a chance he'd have to take. "Then we get wider circulation," he said with a wan smile.

Seidel squinted through a smoky haze. "You got that right."

"Sarge, before you call her, there's something I have to do first."

"What's that?"

Leland glanced at his watch. "I have a Community Board meeting at seven, but first I'll stop off at the borough office and get Chief Hightower's approval."

Seidel gnawed the end of his soggy cigar. "Good luck, Cap."

~~

Chief Lucian Hightower lunged forward in his chair. "You want to do *what*?"

Leland cleared his throat. "Publish his M.O., Chief."

"What in the hell for?"

"So everyone will know who he is. According to the psychiatrist we've consulted, this guy has been getting progressively worse and he may be on the verge of snapping. And if that happens, someone is going to get hurt. I think we have no choice but to go to the press with it." He sat on the edge of his seat and waited for the borough commander to explode.

Hightower sat back and fixed Leland with his big frog-eyes. "How long have these robberies been going on?"

"Since before I got to the Five-five."

"You know my position on pattern crimes, Captain. Why wasn't I told about this sooner?"

Leland could have blamed it on his predecessor. After all, most of the robberies had occurred on Sperling's watch. But instead, he said, "I thought we would have him by now. I've had my Anti-Crime people working on it, but the guy's MO is all over the lot. We can't pin him down, Chief."

"Captain, do you realize that releasing that kind of information to the press is tantamount to calling down an air strike on yourself? You'll be admitting that you have a serious crime problem in your precinct. How do you propose to minimize the damage?"

"By catching the Poet Bandit as quickly as possible," Leland said, not sure he believed that himself.

Hightower grunted. "And how do you figure to do that?"

"Exposure, Chief. We'll publish his composite and everything we know about his MO."

"What else? Are you going to beef up patrols? Shift manpower?"

Leland knew those were the standard cover-your-ass procedures. It was important to look like you were doing something, even if you were just spinning your wheels. "No, sir," he answered. "We don't know where he'll hit next. It would be a waste of manpower and my limited resources. I won't strip officers from one part of the precinct to another when I don't have a clear idea of where he will hit next."

When Hightower didn't interrupt, Leland continued. "The best weapon I have is publicity. The more people who know about him the better the chance we have of apprehending him. The publicity may even discourage him from doing another robbery."

Hightower grunted. "Or at least chase him to another borough."

Leland couldn't tell if the dour-faced chief was kidding or not. Hightower stood up. "If that's what you want to do, it's your call."

"Yes, sir," Leland said with considerably more confidence than he felt.

~~

On his way to the Community Board meeting he reflected on the meeting with Hightower. As he saw it, there was both good and bad news. The good news was that Hightower didn't rip his head off. The bad news was that Hightower, with his constant use of the pronoun "you," had made it clear that Leland alone was going to take the heat for any political fallout accruing from these newspaper stories.

A borough commander who lent support to a losing cause was a de facto loser himself and Hightower didn't get to be where he was by backing losing causes. Hightower had been right about one thing, Leland thought glumly. He, Richard Leland, had made a decision and he alone would rise or fall on its outcome.

~~

This was Leland's second Community Board meeting, but he was getting the hang of it. He knew enough about precinct conditions so that if a specific block or area was mentioned he was confident he would know where it was and the solution to the problem. He also had at his fingertips all the pertinent statistics to answer questions about crime and manpower-related problems.

He was beginning to recognize faces, too, especially the professional complainers—the ones who showed up at every meeting and haunted the station house with the same complaints. He waved to Mrs. Axon, who'd already staked-out her usual seat in the second row. No doubt she'd come to voice her disapproval of double-parked cars on Clinton Boulevard.

As he was about to climb the steps to the dais, a spry octogenarian with a snow-white crew cut cornered him. The handshake was firm. "Captain Leland, Frank Luria. I live on the Hill. Good to see you, sir."

"Mr. Luria. How are you?"

The steely eyes pinned Leland. "Not as good as the old days, Captain."

Leland nodded solemnly, knowing he was about to hear about how good the old days had been.

"I don't see many cops walking a beat. I thought you said you were going to put more police officers on the street."

"I have," Leland said. "There are four more foot cops in your neighborhood."

"Where? I've never seen them."

"Well, the posts are several blocks long, so—"

"*Several blocks*! Why, when I was a lad in Brooklyn, there were cops on damn near every corner. Tim Foley had a beat that couldn't have been more than four blocks long. He knew the names of every man, woman, and child on his beat—*and*—where they lived."

"I know, Mr. Luria, but in those days, cops were assigned to small posts because there was no communication with the station house and it was easier to find them. Besides, crime wasn't as prevalent—"

"You can say that again. I don't think Foley made more than three arrests in the ten years he had that post, but he didn't need to. Just one sharp look from him sent the criminal element scurrying right out of Brooklyn."

Leland had heard all this before. It was frustrating trying to explain that social conditions in the forties were quite different from the present, but at the same time, he, like other cops, had a wistful longing for that simpler time when life—and police work—was so much more manageable. He wanted to explain to the old man that today the proliferation of drugs, guns, and eroding social mores had made police work a managerial nightmare. But he knew Mr. Luria wouldn't understand. His world was fixed in another era and nothing short of bringing back the "good old days" would satisfy him.

Fortunately, Heidi Vancamp called the meeting to order and Leland was saved. While the routine business of the Board was being conducted, Leland scanned the assembled audience. The last time he was here, there were no more than a dozen people, but tonight, by his quick count, there were more than fifty. He leaned across to the Fire Battalion Chief sitting next to him and whispered, "Big crowd tonight, Ed. Anything special on the agenda?"

The chief shrugged, "Not that I know of."

The routine business concluded and the floor was turned over to the audience for the question-and-answer period. Usually, Ronnie Newbert, his Community Relations Officer, would accompany him to these meetings, but tonight she had an exam and had asked for the night off. Leland, confident in his abilities to handle the meeting alone, had granted Newbert's request.

The usual parade of speakers raised the usual problems. Abandoned cars, graffiti, dripping fire hydrants, noisy bars, and vandalism were the major topics of concern. Even without the help of Newbert sitting at his elbow quietly whispering the correct statistics or a brief profile of the questioner, Leland fielded the questions addressed to him knowledgeably and with dispatch.

He stole a quick glance at his watch and was glad that the meeting was almost over. He had a pile of work waiting for him back at the precinct.

Then, Vera Roland, seated in the fourth row, stood up.

The Fire Department Battalion chief leaned toward Leland. "Too bad," he whispered out of the side of his mouth. "You almost made it out of here alive."

Vera Roland, who lived on Seaman Street—the number one drug-prone location in the precinct—was the acrimonious and shrill leader of the Seaman Street Block Association. She'd been a constant thorn in Leland's side since the day he'd arrived in the precinct. In that time he'd done everything he could to placate her, but it was never enough. Now, as he watched the rail-thin black woman striding purposely toward the microphone, he wondered what her latest complaint was going to be.

Then he looked to the back of the auditorium and, to his dismay, saw the Reverend Munyika coming in with his entourage.

Roland's grating voice boomed over the PA system like fingernails across a blackboard. "I have a question for Captain Leland." She paused dramatically. When she was sure she had the full attention of everyone in the auditorium, she continued. "I'd like to know exactly *when* are you going to do something about the dope dealers on Seaman Street? *All* day and *all* night there are strange cars and strange people coming and going. Our children can't play on the street and our old folks can't go to the store without fear of being shot dead by some dope-crazed maniac." She pointed a skinny finger at him. "I have called this problem to your attention time and time again, but you have done absolutely nothing about it. Every time—"

Leland leaned into his microphone. "Mrs. Roland," he said, hoping to short-circuit her harangue, "The Narcotics Division has been notified of the problem. The precinct sector cars and the foot officers have—"

"*I don't want to hear that!*" she bellowed. For a small woman, she had a very big voice. "I'll tell you what. Your police are *afraid* to patrol Seaman Street." A chorus of voices spread throughout the audience signaled their approval by shouts of *"Shame," "Right on,"* and *"Racist cops."*

Now Leland knew why there was such a large crowd. Roland and Munyika had packed the audience with supporters. He was being ambushed and there wasn't a damn thing he could do about it. Shouting to be heard above the voices, he said, "Mrs. Roland, that's simply not true. Every police officer under my command—"

Her shrill voice drowned him out. "You and your *po*-lice don't give a hot damn about the people on Seaman Street. When it comes to black neighborhoods, you overlook the drugs and you overlook the killings." She pointed an accusing finger at him. "*You* are participating in the genocide of African-Americans."

At that inflammatory comment, her followers stood up and began to chant: *"No drugs. No genocide. No drugs. No genocide."*

Leland drummed his fingers on the table impatiently. The only thing missing from this well-orchestrated "spontaneous" demonstration were balloons and campaign hats.

A feisty Heidi Vancamp, not one to let a mob take control of her meeting, slammed her gavel on the table again and again. *"Order! Order!"* she yelled. But it had no effect on Roland's loud and vocal protestors. For the next several minutes, Vancamp, Leland, and the others on the dais, sat helplessly and watched the demonstration run its course.

Outwardly, Leland exuded calmness, but inside he was seething with anger and frustration. He'd called in the Narcotic Division and they had made arrests. He'd assigned more of his people to the street. All this he could have explained to a reasonable person. But Vera Roland was not a reasonable person and had no intention of becoming one. Maybe he hadn't been perfect in his stewardship of his command, but neither he, nor his officers, were guilty of Roland's groundless allegations of racism.

Vancamp, crimson with anger, rapped her gavel. "I will have order or I will have you removed from this meeting. Is that clear?"

The group's response was a series of loud chuckles and catcalls.

Leland groaned inwardly. Vancamp meant well, but she didn't realize how pivotal the situation was. Clearly, Roland and Munyika were looking for any excuse to ignite a full-blown incident and the last thing this meeting needed was the appearance of cops to throw them out. It was just the sort of provocation Roland was hoping for.

Munyika, who had been watching Roland stir up the crowd from the back of the auditorium with a grin of satisfaction, stood up and his voice filled the auditorium. "Ladies and gentlemen," he said solemnly, "let us discuss this peaceably."

He came down the aisle with his arms outstretched like Moses parting the Red Sea. All eyes turned toward him.

"I think we can all agree that Mrs. Roland and the people of Seaman Street have a legitimate grievance. Drugs are rampant on the street. Children are not safe on the street. Old people are not safe on the street," he said in the measured cadence of a TV evangelist. He pointed an accusatory finger at Leland. "Captain, the members of this community want to know why the police department will not protect the lives of our innocent children."

Realizing he had to say something to defuse the situation, Leland snatched the microphone. "Mrs. Roland, Rev. Munyika," he said in a quiet, even voice, "I give you my word that Seaman Street will be cleaned up within thirty days."

There was a stunned silence in the room. Even Munyika was struck dumb. Ronnie Newbert wasn't sitting behind him, but Leland could almost hear his community relations officer groan. The others on the dais, themselves veterans of neighborhood power politics, stared at him in astonishment—and pity. There wasn't a man or woman on that stage who believed for a moment that Richard Leland could deliver on that promise.

Munyika, recovering from his shock, studied Leland with a self-satisfied smile. "I will hold you to that," he said. "The community will hold you to that."

And on that somber note, the meeting ended.

Later, after most of the people had gone, Leland was having a much-needed cup of coffee when he saw Gloria Perez approaching. He'd been watching her out of the corner of his eye as she moved from person to person, no doubt looking for favors and funds for her group. A born politician.

Since he'd had that drink in her apartment, they'd bumped in to each other at a couple of community functions and had engaged in the kind of small talk people engage in when they don't want to talk about anything serious. He'd been cordial, but distant. He told himself he was avoiding her because he didn't want an emotional entanglement, but deep down he wondered if he was avoiding her because of what Chief Drum had said at the Christmas party.

They met at the coffee urn. "These meetings are really hard on you, aren't they?" she said.

As usual, her half-smile, enigmatic and unfathomable, both charmed and irritated him. "I've been through worse," he said.

Her smile turned sunny and his irritation dissipated. He held up his Styrofoam cup. "Want some coffee?"

"No, thanks. The coffee here is almost as bad as Heidi's wine."

"Unfortunately, it's the only coffee around."

"Not true. I'm not a very good cook, but I'm an artist with a Mr. Coffee machine. Care to risk your life?"

Leland was startled—and pleased—with her directness. "Sure," he said. "That the best offer I've had all day."

"You poor man."

~~

Back in her apartment, he sat in the lumpy, familiar chair and sipped her coffee. The truth was, it wasn't a whole lot better than the swill served at the Community Board meetings. "It's very good," he said.

She blew on the hot coffee and examined him with mischievous, large velvet eyes. "You really are a terrible liar, but thanks."

After a few minutes of small talk, she said, "You seem preoccupied, Captain. Thinking about your impetuous promise to Vera Roland?"

"Yeah, I guess I am."

Gloria tucked her shapely legs under her. "Captain, what do you know about Vera Roland?"

Leland shrugged. "She's the president of the Seaman Avenue Block Association and a—" he almost said "a pain-in-the-ass," but he caught himself in time—"a woman very concerned about her neighborhood."

Gloria laughed out loud. "You sound just like a politician."

"Me?" He thought of himself a professional police officer and didn't like being compared to a politician.

"Yes. So calm. So in control. Never a bad word about anyone."

Leland felt the irritation rising again. "You make it sound like a flaw."

"No, just... bloodless. Do you lack passion, Captain?"

"Miss Perez, don't confuse composure with lack of passion."

Gloria ran her glossy-red fingernail around the edge of her cup. "Vera Roland is a dangerous woman," she said softly.

"In what way?"

"She thrives on conflict. The last thing she wants is resolution."

"I don't believe that. She's an advocate for her cause, just as you are an advocate for yours."

The velvet eyes flashed. "Don't compare me to Vera Roland. *I'm* trying to help the people in this community."

"Well, so is Mrs. Roland," Leland snapped. "And she's right. Seaman Avenue is a drug cesspool." He regretted the remark as soon as he said it. Admitting what was tantamount to a failure of the police department—especially to a community activist—was really dumb. At some later date she could use that admission against him. He tried to assess what effect his statement had on her. But he couldn't read anything in those captivating eyes.

"More coffee, Captain?"

He stood up, reluctantly. "No, thank you. I have to get back to the precinct."

At the door she said, "Captain, when it comes to Vera Roland *ten cuidado.*"

All the way down in the elevator he wondered why she'd told him to be careful.

Chapter Twenty

Payday was always a busy day at the precinct. Although most cops had their paychecks electronically transferred into their checking accounts, some still enjoyed the time-honored tradition of bringing the kids—and sometimes the wife—to the station house so they could show them where the old man worked. It also offered an opportunity to talk to friends they didn't get to see during working hours.

Bill Lafferty came skipping down the stairs. "The eagle shit," he yelled, waving his check.

Charlie Reece was standing at the foot of the stairs talking to Mazzeo, Peggy, Elliot, and Oliver. "Good thing they don't pay you what you're worth," he said, "or you'd owe the city money."

"Look who's talking, fat ass. I do more in one day than you do in—" He stopped in mid-sentence and the others turned to see what had silenced motor-mouth.

Nancy Torres was holding the front door open for Hector who, aided by a two-handed walker, awkwardly maneuvered his way through the opening. The six cops stood transfixed in shocked silence. All of them had visited Torres at the hospital many times. He'd looked terrible then, but they'd rationalized that anyone who was hooked up to so many tubes and wires had to look bad. When he left the hospital, they told themselves, he'd bounce back to the old Hector Torres they knew. But now, looking at the frail man with large sunken eyes and rail-thin arms that didn't appear strong enough to hold him up, it was hard to remember the vigorous Hector Torres they all knew.

The quick moment of astonishment passed and they all rushed toward the door. Mazzeo reached out to help him, but Nancy shook her head in a silently 'no', and he pulled back. "Hey, Hector," he said self-consciously, you're looking real good."

Torres's infectious grin was still there. "Eddie, I look like shit, but I feel good. I really do."

"What are you doing here?" Reece chided. "We made arrangements for your check to be delivered to you."

"I was going nuts at home. I had to get out of the house. Nancy drove. She's taking real good care of me."

"He's a star patient." Nancy smiled, but it was a weary smile and, from the dark circles under her eyes, it was clear that this wasn't easy for her either.

Torres stopped to take a breath. "Man, am I out of shape. I brush my teeth and I get winded."

"That walker's gotta be a bitch," Elliot said. "In high school, I broke my ankle and was on crutches for six weeks. I never worked so hard in all my life."

Oliver noticed Torres blinking rapidly. "You okay, Hector?"

"Yeah, it's just my right eye. Sometimes I have a hard time focusing properly. That's my shooting eye. I gotta get that problem corrected or they'll never put me back to full duty."

The six cops exchanged uneasy glances. Not one of them—nor Nancy Torres, judging by the expression on her face—believed for a moment that Hector Torres would ever wear a uniform again.

"What are you talking about?" Lafferty said. "Screw full duty. Take the three-quarters and run. That's what I'd do."

"If I could count on that"—Reece deadpanned—"I'd shoot you in the foot myself."

"I'm serious," Lafferty said. "Three-quarters pay with no taxes. Why would you want to stay in the job?"

"Because I love it," Torres said softly.

Lafferty's mouth dropped open. This was something beyond his comprehension. "You *love* this job?"

"Yeah." Hector blinked away tears. "That's why I'm gonna do whatever it takes to get back to full duty."

Nancy rubbed the back of his neck affectionately and there was genuine concern in her eyes. "His physical therapist tells him he's the hardest working patient she's ever seen. So now he thinks he's superman."

"I know I got a lot of work to do." There was a hint of testiness in his voice that said they'd had this discussion before.

"You try to do too much."

Torres flashed an exasperated grin. "Women. She used to call me a couch potato. Go figure."

"Hey, Hector," Lafferty blurted out. "You remember anything about that night?"

Reece poked his partner. "Billy, for chrissake—"

"No, it's okay, Charlie. The shrink says I should talk about it."

"You seeing a shrink?" Lafferty asked.

"Oh, yeah. And ophthalmologists and plastic surgeons and neurologists and physical therapists and God knows who else. To answer your question, Billy, I don't remember what happened. I went in to break up a fight and the next thing I remember is waking up in the hospital five days later. The squad asked me if I could ID the perps, but..." His voice trailed off.

"Your physical therapist," Mazzeo said, breaking the strained silence. "A babe or what?"

Torres frowned. "Ugly as homemade sin."

"She's just what I ordered," Nancy said with mock sternness.

"How's the baby?" Peggy asked.

"Oh, she's wonderful. My mom is minding her now."

"That's the only good thing about all this," Torres said. "Now that I'm home all the time I get to see her grow every day. She's really something."

Nancy's practiced eye saw that her husband was getting fatigued. "Come on, superman. You promised Captain Leland you'd say hello."

"Okay, boss." He winked at the other cops. "She's worse than Labonte." Then he became serious. "Hey, guys, thanks for what you did at the Joy—"

"Don't thank us," Reece said with a wide grin. "We weren't there."

The six cops silently watched Hector Torres's slow, labored progress toward the captain's office and they all wondered if, under the same circumstances, they would have Hector's courage.

Leland came around the desk and stuck his hand out. "Hector, it's good to see you up and about." Since the night of the incident, Leland had visited Torres regularly both in the hospital and at home. Still, like the others, he, too, was shocked by Torres's emaciated condition.

After some small talk about the new baby and his recovery regime, Torres said, "Cap, I was at the Chief Surgeon's office yesterday."

Leland knew that. Earlier in the day he'd had a long talk with the Chief Surgeon about Torres's prognosis. The Chief Surgeon was a civilian doctor employed by the police department to oversee the medical needs of members of the department. Among his many duties was reviewing the medical records of police officers like Hector Torres to determine the officer's fitness for duty.

"I don't think he believes I can make it back to full duty," Torres said. "But I don't buy that. I'm making great progress. Everyone says so."

Leland saw the passionate light in Torres's eyes and wondered why anyone who'd been through what he'd been through would want to come back for more. He thought he knew what dedication was. He'd always thought of himself as completely dedicated to the police department, but he had to admit that he didn't have the kind of fire he saw in Hector Torres's eyes. And the fact that their goals were so different made it even harder to understand. Leland's goal was to rise as high in the department as he could; Hector Torres just wanted to be a good cop. In the presence of such a man, Leland felt like a fraud.

"Cap, maybe you could put in a good word for me with the Surgeon? I know I never really worked for you, but you can ask any of the bosses, they'll tell you I was a good cop. I can be a good cop again."

"Hector, I know all about you. I'm just sorry that we didn't have more of a chance to work together when I first got here." He glanced at Nancy hoping to get a cue as to what he should say, but she was staring at the floor. "You understand that the Chief Surgeon and the medical board will make the final decision, but I'll certainly do what I can."

"Cap, I hear you've been putting a real full-court press on the Joy. Thanks."

"Hector, if you were here you'd have closed it down yourself by now, just like you did that drug-dealing bodega on Summit. I'm only doing what you would have done. It's just talking me longer."

~~

Leland stood at the window and watched Nancy Torres help her husband into the car. Hector was only thirty-four and before this incident he was in prime physical condition. Now, watching him struggle to get into the car, he could have been an eighty-year-old stroke victim.

The voice of the Chief Surgeon echoed in his mind: *"Captain, Officer Torres will never return to full duty. He has significant neural damage, which will preclude him from ever regaining full use of the right side of his body. I haven't told him this because I don't want to hamper his recovery efforts, which I must say have been truly remarkable."*

As Leland watched Nancy come around and get behind the wheel, he thought once again about the cop's attack on the Joy Lounge. He'd condemned their actions without hesitation then. To his mind there was no room for moral or legal equivocating. As one who has sworn to uphold the law, he couldn't condone what they'd done. But now... Now, he wasn't quiet as certain. There was, however, one thing of which he was certain: Right or wrong, it was the only justice Hector Torres would ever see. Two months ago he would never have thought this way. But two months ago he wasn't a precinct commander. The orderly, comfortable black-and-white world of One Police Plaza that he'd known for so long was gone, replaced by a more complex landscape of infinite and maddening shades of gray.

He looked out at the tenements across the street from the station house. A mother was hanging out a window screaming at her child, who was throwing tin cans at a cat. He was in a different world. A much more difficult world.

~~

"Ain't that some *shit*?" the owner of Fat Adam's Rib Joint said to George Oliver and Jim Elliott.

The two cops stared down at the remains of the meal—a huge mound of gnawed ribs, two half-finished baked potatoes, four empty Heinekens, and empty coffee cups covered by a pile of greasy napkins.

"Hungry bastards, weren't they?" Oliver said. "How much you figure they ate, Adam?"

The fat man surveyed the pile with professional interest. "'Bout ten pounds."

"Maybe we oughta check the local hospital emergency rooms," Elliott said with just the hint of a smile. "See if anyone got their stomachs pumped."

"How'd they get in?" Oliver asked.

"Through the back door."

"They get any money?"

"Shit. I don't leave no money hanging around here." Adam scratched his head. "Who'd *do* somethin' like this?"

Elliott shrugged. "One of the brothers?"

"No way," Adam said emphatically. "Look a that." He pointed an old ketchup bottle filled with a lethal-looking bright red sauce. "They didn't use none of my Fat Adam's Special Soul Sauce." His chuckle made his belly heave up and down. "Too damn hot for white folks."

"I got news for you," Elliott said. "That shit's too hot for me, too."

"That's cause you're practically white," Oliver muttered.

"Will you stop that shit," Elliot snapped. "Just because I'm studying for the sergeant's exam, don't make me no damn Oreo."

"The hell it don't. You—"

"*Hey!*" Fat Adam bawled. "What you gonna do about these people eatin' my damn food?"

"*I'll* take the report," Elliott said, "seeing how I'm the only one on this team who can write a coherent sentence."

"Suit yourself, white boy," Oliver mumbled and headed for the kitchen to see if there were any cooked ribs on the stove.

~~

The twenty-five men and women of the four-to-twelve tour slowly jingled and shuffled into what could be loosely described as a semi-military formation.

As Sergeant Labonte read the roll call, a desperate Billy Lafferty hid behind two tall cops. Charlie Reece had taken the night off and that left him without a radio car partner. Billy glanced up and down the ranks. They'd just gotten three new rookies in to the precinct, whom he'd dubbed Dumb, Dumber, and Dumbest. It was better than even money that Lard-ass Labonte would saddle him with one of these academy wonders who began every sentence with the words: "According to the *Patrol Guide*..." And if that wasn't bad enough, they were so gung-ho, they wanted to go on every damn job within a hundred-mile radius. With no Charlie to keep him out of trouble, he had to find a way to stay away from Lard-ass. The fat sergeant still hadn't forgiven him for bombarding his radio car with piss balloons.

Salvation came to Billy when he heard Labonte say, "Martinelli is sitting on a DOA. He'll need a relief."

"I'll take it," Lafferty said quickly.

"I'll take it, Sarge," Elliot said, glaring at Lafferty. Sitting on a DOA would give him some quiet study time.

Oliver whispered to his partner. "Hey, asshole. Let Lafferty take it. Otherwise I might get stuck with him."

"Lafferty's a hero," Mazzeo said, goosing the little cop with his nightstick. "He shouldn't have to sit on a DOA."

Lafferty batted the nightstick away. "Will you shut the hell up?" he hissed.

"Why shouldn't he sit on a DOA?" someone else piped up. "Superfly will be right at home with all those flies buzzing around the body."

Lafferty shot everyone the finger with both hands. He had been dubbed "Superfly" by the precinct wags after his ledge-walking rescue of Calvin Henderson.

Labonte glared at the little cop suspiciously. Billy Lafferty never volunteered for anything—especially DOAs. "Why are you volunteering?"

"I have no partner tonight. Why break up another radio car team?" He tried to sound sincere, but only succeeded in further raising Labonte's suspicions.

The fat sergeant grunted. "All right. But, don't try anything funny, Lafferty. I'll be up to see you."

"I won't be goin' nowhere, Sarge."

"Oliver, Elliot, give Lafferty a ride to the DOA."

~~

In the car, Elliot said to Lafferty, "Thanks a lot, hump. I could have used the study time."

Lafferty shuddered. "How can you study with a stiff staring at you?" Dead bodies gave Lafferty the creeps. Under normal circumstances he would never have volunteered to babysit a dead body, but he was desperate to stay out of Labonte's way.

"It's a hell of a lot more peaceful than studying at home and having three kids crawling up my leg."

"You're not supposed to be studying on company time," Lafferty said, winking at Oliver. "Doesn't the *Patrol Guide* say that?"

"How would you know? You've never opened the damn book."

As they turned into Edwards Street in the heart of Death Valley, they saw Martinelli standing on the stoop of the building smoking a cigarette. "Uh, oh," Elliot said, chuckling. "It's got to be a ripe one. Martinelli don't even smoke."

Lafferty was beginning to have second thoughts when he saw the ashen-faced Martinelli standing on the stoop. Department regulations required a police officer to remain in the apartment with the deceased, but when the stench was too much, a command discipline was preferable to throwing up.

"I'm your relief, Tony," Lafferty said, getting out of the car. "What apartment?"

Martinelli tossed the cigarette into the street and dove into the back seat of the radio car. "Follow your nose. You can't miss it."

"Bad?"

"A regular meltdown. I think he's been dead since the Mets won their last World Series."

"You spill anything?" At the scene of a ripe DOA, cops often counteracted the putrid odor by sprinkling ammonia or a cheap aftershave lotion about the room.

"A pint of ammonia."

"Do any good?"

"Like pissing in the ocean."

Elliot whooped with glee. "That's what you get for volunteering, Billy."

"Any word about the ME?" Lafferty asked.

"I called the Medical Examiner's office a half-hour ago. They told me what they always tell me. 'We're coming.'"

After the radio car left, Lafferty stayed on the stoop, undecided if he should go up or remain outside. Then he thought about Lard-ass, took a deep breath, and stepped into the building.

Inside the hallway, the stench of death was overpowering. As he started up the stairs, the horrible smell grew worse. On the second floor a door creaked open slowly. An old Puerto Rican woman peered out at him. Her gold teeth glistened in the gloom and he couldn't tell if she was smiling or scowling. "Dead," she muttered. "*Malo.* Junkie... dope... dope..." She gestured as though she were giving herself a needle in the arm.

"Yeah, yeah." Lafferty continued up the stairs. By the time he reached apartment 3F, the stench had enveloped him in a gaseous cloud. He pushed open the door and the rank odor made his eyes water. If there had been any doubt in his mind before, there was none now. *He'd made a big mistake.* Labonte at his worst was better than this.

He put a handkerchief over his nose and mouth and went inside. The body—a swollen brown mass of ooze and putrefaction—was lying on a bed in a tiny bedroom. He didn't see the flies, but he heard their insistent buzzing as they excitedly explored the putrid remains for a suitable place to lay their eggs.

Lafferty had seen enough. He staggered out of the bedroom. Praying the ME, for once, would arrive early, he retreated to the relatively fresh air in the hallway. But even there, after five minutes, he began to feel nauseous. "Screw it," he muttered. "Labonte can stick one up my ass if he wants to. I ain't staying here."

Just as he started down the stairs, he heard footsteps below. *Could that be Labonte? Is that Lard-ass gonna climb three flights of stairs into this stink just to check up on me? He's gotta have a bigger hard-on for me than I thought.*

He peered over the railing. A man was coming up the stairs, but it wasn't Labonte. It was a squat, middle-aged Hispanic and he had that spooky thousand-yard stare. Lafferty stepped back into the shadows and watched the man's progress as he climbed the last flight. He hoped he'd keep going, but the man paused, squinted at the apartment numbers, and shuffled toward Lafferty.

Lafferty stepped out of the shadows. "What can I do for you, pal?"

The man looked right through him and mumbled something in Spanish.

"I don't understand Spanish. Could you—"

The next thing Lafferty knew, he was on his knees trying to focus on the floor's dirty tiles just inches from his nose. He never saw the punch that caught him on the side of the head. As he struggled to his feet, the man disappeared into the apartment. His ears rang as he keyed the mic on his portable radio. *"Ten-thirteen,"*—his shouts echoed in the empty hallway—*"Four-five-two... Edwards... third floor. Officer needs assistance."*

Still groggy, he lurched through the door and into the apartment. He hardly noticed the stench now because it had been displaced by a more pungent and urgent smell—fear. He staggered into the bedroom and gasped, incredulous at the sight before him. "What the fuck...?" *The man was trying to pick up the body.*

The consistency of the body was such that some of it fell apart in his hands while other parts remained stuck to the filthy sheets. A cloud of flies buzzed angrily at the intrusion. Thousands of maggots wriggled for cover.

Without thinking, Lafferty threw himself on the man and slipped a chokehold around his neck.

With the superhuman strength of a psycho, the man dipped forward and swung Lafferty completely over his head. As Lafferty flew through the air, a picture of World Federation wrestlers flashed into his mind and he realized—to his horror—that he was going to land on the body.

The rotting body literally exploded from the impact. The gasses that had built up in the decaying flesh released with a sickening hiss. With slimy body parts clinging to his hands and uniform, Lafferty bounced off the bed and onto the floor.

The man ignored Lafferty as though he were merely one more of the hundreds of flies angrily buzzing about the room, and went back to the task of trying to pick up what was left of the body. Lafferty, fighting back the urge to vomit, fumbled for his gun with sticky, shaking hands. Finally, he got it out. *"Step back you motherfucker,"* he shrieked, *"or I'll blow your goddamn head off."*

The man looked at the gun pointed at his chest, but there was no fear in the eyes. Suddenly, with an animal-like howl, he threw himself at Lafferty. But this time the cop was ready. He sidestepped the rushing man and with all his strength smashed the gun into the man's face, stunning him. Then he drove the gun butt down on the man's head again and again until, slowly, the man slid to the floor.

Lafferty fumbled for his handcuffs and cuffed the man behind his back. On the floor, the man mumbled over and over, *"Mi hijo... mi hijo... mi hijo..."*

Suddenly, Lafferty, gasping for breath, understood what the man was muttering. "Your *son*? Is this... your son?"

The man looked up at Lafferty sorrowfully and repeated, *"Mi hijo..."*

All at once Lafferty's survival instincts, having done their job of protecting him, abandoned him and his other senses came flooding back. He was abruptly aware of the overpowering stench of death. His uniform was a gory mess and bits of slimy flesh hung from his sleeve. Numbly, he looked down at his hand and saw two wiggling maggots futilely trying to burrow into live human flesh. He couldn't hold back any longer. He jerked forward on his hands and knees and vomited on the remains of the body, the maggots, and himself.

When Mazzeo, Peggy, Elliot and Oliver burst through the door, they found him on his hands and knees staring dully at a puddle of vomit.

Lafferty looked up at the cops with watery eyes. "Never volunteer for anything," he rasped.

~~

Mazzeo was waiting for Peggy when she came out of the station house.

"How about I come back to your apartment," he said.

"No, not tonight, Eddie. I'm really bushed."

"Oh, okay. Sure." He stood there for an uncomfortable moment. Then he said, "Hey, how about that expression on Lafferty's face when we crashed into the apartment tonight?"

"Yeah. Old Billy's something else."

"Yeah, he is." Mazzeo stuck his hands in his leather jacket and looked up and down the street. "Well, okay. I guess I'll see you tomorrow."

"Yeah, Eddie. I'll see you tomorrow."

They looked at each other in the darkness. They both sensed something was slipping away, but they didn't know what it was, and they didn't know why.

~~

Peggy went home feeling depressed, angry, and guilty. Over a half-bottle of stale white wine and a plate of leftover pasta, she tried to concentrate on CNN's coverage of an avalanche somewhere in Colorado, but her life—pitiful as it was—kept intruding.

From the beginning of the affair—she hated that word, but what else could she call it?—she'd told herself it was just an infatuation or maybe it was just an occupational hazard of male-female radio car partners. Hell, it happened to people stranded on a desert island, for chrissake. Why not radio car partners? It would soon end, she'd told herself in the beginning, but to her dismay, it had gone on for over a year and she didn't know why. The truth was the affair—relationship?—she hated that word, too, wasn't all that great and she suspected Eddie felt the same way.

In the beginning it had been exciting; meeting in darkened cars, sneaking back to her apartment to steal forbidden moments. But it soon became routine; almost as though they were a married couple. She found herself being unreasonably—and uncharacteristically—jealous of Carol and the baby. She was mortified and guilt-ridden every time she met Carol and had to make small talk. She genuinely liked Carol and, in other circumstances, they could have become good friends.

Peggy thought of her mother, who'd died just before Peggy's thirteenth birthday. Whenever Peggy was about to do something that she knew was wrong, she would always ask herself what would her mom think? Tears welled up in her eyes. Mom wouldn't think much of a daughter who was having an affair-relationship with a married man. Mom wouldn't think much of a daughter who, for her own selfish reasons, was risking tearing apart a family.

Her mom and dad had been married for more than twenty-five years until uterine cancer took her away. Peggy had always suspected that her dad was the only man her mother had ever "known." Through all of her teen years, Peggy had thought her mother hopelessly naïve. But now she envied her. She had had something that Peggy could never have: A first love that lasted a lifetime.

Her cell phone rang, yanking Peggy out of her dismal reverie. It was a private number. She didn't want to answer it. It might be Eddie and she didn't want to talk to him right now. But her curiosity got the better of her. "Yeah?"

"Officer Garrigan?" a tentative voice asked. "This is Helen Jurek." Peggy hit the mute button on the TV just as an aging hippy lady with flowers in her hair was beginning to demonstrate twenty ways to use tofu as a dessert topping.

The name didn't ring a bell. "I'm sorry. Do I know you?"

"From 2315 Morris Avenue? I hate to be calling so late."

Of course. *Helen Jurek!* Cynthia Norville's neighbor! "Robert's mother."

Peggy watched the hippie lady dump a glob of tofu on top of something that looked like turnips. After the trouble she'd gotten into over this incident, she wasn't thrilled to be hearing from anyone connected to Mrs. Norville; especially Mrs. Jurek, whom Peggy suspected had handed her up. "How are you?" she asked coldly.

"Fine. Well, no... that's not exactly true. I'm not fine. I've been thinking about what you said and well, there's something you should know."

Peggy heard something in Mrs. Jurek's voice and clicked off the TV. "What is it that I should know, Mrs. Jurek?"

~~

From the window of his ground floor office, Leland watched the changing of the guard, NYPD style. The late-tour cops, looking tired and drawn, climbed out of their radio cars with arms full of nightsticks, clipboards, and crumpled paper bags containing the remnants of crushed Styrofoam cups and food wrappings—things that kept cops alert and awake through the long night. The day-tour platoon, looking considerably more refreshed, joked or complained to the cops they were relieving about the condition of the car they were going to spend the next eight hours in.

To a bystander, it looked chaotic and haphazard, but between the chuckles and the gripes and the barbs, the two platoons exchanged much needed information—where the latest burglaries had occurred; the location of a stuck-in-the-open position fire hydrant; or the address of an apartment that had been gutted by fire and needed special attention. In the time that it took the tours to trade places, they had exchanged a wealth of information about what was happening in their respective sectors.

There was a knock at the door. "Come in," Leland said without turning around.

Peggy stuck her head in the door. "Captain, can I see you for a minute?"

"Sure."

"I got a call from one of Cynthia Norville's neighbors."

"Come in and close the door."

Leland took notes as he listened to Peggy recount her conversation with Helen Jurek. When she finished, he said, "So the bottom line is Jurek suspects child abuse, but she has no hard evidence."

"Right. She's heard Molly screaming in the apartment several times. She's seen bruises on her, but she's never personally seen Norville hit the child. Cynthia's too clever for that," Peggy added bitterly.

Leland gave her a sharp look. "Don't get personally involved in this, Garrigan."

"I'm sorry, Captain. You're right. So what do we do about this information?"

"Give it to the Special Victims Squad. They'll reopen the case."

Peggy ran her fingers through her hair. "Captain, what if they just go through the motions again?"

Leland was wondering the same thing and then he remembered Lieutenant Fischer, the CO of the Bronx Special Victims Squad. He didn't know him well, but he'd met him at a couple of borough conferences. "They won't just go through the motions," he said emphatically. "I'll see that it gets the proper attention."

After Peggy left, Leland dialed the number and a voice on the other end said, "Lieutenant Fischer, Special Victims."

"Jack, this is Captain Leland."

"Yeah, Boss. What can I do for you?"

"One of my cops submitted a suspected child abuse report on a Molly Norville. You closed the case as unfounded. Last night the officer got a call from a neighbor who now admits she's heard crying from the apartment and seen bruises on the child."

"No problem, Cap. We'll reopen the case."

"Good. I'd appreciate it if you would get on it right away."

"I'm afraid I can't do that. Right now I have every available investigator working on the Satanic Oven Murder."

"Damn. I forgot about that."

A week earlier, a woman living in the Cleveland projects in the north Bronx roasted her two-month-old in the oven. When she was asked why she'd done it, she said Satan had told her to do it. The press, swarming over the Cleveland projects, found a handful of less-than-reliable witnesses who suggested that the woman, and possibly others, were members of a Satanic-voodoo cult. The story exploded onto the front pages of the *Daily News* and the *New York Post* and had been there ever since.

Predictably, Police Commissioner Randall—no doubt at the urging of Charlie Drum—called a press conference and vowed a full and swift investigation into these horrible allegations. What he really wanted was a swift end to these stories splashed all over the front pages, and if it took every detective in the city to make it happen, so be it. The only problem with that kind of knee-jerk, cover-your-ass reaction was that other cases—like Molly Norville's—got put on the back burner.

"I understand, Jack. But get to this case as soon as you can."

"I hear you, Boss. Will do."

Leland hung up feeling uneasy with the thought of Molly Norville in that apartment with her mother.

Chapter Twenty-One

Angela Cosi looked up at the wall clock. It was almost three and she didn't have much time. Quickly, the young bank teller began to gather up her paperwork. She had just thirty minutes to count her money, prove out her drawer, and pick up her daughter at day care.

A bearded man approached. She was going to direct him to another window, but he looked vaguely familiar. She was a brand-new employee and didn't want to get in trouble for offending a regular customer, so she put the "next teller" sign aside and said, "Yes, sir. May I help you?"

Wordlessly, he slipped a note across the counter. When she read: *Give me all your money,* her mind went momentarily blank. She looked up, hoping it was a bad joke, but the dark, penetrating eyes quickly dispelled that notion. Suddenly, she remembered why he looked familiar. She'd seen a police composite sketch of him on the front page of the *Bronx Tribune*. *Oh, God! He's the Poet Bandit.*

Frantically, she tried to recall the proper procedures she'd learned in her training. He put his hand in his pocket, the black eyes pinning her. *The note said he had a gun.* She was taking too long. *That's it! Never stall. What else?* She recalled the next two steps simultaneously: hit the silent alarm and give him the decoy money packet—the one with exploding red dye.

She stared into those black, lifeless eyes and fumbled for the unfamiliar alarm button with her foot. *Where the hell is it?* Suddenly her mouth dropped open. There was a gun in his hand and it was pointed at her. "No... please..." Forgetting the alarm, she opened the drawer and gave him the money packet. He waved the gun impatiently. He wanted everything. *The hell with bank procedures.* She emptied the drawer and slid all the money over the counter toward him. Without hurrying, he stuffed the bills inside his windbreaker and turned to leave.

At that moment, Angela's toe found the silent alarm button and she stepped on it. The bearded man was turning way, but he'd seen what she'd done. There was no surprise or anger in the dark eyes, just a blood-chilling intensity. Without warning he raised the gun and fired a shot into her chest.

Everything went dark and the last thing Angela Cosi remembered was the sound of screaming. Her screaming.

~~

Eddie Mazzeo and Peggy Garrigan were arguing about where to have their delayed lunch when the dispatcher interrupted Mazzeo's pitch for Chinese food.

"Sector John, report of silent alarm at the Fountain National Bank 745 Blackstone."

"Sonofabitch," Mazzeo muttered, turning the car in the direction of Blackstone. "This is the third time today my lunch has been delayed."

Peggy keyed the mic. "Sector John on the way." To Mazzeo she said, "So what's the big deal? There'll still be plenty of greasy egg rolls twenty minutes from now."

Mazzeo maneuvered the car through the traffic, but with no great urgency. Bank alarms were common and mostly false. Between clumsy tellers and glitches in the alarm systems, the precinct responded to at least three false alarms a day.

Then the dispatcher came back on the air: *"Sector John, we have a confirmation of that past robbery by landline. Report of shots fired. Perpetrator described as male, Caucasian, 25 to 35, full beard, wearing a tan windbreaker."*

Reece came on the air. "Sector Baker will back up on that past robbery, central."

Mazzeo accelerated around a slow moving truck. "Ten-to-one it's a phony beard. It's probably in a garbage can already."

After a robbery, the perp often discarded easily identifiable clothing like hats and jackets. As Mazzeo and Peggy approached the location, they were not looking for someone fitting the description. They were looking for a man out of sync with the rest of the pedestrians on the crowded sidewalk.

Two blocks from the location, Mazzeo spotted him. To his amazement, not only was the perp still wearing a beard, the front of his tan windbreaker was stained with red dye from the exploding money packet.

The bearded man spotted the radio car and sprinted down a side street.

Peggy keyed the mic. "Sector John in pursuit of the perp. He just ran west onto Franklin off Blackstone."

Mazzeo snapped a U-turn. The car fishtailed for a moment, but he quickly regained control and darted through oncoming traffic. The intersection was a log-jam of stopped cars and trucks. He mounted the sidewalk and catapulted off the curb. The undercarriage of the car bottomed-out and sparks flew from the muffler. He regained control of the auto just in time to see the bearded man disappear into a tenement halfway down the block.

Peggy shouted over the mic. "Perp ran into 354 Franklin." Before she'd finished her transmission, Mazzeo had slammed on the brakes and was out of the car sprinting for the building.

"Wait for me," she said, jumping out of the still rocking car.

"You cover the back," he shouted over his shoulder. "I'll take the stairs."

By the time she reached the entrance to the building, Mazzeo had already gone in. Cautiously, she slipped through the front door. Inside, she held her breath listening for the telltale sounds of breathing or footsteps. But all she heard was Eddie on the stairs. He was trying to be quiet, but there was no way to stop the jangling of all the equipment attached to his gun belt.

Drawing her gun and pressing her body against the wall, she cautiously made her way down the hall toward the entrance to the cellar at the rear of the darkened hallway.

The cellar door was shut. A good sign: A man in a hurry wouldn't take the time to shut it behind him. Cautiously, she opened it and groped along the wall for a light switch. She found it and flipped it on. Nothing happened. Keeping her body out of the line of fire, she peered down into an unnerving blackness below that smelled of cat urine and coal dust. She fumbled for her flashlight, flipped it on and, holding it away from her body, slowly started down the dark stairs.

~~

Mazzeo stopped halfway up the second flight of stairs and strained to hear above his labored breathing. He heard nothing. Then the nagging questions began: *Does the perp live here? Has he already ducked into his apartment? Did he go out the back way?* If he did, that meant Peggy was going after him alone. He was about to bolt down the stairs, when he heard a soft, scraping noise somewhere above him, the kind of noise made by a shoe crunching broken tile. He looked down. The steps were covered with cracked tiles. The hair on the back of his neck rose. *He was up there!*

Trying to be as quiet as possible, he took the rest of the flight two steps at a time, hoping to close the distance between himself and the perp. He stopped at the third landing, and began to think this might not be a good idea. He was breathing heavily from the exertion. If he was going to take this guy, he couldn't afford to be out of breath. Mazzeo heard faint, but labored breathing above him and took some small satisfaction in knowing the perp was just as out of breath as he was.

He stopped at the fourth landing and listened. The perp was on five, only one floor away from the roof landing. If he made it to the roof, he was home-free. Mazzeo took a deep breath and dashed up the next flight. As he did so, he heard slipping and stumbling as the man made his rush toward the roof. Then, he heard a pounding on a door. *The roof door was locked! I've got the sonofabitch!*

Just then, three gunshots loudly reverberated in the tiled hallway and he dove for the grimy floor tiles. He heard the sound of kicking and a door swinging open. The perp was on the roof.

Scrambling to his feet, he ran up the last flight, down the hall, and looked up. The roof door was ajar. The pungent odor of gunpowder stung Mazzeo's nostrils. As he cautiously climbed the last flight, the door swung shut with a bang. Mazzeo dove to the floor and flattened his body on the stairs before he realized it was the wind.

On the roof landing, he rubbed his sweaty palms on his trouser legs. He knew he should wait for backup, but gripped by the conflicting emotions of fear and anger, he was irrevocably caught up in the mindless excitement of the chase. His mind was fogged by adrenaline and it never occurred to him that he was about to do something that could get him killed. Mazzeo's world had narrowed to just two people. Himself and the perp. And there was no way he was going to let the perp get away.

He pushed the door open and tossed his cap outside. Nothing. He took a breath, kicked the door open and dove out. He rolled twice on the dirty tar, righted himself, and came up pointing his gun at—nothing.

The roof was connected to four more roofs, separated only by three-foot retaining walls. Mazzeo's eyes swept the rooftops covered with clotheslines, assorted debris, and a few pigeon coops. No sign of the perp. "Where the hell is he?" he muttered softly. "He couldn't have just—"

Out of the corner of his eye, he caught a movement. The man came out from behind a pigeon coop and darted across to the next roof. Mazzeo, crouching low to avoid the clotheslines, followed. He'd crossed two roofs and was narrowing the gap. The man wasn't aware that Mazzeo was following him. Then Mazzeo kicked an empty beer can. The man turned and fired blindly at the sound. Mazzeo dove behind the nearest cover—a pigeon coop. At the sound of the shots, the frenzied birds threw themselves against the wire-meshed walls creating a blizzard of feathers.

Mazzeo squinted through a swirl of feathers and dust. The man was examining his weapon. Either he was out of ammunition or the gun had jammed. Mazzeo jumped away from the pigeon coop, dropped into a combat stance, and yelled, "*Police*! Drop it."

As calmly as though he were fighting a duel, the bearded man raised the gun with one hand and pointed it at Mazzeo. The cop, sighting down the barrel of his gun, leveled the sights on the man's midsection. His finger tighten on the trigger. Then a sudden flood of questions stopped him from completing the pull: *Was the perp's gun jammed or empty? Was he about to shoot an unarmed man? Was this guy asking for suicide by cop?*

This wasn't the way it was supposed to be. How many times over a beer at Corr's had he and other cops talked about hypothetical shootouts? And every time, he'd said he'd have no trouble pulling the trigger. But now, confronted with the reality, he couldn't do it.

Suddenly, there was a blinding muzzle flash and a loud crack in Mazzeo's right ear. Instinctively, he squeezed off three quick rounds. The muzzle flash and smoke obscured his vision momentarily. He blinked away the smoke and looked toward the spot where the perp had been standing. He was gone.

Mazzeo threw himself to the ground and crawled toward the shelter of the retaining wall. Warily, he peeked over the top of the wall. He was sure he'd hit him. He must have hit him. So where could he have gone? He'd been standing on the edge of the backyard side of the roof. Perhaps he'd jumped down onto a fire escape? Cautiously, Mazzeo crawled to the edge and gingerly peeked over the side. Five stories below, spread-eagled on his back, the man stared up at Mazzeo with lifeless eyes.

Standing alongside the body, Peggy, Reece, and Lafferty looked up at him. Lafferty was waving a clenched fist and shouting something, but Mazzeo couldn't make out what he was saying. Finally, the buzzing stopped in his head and Lafferty's high-pitched nasal voice came through. *"Way to go, Eddie!"* he shouted. *"Way to go!"*

A worried Sgt. Engle met Mazzeo at the second floor. "Are you okay, Eddie?"

Yeah, Sarge. I'm fine."

Engle led him down the stairs and toward the front door. "I'll drive you back to the house and then—"

"Wait, Sarge. I wanna see this guy."

"Why do you want to do that, Eddie? He's DOA. There's nothing to see."

Mazzeo pulled away. "I want to see him," he said more insistently. He didn't know why, but suddenly it was very important that he see the man who had tried to kill him.

Over Engle's objections, they made their way through the musty cellar and out into the backyard. Oliver and Elliott had arrived and were talking in hushed tones to Charlie Reece. A curious Lafferty crouched over the body to examine for himself the physical effects of a fifty-foot fall. A pale Peggy Garrigan stood apart from the others. She blinked back tears when she saw Eddie and Engle approaching, but she said nothing and made no attempt to come toward him.

Without saying a word to anyone or even acknowledging their presence, Mazzeo walked up to the body and stared down at the face. The man had landed on his back, crushing the back of his skull, but the face was untouched, almost in repose. Mazzeo looked into those lifeless, staring eyes and wondered why this man had wanted to kill him.

Lafferty slapped Mazzeo on the back. "Nice shooting, Eddie. You capped him twice in the chest."

Engle saw Mazzeo's hands were beginning to tremble. He put his arm around the cop's shoulder. "Come on, son. Let's go."

Lafferty looked askance at Mazzeo's filthy, tar-stained uniform. "Buddy, you're a real mess. You've got pigeon shit all over you and—"

Engle spun around. *"Lafferty, for the love of God will you shut the fuck up!"* he bellowed.

To Eddie Mazzeo, Lafferty's voice had been coming from some place very far away. It was so low he couldn't even understand what he was saying. It wasn't even a voice, more like a muffled buzz. But he heard Engle's voice loud and clear, and, inexplicably, he started to laugh. "Sarge," he said softly, "you said fuck. I never heard you swear before."

He was still laughing when Engle and Reece helped him into the back of the radio car. He was laughing so hard he couldn't stop crying.

~~

Since she'd received that heart-stopping telephone call from Captain Leland earlier in the day, Carol Mazzeo's emotions had swung from joy to fear to anger. She was so distraught that at this moment she didn't know what she felt.

At her mother's insistence, she'd taken little Edward over to her house where they agreed he'd spend the night. After three cups of very strong coffee and enduring an endless litany of her mother's platitudes about life and death, she'd returned home to wait for her husband.

And now, alone for the first time since she'd heard the news, she had a chance to reflect on of the implications of that telephone call. And she began to cry.

She was still crying when she heard his car pull into the driveway. She carefully wiped her eyes, ran her hand through her hair in front of the hall mirror, and opened the door.

Eddie was coming up the walk. He was trying to smile, but it wouldn't come. Other than his pallid color, he looked the same as the man she'd kissed and sent off to work this morning as she'd done every morning since their marriage. He didn't look any different on the outside, but she couldn't see inside of him. Dimly, she wondered if she'd ever be able to send him off again without a sense of foreboding, and it suddenly occurred to her that her life—their lives   had been irrevocably altered by today's events.

While she'd been waiting for him to get home, she'd been thinking of what she would say. Should she mention the shooting? Should she ignore it? Should she let him bring it up first? She'd rehearsed opening lines for several alternatives, but now that he was standing in front of her, safe and alive, she'd forgotten what she'd planned to say. Choking back tears, she threw herself at him. "I love you," she mumbled over and over again into his chest, "I love you."

Eddie stroked her hair. "I love you, too," he said softly.

Eddie went upstairs to change. When he came down, Carol was in the kitchen preparing dinner. "What're you making?" he asked.

"Your favorite. Veal Francese."

He made a face. "Don't bother. I'm not hungry."

She hid her disappointment. Making his favorite dinner was the only useful thing she could think of. "You have to eat something. What would you like?"

"I don't know. Something simple."

He rummaged through the cabinet under the kitchen sink and took a bottle of Dewer's. She was surprised. He seldom drank scotch, especially this early in the day. He saw her looking at him. "I'm going to have a drink," he said. "You want one?"

"No." Then she realized that maybe she should have a drink with him. "I mean... okay. Very light."

He used a shot glass for her drink. For his own, he poured directly from the bottle, almost filling the large tumbler.

Over a hastily thrown together dinner of leftover pasta, she furtively watched him. He picked at his food, but he ate almost nothing. Lately, he hadn't been very talkative at dinner, but tonight, he was even quieter. He mumbled short responses to her general questions, but offered nothing to the conversation. He didn't mention the shooting. Neither did she.

When they'd finished eating, he went into the den to watch TV while she cleaned up. Usually, she went upstairs to watch her own programs, but tonight she came into the den to be with him. He was a Ranger fan, but it was evident from his distracted expression that he wasn't enjoying his team's two-goal lead. She wordlessly took his hand in hers and, together, they watched the game.

Eddie shook her and she awoke with a guilty start. It was after midnight, and the game was over.

"Who won?"

"The Rangers."

Wordlessly, they went upstairs. Eddie got into bed, gave her a half-hearted kiss, and mumbled something about being beat.

Carol pulled the covers protectively around her neck and stared at the ceiling, wondering what, if anything, she should say to him. Her mother had counseled her to say nothing. He'll talk about it when he's ready, she'd assured her daughter. At the time, Carol had thought that was good advice, but now she wasn't so sure. Eddie was lying next to her, just inches away, but it might as well have been a million miles.

"Eddie," she said abruptly, "do you want to talk about it?"

His back was to her and he didn't turn around. "There's nothing to talk about. A guy tried to kill me today. I killed him instead. Case closed."

She was astonished by the lack of emotion in his voice. "I know, but... how do you feel?"

"I'm okay," he snapped. "I won, didn't I?"

She refused to be put off by his dismissive tone. Now that she'd decided she wanted him to talk about it, she was determined to go on. "Yes, but it must have been... scary and—"

"Carol. That's what I'm trained to do. It's what I get paid for."

She sat up and pulled her knees close to her body. Tears of anger and frustration welled up in her. He was still lying on his side with his back to her. "It's *not* what you get paid for," she shouted. "And damn it, Eddie, will you look at me when I'm talking to you?"

He rolled over on his back and stared at the ceiling. "Carol, what do you want?"

"Eddie, I'm your wife. I want to help. Don't shut me out."

"I'm not shutting you out. This is something that happened to me. It's something I have to deal with."

"What about me? It happened to me, too. I could have lost you today."

He finally turned to look at her. In the darkened bedroom, lit only by an outside streetlight, she could clearly see his eyes. And in his eyes she saw a sudden flicker of understanding. She'd put into words something he hadn't dared admit to himself. *He could have died.*

He reached out and pulled her close and she covered his face with kisses as he unbuttoned her nightshirt.

After they made love, she lay cuddled in his arms, listening to the low, rhythmic breathing of her sleeping husband. She felt, paradoxically, both contented and distressed. She was delighted that they'd made love—something they hadn't done in quite a while. She attributed their lack of lovemaking to little Edward's arrival. She'd read in a magazine that it wasn't uncommon for men to shun their wives after the birth of a baby. The article had concluded by saying it was usually a temporary condition. Now, lying with her husband, she fervently hoped their lives were about to take a turn for the better.

Nevertheless, a disturbing thought intruded on her bliss. He'd been more physical, more demanding than he'd ever been in their lovemaking. It was as if, by the sheer use of muscle and strength, he could validate his existence. While they were making love, she'd begun to think that this shooting incident was something they could put behind them. But now, she wasn't so sure.

~~

Leland read the last poem of the Poet Bandit:

A flash of light; the sound of doom.
No more noise; the world's a tomb.

"You don't have to be a psychiatrist to figure this one out," Leland said.

Seidel examined the long ash at the end of his cigar, but made no attempt to knock it off. "Actually, Guidron was pretty close with his profile."

Leland eyed the ash precariously perched on the end of the cigar and slid an ashtray, which he now kept especially for Seidel, toward the sergeant. "Who was he?"

"Name is Daniel Toucan, age thirty-three. No living relatives. He'd been in and out of mental hospitals for the past ten years, treated for depression and a half-dozen other psychotic disorders. He wanted to be a poet, but he didn't have the talent. About a year ago, he told his doctor he'd never speak again until the world recognized his poetic genius." Seidel summed it up in his own non-medical vernacular: "Your basic fucking whacko."

"How's the teller?"

"She's gonna be okay. Fortunately, the bullet didn't hit ay vital organ."

"What was Toucan's cause of death?"

"The fall." Seidel finally tapped the long ash into the ashtray. "Actually, it was the landing." He grinned malevolently. "They say it's not the fall that gets you, it's the sudden stop."

Leland met Seidel's wide grin with a stern frown. "It wasn't Mazzeo's bullets?"

"Negative. He took two to the chest, but the ME says he could have survived those. In a sense, it was the bullets I guess. When he got hit, he stumbled backwards and did a two-and-a-half gainer off the roof."

Seidel stood up. As he headed out the door, he said, "Anyway, what difference does it make how he died? The scumbag is dead and we cleared up a shitload of sixty-ones."

"It'll make a difference to Eddie Mazzeo," Leland said aloud to the empty office after Seidel had gone.

He'd spoken to the still-shaken officer about the shooting at length. It had been three days since the event, but Mazzeo couldn't—or wouldn't—admit that the shooting had badly frightened him. And Leland knew why.

After a shooting, a police officer feels elation. He not only survived the confrontation, but he acquitted himself well. But later, when he has time to think, his thoughts turn to the vagaries of death. The perp died. He lived. The outcome was the result of so many intangibles. Instinct. Training. Luck. This time they had all transpired to work in his favor. But the question that would wake him up from a sound sleep for the rest of his career was: *Would they work in his favor the next time?*

~~

That afternoon, Leland went to the weekly borough conference meeting. Hightower was his usual gruff self. He prowled the front of the room like a linebacker getting ready to blitz a quarterback, poking and prodding each of his precinct commanders to explain the rise and fall of crime in their respective precincts. Leland didn't think he was going to mention the Poet Bandit, but just before he closed the meeting, Hightower said, "Congratulations are in order for Captain Leland and the Five-five. They stopped the Poet Bandit."

As the meeting was breaking up, Hightower said to Leland, "Captain, I'd like to see you in my office."

Hightower sat down behind his desk and with a grimace of pain rubbed his knees. "I gotta admit, Captain, I thought it ill-advised to publicize his MO, but it worked. You were right and I was wrong."

"Officer Mazzeo did a great job," Leland said, scarcely believing that Hightower had just admitted he'd been wrong. "I'm writing him up for a commendation."

"Fine. Forward it to me for my endorsement."

"I will, sir."

It had been just eight weeks since Leland had taken over command of the Five-five, but he was beginning to feel good about himself, his command, and even his relationship with Hightower. It had been a rocky first few weeks, but now he felt that he was finally in sync with the job of running a precinct. Things were looking up and maybe two years in the Five-five wasn't going to be all that bad.

Then Hightower said, "You don't have any more pattern crimes in your precinct, do you Captain?"

Leland froze. *The Food Bandits*. They'd struck twice, but that didn't constitute a pattern crime, did it? For a moment, he considered telling Hightower about them, but decided that was a bad idea. The chief would want to know what he was doing about it and the truth was he'd been so busy with more pressing business that he hadn't done anything. "No, sir," he heard himself say and hoping his words wouldn't come back to haunt him. "There are no other pattern crimes in the Five-five."

Chapter Twenty-Two

The maître d', a supercilious man with a pencil-thin mustache and hair so black it had to have come from a bottle, stood behind a glass-etched door depicting the Leaning Tower of Pisa and motioned Lafferty and Reece to go around back.

On the other side of the doors, Lafferty held his hands behind his ears and affected the dumb look of someone who can't figure out what all the pointing and gesturing is about. It wasn't a stretch for Billy Lafferty.

"He wants us to go around back," Reece said for the third time.

"Fuck 'em," Lafferty said without moving his lips. "I ain't going round back. Do I look like I'm delivering bacalao or what?"

Finally, the maître d' grew tired of trying to communicate with the stupid-looking cop with his ears sticking out and opened the front door. "I was trying to tell you to go around to the back," he said.

Lafferty scratched his head. "Jeez, I couldn't make out what the hell you were saying."

"What's your name?" Reece asked.

"Dino Lemonetti. I am the maître d'. Come this way. I show you what happened."

"Hold it, Dino." Lafferty carefully wiped his feet on the doormat. "I don't wanna get your floor all dirty," he said with an ingratiating grin.

The maître d' started to say something to Lafferty, but decided against it. There was no point in talking to this simpleton. "Follow me," he said to Reece.

Reece walked behind the Maître d' and glanced around the dining room. The Casa Blanca was one of the best Italian restaurants in the Bronx.

The food was supposed to be good, but the gaudy chandeliers, smoky gold-veined mirrors, fake brick walls, and gold-leaf cherubs peeking out from behind artificial potted palms was a textbook example of interior decorating clichés run amuck. Lafferty wondered if the cherubs peed into the plants during dining hours.

The maître d' led them to a table near the kitchen entrance. The table was fully set with a white tablecloth, silverware, and assorted wine glasses. There was even a carnation, now dead, stuck in a vase in the center of the table.

"Someone," the maître d' tapped the table with his bony finger, "broke in here last night, set this table, and cooked a meal—including appetizers, wine, and desert."

There was nothing left on the plates except a few dried string beans and some stale rolls. "Must have been pretty good," Lafferty said. "They ate everything." Ignoring the maître d's glare, he added, "You know, if you showed me to this table I wouldn't sit here."

"And why not?" the maître d' asked stonily.

"Too close to the kitchen. All that traffic in and out it's even money you wind up with a bowl of lasagna on your head. Worst table in the joint. Am I right?"

"Apparently it was the perfect table for the burglars," Reece said. It's near the kitchen and you can't see it from the street." Reece nudged the empty wine bottle with his pen. "Good stuff?"

The maître d' swallowed hard. "The best in our cellar. Three hundred and eighty dollars a bottle."

Reece whistled softly. "What'd they eat?"

"Baked clams, tortellini, veal chops, green beans, espresso, Sambuca, cheese cake, and after dinner mints. *All* the dinner mints. They even took the bowl. The only course they missed was the soup."

"Probably didn't want to stuff themselves," Lafferty offered.

Reece noticed the maître d's jaw muscles beginning to twitch. "How'd they get in?" he asked, hoping the question would distract the man from his ball-breaking partner.

"The cellar. They broke the lock."

"Anything else missing?"

"No. Other than the food and the wine, there is nothing valuable left in the restaurant overnight."

"Okay, let's take a look in the cellar."

As they walked through the kitchen, the two cops surveyed the mess left behind by the Food Bandits. The six-burner Viking stove was covered with an assortment of dirty pots and pans. Apparently they'd had a little trouble with the flour canister. There was flour all over the stove, the floor, and the worktable.

"Pretty sloppy," Lafferty said. "If they cook the way they clean up we may find two perps with food poisoning."

The Maître d's tick migrated from his jaw to his left eye. "There is *nothing* humorous about this," he said in a voice quivering with emotion. "My chef is beside himself. He is threatening to quit."

"Why?"

"His kitchen has been abused. He feels personally violated."

"Maybe we oughta send a copy of the sixty-one to the Sex Crimes Unit," Lafferty whispered to Reece as they descended the cellar stairs.

~~

Seidel stuck his head in the door. "Cap, you wanted to see me?"

"Yes."

Leland had been pacing his office. He grabbed three sixty-ones off the desk and waved them at Seidel. "This is the third one of these restaurant burglaries."

"Oh, you mean the Midnight Mangias?"

Leland winced. "Don't say that. Don't ever say that. Food Bandits is bad enough. I've told you, the press loves a catchy handle like that."

"That's where I heard it."

Leland fell into his chair. "What? Who—?"

"Some info babe from the *Bronx Tribune* called me this morning to talk about them." Seidel studied Leland, wondering if he was about to take a heart attack.

Leland buried his head in his hands. "Oh, no. What'd you tell her?"

"Was I gonna lie? She knew all about the burglaries. She just wanted to make sure she had her facts straight."

"Is she going to print the story?"

"That's what they pay her for. What's the big deal?"

"Just yesterday I told Chief Hightower I don't have any pattern crimes in my precinct."

Seidel nodded. Now he knew why Leland was on the verge of a nervous breakdown.

"The chief doesn't like crime waves, Sarge, even if it's only a couple of lunatics eating their way through the Bronx."

Seidel peeled the cellophane from a fresh cigar. These burglaries were annoying him, too. In his thirty years in the department, he'd learned to tolerate a perp doing a crime here and there; that was the way of an imperfect world. But when a guy keeps doing the *same* crime, in the *same* precinct, he's out of line. It shows a lack of respect for the police." "The reporter owes me one," he said to Leland. "I'll tell her to kill the story."

Leland's first thought was first amendment implications. His second thought was Hightower raging at him. "Can you do that?" he asked Seidel.

Seidel stuck his cigar between his teeth. "No problem."

Leland studied his grizzled, disheveled Anti-Crime sergeant. He knew he would probably regret what he was about to do, but he had no choice. If there were another attack by the Midnight Mangias, Hightower would eat *him* for breakfast. Leland had asked the detective squad commander to give these food burglars special attention. The lieutenant had been polite, but in essence what he said was: "Go screw yourself. I have more important things to do than chase food bandits all over the Bronx."

Leland leaned forward. "Marv," he said softly, as though he were afraid of being overheard. "I'm going to give you and your Anti-Crime team a very important assignment."

Seidel leaned forward. It was the first time the captain had called him Marv. "Yeah? What's that, Cap?"

"Get the Midnight Mangias."

Seidel's eyes narrowed. Leland was by-the-book kind of guy. What he was suggesting was definitely not a by-the-book solution. "We're Anti-Crime, not precinct sleuths, Cap. We're not supposed to do long-term investigations. We're supposed to patrol and—"

"You don't have to quote the *Patrol Guide* to me, Marv. I want you and your team to get these people."

Seidel calmly studied the ash at the tip of his cigar as though, at this moment, it was the most important thing in the whole world. But what he really wanted to do was jump up and slap Leland on the back. *Hell, he wanted to kiss him on the lips! This* was why he'd taken that damn sergeant's exam. *This* was why he'd taken over Anti-Crime. So he could do real detective work again! But with his poker face firmly in place, he said, "Boss, I'll do my best."

After Seidel left, Leland said out loud, "Midnight Mangias." In spite of himself he had to chuckle at the sobriquet. It *was* catchy. He just prayed Hightower would never hear it.

~~

Seidel went with Paul Carrington and his partner, Al Soika, to visit the Casa Blanca Restaurante. He'd eaten there a couple of times and the food, mediocre and pricey, confirmed his hypothesis that any joint that spelled restaurant with an "e" on the end was bound to be lousy.

After inspecting the point of entry in the cellar and listening to the pain-in-the-ass maître d' complain about the missing food and wine for the umpteenth time, they left.

Outside, Seidel stopped to read a laminated copy of a review from *the Bronx Tribune* titled "Best Eateries in the Bronx," which had been prominently placed in the front window. The review listed restaurants in the area ranging from inexpensive to expensive. Naturally, Casa Blanca was one of the expensive ones.

Seidel read the review and grunted. "Superior cuisine, my ass. The moron who wrote this must live on cat food." He started to walk away, but then he came back and reread the list of restaurants carefully. "Sonofabitch," he muttered and rushed back into the restaurant.

Ignoring the protestations of the maître d', Seidel yanked the laminated review out of the window and came back outside.

"What's up, Sarge?" Carrington asked.

"Look at this. The Lambros Luncheonette is on the list. So is Fat Adam's Rib Joint. Maybe the perps are using this as a restaurant guide."

~~

Back in the Anti-Crime office, Carrington and Soika gathered around the chalkboard while Seidel copied the review list on the board:

Inexpensive
Lambros Luncheonette
Fong's Chinese Restaurant
Ribs 'n Stuff

Moderate
Song of India
The Fish Shack
Fat Adam's Rib Joint

Expensive
Walter's Steak House
Bonne Bouche
Casa Blanca Restaurante

Next to each of the burglarized restaurants, he wrote the date of the burglary. He stood back to admire his handiwork. "The Midnight Mangias have hit three on this list. It might be a coincidence, but I got a feeling they're working off this list. If we can figure out their pattern, we'll know which one they're gonna hit next."

"Maybe there is no pattern," Carrington said.

Seidel glared at the youngest member of his Anti-Crime team through a cloud of smoke. He was happy that the kid had suffered no apparent lasting effects from the shooting in the hallway. The fact that the perp received only a superficial wound probably helped. But Carrington still had a long way to go before he'd be detective material. "Paulie, how many times I gotta tell you? Criminals are stupid and lazy. That's why establishing the MO is so important. Once a guy is successful in committing a crime, he tends to repeat himself. They got no imagination these guys."

"What do we do if we figure out where the next joint will be?"

"We stake it out."

"Why don't we stake 'em all out," Soika asked.

"I don't have the manpower."

Soika peered at the list. "They hit a Greek joint, a soul food joint, and an Italian restaurant. What's it mean?"

"It means these guys are equal opportunity burglars," Carrington said.

"They didn't hit the Chinese joint," Soika observed. "Maybe they don't like chink food."

"Maybe they're saving it for later," Seidel said.

"There's two rib places on the list. Why would they hit Fat Adam's and not the other?" Soika asked.

Carrington grunted. "You ever eat at Ribs n' Stuff? I had the shits for a week."

Just then, Stan Quigley came in and saw them gathered around the chalkboard. "What's up?"

"We're trying to figure out a pattern to these Midnight Mangias burglaries," Seidel said. "By the way, how'd you make out in court?"

"That wimp of a DA let him cop to an attempt. Why do we bother locking these mutts up?"

Seidel took the cigar out of his mouth. "A philosophical cop is—"

"A lousy cop." Quigley finished the sentence. It was one of Seidel's favorite lines and they'd all heard it a thousand times.

"Where's Kohler?"

"Parking the car. He's on his way up."

Quigley, who was too vain to admit he needed reading glasses, squinted at the board. "What's Bonne Bouche mean?" He pronounced it bonny *boo*-chee.

There was a moment of silence while they all studied the words. Then Carrington said, "I think bonne means good."

More silence. Suddenly, Quigley snapped his fingers, *"Good douche*!"

All eyes turned toward him. "Good *douche*?" Seidel repeated. "Who would name a restaurant good douche?"

Quigley shrugged. "It's in French. Who the hell would know the difference?"

"Only six million Frenchmen and anyone who took high school French, you asshole." He glared at the three cops. "Didn't any of you jackasses take French in high school?"

All heads shook in the negative. Just then, Kohler came in.

"Hey, Tom." Quigley winked at the others. "Come over here. We're trying to figure out what a restaurant name means and we need someone with half a brain."

The big man came over and looked at the board. "Which one?"

"Bonne Bouche."

"A delicate morsel."

Quigley's jaw dropped. "How'd you know that?"

"I took French in high school."

"*You*? You hardly speak English for chrissake."

"Just because I don't say much, don't mean I don't know English. Do you know any French, Shorty?"

As the other cops poked and jabbed at Quigley, Seidel fixed Kohler with narrowed eyes. "Where'd you go to school?"

"St. Catherine of Siena."

"I knew it. Any of you idiots go to Catholic school?"

Silence.

"See. Parochial schools beat the hell out of public schools any time."

Quigley tugged his tie loose. "Sarge, not for nuthin', but you're Jewish. What the hell do you know about Catholic schools?"

"I had a lot of friends who went to *kat*-lick schools and they were all very smart." He flicked an ash into a rusty hubcap on his desk. " Of course none of 'em got laid till they were thirty, but they were smart as hell." Seidel jabbed his cigar at the chalkboard. "There's a pattern there somewhere. But where?"

"Look at the dates," Kohler said. "They went from the inexpensive restaurants to the expensive ones."

Quigley's mouth dropped open again. "Hey, Boss. He keeps this up, you're gonna have to put him in for the Bureau."

"If he gives me the key to the Midnight Mangias, I might just do that."

The other cops, realizing a detective assignment might be at stake, suddenly became very serious and studied the chalkboard with renewed intensity.

"Tommy is right," Seidel said. "They've gone from soulvaki and beer to veal chops and vintage wine. That's a pattern."

"Then that means they'll hit either the steak restaurant or *Bonne Bouche*."

"Maybe. But which one?" He thumped the board with a stubby finger. "What else is here?"

"Look at the dates," Carrington said. "They're about two weeks apart, plus or minus a couple of days."

"Good point. I want all of you to read the complaint reports on these three burglaries. Memorize them. There's gotta be a pattern in there somewhere. "If Carrington is right, we only got four days to figure this out."

~~

The next morning, Captain Leland pounced on Seidel as soon as he came through the door. He led Seidel into his office and before the sergeant had a chance to sit down, Leland said, "Anything yet?"

"Cap, you just gave me the assignment yesterday afternoon."

"Yeah. Right. So you have nothing?"

"I didn't say that." Seidel told him about the restaurant review list and what they knew, or at least suspected, was a pattern. "The thing is," Seidel said, "if we're right, they're going to hit either the French restaurant of the steak joint. I just wish the hell I knew which one."

"I suppose you've already factored in the absence of burglar alarms."

Seidel took the cigar out of his mouth. "Huh?"

"None of the three restaurants they hit had a burglar alarm system."

"Yeah, right." Seidel was outwardly calm, but he was furious at himself for missing such an important piece of information. The only ones he was more furious with were his assholes Anti-Crime cops. "How'd you know about that, Cap?" Seidel asked off-handedly.

"It's in the sixty-ones."

"You *read* the sixty-ones?" Seidel asked in surprise.

"I read *all* the sixty-ones."

"No shit."

The precinct generated over three hundred sixty-ones a week. That was a lot of complaint reports for one man to read, let alone remember what was in them. He himself read only the felonies and serious misdemeanor complaints and most of those he couldn't remember the next day. "Burglar alarms, huh? Tell you the truth, Cap, I missed that."

He expected Leland to go ballistic. Instead Leland said, "Well, okay, then I've given you something to work with."

"Yeah. Let's see what that turns up."

~~

As Seidel was heading up the stairs, he reflected on the changes in Leland since he'd come to the precinct two months ago. The uptight captain whom he met that first day would have exploded at Seidel's admission of oversight. Then it occurred to Seidel that he would never have admitted the oversight to that man. Captain Leland had come a long way since then. If he kept it up and didn't step on his wang, he might even become a pretty good commanding officer.

Stan Quigley had the misfortune to be the only one in the office when Seidel came in. "*Quigley!*" Seidel bellowed. "In my office. *Forthwith.*"

The anxious cop stood at attention in front of Seidel's desk. Everyone in the team knew Marvin was a born shouter. But Stan Quigley had worked long enough for the short-fused sergeant to recognize the difference between a shout that said he was just mad and one that said he was—*mad*. Seidel was *MAD*.

Seidel kicked the door shut. "Quigley, how long you been in Anti-Crime?"

Quigley cringed. That question was always the preamble to a royal chewing out. "Three years, Boss."

"Would you like to remain in Anti-Crime?"

Quigley had no choice but to continue the charade. "Sure, Sarge."

"Would you like to become a detective some day?"

"Sure, Sarge."

"Quigley, what do detective's do?"

"Um, investigate crimes, make arrests—"

"They *detect*! The root word of detective. Isn't that right?"

"Sure, Sarge." At this moment, Quigley would have agreed that pigs could fly.

"Well," Seidel said in a low voice, "it seems you and your cohorts haven't been detecting."

Cohorts? "What ... what do you mean, Boss?"

Seidel slammed the chalkboard with his hand. "Look at this list. Yesterday I asked you and your cohorts to look for a pattern. Have you come up with one?"

"Ah, no. Nothing else since we brainstormed here in your office yesterday."

Seidel chuckled mirthlessly. "*Brain*stormed? You give yourself too much credit. If brains were dynamite, you couldn't blow your fucking hat off, Quigley!"

"Did you find a pattern?" Quigley knew that he had and fervently hoped Seidel would get to the point and stop the pillorying.

"Burglar alarms," Seidel whispered. "What can you tell me about burglar alarms as they relate to these burglaries?"

Quigley stared at the ceiling as though the answer might be written on the paint-peeling ceiling. It wasn't. "Um, I don't know, Boss."

"*None* of them got alarms, Quigley."

"I'm sorry, Boss. I guess I overlooked it. You know, I've been real busy with court and all."

Seidel pulled some change from his pocket and slammed a quarter down on the desk. "Go call someone who gives a fuck."

Quigley knew it was time to shut up. When Seidel did his quarter shtick, he was *really* mad. Anything Quigley said in his defense now would only make it worse.

"Now that I've given you this information, what are you gonna do about it?"

"I'm gonna go outside and call those two restaurants and see if they have alarm systems."

"What a terrific idea. Jeez, you sound just like a real detective."

While Quigley made the calls, Seidel sat with his feet up on his desk, glaring at the chalkboard list. The Midnight Mangias were starting to give him *agita*, and he didn't like people who gave him *agita*. Someone was going to pay for this.

Fifteen minutes later, Quigley hurried back into the office. "*Bonne Bouche* doesn't have an alarm."

Seidel went to the board, took a piece of chalk, and circled *Bonne Bouche*. "Then *that's* the one they're going to hit next."

Quigley slid into a chair. "I'm sorry I missed that, Boss."

The sergeant waved a hand in dismissal. "It's done. Forget it."

Seidel had a quick temper, but he was just as quick to cool down. He knew Quigley was a good cop, but Seidel was a strong believer in keeping the troops on their toes. When warranted, a good verbal kick in the ass was just the ticket. It kept the troops combat-ready.

"Hey, Sarge, you did some pretty good detecting yourself."

Seidel scratched his chin sheepishly. "I missed it, too."

"Then who—?"

"Leland."

"Captain Chaos?"

"Yeah. He may not be much of a street boss, but I gotta hand it to him, he's good with paperwork." Seidel made a drum beat on the desk with both his hands. "Okay, Stan. Give the restaurant a call. Tell them we have confidential information that they're gonna be ripped off and we want to stake out their place."

Quigley stood up. "When do we start and for how long?"

Seidel looked at his desk calendar. "If we're right about the Midnight Mangias' MO, these guys oughta hit it sometime between tonight and the next three nights. But we'll run the stakeouts for as long as it takes." As Quigley was leaving, Seidel said, "And Stan, it's Captain Leland. I don't wanna hear Captain Chaos anymore."

The cop nodded. "Right, Boss. You've got it."

Chapter Twenty-Three

Six weeks after the attack on the Joy Lounge, IAB completed its investigation. Much to the relief of Leland and the cops involved, it ended with a whimper rather than a bang. Without any witnesses, there was nothing IAB could do but close the case. Leland couldn't quite condone what the cops had done, but he was grateful that the precinct had avoided the turmoil and attendant publicity that would have come from his cops being arrested for assault. The net result of IAB's investigation was one command discipline for Billy Lafferty for failure to turn in evidence to the Property Clerk in a timely manner.

The investigation was finally over, but the IAB's presence in the precinct over the last six weeks had created chaos with Leland's statistics. Whenever IAB snooped in a precinct, some cops became skittish about making arrests or issuing summonses for fear of doing something wrong; others simply refused to work out of protest. The net result was that his precinct statistics had plummeted and he would have to do something about that before Hightower got on his case. But at least the pall of the Joy Lounge investigation had been lifted and they could all get back to work.

~~

Peggy Garrigan and Eddie Mazzeo were still laughing over the cause of a family fight they'd just handled as they got back into their sector car.

"Slurping *soup*!" Mazzeo chuckled. "Is that any reason to bash a guy over the head with a coffee pot?"

Peggy wiped a tear from her eye. "Ah, but remember, she said he'd been slurping soup for thirty-five years! That's grounds for justifiable homicide."

"I guess so, but, still—" He stopped to listen to a radio transmission: *"Sector Boy, respond to..."* It wasn't for them and he continued, "When the guy said—"

"Hold it." Peggy turned up the radio and caught the tail end of the message:

"... Morris Avenue. Report of an unconscious child."

Peggy grabbed the mic. "Central, ten-five that last transmission."

"Twenty-three fifteen Morris Avenue, apartment 17C, report of an unconscious child."

Muttering an explicative, Peggy stomped on the accelerator and made a screeching U-turn. "Peggy, that's not our sector," Mazzeo said quietly.

But Peggy wasn't listening. She was busy concentrating on the road in front of her as she weaved in and out of slower-moving traffic.

George Oliver's voice, high-pitched with excitement, came on the air. "Central, put a rush on that ambulance to 2315 Morris. We have a child not breathing."

Peggy flipped on the roof lights and switched the horn to constant siren. As she sped through an intersection, she barely looked to see what was coming and they were almost sideswiped by an oil truck. Mazzeo grabbed for the wheel. "Slow down for chrissake."

She slammed his chest savagely with her right forearm. "You touch that wheel again," she said in a low, even voice, "and I swear to God I'll kill you."

He'd never seen her like this. She'd looked at him as though he were a complete stranger. He braced his feet on the floor and prayed they'd get to Morris Avenue in one piece.

As they pulled up to the building, Jim Elliott burst through the glass doors and held them open while George Oliver, cradling Molly's tiny body in his arms, continued to breathe into her mouth.

Mazzeo jumped out and yanked the back door open while Peggy swept the back seat clear of nightsticks, clipboards, and newspapers. Elliott ran around to the other side of the car and helped maneuver his partner and the little girl into the back seat.

When the five of them were in the car, Peggy slammed the transmission into gear and the car bolted forward. She looked at them through the rear view mirror. "What happened?"

Elliott had taken over the task of breathing into Molly's mouth. Oliver, gasping for air, ran his sleeve against his damp forehead. "Mother said she slipped and fell in the bathtub... the kid stopped breathing right after we got there... no time to wait for a bus."

Mazzeo leaned over the front seat and looked down at the motionless body. Elliott was breathing into her mouth, but there was no response. The child's face was blue. "Central," he said calmly into the mic, "notify Cumberland. We're coming in with a child not breathing. Have a trauma team standing by."

Peggy screeched to a stop in front of the emergency room. Before the car stopped rocking, Molly had been lifted out of the car and onto a waiting gurney. As the trauma team rushed the little girl through the double doors, one doctor jumped up on the gurney, straddled the little girl's body, and started to administer CPR.

Inside the hospital, Mazzeo watched Peggy nervously pacing up and down the corridor. Occasionally, she stopped to peek through the door's small window to see what was happening. But a team of doctors and nurses surrounded the table and she couldn't see anything.

"Peggy," Mazzeo said gently. "We oughta be getting back. We've been out of our sector for—"

She stopped pacing and glared at him. "Eddie, I'm not leaving until I know she's all right."

He'd never seen her like this, but he knew there was no point in arguing with her. He rubbed his chest—still smarting from the blow—and resigned himself to the fact that they wouldn't be leaving the hospital until she was ready.

The door opened and a doctor, a fair-skinned black man with soft brown eyes, came out pulling off his rubber gloves. Peggy rushed up to him. "How's she doing?"

He shook his head. "We lost her."

Peggy stood motionless with her arms at her side and watched the doctor disappear through another door as though she expected him to come back and say it was all a mistake. Then she turned to Mazzeo with tears in her eyes and mouthed the word "why?"

As he went toward her, she saw something over his shoulder and stiffened. He turned. Mrs. Norville had just come through the doors at the other end of the corridor and was talking to someone at the nurse's station.

"You miserable bitch..." Peggy muttered as she brushed past Mazzeo.

She was almost at a dead run before he caught up to her. Norville, still talking to the nurse didn't see them coming. Mazzeo, desperate to keep Peggy away from Norville, shoved her through the nearest door, a linen supply room.

"Let me go!" Peggy shouted.

He stood between her and the door. "You're not going anywhere until you calm down."

She charged him, catching him off guard, and slammed him against the door. Blinded by tears, she flailed at him. He threw his arms around her and pulled her close to him. She continued to pound on his chest, but as he squeezed her tighter, the pounding became weaker. Finally, she stopped struggling and her body shuddered with racking sobs. "Why?" she said in a small, strangled voice. "Why?"

Mazzeo rocked her in his arms and said nothing. Like so many other questions he'd asked himself since he'd become a cop, he didn't know the answer to this one either.

～～

It was after seven o'clock by the time Leland left the precinct. The last three hours had been chaotic. The squad brought Mrs. Norville into the station house for questioning. Minutes later, three high-priced lawyers in very expensive suits showed up and did their best to push their weight around. Elliot, Oliver, Mazzeo, and Peggy Garrigan had to be restrained by Lt. Hanlon and Sgt. Engle from going after the surly lawyers. It was only after Leland threatened to suspend the cops and have the lawyers arrested that peace was restored. In less than an hour, the lawyers found a judge who released Mrs. Norville on her own personal recognizance.

Leland drove back to Queens and stopped in a favorite neighborhood steak house for dinner. After such a trying day, he decided to give himself a treat and eat real food. Since his transfer to the precinct, he'd been living on fast-food and stale sandwiches, which led to chronic heartburn. While he was perusing the menu, he ordered a martini, which led to another, which led to yet another. By the time he was on his fifth martini, he realized he wasn't hungry. He moved to the bar to concentrate on a liquid dinner.

Around eight-thirty, a family came in with a little girl who was around the same age as Molly Norville. She was smiling, obviously happy to be with her doting parents. Leland paid his bill and left quickly.

Reluctant to go back to his tiny apartment, he got into his car and began to drive aimlessly. Soon he found himself back in the Bronx, driving through the streets of the Five-five—his precinct. He couldn't recall precisely when that started, but somewhere along the way he'd begun to refer to it as "his" precinct instead of "the" precinct.

He drove through the squalid streets of the Bulge, stopping momentarily to peer into the Joy Lounge. It was a very different bar from the one he'd seen four months ago. No crowds now; just a bored bartender talking to three bored customers. Even the jukebox was turned down low. He wondered if the bar would go out of business before he had the chance to shut it down himself.

He turned the car onto Clinton Boulevard and made the long climb to the crest of the Hill where the "real" people lived—the wealthy, the powerful, the educated, and—he thought bitterly—at least one murderer.

He pulled into a parking spot in front of Gloria Perez's apartment building and, without giving himself the chance to reconsider, he went into the building, rode the elevator to her floor, and rang the bell.

A shoeless Gloria, wearing a baggy NY Giants sweatshirt over a pair of tight jeans, opened the door. "Well," she said with a look of genuine surprise, "is this visit official or unofficial?"

"Issit a bad time?" he blurted out. *Damn!* He thought. *Did I just slur my words?*

"No. Come in. I'll make coffee."

"I'd rather have a drink."

She studied him with an enigmatic smile. "I think coffee is a better choice."

He heard himself say slowly and deliberately, "Do ya think I had too much to drink?" *Damn.* He *was* slurring his words! And he sounded like a drunken John Wayne. On the way up in the elevator, he'd practiced his opening line out loud: "Good evening, Ms. Perez. I was in the neighborhood and thought I'd drop in." He'd sounded fine then. What the hell happened between the elevator and her front door?

She went into the kitchen to make coffee and he flopped down on the old stuffed chair. There was half a glass of soda and a half-empty bowl of popcorn on the coffee table. He picked up a DVD case and was squinting at the blurry words when she came into the room with a small cup of coffee for her and a huge mug for him.

"*Casablanca,*" she said, handing him his mug.

He felt a tug of disappointment when she retreated to the couch opposite him. *Why did she always have to sit on that damn couch?*

"I'm a sucker for old movies," she explained. "I must have seen that one a thousand times."

"Round up the usual suspects..." He waved his mug and splashed coffee on his hand.

"Oh, did you burn yourself?"

"It's nothing, just first degree burns." He quickly put the mug down and wiped his smarting hand with a handkerchief. He caught her smiling at him. "I amuse you a lot, don't I," he said.

"I've never seen you like this."

"Like what?"

"Drunk."

"Me? Drunk?" He took a sip from his mug and winced as the hot black coffee burned the inside of his mouth.

"Coffee that bad?"

"Hot. Very hot. All right, I may have a slight buzz on."

"Slight?"

"All right, perhaps a little more than slight." He picked up the DVD case. "Watching old movies on a Saturday night?" he asked, changing the subject. "I'd have thought you'd be out on the town with some hotshot lawyer in a three-piece suit."

Her smile turned icy. "What I do on a Saturday night is none of your business. Besides, what are you doing riding around your precinct in your condition on a Saturday night?"

"I'll be goddamned if I know," he muttered.

She studied him over her cup. She'd become accustomed to seeing him alert, confident, and looking as though he could scale Mount Everest at a moment's notice. But now, he sat slumped in her chair looking overwhelmed. "Hard day at the office?" she asked with more concern than she wanted to admit.

"Oh, yeah," he said, after a long pause. "A very hard day."

"Wanna talk about it?"

"No."

For a long while, they both sat in silence drinking their coffee. Finally, he broke the silence. "A little girl died today because the police department—and me, specifically—couldn't get our priorities straight."

She knew who he was talking about. "Didn't they investigate?"

"Oh, they investigated. Unfounded, they said. But, Peggy Garrigan, one of my cops, wouldn't hear of it. She conducted her own—totally unauthorized, I might add—investigation."

"What was the result?"

"The result was that I wanted to give her a command discipline. The result was that I wanted the mother to file a civilian complaint against her."

"Sounds like you were a little harsh."

"Oh, no, not at all. I was doing everything by the book."

"Then why are you so angry at yourself?"

Leland put the cup down with a steady hand. Both the coffee and the conversation were sobering him up. "Because I didn't see Officer Garrigan as someone who was more concerned about a little girl than her own career. I saw her as a threat to *my* career." Leland's eyes clouded with anguish. "And I saw the mother as a threat to my career. That little girl didn't come from a broken home in the Valley. She lived right here on the Hill where mothers take good care of their children."

"So you didn't support Officer Garrigan?"

"No, not right away. It took a little while. I had to be absolutely certain this wouldn't be a career-death experience." He ran his hand across the arm of the threadbare chair. "If I'd supported her right from the start, that little girl might still be alive."

"Don't play the woulda-coulda-shoulda game. You make a decision that you hope is based on good, sound information and you stick with it. God knows I've made some dumb decisions. I work with a limited budget and I have to decide every day which kids will get placed in training programs, knowing full well that those who don't get the opportunity for some sort of job training are probably doomed to a life of crime and drug abuse. Still, no matter how carefully I plan, some kids abuse my trust. The first few times it happened, I was devastated. But now, I've learned that I'm not omnipotent. I can—and do—make mistakes. And," she added softly, "So do you."

"That's for sure," he said bitterly.

"They say the trick is to learn from your mistakes. Have you?"

"I'm beginning to. I've badly misjudged a lot of the people who work for me. Jack Barry is a damn good Operations Coordinator. He's been my guardian angel, trying to keep me out of trouble. He hasn't always succeeded," he added sheepishly, "because sometimes I insist on making an ass of myself and even Jack Barry can't stop me. Do you know Sergeant Seidel?"

"That gruff guy who's always smoking a cigar?"

"Yeah."

"Only by sight."

"When I first came to the precinct, I was convinced that he was going to be my biggest problem. He's outspoken, an iconoclast; given to doing things his way. But, you know what? He's one helluva cop. For the longest time I couldn't figure out why, then it hit me. He loves being a cop."

"Don't you?"

Leland was caught off guard by that question. After a moment's reflection, he said, "I haven't thought of myself as a cop for a very long time. I've been too busy working on my career."

Gloria knew there was no such thing as a "cop type," but looking at the handsome, troubled man sitting before her, she couldn't imagine him doing some of the things she'd seen Five-five cops do. "Were you ever a real cop?"

"Yeah, a long time ago. For a little while."

It was just twelve years, but it seemed like a lifetime ago. He'd come out of the academy and was assigned to the Two-eight in the center of Harlem. Looking back now, he realized it had been the best time in his career. Making arrests and responding to radio runs had been an exciting, new experience for a young man fresh out of college. He was just beginning to shake loose his rookie clumsiness and naïveté when the sergeant's exam was announced. From that moment on, he spent every available minute studying; and it paid off. He wrote number one on the Sergeant's test and never closed the books again.

But he was never a cop again, either.

Gloria's heart ached for him. She knew he was going through a painful transition. He was no longer that smug, self-confident headquarters hotshot she'd seen that first day she'd walked into his office. Instead, he was turning into the kind of sensitive, real human being she'd believed was always there, lying just below the surface. But he wasn't there yet. The battle wasn't over. He was precariously straddling a moral fence and he could fall either way. She tried to think of the words that would help him make the right choice.

"I think," she said tentatively, "that you've done a lot of growing up since you've been in the Five-five."

"Is that what they call it?"

"And I also think you won't be happy until you make up your mind who you are."

He looked at her inquisitively, but he said nothing. She continued. "The question is: Are you going to be happy continuing to be the cold, calculating captain rising through the ranks?"

He was stung by her characterization of him as "calculating," but maybe she was right. "What else can I be?" he asked plaintively.

"Yourself," she said softly.

"You're in the wrong profession, Gloria. You should have been a psychologist."

"It's not psychology. It's common sense."

Glumly, Leland wondered if it was still possible to find the real him. For too long, every move, every decision he made had been made with only one thought in mind: *how will this enhance my career?* Was it too late to return to the man he once was? A man confident in his ability to make decisions based on what he knew was right?

The effects of the martinis had worn off and he was beginning to feel the dull throbbing of what promised to be a world-class headache. He looked at his watch. It was after midnight. "Hey, I'm sorry. I've kept you from your movie."

"No problem. I have the dialogue memorized."

At the door he said, "Gloria, thanks for listening to me cry in my beer."

"Coffee."

"Right. Coffee."

She looked into his hazel eyes, still clouded with uncertainty. For a fleeting moment, she thought he was going to say something, but the moment passed. "Anytime," she said.

For a long time after she closed the door, she remained standing there, holding onto the doorknob, and a remarkable thought occurred to her. If he'd said he wanted to stay, she would have gladly let him.

Chapter Twenty-Four

For the next two nights, Seidel rotated different teams of Anti-Crime cops through his stakeout schedule. The men arrived at *Bonne Bouche* just before closing time and remained in the darkened restaurant until the owner came back the next morning. Seidel had left word to call him forthwith if an arrest was made, but, so far, there had been no late night phone call.

Now it was ten-thirty Saturday night and Seidel was in his office reviewing his team's activity reports. He was about to call it quits when Stan Quigley came in.

"Boss, a problem. Tommy Kohler just called in sick. He was supposed to work the stakeout with me tonight."

"What happened?"

"This morning he was painting his living room and he fell off a ladder. His back went out. He thought it would be better by tonight, but—"

"A clumsy bastard like that has no business being anywhere near a ladder," Seidel muttered. He snatched up the roll call. There was no one else available and it was too late to call anyone in. "Okay"—he tossed the roll call on the desk—"I guess I'll have to work the stakeout with you."

It was after eleven when Seidel came out of his office. "Let's go." As they were heading for the door, Seidel stopped. "Where's the shotgun?"

"What shotgun?"

"Quigley, we're going on a *stakeout*."

"So? These guys *eat*, Sarge. That's all they do."

"That's because no one's ever interrupted them before. They might get cranky as hell when we disrupt their dinner. Bring a shotgun."

~~

It was after one in the morning before the restaurant closed and the help finished cleaning up. As the owner was leaving, he told them he'd left fresh coffee and cookies for them.

Seidel and Quigley sat at a small table in the kitchen, hunched over a small flickering candle, their only light. "Kinda romantic, don't you think?" Quigley said, leering over the candle.

"Not with you, it ain't." Seidel took a sip of coffee and made a face. "Whew, this is god-awful."

Quigley bit into a cookie. "These things are stale. That cheap fucking frog. We're here to protect this hump's restaurant and the best he can do is swill and stale cookies. Talk about your police brutality."

Seidel wasn't listening. He was thinking about what they were going to do if the Midnight Mangias showed up tonight. "Listen up, Stan," he said, interrupting the cop's nonstop tirade against the restaurant's owner. "The best way in here is through the rear window in the cellar. If they show up, you'll hide in there." He pointed to a small, windowless office off the kitchen. "I'll hide in the dining room. Remember, don't you do anything. I'll make the first move."

"Maybe we oughta wait until they finish cooking. It might be something good."

Seidel fixed the grinning cop with a baleful look. "This isn't a goof. We don't know who these two are, but they gotta be pretty whacky to do something like this in the first place. Remember to stay out of each other's field of fire."

Quigley looked concerned for the first time. "You think we're going to have a problem taking them down?"

"I don't know. I always think the worst. That way I get pleasantly surprised. Sometimes."

They were unable to drink any more of the terrible coffee and they moved into the dining room. Seidel tried, unsuccessfully, to get comfortable on one of the velvet banquettes that lined the walls. "I'm too old for this shit," he muttered. "*I'm* the boss. I'm supposed to be home in the crib waiting for a middle-of-the-night call from you guys."

Quigley wasn't listening. He'd taken the tray of cookies with him and was test-biting each one, searching for one that wasn't stale.

It was almost two-thirty when Seidel's eyes snapped open. He'd been dozing, but something had awakened him. "What was that?" he whispered.

Quigley, who'd also been dozing, rubbed his eyes. "I didn't hear nothing."

The sound of breaking glass hitting the tile floor in the cellar brought both of them to their feet. Seidel grabbed the shotgun. "Bingo! Into the office. Quick."

Quigley noiselessly slipped into the kitchen and disappeared into the tiny office. Seidel backed into the dining room and hid behind a fake potted plant.

Soon he heard hushed voices. Peeking through the leaves, he watched a figure come out of the kitchen, spread a white tablecloth, and set two places complete with dinnerware, glasses and silver. The figure was small enough to be a woman but he couldn't be sure in the dim light. From inside the kitchen, he heard the sound of a cork popping. Then a larger figure emerged holding up a bottle. "A nineteen eighty-three Bordeaux"—it was a man's voice—"a great vintage."

The smaller figure spoke and it was a woman. "Wonderful. So what are we having for dinner?"

"I found some veal in the fridge. How does escargot sound for an appetizer?"

They clinked glasses. "Sounds wonderful," she said.

It was time to make their move. Seidel had been on dozens of stakeouts in the past, but it never got easier. The heart still pumped too fast and the hands sweated too much. You planned in great detail who would do what and when. But when the time came, all those carefully made plans had a way of going haywire; mostly because the perps never did what they were supposed to. And when that happened, you had to operate on instinct.

Seidel was mature enough to admit he was afraid, but he felt something else as well—a rush of excitement. It was these two opposing emotions that made police work addicting. Right now, he was wishing he'd retired a year ago, but he knew that later, if everything turned out all right, all thoughts of retirement would be banished from his mind. He struggled to clear his head of these conflicting thoughts. It was time to concentrate on the job at hand.

Hardly breathing, Seidel eased the safety off the shotgun. Even though it made only a soft click, it sounded like a rifle shot to his ears. He took a deep breath and jumped away from the potted plant. *"Police! Don't move!"*

The two Midnight Mangias had just made a toast. The woman was about to take a sip of wine but she stopped, her glass frozen in midair. The man, startled by the sudden intrusion, fell backwards off his chair and disappearing from Seidel's line of sight.

"*Damn it!*" Seidel muttered. Kicking chairs out of his way, he advanced, swinging the shotgun's barrel from the woman to the spot he'd last seen the man; his muscles tensed, prepared to pump off a round.

Quigley crashed though the kitchen door clutching his service automatic in both hands. "Watch it, Stan," Seidel shouted. "There's one on the floor."

Quigley pivoted and trained the gun on the man sprawled on the floor. "Move motherfucker and you're dead," he yelled. Quickly, he advanced toward the man, and then he put his gun up and grinned. "He's out, Sarge. He knocked himself out when he hit the deck."

The woman, who up until now had remained as still as a statue, bolted out of her chair. "Oh, *Donny!*"

Seidel pointed the shotgun at her. "Stay where you are," he shouted in his best snarl. But she paid no attention and knelt by her unconscious man.

Quigley flipped the lights on and the two police officers got their first good look at the Midnight Mangias. The woman cradling the man's head in her lap was a pretty woman in her early thirties. He was a few years older. "What's your name?" Seidel asked him when he saw him coming to.

The man sat up and rubbed the back of his head. "Donald… Hathaway."

The woman stared at the shotgun with wide, frightened eyes. "And I'm his wife, Linda."

Quigley helped the woozy man into a chair. "You okay?"

The man shook his head. "Yeah, I think so."

"Good. Listen up. I'm gonna read you your rights."

When he finished, Seidel said to the man. "I'm Sergeant Seidel. Do you want to tell us what this is all about?" He expected the man to say he wanted to speak to his lawyer, but the man simply nodded. "This is so embarrassing, I don't know where to begin."

"How about the beginning?"

While his wife rubbed the back of his neck, Donald Hathaway recounted the saga of their venture into crime. "Linda and I have been married for almost ten years now. We're both professionals. I'm a stockbroker: she's in computer graphics. We have no children and our combined income has allowed up to live quite well.

"Six months ago, my company had what is euphemistically called a down-sizing. The bottom line is I was let go and I haven't been able to find employment since." He held his wife's hand for support. "Our passion has always been good food and wine. My hobby is cooking."

"He's an excellent chef," Linda offered.

"Thanks, hon." He patted her hand. "In the good old days, we ate out almost every night and frequently entertained at home. Then I lost my job. Funny, I never realized how important fine dining had become to our lives. Things began to change between us. I became irritable and moody. Even our sex life was affected."

She poked him, mortified. *"Don-ny."*

"It's true, Linda. Our marriage was unraveling, Sergeant. Then one day, I saw a restaurant review in the local paper. The article highlighted several local restaurants in the area. We got to talking about what fun it would be to try each of them. Of course, we couldn't afford it, and I said, jokingly, maybe we could break into one of them and I could cook the meal. In the beginning, it was just a fantasy. But then, the more I thought about it, the more it seemed possible."

Quigley spoke up. "If you like food so much, why'd you go to Lambros. It ain't exactly four-star fare."

"True. Officer, I know it sounds self-serving, but I'm basically an honest man."

Seidel and Quigley looked at each other and they were both thinking the same thing: *Let's see what his yellow sheet says.*

"I reasoned—rationalized, I guess is a better word—that if we ate in the most inexpensive restaurant on the list, I really wouldn't be hurting anyone."

"Which one's the least expensive?"

"Ribs n' Stuff."

"Why didn't you go there?"

"I cased the place." Both Seidel and Quigley smiled at the criminal jargon coming out of this amateur's mouth. "There was a burglar alarm system and I had no idea how to circumvent that. I was about to forget the whole thing, but then I took a walk past that Greek luncheonette and saw that they didn't have an alarm system. You know, they really should have one."

"Thanks to you, he's having one installed," Seidel said.

"I'm glad. Well, anyway, we settled for the Greek place."

"Any problems?" Seidel asked.

"None. The food wasn't very good, but we had so much fun. It was scary, but at the same time so—exhilarating. That night Linda and I went home and had the best—"

"*Donny!*"

Seidel wasn't surprised at the revelation. A lot of people got off on doing dangerous, forbidden things. It was a bit kinky for him, but what did he know? "Then what—" He stopped when he saw Hathaway staring longingly at the bottle of wine. "Is that good stuff?"

"Excellent. A haut-médoc. The wine menu lists it at two-hundred and fifty dollars." He caressed the bottle gently and looked at Seidel plaintively. "You know, wine is a living thing. Once a bottle is open, it should be drunk. Otherwise it begins to spoil."

"You're saying we can't stick the cork back in the bottle and save it?"

"Right. Oxygen has already begun the deterioration process."

Quigley, standing on the other side of the table, looked imploringly at Seidel. "I hate to see a good bottle of wine go to waste, Sarge." This from a man who sucked down Bud Lite by the case.

Seidel stared down at the pathetic couple sitting at the table. Despite Hathaway's protestations, he was a criminal. Not only technically, but probably in his heart as well. The ex-stock broker exhibited all the early warning signs. "I didn't hurt anyone," and "I'm an honest person," were the rationalizations of a budding criminal. Hathaway sounded like the politicians who get caught on tape stuffing their pockets with money. He had more respect for a man who took your money at the point of a gun. At least you knew where he was coming from. With a detective's jaundiced view of human nature, Seidel began to wonder about the real reason Hathaway lost his job on Wall Street. Maybe he'd used the same rationalizations in his dealings with his clients.

He had no sympathy for Donny Hathaway, but he did feel sorry for his quiet, frightened wife. She was married to a jerk and he was pretty sure this hadn't been her idea. But one thing was for sure: There would be no great sex tonight.

"Get two more glasses," he said to Quigley. "But we can't drink the whole thing," he cautioned Hathaway. "I gotta save some for evidence."

Doing as they were told, Seidel and Quigley held their glasses up to the soft light of the table candle. "Notice the highlights in the dark ruby color," Hathaway said softly.

"Yeah." Seidel didn't notice anything.

"Now swivel the wine in the glass and sniff it. What does it smell like?"

"Wine," Quigley said very seriously.

"Yes, but is there anything else?"

"Nope, that's it. You smell something else?" he asked suspiciously.

Hathaway stuck his nose in the glass and closed his eyes. "Blackberries, charred oak, a hint of clover, and just an insinuation of tar."

Quigley peered into his glass. "Tar?"

"It takes some practice." Linda Hathaway said. "Donny has taken extensive wine courses. He's very knowledgeable."

Hathaway smiled at his wife, and continued his instruction. "Now take a sip. Suck in some air and swirl the wine around your tongue."

Quigley made a loud slurping sound and a thin trickle of wine dribbled out of the side of his mouth and down onto his sweatshirt. Seidel downed his wine like a shot of whisky.

"Notice the finish." Hathaway said reverently.

Quigley shook the bottle. "What finish? We got half a bottle left."

"The lingering aftertaste, so... full bodied."

Quigley smacked his lips. "Oh. Yeah." Personally, he didn't think much of the wine and was glad he hadn't shelled out two hundred and fifty bucks for this crap. He made a quick calculation. That was equivalent to sixty-two six-packs!

Seidel put his glass down. "Very nice." It was beginning to give him heartburn. "So finish your story, Donny. Why did you move up to the expensive joints?"

"As I said, we really enjoyed the experience, but not the food. So I decided to try one of the moderate restaurants."

"Fat Adam's?"

"Yes. He had no alarm."

"He does now."

Hathaway nodded. "That was a wonderful experience as well. Unfortunately, after that, we were hooked. It was *so* easy. Too easy, actually. If all the restaurants had had alarms, none of this would have happened."

Another rationalization, Seidel noted. "And you decided to go right to the big time?"

"Yes. Casa Blanca is an excellent restaurant. Linda and I have eaten there often. In the good old days," he added less enthusiastically.

"Where were you going to go after you'd run the list?"

Hathaway smiled wistfully. "The *New York Times* has excellent food reviews."

"Were you going to branch out into Manhattan?"

"I'm not sure," he said cautiously.

Seidel saw the look in Hathaway's eyes and knew if they hadn't been caught tonight, the Midnight Mangias would, without a doubt, have started eating their way through Manhattan.

Seidel looked at his watch. It was almost four o'clock and he was getting bleary-eyed. "Drink up, folks, it's time to go."

Seidel watched Hathaway, his wife, and Quigley polish off the rest of the wine. When there was an inch left in the bottle, he stuck the cork in the bottle. "For evidence," he explained.

"What's going to happen to us?" Hathaway asked.

Seidel wanted to scare the hell out of him by giving him a few graphic details about life on Riker's Island, but he didn't want to frighten the woman any more than she already was. "Who knows?" he said. "First offenders like you, they'll probably settle for restitution and some type of community service."

Hathaway blinked. "You mean... I'll have to *pay* for all this?"

Seidel smiled. "You got it." He held up the bottle. "Thanks for the wine, Donny." Then he leaned close to the ex-stock broker and his face turned hard. "One thing for sure, pal. You try this again and you and the misses will be sampling Diet Pepsi in Riker's for a long, long time."

Hathaway blanched at the thought of being locked up with all those *real* criminals.

~~

When Seidel got back from court, he went directly to Leland's office told him the story.

"Great work," Leland said. "Who were they?"

Seidel's eyes were heavy. Except for a catnap in the restaurant last night, he'd been up for over eighteen hours. "A couple of yuppies from the Hill who couldn't afford the good life anymore. Harmless assholes."

"What's gonna happen to them?"

"I made a pitch to the DA. Told him they were no trouble. The usual bullshit. He's gonna ask the judge for restitution and community service." He saw the frown on Leland's face and said, "What'd you expect? Hard time in the joint?"

"No. I was just thinking what it cost us in money and manpower to grab these two. Three RMP teams to respond to reports of past burglaries; processing all that paperwork; forensic assistance; plus the time you and your men put into this. Incredible. All for two yuppies who refuse to grow up."

He was also thinking of what would have happened to him if Hightower had gotten wind of the Midnight Mangias crime spree.

Seidel scratched the stubble of an eighteen-hour growth of beard. "That's what police work is all about, Cap. Sometimes we're forced to squander our resources on stupid things. Problem is, we seldom get to make the choice. But look at the bright side. At least no one got hurt." He yawned and stood up. "I'm gonna go home and sack out."

He saw Leland's glum look and said, "Why the long face, Cap? You should be popping champagne corks. We got the Midnight Mangias."

"I called the SLA yesterday to follow up on the Joy Lounge."

"Those humps are taking their sweet time. Are they ready to close it yet?"

"No. I'm being stonewalled. They promised they'd put this investigation on the front burner, but someone a lot bigger than me has put a hold on it."

"Who?"

"The real owner I expect."

"He's got to have a lot of juice. Archer?"

"I don't know for sure."

Seidel studied Leland carefully. "What will you do if you find out Archer is the owner?"

Leland went to the window and looked out. Two kids were using the precinct's garbage can covers as shields as they flailed away at each other with broom handles. "If I could prove Archer owned the Joy, I'd have it shut down in a heartbeat."

Seidel grunted. He wouldn't have thought it earlier, but now he believed Leland would go head-to-head with Archer even if it meant the end of his career. "I'll keep my eyes open."

As Seidel got up to leave, Leland said, "By the way, Marv, you and your men did a great job. Thanks."

Seidel looked at the captain pensively. "You had a lot to do with it."

Leland slid a stack of reports in front of him and smiled. "Who knows? Maybe someday I'll end up in the Bureau."

God forbid, Seidel thought as he closed the door behind him. Leland was coming around, but he was a long, long way from becoming a boss in the Detective Bureau.

~~

Most commanding officers disliked working late tours, but it worked for Leland. He found it was a good time to get paperwork done without the incessant ringing of telephones and the steady flow of visitors to his office.

It was almost three in the morning when Lt. Hanlon, the desk officer, stuck his head in the door. "I'm sorry to bother you, Cap, but there's a woman on the phone. Said she'd only speak to you. She wouldn't give her name."

Leland looked at the wall clock and stretched. It had to be one of those psychos who got off on calling the police at all hours of the night. He'd been working non-stop since midnight and decided he could use a little comic relief. "Okay, Sarge, put her through."

"Captain Leland?" The voice was tight with emotion.

"Yes, how may I help you?"

"This is... Carol Mazzeo. I met you at the Christmas party."

"Yes, Mrs. Mazzeo. I remember." She was the one who'd spilled wine on him.

"I apologize for not giving my name to the lieutenant, but I didn't want anyone to know I called."

"That's quite all right. What can I do for you?"

"It's after three and Eddie isn't home yet." She paused, as if deciding if she should go on. "I know he's very active, always making arrests, and he tells me he often gets held up at Central Booking processing the arrest."

"That's true, Mrs. Mazzeo. A late arrest can take several hours." While he was talking to her, he opened the sign-out book.

"She cleared her throat. "What... what I want to know is did he make an arrest tonight?"

Leland ran his finger down the list of signatures. Eddie Mazzeo signed out at 12:10 a.m. He'd made no arrest. Leland sat back and rubbed his temples. Obviously, Mazzeo had something going on the side. An image of Peggy Garrigan, Mazzeo's attractive partner, came to mind. Leland slammed the book shut, angry that he'd been placed in this dilemma. If he told Carol Mazzeo the truth—that her husband hadn't made an arrest tonight, it could wreck their marriage. On the other hand, if he lied and the department found out, he'd be in big trouble.

His first impulse was to tell her the truth. It Mazzeo was stupid enough to get involved with another woman, why should he risk his own career? But then he thought of the pretty young woman who'd spilled wine on him. She didn't deserve this. To his surprise he heard himself say, "Eddie made an arrest just before midnight."

He heard a sigh of relief on the other end of the line. "Oh, I see. Thank you, Captain. It's just that I'd like him to be home more often, that's all."

"I'll talk to him, Mrs. Mazzeo. I'll tell him to go easy on arrests."

"Oh, please don't do that. If Eddie knew I'd called you—"

"Don't worry, he won't know. It's commendable that Ed is an active cop, but the department isn't everything; he has a personal life, too." He suddenly thought about Marilyn and added, "There has to be a balance between job and family."

"Thank you so much, Captain." Her voice cracked. "I'm so ashamed to be calling you like this."

"That's all right, Mrs. Mazzeo. Anytime."

After he hung up, he made a note on his calendar to talk to Eddie Mazzeo, super cop.

~~

The following day, right after roll call, Mazzeo knocked on Leland's door. "You wanted to see me, Cap?"

"Yeah, Eddie. Come in and close the door."

He waited until the young cop was seated. Mazzeo glanced around the room nervously. Leland thumbed through a memo, letting him sweat in silence. Then he looked up, tossed the memo aside and said, "Eddie, what are your future plans in the department? You studying for the sergeant's exam?"

"Nah, that's not my bag, Cap. I like excitement. I want Narcotics."

Leland sat back and studied the good-looking cop, who was desperately trying to figure out where this conversation was going. "What does your wife think about that?"

Mazzeo shrugged. "Carol? She'll go along with whatever I want to do."

"How's your arrest activity?"

"Pretty good."

"Disciplinary record?"

"A couple of CDs. One civilian complaint. That's about it."

"Sounds like you're on track."

Mazzeo flashed a winning smile. "Another few months and I should be ready to make my move."

"So there's nothing to stop you."

"Right."

"Except me."

Mazzeo's confident smile faded and he sat up straight. "What do you mean, Captain?"

"Narcotics, or any detail for that matter, requires someone with smarts. Wouldn't you agree?"

"Yeah," Mazzeo answered warily.

"Do you think a married cop with a bimbo on the side is a smart guy?"

Mazzeo turned ashen. "Well… I dunno…"

Leland sat forward and pinned the young cop with hard eyes. "I think any cop who would do that is so dumb that he doesn't deserve to get a detail," he said softly. "Ever. In fact, I feel so strongly about it that I would give that cop a bad evaluation and do everything in my power to see that he never got a detail."

Mazzeo studied the tile floor and his chest heaved under his uniform.

"Eddie, I've been hearing rumors about you," Leland continued.

Mazzeo's head snapped up. "Who? What are they saying?"

"That you have something going on the side."

"That's bullshit, Captain."

Leland took a chance. "It's Peggy Garrigan, isn't it?"

Mazzeo fell back as though he'd been slapped in the face. "Peggy? No way. Why would I do anything with my partner? That doesn't make sense. My wife knows her. There's no way, Captain."

Mazzeo was lying. Leland had learned long ago that when people were innocent, they simply denied the allegation with an irate *no*. Guilty people, on the other hand, felt a compulsion to offer lots of reasons why they couldn't do something wrong. Perhaps that's what Shakespeare had in mind when he wrote: "The lady doth protest too much." He was prepared to come down hard on Mazzeo, but because of his shooting incident, he decided to give the cop some slack.

"Effective tomorrow, I'm splitting you and Garrigan up. We have four rookies coming in. You'll ride with one of them. Any questions?"

Mazzeo started to get up, and then sat back down. "Captain, am I in trouble?"

"Not with me. Not yet. I'm gonna give you one more chance to break this up. But if there's a next time, you're history and you can forget about ever getting a detail."

Peggy was waiting in the radio car outside the precinct. As soon as she saw him, she knew something was the matter.

"What did the Captain want?" she asked when he got into the car.

"He knows about us. He's splitting us up."

"What? How—"

"How the hell should I know?"

"What'd you tell him?"

"I denied everything, but he didn't buy it."

Peggy saw her chances of going to the Bureau flying out the window. "What else is he going to do?" She gripped the steering wheel until her knuckles were white.

"Nothing. He's gonna give me one more chance. If he hears anything about us again, we're shit out of luck."

She allowed herself to breath. "Wow. It could have been worse."

"Yeah, I guess so."

"Who are we gonna work with?"

"There are rookies coming in tomorrow."

"Thank God. As long as I don't have to work with Lafferty."

"This isn't funny, Peggy."

"Neither is working with crazy Billy."

Peggy pulled away from the curb and neither of them said anything for a very long time. Then, finally, Mazzeo said, "This doesn't change anything, Peggy. We'll just have to be more careful, that's all."

Peggy chewed on her lower lip. "Eddie, maybe we are seeing too much of each other. Maybe we should just cool it for a while."

"Maybe you're right," he said, with more relief that he was willing to admit even to himself.

Chapter Twenty-Five

    Leland ripped a page off his monthly calendar and wondered where the time was going. It was already the beginning of February and the "to-do" list he'd started his first day in the precinct was getting longer and longer. For every item he crossed off, he added three more. Every day he came to work determined to chip away at the list, but the precinct's day-to-day crises kept interfering with his plans.

    There was, however, one item he couldn't put off any longer. It was time to make good on his ill-advised promise to Vera Roland to clean up Seaman Street. It had been almost a month since the Community Board meeting, and in that time, he'd found any number of excuses to avoid doing something about it. He told himself he needed more time to train and select the supervisors who would take part in the sweep. He told himself he needed more intelligence about the drug dealers on the block. But the truth was he was terrified that something would go wrong with the operation. He had nightmares in which he saw his career crash and burn in the squalor of Seaman Street.

    In spite of his trepidation, he finally selected the supervisors for the Seaman Street Operation. Lt. Hanlon seemed reasonably competent, but he had an irritating habit of turning everything into a joke. A sense of humor was good—even desirable in police work—but *his* career didn't hang in the balance every time a cop did something crazy. Then there was Lt. Barry with his placid, imperturbable manner. He'd demonstrated his abilities as a good Operations Coordinator, but it remained to be seen if he'd be any help in planning what promised to be a very delicate street operation. Sgt. Seidel was a good street cop, but he was also a loose cannon. Sgt. Labonte was a bull in a China shop who, in three short years in the precinct, had managed to alienate every cop in the command. Sgt. Henry Engle was the best of his sergeants, but he was much too quiet and reticent. He lacked the "take-charge" attitude required of a good patrol supervisor.

Leland's plan to clean up Seaman Street would require imagination, initiative, and energy. Now, he sat behind his desk studying the two lieutenants and three sergeants he'd selected for this assignment with barely disguised disappointment. He seriously doubted these supervisors were up to the task, but they were all he had.

"Gentlemen, I've called this meeting because I want to brief you on my plan to clean up Seaman Street."

Hanlon's chuckle broke the stunned silence.

Leland glared at the lieutenant. "Did I say something amusing?"

Hanlon reddened. "No, Boss. It's just that I've been in this precinct for almost nine years now and Seaman Street was a cesspool before I got here. I've worked for five COs. Every one of them tried to clean it up and every one of them failed. Nothing personal, but it's like trying to keep pigeons from crapping on statues. It can't be done."

Leland wasn't surprised by Hanlon's negative, albeit crude, assessment of the problem. He turned to Engle. "Sergeant, what do you think?"

Engle rubbed his bald pate. "I'd like to see it cleaned up. It needs to be cleaned up," he said more forcefully. "But, Lt. Hanlon has a point. No one's been able to do it in the past."

Leland queried the other sergeants and each of them echoed Engle's opinion.

"Lieutenant Barry, what do you think?"

Barry fixed Leland with his serene blue eyes. "It depends on your plan, Captain. Token drug busts and special attention from sector cars isn't going to hack it. You can't stop arterial hemorrhaging with a Band-Aid."

"What do you suggest?"

"Major surgery," Barry said without hesitation. "A concerted buy-and-bust effort using our people, the Narcotics Division, and anyone else we can get."

"Think that'll do it?"

"That'll just be the beginning. Then comes the hard part: Keeping the street clean. And that means extra and continuous police presence in the area." Barry's eyes never left Leland's. "You know we're short on personnel, Cap. Are you prepared to commit to long-term special attention in that area?"

Leland knew that everything Barry said was true. It would take a huge commitment of manpower to keep Seaman Street clean after the initial sweep. He knew he'd have to do it, he just didn't know how. "I'll do whatever it takes to keep Seaman Street clean," he said. "That's the only way we're going to take back the streets of this precinct."

Barry nodded, but he still looked dubious. "Then it just might work, Captain. What's your plan?"

"First, we begin by gathering intelligence on everything we know about the block. Where do we get that information?"

"Our sector cars are a good source," Hanlon volunteered. "They know the people on the street."

"All right, Lieutenant. That'll be your assignment. Start gathering information from them. I want to know who the good guys and the bad guys are."

"Why the good guys?"

"I intend to enlist their support."

Hanlon grunted. "Vera Roland is supposed to be one of the good guys, Cap, but she'd pour a glass of water on a drowning cop."

"That kind of negative thinking doesn't help," Leland said sharply.

"We'll need Narcotics to do the buy-and-busts," Barry said, verbally stepping between the two men. "From past experience, I can tell you it's going to be a hassle getting them to go along with a precinct project like this."

"I'll handle Narcotics," Leland said. "Their role will be to ID the major players and make the arrests. Our job will be to provide support, traffic and crowd control. Can anyone think of anything else?"

"Helicopters," Seidel said.

"Why?"

"There's going to be a lot of cops on the street. If we don't cover the high ground, they're gonna drop shit on us. They always do."

Leland made a note. "I'll contact Aviation for aerial support. Okay, that's it for now. Start thinking about this operation. If you see any problems, or you think we need to do anything else, let me know immediately."

After the others left, Barry came back into the office. "Captain, does Chief Hightower know about this?"

"Not yet."

Barry's eyebrows went up. "You think that's a good idea?"

"I know what I'm doing, Lieutenant. I want every *i* dotted and every *t* crossed before I tell the chief about my plans. That's what's known as completed staff work."

~~

Lafferty was the last one from the four-to-twelve to get to Corr's. Reece looked up from his beer. "Hey, pard, where you been?"

Lafferty elbowed his way to the bar. "Friar Tuck. He gave me another lecture about low summons activity."

"So what are you pissed about?" Reece said. "Engle is right. You don't write summonses."

"I know. I just wish he'd give me the lecture on company time, not mine." He threw a ten on the bar. "Paddy, give me a beer. I'm dying here." He gulped down half the bottle and slammed it on the bar. "Hey, wait'll you hear what Captain Chaos is up to." He waited until everyone gathered around. "Chaos is gonna clean up Seaman Street," he whispered out of the side of his mouth.

Lafferty's announcement drew a collective groan from the group.

"How?" Mazzeo asked.

"The works. Narcotics, surveillance, undercover buys."

Reece shook his head. "Didn't anyone tell Leland it can't be done?"

Lafferty shrugged. "Who can tell Captain Chaos anything?"

"This gonna be a narcotics operation?" Mazzeo asked.

"Yeah. We get to handle crowd control and run interference for the narcs."

"Great," Oliver said. "Dust off your riot helmets, guys. We're gonna need them."

"I don't get it," Reece said. "There are so many harmless things he could do to make it look like he's running a tight precinct. Why would he take on the one problem that could cost him his command?"

"Because Leland is like Adam and Eve in the Garden story in the Bible," Lafferty said solemnly. "In Paradise, every day was payday. All they had to do was stay away from the apple. But no, they had to go after that fucking apple. Seaman Street is Leland's apple."

There was a startled silence. Everyone assumed that Lafferty had never heard of the Bible.

Reece put his arm around his partner's shoulder. "Billy, I didn't know you were religious."

Lafferty shrugged his arm away. "I'm not. I once spent two months trying to get into the pants of a Sunday school teacher."

Oliver grinned. "You score?"

"Nah. I lasted through Genesis and half of Exodus before she realized what I was after. She told me to take a fucking hike. Not very Christian, you ask me."

Oliver looked at his watch and downed the rest of his beer. "I gotta get home." As he scooped up his change, he said to the others, "I don't know about you guys, but I just hope it's my day off when this Seaman Street shit gets underway."

~~

Leland spent the next several days on the telephone trying to line up his support personnel. The Narcotics Division was his first obstacle and it almost proved to be insurmountable. He'd called the commanding officer of the Narcotics Division, Deputy Chief Alex Duncan, and explained his operation. The chief, who fervently believed that saying *yes* to any request was bound to cause him grief, was unsympathetic and adamant. He had a list of priority operations extending into next year and, given his shortage of personnel, there was no way he could spare people. "Maybe next year," he said as he hung up.

It was politically risky going over a deputy chief's head, but Leland had no choice. He needed the Narcotics Division to pull this off. He flipped through the department's telephone directory and found the telephone number for Thomas Wheeler, the commanding officer of OCCB. The Organized Crime Control Bureau encompassed both the Public Morals Division and the Narcotics Division, and Thomas Wheeler—Duncan's boss—owed Leland a favor.

Two years earlier, Wheeler, then the borough commander of Brooklyn, had presided over an unruly anti-abortion demonstration, which had resulted in massive arrests, injuries to both police and demonstrators, and widespread coverage in the papers. An apoplectic Chief Drum, who'd been watching the demonstration on TV, had instructed Leland to call Wheeler, who was still at the scene of the disturbance, and demand an Unusual forthwith.

Wheeler was a good street commander, but he was also a notoriously poor report writer. Without his support personnel—especially the sergeant at the borough office who wrote all his communications—he was helpless. Leland recognized the chief's dilemma and told him to give him a verbal report over the telephone. Then Leland wrote up the Unusual and gave it to Drum. Drum was so pleased that he personally called Wheeler to congratulate him on one of the best Unusuals he'd ever read. A grateful Wheeler called Leland later to thank him and assure him that he had a friend for life. Now, as Leland dialed the number, he hoped Wheeler's definition of "life" was something longer than two years.

∽∽

Later that afternoon, a grumpy Chief Duncan, the CO of the Narcotics Division, called Leland back. "I've been instructed to cooperate with you," he said icily. "Tell me what you want and when you want it."

Everything was falling into place nicely. Duncan had agreed, however reluctantly, to provide narc undercover "buy" cops and video equipment to covertly surveil the area first. Identifying the dealers, their habits, and drop locations, would be essential to procuring the necessary arrest warrants. Then, when they knew who the bad guys were, and where they were, it was just a matter of sweeping them up.

In spite of his earlier misgivings, Lt. Hanlon entered into Operation Seaman Street with genuine enthusiasm. He instructed his cops to talk to their informants and learn what they could about Seaman Street. Then he debriefed them and added bits and pieces of intelligence to his file and, in the process, amassed an impressive thirty-page Who's Who dossier on Seaman Street.

Hanlon and Barry sat quietly while Leland finished reading the thick report. He closed the book and slid it across the desk. "Nice work, Lieutenant Hanlon."

"Thanks, Cap. It wasn't hard. Every cop in the command is getting excited about this. We haven't done anything proactive in quite awhile."

"Well"—Leland tapped the thick report—"this is a start."

"What's next?" Barry asked.

"It's time to get the chief's permission."

"That's not going to be easy," Barry said.

"Sure it will," Leland said with confidence. "We've put together a great plan. We have Narcotics on board. We've thought of every contingency. All the chief has to do is approve it."

∽∽

Hightower's frog-eyes bulged over the top of his reading glasses. "You want to do *what*?"

A nervous Leland stood rigidly at attention in front of Hightower's desk and said it again. "I want to do a buy-and-bust operation on Seaman Street. It's the worst drug location in the precinct," he added quickly.

He pointed at the thick, thirty-seven-page report sitting on Hightower's desk, which he'd sent to the chief two days earlier. "Sir, I think that report explains fully what I want to do and how I intend to do it."

"I've read it," Hightower snapped. He took off his reading glasses, rubbed the bridge of his nose, and put the glasses back on. "Sit down, Captain."

Leland sat down.

Hightower patted the thick report with a massive hand. "Very thorough report. I think the management books call this completed staff work."

Leland nodded, surprised that Hightower knew that management term.

"How'd you get Tommy Wheeler to go along with this?"

Leland shrugged. "I just explained to the chief what I wanted and he agreed." He tried to read Hightower's face to see if he was buying it, but the expressionless face revealed nothing.

Hightower flipped through the report. "Helicopters, video surveillance, coordinated sweep—" he looked up at Leland—"what, no napalm?"

Leland smiled tentatively, not sure if the remark was meant to be funny or sarcastic.

Hightower pushed the report away from him as though it were a dead rat. "Why do you want to do this, Captain?"

"As I've said, Chief, Seaman Street is the worst narcotics location in my—"

"*Bull dust.* What's the real reason?"

It suddenly occurred to Leland that Hightower probably knew all about last month's raucous Community Board meeting. "I sort of promised some people I'd clean up the area."

"*You* promised? *You* promised to commit the resources of the Narcotics Division, the Aviation Unit, and God knows how many cops to a narcotics sweep in *my* borough?"

A vision of Lt. Barry saying, ""You think that's a good idea?" flashed before Leland's eyes. Once again, the Operations Coordinator had been right. In hindsight, Leland realized it had been a tactical blunder not to get Hightower on board first. But now, he was too deep in the hole to climb out. "Isn't that what they're there for?" he said valiantly. "To give support to patrol?"

"That's not what I'm talking about. You let some rabble-rousing bigmouth goad you into overreacting to a problem that's epidemic in this city. My God, man, damn near every precinct in this city has a Seaman Street. What do you think the Narcotics Division does all day? Sit around waiting for hotshot precinct captains to point out narcotics-prone locations?"

"But Seaman Street is in *my* precinct, Chief."

"You ever hear of proper department channels, Captain?"

"Yes, sir."

"Well, you could have fooled me. Do you call going over the head of Chief Duncan proper channels? Do you call consulting me *last* on this proper channels?"

Leland's normal cautiousness gave way to righteous indignation. "Would you have given me permission to put this plan together, Chief?"

Hightower's bulging eyes narrowed. "I would have asked you a couple of questions first. For example, Captain, have you considered all the things that can go wrong with an operation like this? Have you made contingency plans?"

"I've thought this plan through very carefully. I can't think of anything that can go wrong."

Hightower removed his reading glasses and tossed them on the desk. "Leland, that's the dumbest thing I've ever heard. You're going to have a few dozen cops out there with guns. Some of the bad guys will have guns. A lot can go wrong."

Leland knew that. That's why he'd spent so much time working out his plan. His thirty-seven-page report covered every possible contingency. But he also knew there was one thing he couldn't plan for: the unexpected. And now Hightower was going to beat him over the head with that possibility. Like a true bureaucrat, he was going to take the easy way out and cancel the operation. How could he face Vera Roland? Worse, how could he face the supervisors and men in the Five-five? A man who couldn't keep his word had no right to lead. If Hightower didn't remove him from command, he would have to request it himself.

"Does that mean the answer is no?" he asked bleakly.

Hightower studied him for a long time. Finally, he said, "I didn't say that. In spite of what you think, Captain, this report is not completed staff work. Have you made arrangements with the local hospital to deal with the possibility of gunshot wounds? Are you using only experienced cops and supervisors on this operation? What time of the night are you going to do this? Too early in the evening and you risk the safety of the working-class people who will be coming home at that hour. Too late and you risk missing your targets."

After a half-dozen more questions that Leland hadn't thought of, Hightower tossed the report back across the desk. "Before I make a decision, give me satisfactory answers to those questions."

A relieved, if somewhat chastened, Leland drove back to the precinct to rework the report and answer each and every question put forth by the chief. He was determined, more than ever, to pull off this operation without a hitch.

~~

Sgt. Cox, the Narcotics Division supervisor in charge of video surveillance, sat across the desk in Leland's office and gave him the bad news. "Captain, I thought our targets were supposed to be outsiders."

"That's what I was told." He didn't mention that it was Vera Roland who'd told him that only outsiders came into Seaman Street to sell drugs.

Cox slid an envelope containing grainy eight-by-ten photos across the desk. "We've targeted three dealers. They all live on the block. Most of their customers are neighborhood people, too."

Leland was stunned by this news. The public relations aspect of this operation had suddenly taken a negative tilt. Locking up outsiders was positive PR. People resented strangers coming into their neighborhood and destroying it. But arresting neighborhood people was an explosive proposition. How would mothers and fathers react to seeing their sons handcuffed and arrested? There was no way to do this without inflaming the emotions of people who, all too often, saw the police as the enemy. Leland's operation would only underscore that belief.

As if reading Leland's mind, Cox said, "Locking up locals can get real messy, Cap. I can picture the headlines describing the perps: "Good to his mother; honor student; practically accepted to Harvard; always walks the dog. Did I get them all?"

Leland nodded. The sergeant had indeed recited the mindless platitudes all too often generated by the arrest of neighborhood local thugs.

"Cap, you still want to go through with this?"

Just this morning, he'd gotten Chief Hightower's permission to proceed. Now it was his call to go ahead or call off the operation. He didn't hesitate. "Yes, it's a go."

Cox stood up. "Okay, Boss. Let me know when you're ready."

~~

Lt. Hanlon shouted *"Attention!"* when Leland walked into the muster room and the idle, nervous chatter stopped. Leland's eyes swept across the couple of dozen men and women seated in front of him.

The precinct cops sat on one side of the room; the Narcotics Division people the other. It wasn't just the civilian clothes that set the members of the Narcotics Division apart from his uniformed cops. The scruffy clothing, long hair, beards, and shoulder holsters were all part of a carefully cultivated image to set the Narc cop apart from lowly street cops. Leland looked into the proud, mostly youthful eyes of the men and women and wondered why they risked their lives breaking down doors in the pursuit of drug arrests.

"Captain Purdy," Leland said, "why don't you give us a rundown on what you and your people plan to do?"

The CO of the Narcotics teams was seated in the back of the room checking the warrants with Sgt. Cox. He came to the front of the room and pointed at a map of Seaman Street. "We're primarily after three targets—all dealers who operate in this block. Each team is assigned a perp. We're hoping all three will be on the street. If not, we'll go for the ones at home first. Then we'll take the others in the street."

"What about customers?" Seidel asked.

"If we pick up some customers in the process, that's gravy." Purdy grinned. "It all goes on the sheet at the end of the month."

Purdy's reference to arrest numbers made Leland uneasy. In spite of what the department said, numbers—or quotas, as the newspapers were fond of calling them—were the yardsticks upon which performance was measured. Designating a specific number of arrests, or summonses, smacked of quotas, and it had become a sore spot and a bone of contention between the cops and the brass. "Getting on the sheet," Leland felt, was something that a supervisor should not have mentioned in the presence of subordinates. But this was not the time to discuss it.

Leland said to Lt. Hanlon, "Tell us about the uniform end of this operation."

Hanlon went to the map. "At the signal from Captain Purdy, we'll seal off each end of the block with radio cars and uniformed cops. Two cars will move into the block to remove possible arrestees. Two squads of officers on foot will sweep the sidewalks of all onlookers and generally keep the peace."

"I know you've all been instructed in your specific assignments," Leland said. "Are there any questions?" When there were none, he said, "Be careful out there. I don't want anyone getting hurt." As soon as he said it, he remembered Gloria's warning about Vera Roland: *Ten cuidado.*

After the cops left, he stood alone in the muster room staring at the map. The plan was simple enough. Everyone knew what they had to do. What could go wrong? Before he could dwell any further on that question, a police officer appeared in the doorway.

"Cap, your car's ready."

Leland turned away from the map. "Okay," he said, buttoning up his uniform jacket. "Let's go."

~~

In another day and time, Seaman Street had once been a respectable neighborhood block. The pre-war five-story tenements that lined both sides of the street had been populated by blue-collar Irish, Italian, and Jewish families who took pride in their neighborhood. It would not have been unusual to see housewives sweeping not only the sidewalks in front of their buildings, but the streets as well.

But all that began to change after the war. Men coming back from Europe and Asia wanted a better life for their families. Dreams of a small home in the country with a white picket fence and a backyard where kids could play without fear of being run over by cars and trucks became the goal for men and women starting new families. The GI Bill allowed these men, who otherwise would have gone back to their old jobs as truck drivers and subway conductors and remain trapped in the old neighborhood, to go to college and obtain professional credentials. Well-paying jobs, coupled with low-cost Veteran Administration mortgage loans, allowed these men to pursue their dream homes in the suburbs.

As they were replaced by new minorities, landlords sold out to slumlords, and the cancer of poverty and neglect soon began to eat away at the old neighborhood until Seaman Street became what it was today, a rundown, drug-infested street like thousands more throughout the city.

Captain Purdy and his team of four cops parked their unmarked car in a street adjourning Seaman Street and followed a pre-arranged route through a cellar and backyard that led them into the basement of 394, the tenement in which David Bell, their target, lived.

A disheveled, bearded black man wearing a torn sweatshirt stepped out of the shadows. "Anything yet?" Purdy whispered to his undercover cop.

"No. Bell went into his apartment over an hour ago and hasn't come out yet."

Purdy frowned. He would have preferred to take Bell out on the street. Apartments were dangerous. Too many unexpected things could happen when you had to rush into an unseen, confined space. But he and his team would have to play the hand dealt them.

"Anyone with him?"

"Just his old lady."

Purdy had committed her rap sheet to memory: Numerous convictions for prostitution, possession of drugs, and petty theft. No violent crimes. At least not yet, he thought glumly.

He turned to his team, three men and a young woman newly assigned to the squad. He'd had reservations about taking her along on this raid, but, what the hell, she had to learn the job sooner or later. "Okay," he whispered, "this is it. Keep your cool. I don't want anyone getting hurt. Remember, if there's a cop in front of you keep your goddamn gun pointed at the floor. Any questions?"

There were none. He studied each of the young, earnest faces in the gloom. In spite of their grim smiles, he knew they were afraid. And that was good. Fear—controlled fear—kept one alert. And alive.

Silently, the captain led the way up the stairs to the second floor. Bell lived in the rear of the building. Purdy had men stationed on the roofs and in the backyard below in the event Bell slipped out the back window.

The cops stood to either side of the door. Purdy put his ear to the door. All he heard was the muffled sound of a TV. Stepping aside, he put up one finger and silently mouthed the word "one." When he put his third finger up, two burly cops, firmly gripping a battering ram, rushed the door, which gave way with a loud snap of splintering wood.

Purdy was the first one through the door. He saw Bell rushing toward the window and dropped into a combat stance. *"Police!"* he shouted. *Don't move."*

Bell had one leg out the window, but he hesitated when he saw cops standing in the yard below. Two sets of hands yanked him back into the apartment, threw him to the floor, and handcuffed him.

"Where's the woman?" Purdy yelled.

"Right here." Police Officer Mark Stephens led the handcuffed woman out of the bathroom. Behind him, a grinning Police Officer Margie Cioffi came out holding a dripping wet plastic baggie. "She was trying to flush the works down the toilet, Cap, but I grabbed them first."

Purdy grunted with satisfaction. The little white girl from Long Island had stuck her hand into a filthy toilet bowl. Maybe she'd make a good narc cop after all.

"And the bowl was loaded," Stephens announced with admiration.

When cops busted a drug den, drug dealers routinely tried to flush the works down the toilet. But cops had quickly figured out that tactic. At least one member of a raiding party was tasked with getting to the toilet and snatching the evidence before it disappeared into the city's sewer system. Bu the drug dealers escalated. Some smart-ass drug dealers hit upon the idea of "loading" the bowl with copious amounts of human excrement. A squeamish cop might hesitate before sticking his hand into a swirling mass of turds. To a drug dealer that moment's hesitation could mean the difference between a felony bust and a chump misdemeanor charge.

Purdy nodded to Cioffi. "You did good, Margie. Go wash up."

While the team read their prisoners their rights, Purdy stepped into the bedroom and spoke softly into his mic. "Team leader to Team Two."

"Team Two," Sgt. Cox answered.

"Subject number one under arrest. Proceed with assignment."

"Ten-four," Cox answered.

Purdy idly stared out Bell's dirty window at an apartment across the yard. An elderly woman was talking to her cat as she prepared dinner at the stove. He tried to imagine what Cox and his team were doing. Their target, Adam Jackson, lived in a similar tenement up the block from 394. He knew they faced the same problems his team had faced; get the door down and collar the perp before he could escape or destroy the evidence. And do all that without anyone getting hurt.

After what seemed like a lifetime, Cox's voice, breathless from exertion, shattered the silence. "Team Two to Team leader."

Purdy held the radio to his mouth. "Go ahead."

"Subject not in apartment. Repeat, subject not in apartment."

Purdy swore softly. He'd never worked on a raid that went exactly as planned. Why should this be different? It was time to move on. He keyed the mic. "Team leader to Team Three."

"Team Three," Detective Henry Topple answered.

"Did you hear that last transmission?"

"Affirmative." Topple, the undercover cop who'd made several buys from Adam Jackson, sat in an unmarked car at the top of the block with his partner, Police Officer Helen Webster, who was posing as his girlfriend.

"Any sign of him on the street?"

"Webster was watching Jackson through binoculars. Affirmative. He just got out of a car and he's on the stoop of 439."

"Okay," Purdy responded. "Make your move. The rest of the team stand by and be ready to move in."

Helen Webster started the battered Olds and slowly began to move down the block. Topple switched off the radio and stuffed it and the binoculars under the front seat.

As they approached Jackson, the ever-suspicious drug dealer eyed the unfamiliar car and stood poised on the balls of his feet, prepared to bolt at the first sign of trouble.

The car stopped and Topple rolled the window down. "Hey, my man, how you doin'?"

Jackson recognized a paying customer and came down the stairs away from the safety of the doorway. "Yo, what's happenin'?"

"I need some shit, baby. What you got?"

Helen Webster waited until Jackson was almost at the car before she started to open the door. As she did so, Lt. Hanlon, following Purdy's instructions, gave the word for the two radio cars to move into position at either end of the block, effectively sealing it off.

Adam Jackson, possessing the cunning of a jungle predator, felt the hair on the back of his neck rise. He riveted his attention on the woman. *Something wasn't right.* The bitch was smiling at him. A cocky, self-confident smile. Junkie's girlfriends didn't look like that. *Something was definitely not right here.* He glanced up the block and saw a police car roll into the intersection. He looked down the block. Another one was blocking that end of the street. His eyes swept back to her. *Cops!*

His first thought was to waste these two double-dealing motherfuckers, but his instinct for survival took precedence. Without a word, he spun around and sprinted toward the safety of the tenement. He heard the bitch shout. *"Police! Don't move."*

Without stopping, he yanked a TEC-10 from his waistband and fired a burst over his shoulder. He heard pops of gunfire behind him. Suddenly he was hobbling and there was a stinging in his left leg. He looked down and was surprised to see blood splattered on his $200 designer jeans. Then his leg buckled and he fell sprawling across the steps. Before he could turn and empty the clip into his pursuers, the gun was kicked out of his hand and the weight of several bodies piled on top of him, grinding his face into the broken concrete steps. He felt his arms being yanked behind him and heard the ratcheting sound of handcuffs. The cold metal bit into his wrists.

"Motherfucker," he whispered to the concrete steps. "*Motherfucker!*"

The sound of gunfire had the effect of firing a shot in a cave. Like startled bats, people erupted from tenement doorways. From above, dozens of windows flew open.

From his vantage point seated in a radio car at the top of the block, Leland had been anxiously watching Topple and Webster approach Jackson. At the sound of automatic gunfire, his stomach knotted. Then he watched breathlessly as the undercover cop, his female partner, and backups chase and subdued the drug dealer. It was only when he heard the radio transmission that the perp had been wounded did he begin to breathe again. Then, he watched in dismay as dozens of people began to flood into the street. And he knew the night's operation had just begun.

He keyed his mic. "Lt. Hanlon, get your people into the block. Let's clear the street."

Radio cars with flashing lights rolled down the street as police officers on foot began moving down both sidewalks. Leland's instructions had been clear: They were there simply to keep the peace. Hopefully their uniformed presence would prevent flare-ups. As he made his way down the block on foot, he was pleased to see that his officers, sometimes stern and serious, sometimes joking with onlookers, were doing a good job of keeping the lid on a potentially tinderbox situation. An intense Police Officer Ronnie Newbert, nervously shoving her wire-rimmed glasses back on to her nose, explained what was going on to an angry group of people outside 394.

So far, so good. Then Leland heard the *womp womp* of the helicopter and looked up. Flying no more than a hundred feet above the rooftops, the helicopter slowly made a pass down the block. Leland saw several angry residents pointing up and he almost regretted asking for the helicopter. It only added to the circus atmosphere and now he was afraid its presence might inflame the crowd.

He keyed the mic. "Precinct CO to Aviation Unit."

"Aviation Unit here."

"Pull up, pull up and do not, repeat, do not activate your spotlight."

The helicopter peeled off and rose into the sky. Leland continued down the street. Fifty feet in front of him, the Narcotics team hustled a handcuffed Jackson to an unmarked car and the car quickly sped out of the block. One down, thought Leland, one to go.

As if on cue, Captain Purdy and his team appeared on the stoop of 394 with their manacled prisoner. Another unmarked car screeched to a stop in front of the building and David Bell was hauled away before people on the block even knew what was going down.

Hanlon rushed up to Leland. "Looks like it went pretty well, Boss," he said with a big grin.

"Yes, it does." In his head, Leland had already started writing the Unusual for the borough. He could almost picture Hightower scowling at the last line of the report: *Except for one wounded prisoner, there were no other injuries and no incidental arrests.*

That pleasant thought was suddenly shattered by the sound of an exploding windshield. Leland wheeled toward the sound and saw Police Officers Oliver and Elliott scramble out of their car and sprint toward a building. The windshield was gone. A large chunk of concrete had crushed the car's roof.

"Where'd it come from?" Leland yelled at Sgt. Seidel, who'd been standing right next to the car. The sergeant ran toward the building with surprising speed. "From the roof," he called over his shoulder.

Just then another concrete block shattered on the sidewalk near Leland. Like exploding shrapnel, large chunks of concrete flew in all directions, peppering surrounding parked cars. He felt a sharp pain as a piece the size of a golf ball ricocheted off his ankle.

As though it had been a signal, a shower of missiles came flying off the rooftops. On the street, teenagers, whooping in delight, picked up rocks and started pelting cops with them.

Leland hobbled toward the nearest doorway as a half-dozen cops rushed into adjoining buildings. Leland keyed his mic. "Aviation Unit, this is the Precinct CO. We're taking debris off the roof. Middle of the block."

The helicopter roared overhead and the megawatt spotlight came on, bathing the street in a harsh, surreal white light. As the helicopter dropped lower and lower, the engine noise became a deafening roar.

Leland stuffed a handkerchief into his blood-soaked sock and stared numbly at the pandemonium around him. The light from the swaying helicopter cast eerie shadows across the street and buildings. People and cops ran at each other in waves. Rocks flew through the air; the roar of the helicopter muted the sounds of screams and breaking glass.

Leland hobbled out into the middle of the street and motioned to Lt. Hanlon. The lieutenant hastily formed two ranks and he, Leland, and a squad of cops, dodging rocks and bottles, slowly moved down the sidewalks clearing people as they went. Skirmishes sprung up between knots of people shouting about their rights and cops determined to sweep the streets clear.

The throbbing pain in his ankle was all but forgotten as a stunned Leland helplessly watched his well-planned operation—and his career—unravel.

∾∾

Five floors above, Oliver and Elliott rushed out onto the roof. Above, the spiraling helicopter's megawatt searchlight cast expanding and contracting shadows across the rooftop, making it impossible for them to see anyone.

Oliver dabbed at his cut cheek with a bloody handkerchief. "You see anyone?" he shouted over the *womp womp* of the helicopter.

The tall black cop, shielding his eyes from the bright light above, shook his head.

Suddenly, the helicopter stopped and hovered over a building three rooftops away. *"We have someone in sight,"* the helicopter spotter reported over the radio. *"Running west. Red jacket. Baseball cap."*

"He's coming this way," Elliott said.

Oliver squinted into the glaring light. "You see him?"

Elliot pointed. "Yeah, there, by that pigeon coop."

Now that he knew where to look, Oliver saw a figure hurdle a retaining wall between roofs. Two roofs behind the figure, he saw three uniformed cops chasing after him.

"Come on," he said, pulling Elliot behind the roof-landing wall. "If shooting starts, we don't want to be in the line of fire. If he gets this far, we'll take him."

The figure hopped over the wall onto their roof and sprinted toward the roof door. Oliver dropped into a combat stance and, pointing his automatic at the figure, shouted, "Freeze, motherfucker!"

The man, surprised by the appearance of the cop, skidded to a stop. Then, without warning—or logic—he lunged at Oliver. Oliver ducked and caught only a glancing blow to the head. He slammed the gun into the man's face and the man sank to his knees. Oliver, suddenly realizing that this was the guy who could have killed him and his partner with that concrete block, became enraged. He came down on the man's head with the butt of his weapon and the man fell flat against the tarred roof. Before he could do any more damage, Elliott threw his arms around his partner and dragged him away.

By now, the other cops were on the scene. Mazzeo quickly snapped his handcuffs on the prostrate man. An out-of-breath Lafferty stumbled up and stared down at the man. "Let's throw the motherfucker off the roof," he wheezed.

No one took the suggestion seriously, but they all saw the prisoner stiffen and decided to let him think about that possibility for a while.

A moment later, Sgt. Seidel and Charlie Reece ran out onto the roof. "You get him?" Seidel asked, gasping for air.

"Yeah," Mazzeo said. "It's Oliver's collar."

"Who is he?"

"I dunno," Oliver said. He rolled the prisoner over on his back and shined a flashlight into the bloodied face. In the glare of the flashlight, he was younger than he looked, probably no more than nineteen. Oliver grabbed the youth by his collar and yanked him to a sitting position. "What's your name, scumbag?"

The groggy prisoner shook his head. "Anthony," he said," Anthony… Roland."

"Holy shit!" Lafferty said, peering down at the prisoner. "It's Vera Roland's kid."

~~

At exactly seven-thirty the next morning, Leland was standing stiffly at attention in front of Chief Hightower's desk. He'd stayed on the scene all night to make sure there were no further flare-ups. Then he went back to the station house around six and was cleaning up when he'd gotten the forthwith to the borough office.

Hightower finished reading Leland's Unusual and looked up. "I can't think of anything that can go wrong. I believe that's what you said." From his poker face it was impossible to tell if he was angry or just plain disgusted.

Leland nodded silently. He remembered uttering that brash statement, but it seemed like a very long time ago.

Hightower read from the report. "Two injured perps, four injured police officers, one damaged radio car, seven civilian complaints—so far," he added ominously.

Leland was too numb from lack of sleep to be afraid. It was all over anyhow. Hightower had given him the rope to hang himself and he'd done an admirable job of it. Surprisingly, at this moment he didn't care. He just wanted Hightower to tell him he was transferred and get it over with so he could go home and get some sleep.

"We also arrested three major drug dealers," Leland said with the abandonment of one who knows all is lost.

Hightower's eyes dropped to the report. "It says two here."

"As I was leaving the station house to come over here, Narcotics brought in the third man. They collared him at the Port Authority Bus Terminal. He was about to board a bus to North Carolina."

Hightower grunted noncommittally. "I got a call from Vera Roland this morning. Damn, that woman has an irritating voice." In spite of himself, Leland had to smile, recalling a voice that sounded like fingernails being scrapped across a chalkboard. Hightower continued. "She's made a civilian complaint against you alleging racism, harassment, police cover-up, and Lord knows what else. What do you have to say about that?"

Three months ago, Leland would have been stunned at the thought of getting a civilian complaint, but now he was just too tired to care. "We didn't target her son, Chief. We didn't even know who he was until he told us."

"Sit down, Captain." Leland was caught off guard by Hightower's disarming tone. Hightower rocked back in his swivel chair. "It wasn't pretty, but essentially you accomplished your mission."

"Yes, sir. I believe we did," Leland answered cautiously.

"However, you've only won the battle not the war."

"Sir?"

"The drug dealers will be back. The lure of money is too strong. They'll be back unless you keep them out."

"I'm not going to let them come back," Leland said with a conviction that surprised even him. A moment ago he'd given up, believing that his patrol career was finished. But he didn't want it to be over. He and his cops had done something good for the neighborhood and he wanted to stay and finish what he'd started.

"Cleaning up Seaman Street has been good for morale," Leland said tentatively. "Charlie Reece, the PBA delegate, came to me last night and thanked me. He said it's been a long time since they've done something that they've been proud of. My cops are feeling good about themselves again."

Hightower grunted. "Go on home and get some sleep."

As Leland reached the door, Hightower said, "Oh, Captain—"

Here comes the axe, Leland thought.

"All and all, that was a decent job you and your people did last night. Well done, Captain."

A stunned Leland could only nod in thanks.

Chapter Twenty-Six

Richard Leland drove back to the precinct feeling good about himself and his cops. It was true that the Seaman Street operation had not been a textbook example of a well-run drug sweep. Still, they'd arrested the targeted drug dealers and kept the collateral damage to a minimum. Hightower's praise, while not effusive, put the stamp of approval on what had been a very difficult—not to mention a potentially career-busting—gamble. Maybe the precinct was beginning to shape up after all. Maybe he was beginning to make a difference. Maybe there was light at the end of the tunnel.

Or maybe not. His euphoria was short-lived when he turned into the precinct block and saw the Rev. Munyika and his followers blocking the street in front of the precinct.

Lt. Barry stood on the station house steps shouting instructions through a megaphone to a handful of frustrated cops. They were doing their best to move the demonstrators off the street and onto the sidewalk, but it was hopeless. The cops were no match for the unruly demonstrators who outnumbered them fifteen to one.

Munyika's voice, amplified by a megaphone, reverberated off the ancient tenement walls like the voice of an Old Testament Prophet. *Down with the fascist pigs! Stop racist brutality!"* he intoned. The demonstrators picked up the chant. *"Down with the fascist pigs! Stop racist brutality! Down with the fascist pigs! Stop racist brutality!"*

Leland pushed his way through the crowd toward Barry. "When did this start?" he shouted over the chanting.

"They just got here," Barry yelled in his ear. "I called the borough and requested the Task Force, but they said we should handle it ourselves."

"Call in all the sectors."

"I did."

Leland glared at Munyika with seething anger. This was uncalled for. Hadn't he asked Munyika to talk to him first? Hadn't he said that he would cooperate with whatever he wanted to do? Leland pushed his way through the hostile demonstrators and stopped in front of Munyika.

The Reverend looked down at Leland and clicked off his megaphone. "You really fucked up this time, Captain," he said chuckling. "*A Normandy invasion of Seaman Street*! What in the hell was you thinkin'?"

Leland ignored the sarcastic grin on Munyika's face. "I asked you to talk to me first," he shouted over the chanting. "This demonstration is unnecessary and unlawful. You don't have a permit to do this."

"No permit? Well, then I guess you'll just have to arrest all of us, Captain."

That was exactly what Munyika wanted, but Leland had no intention of throwing more fuel on the fire. "That won't be necessary," he said, trying to keep his anger under control.

Munyika clicked on his megaphone and pointed it in Leland's face. "*Stop the fascist pigs,*" his voice boomed out. "*Stop racist brutality.*"

It took almost an hour for the last of the sector cars to finish up their assignments and hurry back to the station house to assume crowd control. Munyika waited patiently until the last of the radio cars arrived and then turned off his megaphone. "That's it," he said to his assistants. "Tell everyone to go home."

From his office window, Leland watched in amazement as Munyika and his followers suddenly dispersed. Within five minutes, they were gone. Except for a couple of overturned garbage cans there was no indication that there had been a demonstration here.

Lt. Barry came into the office. "I called the borough and told them the demonstration is over."

Leland continued to look out the window. "Why did he leave?"

Barry shrugged. "No press coverage or maybe he just wanted to send you a message that he can disrupt your precinct anytime he wants."

"But he didn't disrupt anything."

"I'm afraid so, Cap. Now we have a two-hour backlog of jobs. The borough wants a full report on that and an Unusual on the demonstration."

Leland recalled the self-satisfied smile on Munyika's face as he watched more and more radio cars respond to the precinct. He knew if they were here, they couldn't be handling jobs in their sectors. His plan had been to disrupt the precinct and he'd done just that. There was no doubt in Leland's mind that he would do so again, and Leland didn't know what to do about it.

~~

Seidel had watched the demonstration from his office window. Now he was watching a teenager on the tenement roof across the street exercising pigeons. The kid was waving a long pole with a white rag attached to it as dozens of pigeons swooped and darted around him.

"I don't get it," he said to Stan Quigley and Tom Kohler, who were standing behind him. "Why would you pay good money to have pigeons shit on your head? You can go to any park in this city and they'll do it for free. It seems to me—" He stopped to watch the precinct detective car pull up in front of the station house. Two detectives got out and opened the back door. Alvin came out of the back seat in handcuffs. Seidel took the cigar out of his mouth. "Well, I'll be goddamned..."

Five minutes later, Seidel slipped into the squad office and peeked around the corner. Alvin was sitting in the holding pen looking askance at a transsexual cross-dresser who looked amazingly like Cher. Seidel darted across the open space and into the office of Lt. Angelo DeMarco, the precinct squad commander. DeMarco and Seidel had been detective partners in Midtown Manhattan for eight years.

DeMarco looked up from a report and shook his head. "Whatever you want, the answer is no."

"Who says I want anything?"

"I know that look, Marv. Either you just got laid or you want something. Clever detective that I am, I know you haven't gotten laid since the Spanish American War, so I deduce that you want something and the answer is no."

"What've you got Alvin for?"

DeMarco sighed and tossed the report into an overflowing 'in' basket. "What's it to you?"

"Don't give me that squad commander shit. I taught you everything you know."

"Yeah, and everything you taught me has gotten me into trouble." DeMarco sat back and looked up at his old partner. "Possible possession of stolen property."

"No shit? You got him good?"

"Not necessarily. The Four-four squad busted a burglar who's looking at heavy time. He coughed up a few names. Alvin was one of them."

"Are you gonna book him?"

"I'm waiting for a call from the DA to okay the warrants."

"If it's a no-go, Alvin walks?"

"Yeah."

"Do me a favor."

DeMarco picked up the report again. "No. I almost went to jail the last time I did you a favor."

Seidel sat on the edge of DeMarco's desk and pushed the report aside. "Angelo, I'm trying to close the Joy Lounge."

DeMarco held his head in his hands. "Marv, why don't you retire and go play golf in Florida and leave me alone?"

"If Alvin's gonna walk, just give me five minutes alone with him," Seidel explained.

"Are you nuts? Those days are over."

"I won't lay a finger on him. I just want to give him a good substantial scare."

DeMarco looked doubtful.

"Come on," Seidel said. "You of all people know how it works. You wrote the book on it."

DeMarco shrugged modestly. In his younger days, Angelo DeMarco had become a living legend for his ability to shake an admission out of a perp. And he did it without laying a finger on him. The nattily dressed detective would come into the interrogation room, smile at the perp, and say, "Look, I know you did it. You know you did it. Why don't you save us all a lot of time and trouble and just 'fess up?"

If a change of heart was not immediately forthcoming, he would ask everyone to leave the room. And then he would go into his act. The smile would fade, replaced by the vacant look of a contract killer. Then he'd make a big show of taking off his suit jacket and smoothing it before draping it across a chair. Then came the best part. He would undo a cufflink—Angelo DeMarco was probably the only detective in the NYPD who wore cufflinks on a daily basis—and carefully roll up his sleeve. He seldom got the second cufflink off before the perp had an epiphany and was suddenly struck with the urge to cooperate.

"It was the cufflinks," Seidel said. "That was a stroke of genius."

DeMarco smiled depreciatingly. "I think it was the whole effect. It took me a long time to perfect that act."

"Give me five minutes with him, Angelo."

DeMarco studied his mentor for a long time. "Okay. But only if we're gonna cut him loose."

"Absolutely. I'll be in my office."

~~

An hour later, DeMarco called. "The DA won't go along with the collar. You've got five minutes with Alvin, and then he's free to go."

Alvin was sitting alone in DeMarco's office when Seidel came in. Alvin eyed him warily. Seidel sat in DeMarco's seat and fired up a cigar. He took his time, studied the faint glowing ash, and said, "Alvin, you're in a whole heap of trouble."

"I didn't do nuthin'. I don't even know what the hell I'm doin' here."

"A snitch got his balls caught in a vice. He's willing to testify in court that you bought stolen property from him."

"Bullshit."

"We'll know soon enough. The judge just signed the search warrant. Even as we speak, the cops are on their way to toss your apartment."

Alvin's laughter shook his whole body. "They can search all they want. They ain't gonna find shit."

"Got rid of it already? Alvin, you're smarter than you look."

Alvin flashed a self-satisfied grin.

Seidel squinted at the fat man through a blue haze. "What about the kilo of coke?"

Alvin stopped smiling. "What you talkin' 'bout?" Then it hit him. That old sonofabitch sergeant was gonna flake him. "Goddamnit, Seidel. Don't you be trumping me with no damn kilo of coke. I got you the cop's gun. What the hell more do you want?"

"Who owns the Joy?"

Alvin glared at Seidel. "I do."

"You're only the front man. Who's bankrolling it?"

Alvin folded his arms. "I got nuthin' to say."

Seidel picked up the telephone receiver. "One phone call, Alvin. You tell me who the owner is and that kilo will disappear before the cops get there and you walk out of here. Otherwise, you're looking at hard time for a key."

By this time, Alvin was sweating profusely. He looked at Seidel. He looked at the telephone. "You're just shinin' me on," he said with little conviction.

Seidel stared back silently and puffed on his cigar. Sometimes saying nothing was the best way to keep the pressure on.

Alvin wiped his wet forehead with a handkerchief. He looked up at the cracked ceiling. "Thaddeus Archer," he whispered.

"You sure?"

"Yeah, I'm sure. Now make that damn phone call."

Seidel snatched up the phone and punched in a number. "It's me," he whispered into the telephone. "Deep six the key." He hung up and sat back. "Alvin, you're free to go."

Downstairs in the Anti-Crime office, Quigley stared at the telephone. "Who was it?" Kohler asked.

"Seidel. He told me to deep six the key."

"What key?"

"I don't know what the hell he's talking about."

~~

"Senator Thaddeus Archer, " Seidel said.

"He *does* own the Joy Lounge?" Leland looked at Seidel incredulously. "How do you know?"

"Alvin told me."

Leland was about to ask why Alvin had told him, but he was learning not to ask too many questions. "Are you sure?"

"I'm sure."

Leland fell back in his seat, relieved that he'd finally found out who owned the Joy. But now he realized he would have to do something about it and he wasn't sure what to do.

~~

For the rest of the week, he thought about how he should approach Archer. The senator kept a small office on Taylor Street, but Leland didn't think that would be a good place to confront him. Then, on Friday, a telephone message from the borough solved his dilemma. The message said there was to be groundbreaking ceremony on a new State Motor Vehicle Bureau office building next Monday. Archer and the mayor would be there and Leland was ordered to provide the detail.

Breaking ground on a new Department of Motor Vehicle office building lacked the cachet of erecting a hospital or a school, but Archer and the mayor were up for reelection and they both deemed it worthwhile to take the time to appear before a sparse and lackluster Bronx audience.

The speeches were over quickly and as soon as the photos were taken, the mayor jumped into his Escalade and fled back to the borough of Manhattan, which, as far as he was concerned, *was* New York City.

Leland waited for the last of Archer's constituents to leave before he approached.

"Senator Archer, how are you, sir?"

"Fine, Captain Leland, just fine," he said expansively, as though he were still talking to one of his constituents. "It's always a thrill to witness the beginning of a new building, don't you think?"

"And sometimes it's just as thrilling to see one close."

"I don't understand."

"The Joy Lounge."

Archer glared at Leland. "Captain, you are becoming quite tedious about this Joy Lounge," he said sternly. "I thought I made it clear the last time we spoke that you were squandering valuable resources on something that did not merit that kind of attention. I took into consideration that you were new to the precinct, but now you've been here long enough to know better. Frankly, I'm disappointed with your performance. I'm having lunch with the mayor tomorrow and I may suggest to him that the precinct could use new leadership."

In his previous life, Leland would have been struck dumb at the thought of a state senator bad-mouthing him to the mayor, but that was then and now was now.

"I know you own the Joy," Leland said softly.

Archer's face contorted first in anger, then dismay, and finally, just a flicker of fear. He took Leland's arm and led him into the alcove of a building. "For the record, I do not own that bar and I'll have your head on a platter if you spread that malicious falsehood."

Leland was taken aback by the vehemence in the senator's tone and suddenly had second thoughts about just how good Seidel's information really was. But it was too late to back down now. He looked the senator in the eye. "I have proof," he lied, "and I won't hesitate to hand it over to the press." In spite of his fear, he was enjoying Archer's discomfort. "During the cold war," he added, "I believe they called this a mutual assured destruction situation."

"Meaning?" Archer asked coldly.

"If I go down, you go down."

"What do you want?"

"I want the Joy Lounge closed. As the owner, you're the only one who can do that."

Archer straightened his tie and smoothed his jacket. The anger and the fear were gone. He was in control again. "I don't know what you're talking about, Captain."

He started to walk away, but Leland grabbed his arm. "You have one week, Senator."

Without a word, Archer pulled away and hurried to his waiting car.

Leland watched him go and wondered if he'd just hammered the last nail in his career. If Seidel was wrong, Archer would destroy him. Slowly, he walked to his waiting radio car. There was nothing he could do but wait for the axe to fall—or for the Joy Lounge to close.

∾∾

It took Hector Torres a painfully long time to make it down the cellar stairs to his basement. Before he'd been hurt, he would have hopped down the dozen stairs two at a time, but now that wasn't possible. He'd always liked to do everything quickly, which was why he found using a walker especially frustrating. He'd left the damn walker at the top of the stairs and, using the banister for assistance, had managed to make his way down to the basement without falling.

"Please come in. The doctor will see you now..."

He eased himself into his recliner, panting and dripping with sweat from the exertion. While he caught his breath, he glanced around the room admiring his handiwork. The finished basement—his pride and joy—had always been his favorite part of the house.

When he and Nancy had first moved into their new home, he didn't know a screwdriver from a hammer. Why should he? He'd had no need for tools growing up in the cramped tenement on 115th Street in Spanish Harlem.

But all that changed the day a building contractor told him it would cost him $5,000 to finish the basement. Stunned at the astronomical cost, he decided he would do it himself. First he talked to guys at the precinct and neighbors about what kind of tools he needed. Then he went to the library and read a mountain of books on how to finish a basement. It took the better part of a year to do the job and, surprisingly, it went without a hitch—if he didn't count the ceiling tiles that fell down because he'd forgotten to staple them.

Nancy always kidded him that he spent so much time in the basement that he was in danger of turning into a mushroom. The truth was he felt at peace here. It was a room he'd built with his own hands and he was surrounded by all the things that mattered to him. One wall was covered with family photos—now mostly little Maria and Nancy. Another wall was reserved for photos of him playing on various high school and precinct teams. Behind the bar on a shelf was a neat row of gleaming trophies that he'd won in track and baseball. His collection of Dixieland CDs, neatly stacked and catalogued, sat on a shelf he'd made especially for them.

Whoever heard of a Puerto Rican liking Dixieland? was the usual comment the first time someone saw his extensive collection. "What the hell." he'd reply with a wide grin, "we don't all have to like Tito Puente."

He looked for any excuse to hold parties in his newly finished basement—a holiday, a neighbor's birthday. He even had a Bastille Day party one July. His friends and neighbors affectionately called it "Hector's cave."

"I'm recommending you for a medical disability discharge…"

Hector blinked back tears and looked at photos on his "cop wall." There was a photo of him in his rookie grays. There was one of him at a Medal Day ceremony when he'd won a commendation for foiling a liquor store robbery. And there, clustered together, were photos of five years of precinct picnics. All the guys he'd worked with were there on that wall—Eddie Mazzeo, George Oliver, Jimmy Elliot, Peggy Garrigan, Sgt. Engle, Lt. Barry, and goofy Billy Lafferty making rabbit ears behind Charlie Reece's head in all five photos.

Since he'd been hurt, they'd kept in touch with phone calls and visits. Even the new CO, Captain Leland, stopped by every week. The guys called him Captain Chaos, but he didn't think that was a fair nickname. The captain seemed like a really nice guy. He always took some time to play with little Maria and he never failed to ask Nancy if there was anything he could do.

Hector knew the guys visited him to cheer him up, and he had to admit he got a chuckle hearing about Captain Chaos' latest screw up, but most of what they had to say was unintentionally painful. Listening to them talk about Seaman Street, arrests, the Munyika demonstrations, even the shadowy presence of IAB, made his heart hurt because he wasn't one of them anymore. He would never be a cop again. Not after today.

"I'm recommending you for a medical disability discharge…"

Hector put the letters he'd written to Nancy and baby Maria on the table in front of him. He hoped they would explain everything. He took his Glock out of its holster, ejected the magazine, wiped away a light coating of dust and slammed the magazine back into the gun. When he was working—*when he was still a cop*—he cleaned his guns at least once a week. But there had been no need to clean his guns since that December night.

He stared at the weapon in his hand. Since the chief surgeon had given him the bad news, he'd given a lot of thought to what he was about to do. He knew all the arguments—both pro and con—by heart. It was the coward's way out. It was giving up. And worse, despair, he knew, was a mortal sin in his Catholic religion.

But there was the other side of the argument. His eyesight was getting worse. The ophthalmologist tried to be encouraging, but Hector was a cop—at least he used to be—and he was able to read the truth in the doctor's eyes. He was going blind.

He might be able to live with being blind, but he couldn't live with being a cripple, too. He'd lost all sensation in his right leg and it dragged behind him like an appendage that didn't belong to his body. There was neural damage. Where would that lead? Would he become a vegetable? Of course not, the doctors lied. He couldn't bear the thought of subjecting Nancy to bathing him, changing him, taking him to the bathroom as though he were a helpless baby.

There was insurance. Nancy and Maria would be provided for. God knows they would be better off financially without him.

He worked the slide, driving a round into the chamber. He picked up a bullet from the pile on the table and studied it. It was so small. It was hard to believe that something so small could end his life. End a world.

He took one last look around his beloved finished basement, put the barrel in his mouth, and pulled the trigger.

~~

Billy Lafferty and Charlie Reece came out of a tenement across the street from the Joy Lounge. They'd just adjudicated a family fight and it had gone reasonably well; there were no serious injuries to either party and the boyfriend agreed to move out until the dust settled.

Lafferty looked across the street at the Joy. "Whoa, what's going on?"

Two workmen were nailing plywood sheets across the windows and door.

"What's up?" Reece asked one of the workmen.

He shrugged. "The bar's closed. That's all I know."

Lafferty and Reece looked at each other and grinned. "Well, I'll be goddamned," they said in unison.

~~

Lt. Barry and Leland were behind the desk talking to Lt. Hanlon when Reece and Lafferty banged through the double doors.

Hanlon peered at them over his reading glasses. "Why aren't you guys in your sector?"

"We had to deliver the good news in person," Reece replied.

"The Joy Lounge is fucking closed!" Lafferty shouted, pumping his fist in the air.

"What are you talking about?" Barry asked.

"We just came from there. Two guys are nailing plywood over the door."

Barry turned to Leland. "You did it, Cap. You closed the Joy."

Leland shook his head, scarcely believing that the hated bar was finally gone. "We *all* closed the Joy."

While they were high-fiving each other, the phone rang. Barry picked it up. "Five-five, may I help you?"

He turned ashen, and then muttered, "Oh, sweet Jesus..."

Leland saw his bleak expression. "What is it?" he asked.

Tears welled up in the lieutenant's eyes. "Hector Torres just shot himself."

~~

To the casual observer, all police offices' funerals look the same. There's always a police honor guard, ranks of sorrowful fellow-officers, and a sad eulogy to describe a life snuffed in its prime.

But the truth was that every police officer's funeral was unique, and what made it unique was the body in the casket, and the surviving family members. Hector's grieving family consisted of Nancy and a dozen of Hector's aunts and uncles, many of whom had flown up from Puerto Rico. Standing behind the family, among the ranks of uniformed officers, were Reece, Mazzeo, Garrigan, Elliot, Oliver, Reece, and dozens of others from the Five-five.

But what made Hector Torres's funeral even more unique was the music. Usually a piper from the Emerald Society Pipe Band was on hand to play the mournful *Amazing Grace.* But for Hector Torres's funeral the cops from the Five-five had hired a Dixieland band. As the casket was carried from the small church, the Second Line Band struck up the mournful chords of *Just A Closer Walk with Thee,* a traditional gospel tune that is still played at funerals in New Orleans. The tune, unfamiliar to most, was a cross between down-home blues and a dirge and it made heads turn in the ranks. The trumpet and clarinet, carrying the plaintive melody soaring over the soft baritone of the trombone and the tuba, brought a tightness to the throat and a glistening in the eye, but at the same time, it was a tune that made one want to tap one's foot.

~~

After the funeral, the cops from the Five-five took the Dixieland band back to Paddy Corr's and paid them to play the same handful of tunes over and over again until Paddy Corr couldn't take it anymore and threw them all out.

The cops stood on the sidewalk outside Corr's. It was after midnight. They'd been drinking steadily since the funeral, but not a man was drunk.

"Well," Mazzeo said, "I guess that's it."

"I guess so," Reece said.

"Right." agreed Jimmy Elliot.

It was clear that no one wanted to go home. It was as if they all sensed that something was missing, that something had been left undone.

And it was Lafferty, watching the band members load their instruments into their van, who realized what that something was. "Yo, guys," he called out. "Not so fast. You got one more tune to play."

~~

Five minutes later, the band and the cops were standing in front of the darkened Joy Lounge.

The cops stood at attention in the street, looking at the plywood that covered the windows and door, and thinking about Hector Torres. Then, after a moment of silence, Lafferty nodded and the band launched into one final chorus of *Just A Closer Walk with Thee.*

As the music reverberated off the tenement walls, windows opened one by one and heads appeared. It was almost twelve-thirty in the morning, but no one complained. The neighborhood, along with the cops, listened in respectful silence. The sounds of the instruments wafted up, over the tenement roofs, and into the gray clouds above.

When the tune ended, Charlie Reece said, "That's it. It's time to go home."

Everyone nodded. It was, finally, time to go home.

~~

It took a full five months for the fallout from the "Seaman Street War"—as it had come to be called—to finally blow over.

To no one's surprise, Kawasi Munyika and his pickets returned to the Five-five day after day for the two weeks following the night of the Seaman Street War. The demonstrations were raucous, loud, and contentious. More than once, Leland thought arrests would have to be made, but that drastic action proved to be unnecessary.

The demonstrations didn't go as Munyika planned. In spite of the antics that had gotten him face time on TV in the past, the media gave him scant attention this time and he soon grew tired of playing to an empty house. By the end of the second week, Munyika found a cause that required his immediate attention—a bogus racial discrimination issue in a fast-food restaurant in Brooklyn—and everything returned to normal in the Five-five.

As normal as things could be in the Five-five.

As a result of the blizzard of civilian complaints lodged by Vera Roland and company against every member of the Five-five—including Leland—the Civilian Complaint Review Board conducted a massive and thorough investigation that lasted into the middle of April. In the end, they were all exonerated, except Billy Lafferty, who was given a command discipline for calling a hearing officer an asshole.

Winter gave way to a chilly, damp spring that lasted into late June. Then the summer appeared with a vengeance. The temperatures the first week of July never dipped below ninety.

Summer is the season the New York City Police Department dreads the most. Hot weather, crowded conditions, and short tempers are a recipe for calamity in the ghettos of the city. And Death Valley in the Five-five was the worst of those ghettos.

It was just after six o'clock on the morning of July 14th when Leland's alarm went off. Half asleep, he clicked on the Weather Channel. Temperatures had been unseasonably high since June, but now the city was in the grip of a heat wave that seemed as though it would go on forever.

The weatherman, a clean-cut young man with blow-dried hair, was absolutely delirious with joy as he explained that the thermometer was expected to hit a hundred by three this afternoon. Leland clicked off the smiling face in disgust.

Like every other precinct commander in the city, Leland had been carefully monitoring the weather. After five days of record-breaking temperatures, tempers were raw and the city was a tinderbox that could go up in a flash. Even though most of the current precinct COs weren't even born in 1964, thoughts of the infamous Harlem Riots of that year were never far from their minds and each prayed that nothing like that would happen in their precinct.

In the summer of '64 an off-duty police lieutenant shot and killed a fifteen-year-old boy whom he mistakenly thought was a burglar. For the next two nights, mobs rampaged through the streets of Harlem looting, burning, and fighting the police and firefighters with bricks and bottles. When the police finally regained control of the Harlem streets, the rioting shifted to Bed-Sty in Brooklyn. When the smoke cleared weeks later, the toll was one dead, hundreds injured, and millions of dollars in damages to burned-out buildings and stores.

Ever since that summer so long ago, the police department held its collective breath at the beginning of every summer, wondering if this was the summer that would ignite the city again.

Leland's major concern was his two trouble spots: the Bulge and Death Valley. In hot weather, people sought relief from cramped, stuffy apartments by spilling out into the streets. And as the mercury rose, so did the number of murders, assaults, and family fights.

As Leland poured his first cup of coffee of the day, he called the precinct.

Lt. Hanlon picked up the phone. "Five-five."

"Captain Leland. How did we do on the late tour?"

"Not bad, Boss. Three arrests for assault and two stolen cars."

Leland hung up feeling a little better, but not much. That grinning weatherman had promised at least three more days of ninety-plus temperatures.

∾∾

Due to a mistake by a new roll call clerk, Mazzeo and Peggy were put into the same radio car. Since they'd stopped being radio car partners, they hadn't seen much of each other away from the job either. They told themselves it was because they were afraid of getting caught by Leland.

The dispatcher mercifully interrupted the stilted small talk they'd been engaging in to fill the awkward silence.

"Sector Boy, respond to six-seven-two Carlyle Avenue, Apartment 5F. Report of a woman in labor."

Five minutes later, Mazzeo and Garrigan stood to either side of the door of apartment 5F. They'd learned not to take any job description at face value. "A woman in labor" call could be just that—or a psycho with an AK-47.

Mazzeo tapped the paint-chipped door with his nightstick and a wide-eyed black man in his late twenties opened the door. "She's in here," he said, leading them through the kitchen where an eight-year-old was feeding a bottle to an infant strapped into a high chair.

The tiny bedroom's only light was the flickering glow of three votive candles burning before a statue of the Virgin. A woman in her mid-twenties lay writhing among a rumpled pile of bedclothes.

"Let's get some lights on," Peggy said.

The husband flipped on a ceiling light and Peggy gently removed the blankets from the perspiring woman. The amniotic sac had burst and the sheets were soaked.

"Hang on," Peggy said, brushing damp hair out of the woman's eyes, "An ambulance is on the way. What's your name?"

"Tamicka." The woman clutched her stomach and grimaced in pain.

"Are those your two kids out there?" Peggy asked.

Tamicka nodded, clenching her teeth.

"Do you feel like you have to go to the bathroom?"

Again a nod.

"How long between contractions?"

"Two minutes, five minutes, I'm not sure."

"Tell them to put a rush on the bus," Peggy whispered to Mazzeo. "She's ready."

Just as Mazzeo finished the call, he heard a blood-curdling scream. He rushed back in and saw Peggy peering between the woman's legs. She looked up at him with a mixture of fear and awe. "The baby's coming. I need clean towels."

Mazzeo stared at the woman, slack-jawed. He and Carol had elected to have their baby by natural childbirth. There had been nothing to it. He'd even recorded the event on videotape. It had been a wonderful experience—but the delivery had taken place in a hospital with doctors, nurses and all the proper equipment readily available. He looked around the cramped bedroom. *They had nothing.*

Peggy shouted, *"Eddie. Now!"*

Mazzeo jumped and ran out to the kitchen with the husband to look for towels.

Peggy gently pushed the woman's legs apart. "Just take it easy, Tamicka. There's nothing to it."

"The woman's eyes snapped open. "You ever have a baby?"

"Um, no."

"Well, I've had two. Don't you tell me there's nothing to it." She screamed and clutched her stomach.

"Okay, okay," Peggy said soothingly. "Try and relax. How about another call on the ambulance," she shouted into the kitchen.

Mazzeo came back with an armful of towels. "They're only a couple of blocks away."

Peggy placed two under the woman's buttocks and draped towels over her abdomen and each thigh. Tamicka, who'd been grunting rhythmically, gasped. Peggy looked down and saw black hair begin to emerge from the vagina.

"Oh, my God..." she whispered.

Trying to remember what she'd been taught in the police academy, she climbed up on the bed and positioned herself between Tamicka's legs. *Childbirth is a natural phenomenon,* the supercilious ass of an instructor had said. *All you have to do is catch the baby on the way out.*

Yeah, right.

She placed one hand under Tamicka's vagina and positioned her other hand to guide the baby out. *Please,* she prayed, *let's have no complications.*

Tamicka grunted and the baby's head began to appear. Soon it was all the way out. Peggy stared in dismay. *The umbilical cord was wrapped around the baby's neck.*

"Eddie, you'll have to unwrap the cord," she said in a hoarse whisper. "I'll hold the baby's head."

Mazzeo, who'd been standing next to the wide-eyed father, climbed up on the bed next to Peggy and gently began to uncoil the cord.

"Easy," Peggy said.

"I *am* doing it easy," he snapped.

"We don't want it to break, do we?" she said through clenched teeth.

"No, we don't." Gently, he unwound the cord.

Peggy held the baby's head and carefully lowered it to allow one shoulder to come out. Then she raised the head slightly, the other shoulder appeared, and then, the rest of the baby gushed out.

It was a girl. A wave of exhilaration swept over Peggy. *She was holding a brand new life in her hands.* The brief moment of intense joy and sense of wonder was shattered by the noisy arrival of the EMT team.

While one paramedic took the vital signs of the mother, the other inserted a bulb syringe in the baby's nostrils and sucked the mucus and blood out. The air passages cleared, the baby let out a loud, lusty squeal to protest her entry into a harsh world.

Peggy and Mazzeo, bystanders once again, stepped back and watched. When the team determined the mother and baby were stabilized, they lifted her onto the gurney and wheeled her out of the apartment.

The two officers stayed behind to get the information from the wildly grinning father who couldn't stop shaking their hands. After they'd finished the paperwork, they remained in the apartment while the father left to round up a babysitter for his other two kids. A few minutes later, an old woman with a snaggletooth-grin appeared and told them that the father had already left for the hospital.

Outside, in the dimly lit hallway, the air was heavy with the smell of frying food, exotic spices, and blaring televisions. Peggy, suddenly exhausted, stopped and leaned against the wall.

"You okay?" Eddie asked.

"Yeah, I'm fine. Eddie, can you believe that?" she said with wonder in her voice. "One minute there's four of us in the room, the next there's five. I've seen the films and heard mothers talk about childbirth, but I never thought it could be so... so beautiful."

Mazzeo, uncomfortable expressing emotions, merely grunted. "Yeah, I'm glad everything worked out okay."

"Did you see the way Tamicka looked at her husband after the baby was born? There was such... love."

Mazzeo shrugged. "I didn't notice."

Tears welled up in her eyes. "It's made me realize something," she said.

"What's that?"

She touched his cheek the same way she did that first time in her apartment. "We can't be together anymore."

He pushed her hand away. "Come on... what are you talking about?"

"In there... it made me think of you and Carol and little Edward. I have no right to come between a family."

"Peggy, that's—"

She held his face with both her hands. "Listen. You and I have had something very special and nothing can change that. But there's no future for us. I think I've known all along you'd never leave Carol. You love her too much. And that's good. I'm not ready to settle down anyway. There's so much I want to do." His arms hung by his sides and his face contorted with mixed emotions. "But... you saved my life, Peggy."

"And I'm going to do it again." She looked up into his dark brown eyes, now clouded by confusion. "You know I'm right, don't you?"

He swallowed hard and nodded silently.

She slipped her arms around his neck. "Eddie, give me one last hug."

In an apartment down the hall, a child squealed in delight; in another apartment, someone dropped a frying pan; and in another apartment, a TV blasted an MTV video. But Peggy and Eddie heard none of it. They stood in the dimly lit hallway clinging to each other—a human island surrounded by their own sea of silence.

~~

The Five-five-precinct station house was not air-conditioned. Even if the City, in a paroxysm of largesse, had decided to install air conditioning, the old wiring snaking through the crumbling lathe walls wouldn't have been able to handle the extra electrical load.

Leland's "air conditioning" was an ancient pedestal fan that was impressively noisy, but completely inefficient. The eighteen-inch blades, powered by a motor that sounded like a runaway Volkswagen, did little more than push hot air from one side of the room to the other.

Leland stood by his open window, watched the day tour take over from the late tour, and wondered, once again, if this was going to be *the* summer.

A blast of hot air drove him away from the window and back to his desk. It was only 8 a.m.

~~

At two-fifteen that afternoon, as the temperature broke through the one-hundred-degree mark, sixteen-year-old Lucy Williams was standing in front of a meat display in Kim's Market struggling to make a very difficult decision. The heavy-set black girl screwed up her face in concentration and studied the two choices before her. The shiny tin of smoked turkey looked real good. But, then again, so did the ham. After considerable thought, she reached out a pudgy hand, selected the ham and stuffed it under her blouse. On her way out, almost as an afterthought, she picked up a bag of potato chips.

As she was at the counter paying for the chips, Kim saw the huge bulge under her blouse and poked it with a bony finger. "Hey, what you got there?" he shouted shrilly.

"I ain't got nuthin'," Lucy muttered.

He lifted her blouse, revealing the canned ham. His eyes widened. "You steal from me."

Lucy threw the can on the counter. "I didn't steal shit, you yellow motherfucker."

She turned to leave, but Kim blocked her way and yelled something to his wife.

Lucy didn't understand Korean, but she was pretty sure he'd told his old lady to call the cops. "Get outta my way, motherfucker," she said indignantly. She tried to push past him, but even her 195-pound bulk couldn't move the little man.

"You stay," he shouted in her face. "Police come arrest you."

All the shouting and arm waving was beginning to make her nervous, and the little man's piercing voice was hurting her head. She shoved him hard this time. He pushed back. *"You stay. Police come!"*

Kim's wife came out from the back of the store just as Lucy smacked him. The wife screamed. Kim felt something sticky and put his hand to his cheek. His hand came away covered with blood.

Lucy had slashed him from his left ear to his jaw line with a razor blade she'd been holding between her fingers. A four-inch piece of loose flesh hung from his cheek.

Wide-eyed with fear and fury, he slammed her bulk against a row of canned peaches. The impact jarred the cans loose and they cascaded to the floor. She tried to elbow her way past him, but she slipped on a can and went sprawling across the floor. Kim jumped on her back. As his blood squirted over him, her, the floor, and the rolling cans, she tried to buck him off while she rooted among the cans for the razor blade she'd dropped.

Fortunately for Kim, the cops arrived before she found it.

~~

Lt. Hanlon looked up as Jim Elliot and George Oliver came banging through the doors with a handcuffed Lucy Williams. *"Get your motherfuckin' hands off me you motherfuckers,"* she shrieked.

"What've you got," the lieutenant asked Elliot.

"One for assault." Elliot leaned close to the desk and whispered, "She cut the Korean grocer."

The lieutenant's eyebrows shot up. "Kim?"

"Yeah. The shit's on," Elliot said knowingly.

"George, take her in the back," Hanlon said. "Jimmy, you stay here and give me all the details. The captain's gotta know about this."

~~

There was a knock at Leland's door and Lieutenant Hanlon stuck his head in. "Got a minute, Cap. This is important."

Leland pulled his sticky shirt way from his body. "Sure, what's up?"

"Elliot and Oliver brought in a female for assault. I don't know if you heard them."

"Yes, I heard them." Leland had trained himself not to jump up and investigate every time he heard shouting and cursing outside his door. He'd learned that if the incident required his attention, he'd be told soon enough. "What's up?"

"She cut Kim."

"The Korean? Bad?"

"Yeah, and it gets worse. She's black."

"Oh, my God."

Shortly after his transfer to the precinct, he'd noticed an inordinate number of sixty-ones for assaults, thefts, and disputes emanating from Kim's Market. He'd called Ronnie Newbert, his Community Relations Officer, into his office.

"Why all these sixty-ones from Kim's Market?" he asked her.

"About a year ago, Kim opened up a store on Dumont Avenue—sort of a green grocer and supermarket," Newbert explained.

Leland looked at the wall map and noticed that Dumont was in the heart of the Bulge. "Go on."

"Right from the get-go there was trouble. The locals, mostly kids, started ripping him off. Shoplifting, snatch and run. That sort of thing. Most of the merchants in the Bulge are intimidated. They get ripped off;

they don't do anything about it. Not Kim. Every time he catches them stealing, he confronts them. They call him a racist. He calls them thieves."

Leland knew all too well what that could lead to. He recalled reading about the community relations nightmare caused by a neighborhood boycott of a Korean grocery store in Brooklyn back in 1990 that lasted for almost a year.

"You think we're going to have a problem?" he asked Hanlon.

"I think so, Boss. This is an issue made to order for Munyika."

"Okay. Let's start shifting manpower. Take two sectors from the Hill and assign them to the Bulge."

"Will do."

As Hanlon was leaving, Barry came in. "I called the borough and gave them a heads up," he said.

"Good."

"Where's Ronnie Newbert?"

"She's out there now, trying to get a feel for the mood of the neighborhood."

"Keep me posted."

After Barry left, Leland looked at his watch. Almost three-thirty. He was supposed to have dinner with the Janssens at seven. Maybe the lieutenant was overreacting. Maybe Munyika was picketing somewhere in New Jersey. Maybe he was on vacation. Maybe he'd been hit by an eighteen-wheeler crossing Bruckner Boulevard.

Ten minutes later, Barry stuck his head in the door. "Munyika and thirty followers just arrived at Kim's."

"What are they doing?"

"Setting up picket lines."

~~

Five minutes later, Community Affairs Officer was sitting in Leland's office.

"What did you find out?" Leland asked.

"If it wasn't for Munyika and his bunch agitating, it'd be no big deal, Cap. You see, the thing is, Lucy Williams is disabled. She has the I.Q. of a burned-out light bulb. She's a habitual truant and she's been busted for shoplifting six times in the last year."

"She doesn't sound like the kind of person Munyika would want make a cause célèbre," Leland said hopefully.

"She'll do until something better comes along."

Leland wasn't happy with Newbert's description of Lucy. If she was all Newbert said, she could be easily manipulated by Munyika. "What's the black community saying?"

"There's really no such thing as *a* black community anymore, Cap. We've had such an influx of immigrants in the past ten years that each ethnic group has carved out its own piece of the neighborhood. In this precinct, we have a sizable number of Haitians, Nigerians, and Jamaicans. She pushed her glasses up on her nose and grinned. "To a white man, we may all look alike, but I promise you we're all very different with different cultures and values." Newbert smiled ruefully. "The melting pot we ain't."

"Who shops at Kim's?"

"Mostly Haitians. And they come with a whole lot of emotional baggage. They're still smarting about the way our government handled the relief after the earthquake a couple of years ago. All kinds of aid was promised, but they think we reneged on our promises to get the country back on its feet. Being labeled AIDS-carriers hasn't helped their self-esteem, either. When an ambulance shows up, some paramedics don't want to touch bleeding Haitians—neither do some of our guys, for that matter. On top of all that, they have what I call the West Indies marketplace mentality. Back home, they shop in open-air markets. Custom says you wanna buy a mango or whatnot, you try it first."

"I can't do that in my supermarket. Everything's wrapped in plastic," Leland said.

"Same with mine. The Haitians don't like that and that's why they shop at Kim's. He doesn't wrap anything and he stocks tropical fruit. Problem is, I guess in Korea they don't sample fruit. He sees someone munching on a mango in his store and he thinks he's being ripped off. Another thing. The marketplace mentality says you never pay the posted price. When they try to bargain with him, he gets mad and says they're trying to cheat him."

"Hasn't anyone told him about these customs?"

"I did." Newbert shrugged. "But he's real suspicious and defensive. People complain the dude don't smile. Well, hell, none of them smile. It's a sign of impoliteness in Korean society. Same thing with direct eye contact. But the Haitians think the Koreans are dissing them. Even giving change can cause a hassle. Korean females are taught to avoid physical contact with men, so they drop the change on the counter. The men think they're being disrespected."

"So the problem is more than just theft."

"Right. It's a serious clash of cultures. Don't get me wrong, Cap. Kim gets ripped off all the time. But it's these cultural differences that exacerbate the problem and it's these kinds of problems that Munyika feeds off."

Leland was impressed with the young officer's knowledge of the neighborhood's sociology. "Thanks for the briefing," he said. "Get back out on the street and keep in touch."

As Newbert was leaving, Leland said, "Hey, Ronnie. How do you know so much about these groups?"

Newbert grinned. "I have my sources. My math professor is Korean and my boyfriend is Haitian."

Chapter Twenty-Seven

Leland pulled up to the corner of Dumont and Morton and into a scene of mass confusion. An angry crowd of over thirty men and women had gathered across the street from Kim's Market and were loudly chanting obscenities. A few hoisted a handful of hastily written signs proclaiming NO MORE MONKEYS IN OUR COMMUNITY and KOREANS UNFAIR TO THE COMMUNITY.

Every available precinct radio car was on the scene, but the harried handful of cops in Robin-blue riot helmets were no match for the larger, more aggressive throng.

Leland grabbed Labonte, who was beet-red and sweating profusely in the ninety-plus temperature. "Where's Munyika?"

Labonte wiped his face with a sopping wet handkerchief. "He was here, but he left. He said he's coming back."

Leland assessed the growing crowd. "You need barriers," he shouted over the shouting. "You're not going to hold them without barriers."

"I know, Cap. I set up a temporary headquarters over there. My driver's making the call to the borough now."

Leland glanced toward a row of stores across the street. There was a private taxicab service, a bar, and a Laundromat. All the other stores were boarded up. "Where?"

The sergeant pointed. "The barbershop." The only evidence of its intended use was a crudely hand-painted sign offering "haircuts and the latest styling."

A howl went up from the crowd and both Leland and the sergeant turned to see the cause. Two Koreans had come out of the store carrying a ladder.

"What are they doing?" an astonished Leland asked.

"Looks like they're going to tape the window," Labonte replied. "Before we got here, someone threw a rock through it."

"Get them out of there, Sarge. They're only exciting the crowd."

Labonte hitched up his gun belt in exasperation. "You don't know these Koreans, Cap. They wouldn't give a rat's ass if the entire North Korean army was across the street. They're gonna fix that goddamn window, no matter what."

"Well, see if you can talk them out of it. I'll check on the status of reinforcements."

There were no customers in the barbershop, just the owner, an elderly black man, and Vic Martin, the sergeant's driver, who was arguing with someone on the phone. The old man peered through his dirty window and shook his head. "Damn shame," he muttered. "Damn shame."

A frustrated Martin shouted into the phone. "I'm just telling you what the sergeant said. We need barriers *now*."

"Who are you talking to, Martin?"

"Sgt. Luff at the borough."

Leland took the phone. "Sgt. Luff, this is Captain Leland. What's the problem?"

"Cap, we don't have a barrier truck available right now."

Leland glanced out the window. The cops, standing shoulder to shoulder, were using their bodies as human barriers, but the thin line wasn't going to be able to hold this group much longer. "Sergeant, I don't care if you bring those barriers out here on bicycles. I want them here *forthwith*. Understand?"

The sergeant's response was muffled by a booming amplified voice outside. *"Brothers and sisters—"* Leland handed the phone to the cop and went to the window to stand next to the old man.

Kawasi Munyika, towering over the crowd, was wearing his usual uniform—gold chains and a multi-colored Dashiki. "Brothers and sisters," he repeated. "I speak for all of you in this community when I say that we are not going to stand by and watch one of our sisters get assaulted by one of *them*."

A chorus of voices howled their agreement. Munyika had a hypnotic effect on the crowd. All eyes were upturned toward him as they regarded him in rapt silence. At least the lull gave the exhausted cops a much-needed break.

The old man grunted. "That fool don't speak for me. He speak for that rabble out there. Look at 'em. Not one of 'em done a lick of work in their useless lives."

When Leland came outside, he saw Labonte arguing with a Korean standing on the ladder. He didn't seem to be having much success. The man gestured wildly toward the crowd and continued to cover the cracks with duct tape.

Munyika's deep, resonant voice reverberated off the surrounding buildings. "Two hundred years of slavery and now *this*." He jabbed a ring-bedecked hand in the direction of the Korean market. "*Foreigners* coming into our community to take away our *jobs*, our *money*, our *opportunity*, our *dignity*."

He spoke in the measured cadence of an Evangelical preacher and it had the desired effect. Cries of "Amen" and "Right on" rose from the crowd.

"Well, I am here to tell you that all this will *cease* as of this moment."

As Munyika was talking, four radio cars with blue barriers sticking out of open trunks, pulled up at the scene. Leland helped the cops drag the barriers out and set them up along the curb line. He felt some measure of relief when they were finally in place. At least now, the crowd could be contained. He walked across the street to get a closer look at the man who could ruin his career.

Munyika bellowed into his bullhorn. "I am serving notice on this city right here and now that this community is not going to take this any longer. We will not be enslaved by no foreigners who can't even speak no English."

That last line brought smiles to the faces of the cops who were listening intently to the reverend.

"*What are we gonna do?*" a voice from the crowd called out.

Munyika spread his arms out over the crowd like an Old Testament prophet. "We are going to boycott this store. As Jesus did, we are going to drive the moneychangers from the Temple. From the *Temple*! From the *Temple*"

As the crowd picked up the chant, his assistants helped Munyika down from the overturned garbage can.

Munyika saw Leland approaching. "Ah, my good friend, Captain Leland. Have you come to arrest the owner of that store for assaulting that poor unfortunate young girl?"

"The matter is under investigation by the District Attorney's Office, Reverend." Leland was aware of the hostile looks from the surrounding crowd and tried a smile. "We're just here to keep the peace."

Munyika's eyes narrowed. "And how you gonna do dat?"

Without the bullhorn and the audience, Leland noted, Munyika had reverted to street speech.

"You have every right to demonstrate. We just have to go over the ground rules."

"Such as?"

"Are you planning on setting up a permanent picket line?"

"Are you tellin' me I can't?"

"Not at all."

"What are your rules?"

"Your people will have to remain behind these barriers. Keep the noise level down, especially after ten o'clock. And no one is to interfere with shoppers coming and going into the market. If your people will follow those rules, I'm sure we'll have no problem."

Munyika folded his arms and looked down on Leland with a smile dripping contempt. "You got that all wrong, Captain. We're gonna picket right in *front* of that market. That's the way a boycott works."

Leland was afraid that was what he was going to say. "Reverend Munyika, I'm sorry, but you'll have to follow the rules."

"Or what?"

Leland realized, too late, that he'd painted himself into a corner. All the books he'd ever read about street confrontations cautioned: *Never give ultimatums*!

Munyika repeated his question. "Or what, Captain?"

Leland cleared his throat. "If the law is broken, arrests will be made."

"We'll see." Munyika turned away. "Where's the damn press?" he snapped at an aide.

"They've been called, Reverend. There're on the way."

Most of the picketers left with Munyika. The handful remaining listlessly ambled back and forth calling out an occasional obscenity as a customer went into the market.

Leland welcomed the opportunity of relative calm to regroup. Under his direction, the hastily erected barriers were repositioned. In the meantime, a detail of two sergeants and twenty police officers arrived from the precinct. Leland explained the sensitive nature of the demonstration and what he expected from them. If this situation ignited, he didn't want his police officers to be the cause.

An unmarked car pulled up and Seidel got out. "How's it goin', Cap?"

"Right now? All right. I think we have enough cops and barriers to contain them."

Seidel, squinting through a cloud of smoke, studied the demonstrators. "You think those barriers will contain them, huh?"

"There are only ten pickets."

"That's because the press isn't here."

Leland had been wondering where the press was. He heard Munyika's aide say he called them and they were on the way. "Maybe I got lucky," he said, hopefully. "Maybe there's a big subway fire in Manhattan and they're all covering it."

Seidel grunted. "You can bet your pension Munyika will be back by six."

"How do you know that?" Leland asked, mildly irritated that his Anti-Crime sergeant always seemed to know something he didn't.

"It's four-thirty now. In the old days, anyone hoping to get their demonstration on the six o'clock news had to have their demonstration underway by four."

"Why?"

"The TV stations used film then. They needed time to get back to the studio, develop the film, edit it, and find a suitable spot for it in the broadcast. Now, with everything live, the demonstrations don't have to start until six."

"How did you know that?" Leland asked in exasperation.

"I was a cop in Intelligence for a couple of years. We could always tell the professional agitators from the amateurs by the way they orchestrated the press."

"And Munyika's a pro."

"You got that right."

"What do you know about Munyika?" Leland asked.

"What do *I* know? Captain, Munyika is the guy who can torpedo your career. And you're asking me?"

"I called the Intelligence Division for a rundown," he said defensively, "but they didn't have much to tell me about him."

Seidel grunted. "Since the Handschu Decision, the court's clamping down on our intelligence-gathering activity. The department is scared shitless of lawsuits when it comes to guys like Munyika. I'm surprised they even admitted to hearing about him."

"I'll bet you know all about him, don't you Marv?"

Seidel flicked his cigar stub into the street and it landed in a shower of sparks. "His real name is Leonard Smalls. He's got a yellow sheet as long as a donkey's dong. The usual. Burglary, grand larceny, and assaults busts. He did nine years in the slammer for manslaughter. Claims he got religion in the joint."

"Sounds like you don't buy it."

"Nah. Mutts like Munyika don't get religion. He figured out it's a whole lot safer and profitable being a con man. Munyika remind you of anyone, Cap?"

"Yes, he does, but I can't put my finger on it."

"I'll give you a clue. *National Geographic.*"

"That's it. He looks like those Masai warriors."

"It's an image he cultivates. He tells the poor saps who follow him that he's a descendent of Masai kings. What a crock. Leonard Smalls was born in a one-traffic-light town in southern Mississippi. If he's descended from African royalty, I'm Prince Charlie's illegitimate brother."

The very thought of this cigar-smoking, iconoclastic Jewish police sergeant being even remotely related to the British family made Leland grin. "Earlier you said something about not having enough barriers and men. What'd you mean by that?"

Seidel watched the stream of pickets listlessly tracing an elongated semicircle behind the barriers. "When Munyika comes back, he's gonna have a whole lot of people with him and he ain't gonna let you herd him behind those barriers."

That is essentially what Munyika had told him. "What will he do?"

Seidel jerked his head toward the Korean market. "Set up in front of the store. He wants to be in your face and in Kim's face."

"How can you be so sure?"

Seidel shrugged. "Can you think of a better photo op?"

Seidel headed for his car. "If I was you, Cap, I'd call for the cavalry."

Leland hurried back to the barbershop and called the borough. Sergeant Luff answered.

"This is Captain Leland. I'm going to need more people over here."

"How many demonstrators you got, Cap?"

"Right now, about ten. But more are coming."

There was a pause, and then the sergeant said, " Captain, you got more cops than demonstrators."

Leland was tired of quibbling with an administrative sergeant. "Let me talk to the Chief," he snapped. He didn't really want to talk to Hightower, but he knew he'd get nowhere with this palace guard hack.

"The Chief's at a meeting at OPP," the sergeant said airily. "But Chief Zeigler is here."

"Fine. Put him on."

It wasn't fine. Walter Zeigler, the oldest deputy chief in the department, was known as "space junk" to the cops in the Bronx. In his forty-one years, Zeigler had tripped, stumbled, and staggered his way up the ranks, shattering all existing *Peter Principle* records. He'd gone into the hospital a year earlier for a gallstone operation, but some irreverent cops started a rumor that he'd had a brain CAT scan and nothing showed up on the X-rays. The cops even managed to convince some of the more gullible civilian members of the department that Deputy Chief Walter Zeigler was going to appear on the cover of the *Journal of the American Medical Association,* billed as the man without a brain.

Charlie Drum despised Zeigler, but the devious Chief of Department had found a use for him. Leland remembered the day Drum transferred Zeigler to the Bronx. "Zeigler is gonna reach mandatory retirement in a year," a gleeful Drum had explained. "But in the meantime, he'll drive Lucian Hightower crazy."

"What's the problem, Captain?" The voice on the telephone was meant to be gruff, but Zeigler came off sounding like Don Corleone with emphysema.

"Chief, I'm requesting additional personnel for this demonstration."

"How many demonstrators do you have?"

"Ten. But I expect a lot more to show up soon. I spoke to the Reverend Munyika a while ago and he said—"

"Are they there now?"

"No, but—"

"Captain, I'm very busy. If a large group shows up, call back."

Leland slammed the phone down. "I'll bet he's busy," he muttered as he went out the door. "Probably has a whole coloring book to finish before the end of the tour!"

Leland stood on the sidewalk fuming. He was a precinct commander, for God's sake. He was supposed to be able to call on the full resources of the borough—the entire department, if necessary. It was as though no one wanted anything to do with this demonstration. Then it hit him: *No one did want anything to do with this demonstration.* Hightower had nothing to gain and everything to lose by involving himself in a racial confrontation with Munyika. He, Richard Leland, and his Five-five cops were going to have to handle this all by themselves.

It was just after five. Things were quiet and there was no sign of Munyika. Now, Leland decided, was a good time to talk to the Koreans.

Kim was back from the hospital. His left cheek was packed with a thick dressing held in place by bandages wrapped around his entire head. Swelling had partially closed the left eye, but the right one was open wide in anger as he berated Leland.

"They steal from me! They try to kill me! They try to ruin my business! What you going to do?"

"Keep the peace," Leland said in a calm voice which he hoped would soothe the excited Korean.

"*Peace*? I have no peace since I come here." He struggled for the proper words. "Two year ago I come here. My family, we do best we can. They call us names. They steal. This not peace."

Leland sympathized with the man's frustrations. "Mr. Kim, the police department's job is to keep the peace and that's what we're going to do. I promise you no one will interfere with your business. You'll be safe. If necessary, I'll provide police escort to and from your home."

"We live upstairs," Kim muttered, gingerly touching the dressing on his cheek.

Kim's extended family nervously huddled in the narrow aisles between the cans and boxes. Including women and children, Leland counted thirteen. He couldn't imagine that many people sharing one small apartment.

As if reading Leland's mind, Kim said, "It very hard to make money in this business. I need family to help."

Suddenly, Leland felt like an intruder. He was in their home. He looked at the frightened faces of the children peeking at him and turned away. "Mr. Kim," he said. "Everything will work out."

Kim regarded him with the sullen, hostile look of a man who has experienced a lifetime of duplicitous authorities. "We see," he said.

At five-thirty, just as Seidel had predicted, TV vans from the three major networks began arriving. Quickly and efficiently, like an army preparing for battle, technicians unpacked their equipment, aligned satellite dishes, cranked up generators, and studied the rows of dials and gauges that told them they were attached to the mother station by an invisible, but technologically sound, umbilical cord.

On-the-air field reporters of both sexes fussed with their hair and consulted their producers about the best camera angles and story lines. By six o'clock, everything was in readiness.

Leland made another call to the borough, but Hightower still hadn't returned from the meeting at One Police Plaza. Leland had worked for Hightower for eight months now and he was just beginning to come to the conclusion that Hightower was an effective and competent borough commander. But now, he wasn't so sure. Maybe Drum had been right when he'd said that Hightower didn't know how to prioritize his problems. Exasperated, Leland wondered what meeting at the Puzzle Palace could be more important than what was going on right here in Hightower's own borough.

The sound of muffled chanting in the distance brought him out of his foul thoughts. The mood in the street was suddenly tense with anticipation. The handful of demonstrators, who'd been listlessly shuffling behind the barriers, started chanting again. One by one, the cops standing by the barriers snapped their chinstraps and pulled the straps tight. Quietly they removed their nightsticks from their belt holders and wrapped the sticks' thongs tightly around their hands. Reporters spoke into microphones getting last minute sound levels.

From across the street, Leland heard a technician shout to a cameraman. "It just hit a hundred and two, Ralph. A new record."

The chanting grew louder as the group—almost a hundred strong—came around the corner and into view. The Reverend Munyika, towering over the heads of his followers, led them down the middle of the street. The crudely handwritten signs were gone, replaced by professionally printed ones that said, "Koreans are Racists" and "Koreans Must Go."

Leland grabbed Ed Mazzeo. "Go to the barbershop and tell Martin to call the borough. Tell them we have at least a hundred demonstrators on the scene and we need reinforcements forthwith."

Yelling over the chanting, Leland directed his men to fan out across the street. The two sergeants and nineteen cops did as they were told, but they made a pitifully thin blue line. Leland knew they were about to face a critical test. The cops of the Five-five could act like disciplined professionals—or they could act like a mob who just happened to be wearing blue uniforms.

Leland stood in front of his men and directed the advancing group of demonstrators toward the barriers to his left. But Munyika, ignoring Leland and doing exactly what Seidel said he would do, veered to the right and headed directly toward the Korean market.

Leland yelled to his detail to form a cordon around the entrance to the store. The cops, rushing past the crowd, formed a ring in front of the store. With sticks held chest high, they began to push the demonstrators off the sidewalk and back into the street. There was an eruption of blinding flashes as photographers closed in, hoping to capture the perfect front-page photo op.

Leland stood in the doorway of the market and yelled instructions into his bullhorn. *"Please move across the street behind the barriers,"* he kept repeating.

But they weren't moving. Then, suddenly the chanting stopped. In the startling silence, Munyika emerged from the crowd and slowly walked toward Leland. There was another blinding explosion of flashes. Klieg lights clicked on. Cameramen and crews shouldered their way into the crowd.

Munyika looked down at Leland with distain. "We are not demonstrators," he said loud enough to be heard by the media microphones which had been thrust over the heads of the crowd. "We are here to boycott a racist merchant." His voice rose as he played to the cameras. "We are here to show our solidarity with our brothers and sisters in this community. We will not allow foreigners to show disrespect to our defenseless sisters."

"That's your Constitutional right, Reverend Munyika," Leland said, "but you and your people will have to move across the—"

Munyika staggered backward as though he'd been struck. *"People?"* he bellowed. He turned to face the TV cameras, which the crowd had permitted to move to the front for an unobstructed view of their leader. "Did you hear what this white policeman called us? You *people*? We know what *people* means don't we?" There were shouts of *"Oh, yeah"* and *"We do"* from the crowd.

"It's a code word used by white racists to separate us from the mainstream of society. But that damnable code word will not work any longer. We *are* the society here. We *are* the community."

Just then, a black woman in her mid-thirties came through the crowd. She was well-dressed and apparently had just come from work. She looked around, bewildered by all the people.

Munyika addressed her. "Sister, have you come to join us in our protest?"

The woman shot him a look that said she had no time for his foolishness. "I've come to do some shopping. I got a dinner to cook."

"We are boycotting this racist grocery store and we ask you to shop elsewhere."

"Where elsewhere?" she snapped. "This is the only grocery store for miles around." She took a step, but several men moved around in front of her. She tucked her handbag under her arm like a football and pushed the man in front of her. "Out of my way, fool," she shouted.

He pushed her and she staggered backwards. Leland stepped between them. "I said no one will be interfered with."

The man who had done the pushing couldn't have been more than eighteen. "What you gonna do about it?" he sneered.

Leland leveled his gaze at the young man and somewhere in the back of his mind he realized that what he did next could have a profound impact on his career. "I'll have you arrested," he said calmly.

The woman tried to pass again, but the man shoved her again.

Leland turned toward the nearest police officer. "Officer, arrest this man." It was only after he said it that he realized he'd made a terrible mistake. He'd just asked the last cop in the precinct he'd want to make an arrest in front of a bank of TV cameras.

Billy Lafferty grabbed the man's arm. "Come on, pal. You're in."

Without warning, the man punched Lafferty in the face. Then, to Leland's horror, an enraged Lafferty did exactly the wrong thing. He stepped back, swung his stick over his head and came down on the man's head with a hollow *thunk*.

And all hell broke loose.

As flash strobes exploded and cameras jockeyed for position, a scuffle broke out between the cops and the demonstrators. In the melee, someone shoved a young child in front of a cop who tripped over the small body and fell on top of him. More strobes flashed.

It was over as quickly as it had begun. The arrested man, now in handcuffs, was hustled to a waiting radio car and rushed away from the scene. Except for a few scratches and some ripped clothing, no one was seriously injured.

Munyika, realizing he'd gotten what he'd wanted from the incident, became the peacemaker. "Brothers and sisters," he said in a reasonable tone, "we do not want violence, but the boycott will continue. Tomorrow, and for as long as it takes to drive the racists from our midst, we will be here, and no amount of police with their sticks and their guns will deter us from our holy purpose."

After holding a brief news conference for the TV reporters, Munyika and his aides—making sure they were out of sight of the cameras— climbed into a black Escalade and sped away.

The reporters converged on Leland for a statement. He tried to respond to a question about his use of the word "people," but the more he tried to explain, the worse it sounded. Mercifully, the reporters cut off the interview. They had more than enough footage to last them the rest of the week.

As a dejected and exhausted Leland was walking toward the barbershop to call the borough, seven radio cars with lights flashing, pulled up. A puzzled lieutenant jumped out and ran over to Leland. "The borough sent us. I have twenty cops with me. Where's the demonstration?"

If Leland hadn't been so depressed, he would have laughed.

Chapter Twenty-Eight

When Leland got back to the precinct, he had a message from the borough office telling him to report to Chief Hightower's office at 0800 hours tomorrow morning.

He was exhausted and just wanted to go home and go to bed, but first he had to write up the Unusual for the borough. Then he had to read and sign the two-inch thick stack of reports that had piled up while he was making a fool of himself on TV. And finally, he had to respond to a dozen must-return-call messages from people he'd never heard of.

By the time he got home, it was after midnight. He hadn't eaten since noon, but he wasn't hungry. His ancient window air conditioner was trying valiantly to cool the hot, muggy air in the tiny apartment, but it was losing the battle. He made himself a martini, stripped down to his shorts, and collapsed on the living room couch.

With Bach's Third Brandenburg Concerto playing on the stereo, he sat in the darkened room exhausted, angry—and scared. He'd been a CO for only eight months, but if felt like a lifetime. By nature, he was self-confident, but he was beginning to wonder if he'd be able to take this pace for the next two years. Maybe he wouldn't have to. If today's performance was any indication of his leadership abilities, he wouldn't last two years. And after tomorrow's meeting with Hightower, his tenure in the precinct might be a moot point.

He was half asleep on the couch when the telephone rang. It was a clerical sergeant from the borough. "Captain, you have a meeting tomorrow at 0800 hours."

"I know. At the borough office."

"No. That's been cancelled. Tomorrow 0800 hours at the Chief of Department's office."

Leland put the telephone down slowly. The only man he wanted to see less than Hightower was Drum. Precinct COs were never summoned to the Chief of Department's office for social chats. He could well imagine what Drum wanted to see him about. He'd missed the news on TV, but he'd seen the papers. Police Officer Lafferty had made the front page of the *Daily News* with a photo of him bringing his stick down on the head of a defenseless demonstrator. Leland was certain that somewhere in the pile of photos taken this afternoon, there was a photo of the man punching Lafferty first. But he was cynical enough to know that a photo of a cop getting punched wasn't nearly as eye-catching as a flailing nightstick. The *Post's* front-page showed a cop sprawled on top of a young child. The caption read: INNOCENT CHILD TOPPLED IN STREET BRAWL. *Street brawl?*

Leland drained the remainder of his martini. It was after one by the time he'd taken a cold shower and climbed into bed where he slept fitfully for the next five hours.

~~

At 0745 hours, Leland, dressed in full uniform, walked into the Chief of Department's office. Most of the staff worked a ten-to-six tour and the office was quiet at this hour. Only a skeleton crew—a few civilians and Charlie Joiner, Chief Drum's clerical sergeant—was there.

"Hey, Charlie, how's it going?" Leland asked.

The sergeant looked up. "Hectic, Captain."

Leland detected something in the sergeant's wary look. Embarrassment? Pity?

Joiner pointed to a door. "You can wait in the Chief's conference room," he said, burying his head in the morning's mail.

As Leland walked toward the conference room, he looked around for a familiar face, but all heads were down, intent on their work. These were people he knew. People he'd worked with. Was it his imagination or were they avoiding him?

Five minutes later, Joiner stuck his head in the door. "The Chief will see you now. You can use that door." He indicated a door connecting the conference room with Drum's private office.

A uniformed Chief Hightower was seated in one of two chairs in front of Drum's large desk. Hightower's presence was surprising—and encouraging. Drum never "Drummed" a precinct CO in front of witnesses. The borough commander nodded curtly to Leland and returned to reading a copy of Leland's Unusual.

From behind his desk, Charlie Drum studied Leland. The hooded eyes revealed nothing. "Sit down, Captain."

Drum studied them both in silence. Silence, Leland knew from experience, was one of Drum's favorite tactics. It gave the victim a chance to sweat, to dwell on his past sins, to think about his fate. One hapless quarry had described the experience to Leland as a feeling of drowning in silence. He'd claimed his whole life passed before his eyes. Leland wasn't having that experience, but beads of sweat were taking the stiffness out of his starched collar. Leland's eyes went to a copy of the *Daily News* on Drum's desk.

"All right," Drum said, puncturing the ominous silence." Who wants to explain this—debacle?"

Leland groaned inwardly. It was all in the Unusual, a copy of which was right there on his desk alongside the *News*, but Drum was going to make him explain it all over again.

"*You* were there, Captain," Hightower said in an icy tone. "Why don't you explain it?"

And *you* should have been there, Leland said to himself, and wondering why Drum wasn't jumping all over the borough commander for not being at the scene. He didn't know what, but something was going on between these two titans and he knew he would do well to tread very carefully.

Leland briefly recounted yesterday's events. When he finished Hightower said, "Captain, you should have realized that two and twenty wasn't going to be enough. Why didn't you ask for more assistance?"

Leland stared at the cap on his lap and fidgeted with the gold braid. An Unusual was supposed to contain everything pertaining to an incident. But there were certain delicate things that had to be left out. How could he say that Chief Zeigler, Hightower's second-in-command at the borough, refused to send more personnel? Drum and Hightower knew Zeigler was an incompetent fool, but it wasn't his place to point that out to them. But now he had no choice.

"I did speak to Chief Zeigler," he said quietly. "I requested more personnel."

Hightower's frog-eyes bulged even more. "You asked Zeigler for help?" It was apparent from his question that he wasn't aware that they'd spoken. But that wasn't surprising. Zeigler wasn't about to tell Hightower he'd dropped the ball at the borough level. "What did he say?" Hightower growled.

"He said I had enough people and to call back if more demonstrators showed up."

Hightower's jaw muscles knotted and he shot a look at Drum and both Drum and Leland knew what he was thinking: An incompetent fool like Zeigler had no business being an assistant borough commander and Drum had been the one who'd put him there.

"The damage is done," Drum said in a reasonable tone that was very much out of character for him. "Munyika got his TV airtime and headlines. Now it's time for damage control. Lucian, how do you plan to handle this boycott?"

"The same way I handle all demonstrations. Munyika will have to abide by the rules. Picket lines will be set up across the street from the market. There'll be no violence and no one will interfere with the man's place of business."

Leland was relieved—and somewhat surprised—that Hightower agreed with him.

Drum shook his head. "That won't fly, Lucian. Munyika's life-blood is publicity. As long as he has the media's attention, he'll be a thorn in our side. For chrissake, we all know he's been looking for an opportunity to garner national exposure. This could be his ticket to national prominence and, by God, the NYPD will not be the one to give it to him. I will not let him be the spark that sets this city ablaze."

"What do you suggest?" Hightower asked curtly.

"Deny him that publicity."

"How do we do that?"

"By doing nothing."

"Nothing? They'll camp inside the Korean's store."

Drum idly formed a wedge with ten miniature Roman soldiers. "I'll admit it will be tough for awhile, but eventually the media will get bored, Munyika will get bored, and they'll all go away."

"And in the meantime, they'll put that Korean out of business."

An image of Kim's thirteen family members flashed in Leland's mind and he heard the man's words in his mind: *"We don't make much money at this."*

Drum fondled a miniature Roman Centurion. "That would be unfortunate, but we have to look at the big picture here. Munyika is a royal pain in the ass. Every time he shows up somewhere, we have to assign a detail of cops to protect the sonofabitch. He's costing us a fortune. A fortune, I might add, we don't have in the budget." Drum slammed the toy soldier down on his polished desk. "I want Munyika and his half-ass causes to shrivel up and die. The only way to do that is to ignore him."

"And in the process ignore the law?" Hightower said evenly.

"What are you talking about?"

"Munyika intimidates people. Without police protection, no one will shop in that store. They'll put that Korean out of business. If the mafia did that, we'd call it extortion."

Drum's eyes narrowed. "What are you implying, Lucian?"

"A double standard. The law of this land doesn't apply to blacks and Koreans."

"Bullshit! Munyika's black isn't he?"

"And so are the people who shop in that market. Kim may be a surly, sour-faced sonofabitch, but he's the only show in town. There *are* no other stores like his in the neighborhood. If he goes out of business, where do these people shop?"

Drum, tired of playing with his soldiers, sat back and made a bridge of his fingers. "That is not my concern. The best utilization of manpower and resources with a very limited budget are my only concerns."

"And to hell with the United States Constitution?" Hightower shot back.

Drum got up and went to look out a window overlooking the promenade thirteen floors below. From this height, the people scurrying into the building looked like industrious ants. He felt a surge of pride. Most of those ants, in one capacity or another, worked for him.

"Chief Hightower," Drum said, "you will comply with my policy of non-confrontation. Is that clear?"

Hightower's jaw muscles were knotting again. Leland looked away. He wasn't certain if he felt pity for the man or admiration. "Yes," Hightower said in a barely audible tone. "It's perfectly clear."

Still looking out the window with his hands behind his back, Drum said, "That'll be all, gentlemen."

As Hightower and Leland were walking toward the door, Drum turned. "Captain Leland, I'd like to talk to you for a moment."

Hightower shot Leland a withering glance and closed the door behind him.

Drum returned to his desk, but he didn't invite Leland to sit down. "Did you see yourself on the news last night?"

"No, sir. I got home too late."

"You didn't miss much," Drum said dryly. "Damn it, Richard, you should know better than to use a word like 'people' in that situation."

Leland was weary of explaining that he meant no disrespect. "Yes, sir," he said. "It won't happen again."

Drum went on as though he hadn't heard. "Bad enough you use the word, but then you go ahead and make an ass of yourself trying to explain it."

"Chief, I thought I could—"

"Watch the press," Drum interrupted. "Especially TV reporters. They're slick and they hold all the cards. Remember, they're the ones who get to do the editing. Not you. Don't get caught with your pants down again."

"No, sir. I won't."

"All right." Drum picked a report out of his in-basket. "Go back to work and try not to step on your dick for the rest of the day."

A puzzled Leland left the office with a lot of unanswered questions in his mind. Why hadn't Drum taken Hightower to task? It was his borough. He should have been there. And why was nothing said about Zeigler's incomprehensible actions? And most of all, why was Drum so calm? He's seen the Chief of Department go ballistic over much less. There was something going on, but he couldn't figure out what it was.

He was also angry. He'd been treated like a child and castigated for events that were beyond his control—or were other people's mistakes. For the first time, he began to have genuine sympathy for the stream of precinct COs he'd seen "Drummed" out of their commands.

Leland took the elevator to the basement garage. Just as he was opening his car door, Sgt. John Wallace stepped out from behind a column. "Hi, Cap."

Leland grinned. "So this is this where Drum put your desk."

"Don't give him any ideas." He looked around furtively. "How'd it go with the Chief?"

"I still have my command."

"I saw you on the news last night. You got mugged."

"I can't blame the media, Johnny. I self-destructed."

Wallace kept glancing around as though he was afraid to be seen with Leland. "Boss, Drum hung you out to dry," he whispered.

"What do you mean?"

"Cap, I've been in patrol most of my time in the job. Since when does a precinct commander, especially a new one, handle someone like Munyika alone?"

"You can't hang that one on Drum. Hightower should have been there, but he was at some damn meeting."

"He was here. In a meeting with Drum."

Leland was stunned. "Didn't anybody tell Drum what was going on in the Bronx?"

"I did. I got the call from the borough. They wanted Hightower to know about the problem developing up there. I personally relayed the message to Drum."

"What'd he say?"

"Thanks."

"Thanks? That's it?"

"Yeah. Hightower didn't know about the demonstration until it was over. Drum kept him in the dark and let you swing in the wind." Wallace looked at his watch. "I'd better get back. I'm still number one on Charlie's shit list."

~~

At first, Leland didn't get it. But by the time he pulled up in front of the Five-five, he'd figured it out. Johnny Wallace had misinterpreted events. Drum wasn't trying to put the screws to *him*. He wanted Hightower to look bad, and if Richard Leland, a lowly precinct commander, got hurt in the process, well, that was just acceptable collateral damage.

He recalled the cavalier way Drum had dismissed the possibility of Kim losing his business and realized that, to Drum, people like Richard Leland and Kim meant little more than the miniature toy soldiers he played with.

When he'd been sent to the Bronx, he knew he was being thrown into the middle of a Drum-Hightower war. He was prepared to protect his rear from Hightower. Now, he would have to protect his rear from Drum as well.

Chapter Twenty-Nine

As he'd been doing every day since the start of the picketing, Leland went to Kim's to assess conditions. He didn't like what he saw. There were more than thirty picketers in front of the store and they were harassing anyone who attempted to enter the market.

When he got back to the precinct, Barry was waiting for him.

"No dice, Boss. The borough said they won't be giving us any manpower to cover the demonstration."

"That ridiculous," Leland said. "There's a mob of demonstrators marching in front of the store. We don't have the people to handle this *and* the normal precinct assignments."

Leland realized a precinct was expected to handle small, local demonstrations within the confines of its borders, but the Munyika boycott, which promised to be a long drawn-out affair with a potential for violence, was beyond the capability of a single precinct. Only the borough command, with its ability to draw on manpower from every precinct in the Bronx, could coordinate the large numbers of cops required.

Leland put a call into the borough and the gruff voice of Chief Hightower came on the other end of the line. "What's the problem, Captain?"

"We were told the borough won't provide manpower to cover the Munyika demonstration."

"That's right."

"Chief, this demonstration may get unruly. I don't have the people to—"

"Put your Anti-Crime people back in the bag. I'm sure you have a few steals hanging around the office. Use them."

"Steals" were cops who were supposed to be on patrol, but who were taken back inside to help with the extra paperwork. But Leland, as part of his efforts to tighten up the command, had returned all of them to patrol months earlier. By trying to run an efficient command, he'd left himself with no cushion of people to fall back on at a time like this.

"I don't have any steals," he said in frustration.

"Then do the best you can. If you fall below minimum manning, I'll arrange for adjoining precincts to cover your sectors. After all," he added, "how many men do you need to do nothing?"

On the other end of the line, a fuming Leland drummed a pencil on the desk. Hightower could hide behind sarcasm. He could blame it on Drum's ill-advised "do nothing" policy, but what he was really doing was distancing himself from the problems that were bound to come from Munyika's boycott. If he, Leland, blew it, Hightower could say, "Captain Leland was in command." And everyone would know, of course, that Leland was Charlie Drum's man. In his frustration, he felt like the only child in the middle of a particularly nasty divorce.

Well, he wasn't going to roll over on this one. Two could play the power game. He'd vowed he would never invoke the name of the Chief of Department, but he'd had enough of Hightower and his "hands-off" policy. "Does Chief Drum know about this?" he asked pointedly.

"It was his idea," Hightower snapped back.

Leland fell back in his seat. "Why?"

"Your ex-boss just finished reading a book on military cohesion. As he explained it to me not more than ten minutes ago, people who are part of the same unit work together better than a mix of people from different units. He thinks your people will do a better job than a detail from nine Bronx precincts." The scorn in his tone left no doubt about what he thought of that idea.

Leland hung up and stared at the telephone for a very long time. He was only too aware of Drum's penchant for reading books on military tactics and strategy, which he sometimes tried to incorporate into the police department with disastrous results. What the Chief of Department never seemed to grasp was that a forty-odd thousand-member police department was not the same as a standing army. But whatever Charlie Drum's tortured reasoning, the fact was Leland had been placed squarely at the center of ground zero. If anything went wrong, it would be his, and only his, responsibility.

So be it. He would just have to make sure he kept the lid on. In situations where racial tensions ran high, any number of flashpoints could set off a major disturbance. His first order of business was to minimize those flashpoints.

Weather was one such flashpoint. The good news was a sixty-percent chance of rain was forecast for the next two days. The bad news was the heat wave was continuing with no sign of deliverance. Leland prayed the weatherman was right for a change. Rain was the police officer's friend. It cooled things down and kept people off the street. It also discouraged picketing. Even the most diehard Munyika supporter didn't like standing out in the rain.

His cops were another flashpoint. They were grumbling about the way this demonstration was being handled. They wanted the cop's quick solution: arrest anyone who refused to remain behind the barricades; arrest anyone who used a bullhorn without a permit; arrest anyone who interfered with Kim's customers. But what they didn't know—Leland hadn't told them—was that Drum had issued orders expressly forbidding that kind of action.

Charlie Drum was right about one thing: Munyika would welcome a confrontation with the police. Professional agitators were adept at using verbal abuse to incite cops to overreact and Leland would have to make sure that his cops didn't get sucked into Munyika's trap.

He called Jack Barry into his office and together, but relying mostly on Barry's intimate knowledge of personalities, they culled from the precinct roster all the hotheads, the quick tempered, the unseasoned rookies, and anyone else they deemed might not be able to handle the pressure that comes from standing three feet away from people who are screeching obscenities in your face for eight straight hours.

Lafferty's name was at the top of the list. To make sure the the list remained confidential, Leland directed Barry to personally draw up the list for the boycott detail. He didn't need his three PBA delegates storming into his office, complaining about selective discrimination.

Leland sat back and rubbed his tired eyes. He'd been here since six o'clock and now it was almost four. "Who's turning out the four-to-twelve, Jack?"

"Engle."

"Tell him I'll want to talk to the platoon."

"What about, Cap?"

"I want to explain the boycott policy."

"Do you think that's a good idea?"

No, he didn't think it was a good idea, but what else could he do? "They have to know the ground rules," he explained.

"Maybe it would be better to do it with a memo."

Leland knew what Barry was driving at. Drum's do-nothing policy was going to be a hard sell to the cops. "No, it's best that I talk to them."

~~

Leland stood behind the desk and forty-six sullen faces stared back at him. He'd just explained the ground rules and had been fielding questions from irate cops for over ten minutes. It was Charlie Reece's turn. "Cap, let me see if I have this right. We're not gonna make Munyika and his crowd stand behind barriers like picketers have to in every other demonstration I've ever worked?"

Leland nodded, weary of answering the same question yet again.

"And they're gonna be allowed to stand in *front* of Kim's store?"

"That's right."

"So we're there to do nothing."

"I didn't say that. We'll be there to keep the peace."

"But we can't make arrests."

"That's right."

Reece scratched his double chin in exasperation. "Cap, with all due respect, that's bullshit." There were murmurs of support from the ranks. "How can we be expected to stand by while Munyika puts Kim out of business?"

"That is not the intent of the policy. By not making arrests, by not confronting him, we will deny him the publicity he seeks. If there's no confrontation, the press will lose interest. Munyika will lose interest. I expect this demonstration to be over by the end of the week."

More hands went up, but he was tired of trying to sell a policy he himself didn't believe in. He'd done his best. He had clearly stated the policy and they would have to live with it. "Sergeant, post the platoon." he said to Engle.

Barry followed Leland back into his office. "They were pretty rough on you."

"I don't blame them, but it's important that they know exactly where the department stands. This Kim boycott is a potential powder keg, Jack. I can't afford to have it blow up in our faces." He felt a quick stab of guilt as he realized that his major concern was that it not blow up in *his* face.

As Barry was leaving, a weary Ronnie Newbert came in. Leland motioned her into a seat. He'd sent her out into the street to check on the last, and most dangerous of all, flashpoint: rumors. Rumors, if left unchallenged, could fan the flames of racial tension into a firestorm. His

Community Affairs Officer's eyes were red from lack of sleep. She'd been out on the street till well after midnight the night before, putting out brushfires before they turned into full-scale conflagrations. And she was back out there at seven this morning.

"What are they saying out there?" he asked.

"Around seven last night I heard some people whispering that the cops had beaten Lucy and she was in a coma. I gave the community leaders the phone number for Corrections and told them to check it out. It took one phone call to squelch that rumor.

"Then around nine-thirty, a rumor started flying around that Lucy was pregnant and the cops had kicked her in the belly, causing her to miscarry. I told them to call Corrections again." She chuckled. "Man, those Corrections guys gotta love me.

"Around eleven, some mope on the picket line started spreading the story that the cops had hung Lucy in her cell and made it look like a suicide. I told him, 'Fool, don't you think that if that story was true it'd be all over the TV news? Why don't you go watch the TV and tell me if they're reporting that story.' The others laughed and that shut him up."

She pushed her glasses up on her nose. "It ain't exactly textbook community relations, Cap, but sometimes you gotta talk trash to them."

Eight months ago he would have chastised her for that kind of behavior. But now—well now, he knew it was just good police work.

"So that's it for the rumors?"

"For the time being. That Munyika crowd has a vivid imagination. When I go back out, I wouldn't be surprised to hear that Lucy was just sold into slavery."

Leland stood up. "Come on, Ronnie. Let's take a ride over to Kim's."

~~

Jimmy Elliot turned the radio car into Clinton Blvd. "What did you think of Leland's speech?" he asked Oliver.

"Charlie's right. It's bullshit."

"I think the captain may have a point."

"What the hell are you talking about?"

"It could be the way to diffuse Munyika."

"Man, since you've been studying for the exam, you've become a real pussy. If you were in the cavalry, you'd be riding sidesaddle. You know that?"

"Would you get off my back about the sergeant's exam? All I'm saying is there's more to this than your myopic ass is capable of seeing."

"So, let me ask you one thing. Are you happy with this policy?"

Elliot drummed the steering wheel for a moment. "No."

"See? That's what I mean. You can't make up your own goddamn mind any more since you've got your head stuck in those books."

They were stopped at a traffic light, when Leland and Newbert drove by.

"Chaos is heading for Kim's," Elliot said.

"Yeah, he'll straighten the whole thing out. Probably tell Kim to go back to Korea."

~~

Leland was pleasantly surprised to see that there were only five listless pickets on the scene. "Small group. Not bad."

"It's early," Newbert said, throwing cold water on his small flame of hope. "Most of Kim's business is in the late afternoon when people come home from work. I guarantee there'll be a whole lot more pickets then. Jeez, will you look at that?" She pointed at a demonstrator carrying a sign that said: "MELANIN SUPERIORITY."

Lt. Hanlon came over to the car. "How's it going?" Leland asked.

"It's been quiet, Cap. Only a few shoppers so far."

"Did they go in?"

"No. The pickets got on their case and they left. Isn't that harassment, Boss? Shouldn't we be locking them up for that?"

"No," Leland snapped. "We're not gonna give Munyika the satisfaction of an arrest confrontation over a little verbal abuse."

"But no one's gone into the store all day. How's Kim gonna make a living if—"

"Lieutenant"—Leland yanked the door open and got out— "let's move those barriers across the street," he said, changing the subject.

Two days ago he'd personally helped set up those barriers in the location where he thought the picket should be. But that was before Drum's "no confrontation" order. Now, the ignored rectangle of blue barriers stood as a disturbing reminder of the police department's—and Richard Leland's—impotence.

"Where do you want them, Cap?"

"In front of the store."

Hannon scratched his head. "In *front*? That'll make it even harder for customers to—"

"You heard me. And make sure you put a row in front of the window. I don't want someone 'accidentally' breaking it."

While Leland was talking to Hannon, he'd been watching the store. Behind the duct-taped plate glass window, Kim, and several family members, stared out at him with anger and fear in their eyes. Their expressions reminded him of photographs he'd seen of Vietnamese prisoners. But this wasn't Vietnam and they weren't prisoners. This was the United States and they were the lawful proprietors of a place of business. And they were not being allowed to conduct business.

"Come on, Ronnie," Leland said reluctantly. "Let's go talk to them."

~~

"*They ruin my business,*" Kim shouted at Leland. "No customers. No money. How I eat? How I pay rent?"

"I understand," Leland said soothingly. "But our hands are tied. They have a right to picket."

"*Right*? They have right to put me out of business? Don't I have right?"

"Yes, you do," Newbert interjected. "But we can't pick sides. We're here to protect everybody's rights"

Kim's eyes flashed in anger. "I do not believe you. You do not protect me."

And on that acrimonious note, Leland and his Community Affairs Officer left the store. As they crossed the street to the car, two TV vans pulled up. A pretty redhead, whom Leland recognized as an anchorwoman for a local affiliate, rushed up to him. Up close, she wasn't quite as attractive. Perhaps it was the heavy orange makeup that made her look hard. But she did look cool. In spite of the oppressive heat, she wasn't even perspiring.

"Captain," she asked breathlessly. "What time is Munyika due?"

"I'm not expecting him," he answered.

She shot him a petulant look and turned to her cameraman. "Bernie, we'll set up across the street."

"Do you have a feeling that she knows something we don't?" Newbert asked.

Leland beckoned to Hanlon. "Lieutenant, it looks like Munyika is going to be showing up sometime soon. I want everyone on the barriers. Get all your people off meals and breaks."

While Hanlon scurried about retrieving the members of his detail, an uneasy Leland paced up and down, recalling his last—and less than auspicious—encounter with the reverend. He reminded himself to watch what he said.

Ten minutes later, Munyika, followed by a caravan of six cars, pulled up in his Escalade. Without a word, the twenty-five people, equipped with their own signs, quickly joined the five pickets who'd been lethargically lounging against the barriers. An aide handed Munyika a BLACK SOLIDARITY sign and the reverend, wearing an ornate orange Dashiki and matching beaded pillbox hat, joined the others, who were now animatedly walking up and down the sidewalk shouting, *"Do the right thing! Do the right thing!"*

The two TV cameramen moved in for the requisite close-up of the angry, chanting faces. A few minutes later, Munyika handed his sign to an aide and came out from behind the barriers. As though he were directing a movie, he positioned himself so that the cameras would be able to get the demonstrators and Kim's market in the background.

He motioned to the two reporters and dutifully they, and their camera crews, moved toward him. The woman, who'd spoken to Leland earlier, asked the first question. "Reverend Munyika, you and your fellow-demonstrators were just chanting 'Do the right thing.' What is the right thing?"

Munyika, displaying his skillful use of the media, turned and addressed the cameras directly. "For too long now, we have had outsiders come into our community and take away jobs and opportunities from our young people. In return, what do we get? Disrespect, physical abuse, and price-gouging. These inequities must stop and I am here to see that they do."

The second reporter, an older man with the blasé look of someone who'd been in the business long enough to know bullshit when he heard it, said, "Reverend Munyika, how do you propose to reverse these so-called inequities?"

Munyika's eyes flashed in anger at the reporter's use of the phrase "so-called," but he didn't react. "There are many ways for the outsiders to atone for the economic crimes they have perpetrated against our community."

He paused so the camera microphones could pick up the chanting: "*Do the right thing! Do the right thing!*" Then he continued in the measured cadence of a TV minister. "I call upon them to share their entrepreneurial skills with us by providing jobs for the people who live in this community. I call upon them to give back some of the obscene profit they make from the people of this community. I call upon them to contribute to the educational and training needs of the people in this community."

"Reverend, I've spoken to Kim," the male reporter persisted. "He says his profit margin is very small. If that's the case, he'd not earning, as you characterize it, obscene profits."

Munyika had had enough of this reporter's nitpicking and turned his considerable charm on the woman reporter. "I ask you," he said with a knowing grin. "When have you ever heard a business man admit to making a profit? I don't care what they say." He pointed a long finger toward the Korean market. "These outsiders are making money off the blood, sweat, and tears of our people and all we ask is our fair share of those profits."

The male reporter attempted to ask another question, but Munyika waved him off. "That's all I have to say at this time."

Surrounded by a swirling circle of aides, Munyika disappeared into the back of his Escalade and sped away. Minutes later, the pickets who had arrived with him were back in their cars and they, too, left. Soon after that, the TV crews pulled the plugs on their equipment and departed, leaving the street as it was with the same five lethargic demonstrators and fifteen bored police officers to watch them.

Leland had watched Munyika's performance with grudging admiration and—anxiety. Any man who could manipulate the media the way he did was indeed a formidable adversary. At this moment, he was glad that Drum had insisted on his "no confrontation" order. He didn't relish going head to head with a man who was clearly a master of confrontation politics.

"Back in the deep end of the pool I see."

Leland turned to see Gloria Perez smiling at him and he immediately came out of his funk. "If this keeps up, I'm gonna have to learn how to swim."

She cocked her head. "You keep using words like 'people' and you might be better off drowning yourself."

Leland winced. "You saw the news?"

"Oh, yeah. Don't they give you guys any training handling the press?"

Leland bristled at her implied criticism. Was he always going to react to her this way? One minute glad to see her, the next wanting to kill her? He was going make up an excuse about being preoccupied with the demonstration, but instead, he said, "I screwed up. I shouldn't have used that word."

She looked at him curiously, as though she were trying to make up her mind about something. "It's an unusual man who'll admit to making a mistake."

He looked into her eyes to see if she was serious or putting him on, but there was no clue in those lovely eyes.

"Are you up to admitting to making another mistake, Captain?"

He grinned. "Another one?"

"Kim's Market."

Leland's smile vanished. "What do you mean?"

"What you're allowing to happen here is unconscionable."

He almost blurted out that none of this was his doing, but she was a civilian and a nosy one at that. The department's tactical decisions were none of her business. "Our job is to remain neutral," he said evenly.

"What about justice? What about doing—as the Reverend Munyika stated so eloquently—'the right thing'?"

"It's a complex issue," he muttered in frustration. It wasn't easy disagreeing with someone he agreed with.

"I don't think it's complex at all. The police department is evading its responsibility because it's afraid of antagonizing a fool like Munyika. God forbid the New York City Police Department should look bad on TV."

"The New York City Police Department did look bad on TV and I was the cause."

"At least you were trying to do your job."

The sound of shouting made them both turn toward the market. A woman attempted to enter the store, but the heckling pickets turned her away. "Why are you letting them picket right in front of his store?" she asked.

"Department policy."

"Since when is it department policy to let people disrupt a man's ability to earn a living? I've never seen pickets permitted to interfere with customers."

"What you may or may not have seen, Ms. Perez, is irrelevant," he said in exasperation. "There is no set policy about such things. Each situation must be evaluated on its merits."

"You're hopeless. You know that?" And on those words she whirled on her heels and walked away.

Ronnie Newbert had been sitting in the car across the street and had seen them in heated discussion. When Leland got into the car she said, "That Perez broad is some pain in the ass, isn't she?"

"Let's go back to the station house," he muttered.

He was angry at himself for getting into an argument with her and disappointed that the tentative truce between them had shattered so easily. When she'd first approached him a moment ago, it seemed to him that her smile was friendlier, less enigmatic. He could now admit that he was happy to see her. He enjoyed talking to her. She was attractive, intelligent, and he was even beginning to appreciate her droll sense of humor. He was even beginning to hope that their professional façades—he, police captain, she, community activist—were beginning to dissolve as well.

But what dissolved was his euphoric mood. Obviously, her change in attitude had all been in his imagination. She was still the same strident community activist she'd always been. What could he have been thinking?

From behind the barriers, Eddie Mazzeo watched Leland's car pull away. "I don't get that guy," he said to Charlie Reece. "I was just beginning to think he had some balls, but I guess I was wrong. He's letting Munyika shit all over him."

Reece shook his head sadly. "I've seen a lot of COs come and go. A few were certifiable assholes, most were okay, and a very few were good bosses. You know what separates the few good ones from the others? *Cojones*. The guy who is willing to put everything on the line when he knows he's right is the one who becomes a good CO. Take Leland—" He was interrupted by the sound of jeering pickets turning another customer away from Kim's. Reece continued. "I thought he had the makings of a good boss, but I guess not. He's just another gutless wonder from the Puzzle Place."

Mazzeo looked across the street and saw another intimidated shopper turn away from Kim's. "The bosses downtown gotta be watching his performance here real carefully. I'll bet they figure he'll make a terrific deputy inspector."

Chapter Thirty

July turned to August and August turned to September with little relief from the stifling heat wave that refused to go away. Meteorologists were calling it the hottest summer New York City had seen in the last hundred years. And, in the midst of this sweltering never-ending summer, the Munyika's boycott—to everyone's dismay—was still going strong.

At the beginning of every tour, Leland visited Kim's Market to personally assess conditions. He'd been doing it for so long it had become a depressing ritual. Every day he saw the same sorry spectacle. The demonstrators—ranging in numbers from five to seven—stood on the sidewalk in front of Kim's store, heckling the people working inside and the occasional shopper who braved the gauntlet of threats and obscenities. Stern, helmeted police officers with arms folded watched the proceedings in restrained, seething silence. Nearby, a small gathering of reporters, weary with what had become a boring assignment, stood around a solitary TV truck talking shop and drinking coffee.

In the eight weeks since the start of the demonstration, the pickets had settled into a dreary routine. A few showed up in the morning, a few more arrived in the afternoon, and a couple of dozen more showed up later in the afternoon in time to hassle Kim's customers who were coming home from work.

The cops, too, had settled into a routine. On a rotating basis, they visited the barbershop to use the restroom facilities or just to get a respite from the heat and the mind-numbing job of watching pickets shuffling aimlessly up and down the sidewalk.

Munyika came less and less, and then only to hold a press conference when he judged interest on the part of the press was waning. The cops always knew when he was coming because additional TV vans and reporters, tipped off by Munyika's efficient PR staff, would suddenly increase in numbers.

On those occasions when he came, he would arrived with a flourish and state his demands, which were growing more and more outrageous. Reporters would ask a few half-hearted questions, and then it was over. Munyika and his entourage would leave, and the press, the demonstrators, and the cops would return to their routines.

It was all in accordance with Chief Drum's plan, but as the days turned to weeks, Leland became more and more troubled with Drum's untenable policy. The Koreans had a right to run their business without interference. The neighborhood residents had a right to shop unopposed. And police officers should not be placed in a position where, day in and day out, they were not allowed to enforce the law.

Leland, accompanied by Ronnie Newbert this time, parked across the street from the market. He caught a glimpse of Kim through the window, still cracked and duct-taped. The Korean was still wearing a thick dressing over his cheek. "How's he doing, Ronnie?"

"I don't know how he hangs on, Cap. A lot of people in the neighborhood feel sorry for him, but they're afraid to cross Munyika. How long can this go on?"

Leland detected an accusatory tone in his Community Affairs Officer. He couldn't blame her. It was a question he'd been asking himself for weeks. He never dreamed the boycott would last this long. "I guess until Munyika gets what he wants," he said halfheartedly.

"But what does he want, Cap?"

"According to his press conferences, he wants the Koreans to hire more minorities and donate money to community causes."

"Which, incidentally, he controls," Newbert shot back. "Besides, Kim doesn't have any money to donate."

"Munyika knows that, but he's betting someone will come up with the money. When a Brooklyn Korean grocery store was boycotted back in 1990, the Korean Merchants Association pumped eight thousand dollars a month into the store to keep the owner above water. Maybe Munyika figures they'd rather give him some of that money up front and cut their costs."

Leland recalled what Hightower had said in Drum's office and the borough commander had been absolutely right. What Munyika was doing to Kim was nothing short of extortion.

Leland saw the glum, sullen expressions on his cops and wished there was something he could do for them. Policing any demonstration was tedious, but this one was particularly onerous because there seemed to be no end in sight, and every day they were forced to stand by helplessly while Munyika and his followers slowly squeezed the economic life out of the Koreans.

He was also painfully aware that as the demonstration dragged on, the gulf between him and his cops was widening. And that troubled him the most. He'd just begun to establish a rapport with them, especially since the Seaman Street operation and the closing of the Joy Lounge. But these last eight weeks had used up all that hard-earned goodwill. Now his cops ignored him and talked to him only when asked a direct question.

Eddie Mazzeo, Peggy Garrigan, and Charlie Reece stopped talking when Leland approached.

"How's it going?" he asked.

There was a prolonged moment of silence and Leland thought no one was going to answer him. Finally, Charlie Reece, in his role as PBA delegate, felt compelled to keep the dialogue open. "About the same, Cap, he said. "I don't know how Kim does it. I've been here for three hours and he's only had one customer."

"He won't last much longer," Mazzeo said bitterly. "He'll probably be replaced by a crack den. Just what this neighborhood needs."

Peggy saw the belligerent expression in Mazzeo's eyes and stepped in front of him. "Cap, who are these pickets? How can they afford to do this day after day?"

"The Intelligence Division says they're being paid by Munyika's organization."

"Unbelievable," Mazzeo said. "A bunch of unemployed bums trying to put a working man out of business. Is this a great country or what?"

Reece shoved Mazzeo behind him. "How long do you think this is gonna go on, Cap?"

"I don't know, Charlie. I just don't know."

"Captain"—Newbert called from the car, mercifully ending the awkward silence—"Lt. Barry called. You're wanted back in the house."

~~

When Leland walked through the door of the station house, an anxious Barry was waiting for him. "There's a Mr. Bernard Cohen to see you."

"Who is he?"

"Kim's lawyer."

Bernard Cohen, a lean man in his early forties, radiated the no-nonsense demeanor of a man who has little time for idle chatter. He sat down across the desk from Leland and ran his hand over his sparse hair. "Thank you for seeing me, Captain Leland," he said, sliding his business card across the desk. "I represent Mr. Kim."

Leland studied the card and noted that Cohen was a partner in a midtown law firm.

"What can I do for you, Mr. Cohen?"

The lawyer smiled, but there was no warmth in it. "You could do something about those people who are trying to put my client out of business."

Leland sighed inwardly. "The police department is doing all that it can, Mr. Cohen."

This time, Cohen didn't even attempt to smile. "Captain, you and I have a serious disagreement about that. My specialty is labor law and I must tell you that I have never in all my years of practice seen pickets permitted to demonstrate directly in front of man's place of business and interfere with his livelihood. Have you?"

Leland said nothing. He'd long since stopped defending a policy he didn't believe in.

Cohen continued. "Captain, have you ever wondered how Mr. Kim has been able to withstand this siege?"

"I wouldn't characterize it as a siege."

"The Korean Merchants Association has been contributing thousands of dollars a month to Mr. Kim's business so he can pay his rent, utilities, and feed his family."

"That's very commendable of them."

"Yes, it is. And they're doing it because they think there's an important point to be made here. Namely, that no one has the right to deprive a man of his livelihood because of the color of his skin."

"I agree with that."

"Do you? It's hard to tell, Captain."

Leland was stung by the sarcasm in the attorney's tone. "Mr. Cohen, I am following police department policy, which is to keep the peace and remain neutral. As I'm sure you know, this has been an extremely volatile situation and, since that first day, no one has been hurt."

"Except," Cohen added pointedly, "Mr. Kim and his family." He stood up. "Captain, if the police department won't protect Mr. Kim's rights, then I intend to petition the court to make you. Tomorrow morning I am going before Judge Tollinger to request a restraining order enjoining the pickets from demonstrating within fifty feet of Kim's Market."

Leland nodded noncommittally, but inside he was overjoyed. A court action would break the stalemate. The court had the power to overturn Drum's ill-advised strategy and even Charlie Drum wouldn't defy a court order. "I want you to know," Leland said, "that we will enforce any restraining order handed down by the court."

Cohen nodded curtly. "Mr. Kim will be glad to hear that."

~~

It was almost six o'clock when Leland got a phone call from Sgt. Engle. "Captain, I thought you should know. We just got word that Munyika is going to give a press conference in a couple of minutes."

The press conference was already underway when Leland pulled up in front of Kim's. He stood behind the bank of TV cameras and listened to the redheaded reporter ask a question. "Reverend Munyika, it's our understanding that Kim's lawyer is going into court tomorrow morning to seek a restraining order against you blocking the store. Will you abide by a restraining order if one is issued?"

Munyika's smile reflected his utter lack of unconcern. As he turned to the cameras to deliver his answer, he saw Leland standing in the back of the crowd and their eyes locked. "I don't care what the court—or the police department—says. We have a righteous cause that supersedes any mere piece of paper."

"So you will disobey a restraining order?"

Munyika continued to stare at Leland. "Yes, I will."

Leland's stomach knotted. When Cohen had told him about the restraining order, he'd been elated, but now he realized that, far from solving his problems, a restraining order simply played into Munyika's hands. Since the beginning, he'd been looking for a confrontation, which Drum's strategy—Leland grudgingly had to admit—had denied him. Now, enforcing a restraining order would give him the confrontation he so desperately wanted.

When Munyika finished speaking, Leland started back toward his car. It was important that he talk to Hightower and work out a strategy. Whether he wanted to or not, the chief was finally going to have to get involved in this. Enforcing the restraining order would take more cops than Leland had at his disposal. In spite of his misgivings about going up against Munyika, he was relieved that this intolerable stalemate was finally going to be broken.

The redheaded reporter spotted him and, trailed by her camera crew and the other TV reporters, rushed toward him. The klieg lights of three cameras momentarily blinded Leland as three microphones were thrust in front of his face.

"Captain, you just heard the Reverend Munyika say he will defy a restraining order. How will the police department respond to that?"

Leland, wishing he'd made his getaway, turned to face the bank of cameras. He knew better than to state a policy decision on TV without consulting Drum or Hightower, but this was a clear-cut issue and he saw no problem in declaring what had to be the department's position. "The police department will enforce the provisions of the judge's restraining order," he said.

"And what if Munyika resists?" another reporter shouted out.

Leland sighed inwardly. They never give up. "We will take whatever action we deem necessary."

"Including arrests?"

"Including arrests." As soon as he said it, a little voice inside him told him he'd made a big mistake.

~~

That night in his stuffy apartment, Leland watched the eleven o'clock news, sitting in front of the TV, clothed only in shorts. He winced when he heard himself say: *"Including arrests."*

"Congratulations, schmuck," he said, waving his martini at the TV. "You may have just self-destructed on the eleven o'clock news."

He changed the channel to watch the end of a Yankee game when the phone rang. It was Gloria. He hit the mute button and sat up straight. He hadn't spoken to her since their argument in front of Kim's.

"I just saw the news. Congratulations."

"For shooting myself in the foot again?"

"No. For sounding like a responsible member of the New York City Police Department."

Leland grunted. "As usual, we see things differently."

"What are you talking about?"

"I should have conferred with Chief Hightower."

"What else could you have said? You have to honor the court's restraining order."

"I guess so," he said hesitantly. Munyika and this whole boycott fiasco had shaken his confidence and he wasn't sure about anything anymore.

"Well, anyway. I just called to give you an 'attaboy.'"

"Thanks."

There was an awkward silence as he tried to think of what to say next. For an instant, he thought about asking her out to dinner, but this latest twist in the Munyika boycott promised to keep him busy for the foreseeable future.

"Well," she said, finally breaking the silence. "I'll see you around."

"Yeah," he answered. "I'll see you around."

Before he could say anything else, he heard a click on the other end of the line. He slammed the phone down, angry with himself for acting like a damn high school kid asking for his first date.

The phone rang again. Thinking it was Gloria, he snatched it up. "Hello?"

"Captain Leland, Lt. Hanlon here. I hate calling you at this hour, but I just got a telephone message from the Chief of Department's office. You're to report to Chief Drum's office at 0800 hours tomorrow morning."

Leland put the phone down slowly. That message could mean only one thing: He's screwed up big time. But of course he knew that. What he didn't know was: How badly? He picked up his half-finished martini and put it back down. Even vodka couldn't help now.

~~

Charlie Drum slammed his hand down on the desk and half-dozen miniature Roman legionaries toppled over. "Goddamn it, Richard, what's the matter with you? You're a mere *captain*. You don't make policy and you don't speak for the police department."

"I'm sorry, Chief, but they ambushed me. I had no intention of—"

"If you must talk to the press, talk for chrissake, but don't *say* anything."

Leland nodded. It was easy for him to criticize, but he wasn't the one with three cameras in his face. "Chief, perhaps I shouldn't have said anything, but what I said was true. If there's an restraining order, we have to honor it."

Drum was about to respond when the phone rang. He listened for a moment. "Yes, send him in."

Lucian Hightower came in. He acknowledged Leland with a silent, grim nod, probably wondering why Leland was in Drum's office ahead of him.

"Lucian, I guess you know why I've called you two here."

"The restraining order."

"That and Captain Leland's TV performance."

Hightower shot a glance a Leland. 'I don't approve of him giving press conferences without checking with me first, but, mercifully, he didn't say anything wrong."

Leland felt the deep gratitude of a drowning man who has just been thrown a life ring. Even if it was a left-handed compliment.

Drum's eyes narrowed. "He didn't say anything wrong?"

"No. If the court issues a restraining order, we'll have to enforce it."

"We don't have to enforce a *civil* restraining order," Drum said with the self-satisfied smile of one who has discovered a loophole that only he knows about.

"Maybe we don't have to," Hightower said warily, "but we do it all the time."

Drum picked up his fallen legionaries and put them back in formation. "We will not enforce this one."

Hightower's eyes narrowed. "On whose authority?"

"The City's attorneys. I had a meeting with them last night."

Hightower studied Drum, trying to figure out what the hell was going on in that convoluted mind. "In my thirty-seven years in the department, I can't remember a time when we didn't enforce a civil court order, especially where public safety is concerned."

"Well, there's always a first time."

Hightower sprang forward with such suddenness that Drum recoiled. "In the name of God, what are you trying to prove? We've followed your instructions, which have done nothing but hurt the Koreans, made Munyika look good, shattered the morale of the police officers in the Five-five, and, in general, made the police department look like a horse's ass. Do you want to continue that policy in the face of a court order?"

Drum quickly recovered his composure. "Yes, I do. And for the same reason as before." To get away from Hightower's frog-eyed glare, he went to the window and looked toward City Hall. During the winter months City Hall could be clearly seen, but now the leaves were in full bloom and he could only see the top of the building poking above the green canopy. "I will not give Munyika the satisfaction of a confrontation."

"He doesn't need a confrontation," Hightower said bitterly. "He's getting plenty of publicity just making us look like fools."

Drum turned away from the window. "You're wrong. He's getting less and less TV coverage. The media is getting bored with him."

"How can you say that? Every time he calls a press conference—"

"Lucian," Drum said sharply. "Let me see if I can make it real simple for you. Munyika thrives on publicity. He gets publicity from TV. Those whores in the TV media are drawn to confrontation. Deny Munyika his confrontation and we deny him publicity."

"But at what expense?" Hightower asked in exasperation. "We've appeased this man for too long. It's been more than eight weeks. It's time to draw a line in the sand. A restraining order will be the perfect excuse for changing our policy—"

Drum held up a silencing hand. "Perhaps I didn't make myself clear. I didn't call you two here to ask for your suggestions. I called you here to give you your instructions. You will not enforce that restraining order. Is that clear?"

"Perfectly," Hightower answered in a voice constricted with rage.

"And you, Captain Leland, will not conduct any more press conferences. Is that clear?"

Leland nodded silently.

Drum sat back down in his high leather-backed chair. "I'm glad we all understand each other. That'll be all," he said with a dismissive wave of his hand.

∼∼

Leland rode the elevator to the basement garage with mixed emotions. He was grateful he'd dodged the bullet again, but Drum's insistence on continuing his absurd policy had put him in an untenable position. *Not enforce the restraining order?* How could he face his cops? How could he face Kim? How could he face Gloria?

He went back to the precinct and tried, without much success, to concentrate on the daily business of running a precinct. Around six o'clock, he gave up. He was just going through the motions and was accomplishing nothing. He glanced at his calendar to see what he had to do tomorrow and groaned. There was a Community Board meeting tonight, which he'd completely forgotten about. He would have skipped it, or sent someone else, but he'd been asked to speak about crime prevention. As he was locking up his desk, Lt. Barry came in and tossed some papers in the in basket. "The mail just came, Cap."

"Thanks, Jack." Leland glanced at the Special Orders on top of the pile. Five lieutenants were being promoted to captain tomorrow. Tim Frazer was one of them. Curious to see where Frazer was being assigned, Leland's eyes scanned down the "transferred to" column. He sat down heavily on the desk and read the line again. *Captain Timothy L. Frazer will continue in his assignment at the Chief of Department's office.*

Drum had violated his own policy—a policy that had gotten *him* into this mess in the first place. He dropped the Special Orders in his in basket and walked out the door.

~~

The Community Board meeting was mercifully brief. After his talk there were few questions and the meeting ended quickly. As Leland finished talking to a woman who'd been complaining about low flying airplanes, Gloria came up to him.

"In spite of your misgivings, I see you survived yet another harrowing TV appearance."

"Barely." He had no intention of telling her about his run-in with Drum—or the Chief's decision to ignore the restraining order.

"I'm so glad Kim is finally going to get some relief from Munyika." When he said nothing, she continued. "I had a long talk with him this afternoon. Do you have any idea what he had to go through to open that store? By our standards, the startup costs are low, less than ten thousand. But he couldn't get that money from a bank. What bank would lend money to a man who is an immigrant who can hardly speak English? He raised it by borrowing from friends and relatives. He cuts his overhead by using family members to run the store. Fortunately, Kim and his family have a good work ethic. They think nothing of putting in twelve or sixteen hours a day."

Leland felt bad enough for Kim without hearing this. "Why are you telling me all this?" he asked.

"Just so you know how unfair it is for Munyika to demand a cut of Kim's 'obscene profits.' And as for jobs, forget it. If he had to pay his family a regular salary, he'd have to fire them all. To hear Munyika talk, you'd think Kim was Wal-Mart."

Leland was getting the distinct impression that he was being lectured to and he didn't like it. "I understand the issues," he said.

She looked at him curiously. "Do you? Do you really?"

"Of course I do, but none of that is relevant to me. My job is to remain neutral."

She was still looking at him with that curious expression. "You're dealing with human lives."

"I know that," he said evenly. "What else can I do?"

Angered by his detached tone, she said, "I guess you don't have to do anything except enforce the restraining order." She turned and walked away from him.

~~

Billy Lafferty clicked the microphone button several times. "I don't think the radio's working. We haven't gotten a call in over twenty minutes."

An exasperated Charlie Reece slapped the steering wheel. "You're unbelievable, you know that? You're always bitching about too many jobs, now you're complaining because there's not enough."

"I don't mind jobs. I just like them spaced out, that's all."

"This is the police department, schmuck. You wanna work by appointment, you shoulda been a hairdresser."

Lafferty looked at his watch. "It's seven-thirty. Let's take a run by Kim's."

"That's not our sector."

"I just want to see what's going on."

"There might be bosses from the borough there. You don't need to get on anyone's else's shit list."

"Charlie, no boss outside this precinct has set foot within a mile of Kim's."

Lafferty wasn't often right, but he was this time. The Kim "problem" was a powder keg ready to explode and any boss who valued his career didn't want to be anywhere near the impact zone when it happened. Reece made a U-turn.

As the radio car pulled into the curb across the street from Kim's, Lafferty thumped the dashboard. "Ain't that some shit? They're all over the front of the store. How's anyone supposed to get in there?"

Lt. Hanlon rapped the roof of the radio car and Lafferty lowered his window. "What are you doing here?" the lieutenant asked. "You're out of your sector."

"We just stopped by to see if you wanted some coffee," Reece, ever the diplomat, said.

"Thanks. I just had some."

"How are things going?" Lafferty asked.

"For Munyika, pretty good. For Kim, not so good. I swear to God I don't know how he stays in business. I've been here since four and he hasn't had more than three customers."

"I don't know *why* he stays in business," Lafferty muttered. "These fuckin' mutts don't deserve a decent store. Kim should—"

He was interrupted by a howl from the crowd. One demonstrator yelled at an elderly woman who was heading for the store, *"Hey, Aunt Jemima, go shop in one of the brothers' stores."*

"That's what they've been doing all day," Hanlon said. They torment anyone who attempts to go into the store. Most of them leave. I don't blame them."

"She looks like a feisty old broad," Lafferty said. "A buck says she goes in."

"You're on," Reece said.

After a couple of minutes of finger pointing and shouting from both sides the woman shoved her way through the jeering crowd and left.

Lafferty muttered an oath and threw a dollar bill on the seat, then he snatched it up and yanked the car door open. "Goddamn it. *I'm* gonna go in there and buy something."

An alarmed Hanlon slammed the door shut. "Like hell you will. Get back to your sector."

Reece put the car in gear. "It's time we were going."

As they pulled away from the curb, Reece snatched the dollar out of Lafferty's hand. "And that's my dollar, fucko."

Chapter Thirty-One

The next day, Billy Lafferty, late as usual, barged into the locker room gleefully rubbing his hands together. *"All right!"* he shouted. The other cops, in various stages of undress, looked up. "I just heard it on the radio," he explained. "Kim got a restraining order against Munyika. Now we're gonna kick some ass."

"*We?*" Mazzeo asked. "You haven't worked a day on the demonstration."

Lafferty shrugged. "That's because my talents as a street cop are too valuable to be wasted watching a bunch of mopes walking a picket line. That's for dolts like you."

Someone tossed an empty coffee container over the lockers and Lafferty batted it away. "Missed me, hard-on," he shouted to his unseen assailant.

Mazzeo buffed his shoes. "Billy has a point. Leland's gonna have to let us make some collars."

"You guys talk like you're going on a picnic," Elliot said, strapping on his vest. "If we try to move them behind barriers across the street, Munyika and his crew ain't gonna go quietly."

Reece stuck his head around a locker. "Jimmy's right. Munyika is gonna want to get a lot of mileage out of this."

"Let 'em," Mazzeo said. "I'm sick of standing around watching a bunch of skells put Kim out of business. I figure it this way: Either we act like cops or we shouldn't be there. If Munyika wants to mix it up, that's okay by me."

~~

As soon as the day tour platoon turned out, Leland went directly to Kim's, more apprehensive than usual. This morning he'd been officially notified that the judge had signed the restraining order. Anticipating trouble, he'd increased the detail by two sergeants and twenty cops. In doing so, he'd stripped the precinct's coverage and the borough had to send in four additional radio cars to cover radio runs in the precinct.

As soon as he pulled up to Kim's, he could see that the level of tension had been ratcheted up a couple of notches. He counted thirty-five pickets. And there were a lot more TV cameras on the scene. Only the local affiliates had been covering the boycott, but now, to his dismay, he saw camera crews from ABC, CBS, and CNN.

The Reverend Kawasi Munyika has finally gotten the national exposure that he'd so desperately craved, Leland thought glumly. Now it was a whole new ballgame. The eyes of the whole world were on the Five-five—and *him*.

The beefed-up contingent of demonstrators chanted *"People's Freedom Legion"* over and over again for the benefit of the cameras trained on them.

A battery of photographers checked their equipment, getting ready for the confrontation that was sure to come.

Leland found Lt. Hanlon. "Have you seen Chief Hightower?"

"No, Boss."

Leland had been told that Hightower would be here. *Where the hell was he?* Right now, Richard Leland was the ranking officer, and if the borough commander didn't show up, he would be the one who would have to announce that the New York City Police Department had no intention of enforcing the restraining order.

He just finished going over his orders with Hanlon and his two sergeants when he saw Munyika's Escalade coming down the street. He looked at his watch. Nine-thirty and still no sign of Hightower. Munyika got out of the car, waved to the reporters, shook hands with a couple of onlookers, and joined the demonstrators in front of Kim's.

The actors were taking the stage, Leland thought with growing apprehension. The only players missing were Cohen—and Hightower. He prayed the chief would get here before the lawyer.

As if on cue, Cohen pulled up to the curb in a taxi and got out waving the document in the air for the benefit of the cameras. Camera crews and reporters converged on him as he strode toward Leland, who was standing alone in front of Kim's Market, silently cursing Drum and Hightower.

The dour-faced attorney stopped in front of Leland. Leland's eyes swept the crowd, hoping to see Hightower's car coming down the street.

There was no sign of his borough commander, but he did see Gloria standing across the street watching him intently. Leland's stomach knotted and he wished he were anywhere but here.

In a loud voice for the benefit of the cameras, Cohen said, "Captain Leland, I have here a restraining order signed by Judge Tollinger. It enjoins the demonstrators from picketing within fifty feet of Kim's Market."

Out of the corner of his eye, Leland noticed that Munyika had stopped marching and was intently watching him. Leland read the order, hardly paying attention to the legalistic jargon. What did it matter what the words said? He wouldn't be enforcing it anyway. The chanting grew louder in his ears. Every camera and microphone was trained on him, waiting for him to speak. Every police officer, poised behind the barriers, watched silently. He looked out over the heads of the reporters crowded around him. Still no Hightower.

"Mr. Cohen," he said evenly, "this is a civil restraining order. The police department is not required to enforce a civil order."

There was an immediate explosion of strobe lights as the photographers reacted to the police department's stunning capitulation.

Cohen, at a momentary loss for words, recovered quickly. "Captain," he hissed, "this is... preposterous. There is absolutely no precedent for this."

"Mr. Cohen, I am following the instruction of the city's Corporation Counsel."

His face contorted with fury, Cohen snatched the restraining order from Leland. He turned toward the cameras and dramatically waved it in the air. "It's a sad day for justice in this city when the New York City Police Department refuses, even when so ordered by the court, to protect the rights of one of its citizens."

The redheaded reporter pushed her way to the front. "Mr. Cohen, what will you do now?"

"I will confer with the court. But I'm serving notice on the city and the police department that I am holding them responsible for any and all personal and property damages that may occur as a result of the police department's refusal to protect my client."

As a furious Cohen disappeared into Kim's store, the reporters rushed to Munyika, who'd been intently listening to the exchange.

"Reverend Munyika," a reporter shouted out, "do you see this as a victory for your side?"

"Absolutely," he said confidently. In truth, he was disappointed. He'd been hoping to spark the kind of out-of-control melee that would guarantee him the spotlight of national television. But he hid his frustration with a toothy grin. There would be another time. "As I've said all along, we are totally within our rights to demonstrate here and"—he made eye contact with Leland and winked—"I'm happy that the police department has finally acknowledged that right."

The redheaded reporter saw a handful of cops in a heated discussion and her reportorial instincts told her there was a story here. Before Leland could head her off, she rushed over with her crew and thrust the microphone into the center of the group. "What do you police officers think of the department's policy not to enforce the injunction?"

Mazzeo was about to say what he thought, but Peggy Garrigan stepped in front of him. "We don't have an opinion," she said evenly. "We're neutral and we do what we're told."

Leland, grateful for her words, exhaled slowly. The other cops stared stony-faced at him as though this had been his doing.

Within minutes, the TV crews and photographers had packed up and left. Shortly after that, Munyika, tired of picketing without an audience, hopped over the barriers and headed toward his car. He saw Leland standing on the other side of the street. With the self-satisfied smile of the victor, he shouted, "Some days it don't pay to get out of bed, do it, Captain?"

"You're right," Leland said gamely, "but you never know which days."

Munyika was still laughing when he climbed into his Escalade.

Hightower's car pulled up just as Munyika's car squealed away from the curb. Hightower jumped out. "Am I too late?"

"Yeah," Leland said bitterly. "You're too late."

Hightower's practiced eye swept the scene, mentally making sure that the cops and barriers were properly placed. "I meant to be here sooner."

Leland didn't trust himself to look at the chief. He concentrated on watching Munyika's Escalade disappearing down the street. "Traffic can be a bitch this time of day," he said through clenched teeth.

Hightower gave him a sharp look, but Leland was too furious to care. Then he heard himself say, "You missed your chance to get on TV, Chief, and so I had to do it. I know Chief Drum told me to stay off the tube, but what could I do? It was either me or one of my sergeants. I figured I'd better do it since I have a hell of a lot more experience making an ass of myself than they do."

Hightower opened the back door of his car. "Get in." To his driver, he said, "Frank, go get a cup of coffee or something. I'll call you when I need you."

Leland climbed into the back of the car, resigned to the fact that he'd finally blown it. He'd always been able to mask his feelings—a talent he honed in the tinderbox atmosphere of One Police Plaza—but he couldn't do it anymore. And furthermore, he didn't want to.

To his surprise, the thought of getting dumped out of the Five-five no longer held any dread for him. The only emotion he felt—and one that amazed him—was regret. He wouldn't get the chance to finish the things he'd stared in the Five-five. It had taken him ten months, but he'd finally begun to turn things around. Until this Kim-Munyika fiasco, morale was up, as evidenced by a dramatic drop in sick time and a sharp increase in his arrest and summons stats. And his cops weren't nameless faces anymore. He knew who the good ones were and who the bad ones were. He'd been rewarding the former by recommending them for details, and he'd been doing his best to adjust the behavior of the latter. To his astonishment, he was actually beginning to enjoy being a precinct commander. But now, it was all over and everything he'd worked so hard to achieve was about to blow up in his face.

Hightower got in beside him and slammed the door. "You think I left you out here to swing in the wind alone?"

Leland's fury deadened his caution. "Yes, that's exactly what I think."

"Then you don't know me very well, Captain."

Leland glared at his boss. "I guess I don't. You're not an easy man to know."

Hightower grunted. "That's true. I can be a demanding sonofabitch, but that's my job. I'm not here to hold the hand of my precinct commanders."

"I don't need anyone to hold my hand, Chief. Just a little support will do." He jerked a finger toward the cops standing around the barriers. "Since the beginning, I've had to handle this with just my people. Have you any idea what that's done to their morale?"

"That was Drum's call," Hightower reminded him.

Charlie Drum. Leland fell silent as he thought about the exasperating Chief of Department. They'd never been friends—Leland doubted anyone could be friends with someone like Charlie Drum—still, he'd expected some degree of loyalty from the man he'd worked for so hard and so long. Instead, Drum had purposely put him in the line of fire in his attempt to bring down Hightower. It suddenly occurred to him what he should have known all along: Charlie Drum neither liked nor disliked people. To him, people were just pieces on a chessboard. Like all good chess players, he knew it was sometimes necessary to sacrifice a valuable piece in order to win the endgame. Leland wondered if Drum considered him a valuable piece or just another pawn. But what was the difference? The end result was the same.

Hightower, smarting from Leland's accusatory tone, said, "I don't owe you an explanation, Captain, but I'll give you one anyway. I was at the PC's office trying to convince him to override Drum."

Despite his fury, Leland felt a grudging admiration for Hightower. In making an end-run around Drum to appeal directly to Commissioner Randall, Hightower had put himself in a politically dangerous situation.

"What did he say?" Leland asked.

"Just what I was afraid he'd say. 'Chief Drum has a handle on it. I trust his judgment.'"

"I can understand Randall saying that," Leland said in frustration. "But how could the Corporation Counsel go along with it?"

"Captain, what do lawyers always say when they know they will have to deal with the consequences of their decision? *Do nothing*. And I'm sure Drum also pointed out to them that Munyika can cause a hell of a lot more trouble for the city than one Korean grocer. For chrissake, get it through you head, this is about cost-benefits, not justice."

Leland was dismayed to hear Hightower matter-of-factly reduce the human issues involved to such a cold common denominator. Leland had always thought of himself as politically mature, but he never imagined the police department would acquiesce in the destruction of one man in order to avoid trouble with another. "So, that's it?" he said bleakly. "We do nothing?"

Hightower opened the door. "We can do nothing."

Leland got out and turned to face his borough commander. "Let me ask you a question, Chief. Do you think this is right?"

"Hell, no," he growled. "Of course it's not right."

Chapter Thirty-Two

Fall came late, no doubt due to the heat wave, which finally broke the last week of September. And now, just three weeks before Thanksgiving, the weather had turned crisp, a harbinger of the winter weather to come. Still, a handful of red and yellow leaves stubbornly clung to the branches in a desperate effort to stave off winter.

Autumn was a season of change, but some things didn't change, at least not in the Five-five precinct. There was no let-up in the Kim boycott and each passing day meant Kim was one day closer to closing. Only a day earlier, Cohen had called Leland to tell him that the Korean Merchants Association was running out of support money and patience. Leland thanked him for the information and assured him, once again, that the police department would remain neutral and committed to maintaining the peace.

Those words rung hollow in his ears. He'd been saying them for so long that he almost believed them, but then he'd see Kim, staring out at him through the cracked window with those accusing almond-shaped eyes; he'd watch demonstrators heckle timid shoppers until they turned away from the market; and he knew that what he'd been repeating over and over again for the past four months, like a mantra, was a lie.

While the Kim-Munyika drama played itself out in one corner of the precinct, life went on in the Five-five. Radio calls were answered, arrests were made, summonses were issued, the sick and injured were tended to, and the hundreds of reports generated by all this work were duly submitted and filed.

The day-to-day work continued, but an unmistakable pall hung over the Five-five. New York City cops were renowned for their gallows humor. They always found something to laugh about no matter how bad things were. But there was little laughter in the Five-five now.

Leland had grown used to their sullen stares and laconic responses to his attempt at dialogue. He knew they blamed him for what was going on at Kim's Market, but what bothered him more was that they blamed themselves for the part they were playing in the destruction of Kim's business. To a cop, the worse thing he can do in the face of lawlessness is to do nothing. And they had been doing nothing for over four months.

Ronnie Newbert stuck her head in the door. "Cap, got a minute?"

"Sure. Come in."

She slid into a chair and stared at the floor. She was exhausted. She'd been going non-stop since the first pickets showed up at Kim's. Every day, she roamed the streets squelching rumors, assuaging the ruffled feathers of community groups that felt they weren't getting the protection they deserved, and mediating between groups that thought the cops weren't doing enough and groups that thought they were doing too much. But the long frustrating hours had taken their toll and the enthusiastic spark had gone out of her eyes.

She picked an imaginary piece of lint off her slacks. "Captain, I'm putting in for a transfer."

Leland winced. He knew it was only a matter of time before some smart boss offered someone as talented as she was a better opportunity, but he didn't want to see her go. It was selfish, he knew, but he didn't want to lose her valuable skills, especially while the boycott continued. "You have a shot at a detail?" he asked.

"No." She wouldn't look at him. " I want to go to another precinct. I think it's time to move on."

Leland's heart sank. She wasn't even leaving for a better opportunity. She just wanted out. And if she wanted out so did the rest of the command. "Ronnie, talk to me."

She pushed her glasses up on her nose and her eye sparkled with tears. "I can't deal with this Kim thing anymore, Captain. Every day I meet people—white, black, Asian—and they all ask me the same thing: When are we gonna do something about Munyika? I don't know what to tell them anymore."

"I hear what you're saying, but I really need you here."

"I know you do, Boss. That's why I waited. I figured this would end, but it hasn't and I'm tired—and angry."

"At me?"

"No. I know you're stuck in the middle of this just like the rest of us. I'm angry at Munyika and what he represents." She blinked away tears. "Guys like him hold all black people hostage to stereotypes. He says he wants jobs for his 'people.' That's a lot of crap. You see who's walking that picket line. Ain't one of 'em has had a real job in his whole life. You offer those people a job in Kim's Market and they'd laugh in your face. Twelve hours a day, seven days a week for chump change? No way. They just want to get paid for making believe they're working."

"Ronnie, if others in the neighborhood feel the way you do, why don't they break the boycott?"

"Because they're afraid of Munyika. Most of the people who have been turned away are hard-working people, but Munyika tells them that if they shop at Kim's they're Uncle Toms and Aunt Jemimas. It's all bullshit, but it works. No black person wants to be thought of as an Uncle Tom or an Oreo. That's what I mean about being held hostage to our own stereotypes. I'm black *and* a woman. Believe me, I know discrimination. It's always been there, it may always be there, but it's not gonna stop me from succeeding."

She took off her glasses and rubbed them furiously with a handkerchief. "My older brother is in dental school. He's there because of a partial scholarship and three part-time jobs. I became a cop because the pay is good and it allows me to pay the tuition at NYU. I'm not blowing my own horn. There are plenty of blacks doing what my brother and I are doing. I just hate to see someone like Munyika ridicule people for trying to make it in this world. I don't care what color they are."

She put her glasses back on. "There's another reason why people like Munyika get a following and it pains me to talk about it. What have rabble-rousers like Munyika been saying for years? That we don't get the chance to succeed in this country because we're a minority, because we haven't received the proper education, because we don't have the capital to start up our own businesses. Then these damn Asians come along. Minorities like us, only maybe worse off. They're yellow, they have slanty eyes, they don't speak English, and they have no money. And damn if they don't go and get *successful*! They scrape a few bucks together from family and friends, add a lot of sweat equity, and *bam*! They start living the American dream. While they're doing that, they send their kids to the same crummy ghetto schools we complain about. As soon as these kids learn to speak English, they shoot to the top of the class. Captain, Munyika hates Kim because he makes a liar out of him."

Leland hadn't thought about it quite that way, but, then again, he wasn't a minority. "Ronnie, someday you'll make a great sociologist," he said.

She smiled ruefully. "Thanks, Boss. But sometimes a little knowledge is a dangerous thing. I know what Munyika is doing and I just can't be around it anymore."

Leland knew he could block her transfer, but he wouldn't do that. It wouldn't be right to penalize her just because she was good at her job. "Okay, Ronnie, give me the transfer request and I'll sign it."

She stood up, blinking away tears. "Captain, I'm sorry."

"Me, too, Ronnie. Me, too."

~~

That afternoon, Leland made his daily trip to Kim's. Munyika was making one of his rare appearances when no TV cameras were present. Leland was talking to Sgt. Engle, but he was watching Munyika laughing and joking with a handful of demonstrators. Like a good field general, he was keeping his troops happy. *He's doing a hell of a lot better job than I am*, Leland thought, ruefully eyeing a dozen sullen cops manning the barriers.

Suddenly, Leland had a thought and as Munyika was heading for his car he intercepted him. "Reverend Munyika, could I have a word with you?"

"Certainly, Captain. I'm always at your disposal," he answered, supremely confident. And why shouldn't he be? He'd gotten everything he wanted – national TV coverage, an impotent police department, and a Korean grocer who was about to go out of business.

"Alone," Leland added.

Munyika's eyes narrowed and the smile turned wary. He nodded to his entourage and they moved a few paces down the sidewalk.

Munyika looked down at Leland. "What do you want?"

"I want to know how long you're going to keep this up."

"Until our demands are—"

Leland dropped his voice. "Cut the bullshit, Munyika. There are no TV cameras around now. Just you and me. How long?"

Munyika regarded Leland with dull, hard eyes. "Okay, let's you and me talk man-to-man. I'm gonna keep this up until I put that little yellow motherfucker out of business," he said softly. "Does that answer your question?"

Leland nodded. "Yes, it does," he answered, feeling better than he had for a very long time.

~~

Leland was up the whole night, pacing his tiny living room, thinking his plan through. It was risky—hell, who was he kidding? *It was the mother of all career busters.* All night long, he reviewed the pros and cons. Unfortunately, his plan contained mostly cons and that's why it wasn't until three in the morning that he finally made up his mind. And as soon as he did, a wondrous calm came over him. He felt at peace with himself—a peace he hadn't felt in a very long time.

~~

The next day, Leland purposely arrived at the borough office after 6 p.m. He knew most of the staff would be gone and he'd find Hightower alone. What was about to take place could get noisy and he wanted as few witnesses as possible.

The chief was at his desk reading a crime analysis report when Leland knocked on the open door. Hightower looked up in surprise. "Do we have a meeting scheduled?"

"No." Leland came in and slammed the door behind him.

"Why don't you close the door," Hightower said, glancing at a photo of the PC that had been knocked awry.

"I want to talk to you about Kim."

Hightower's frog-eyes blinked once, slowly. "Now what?"

"It's time we broke the siege."

Hightower's expression was neutral. "*We*? You got a mouse in your pocket, Captain?"

"You and me."

Hightower sat back and folded his hands behind his neck. "What brought you to that conclusion?"

"Drum's strategy isn't working."

Hightower grunted. "Did you ever think it would?"

"No."

"And now you want to do something about it."

The use of the singular pronoun didn't escape Leland. "That's right. I want us to enforce the restraining order."

"And give Munyika the publicity he's looking for?"

"He's already got the publicity. That's not what he wants now."

"Really? What does he want?"

"More than anything, he wants to put Kim out of business."

"Who told you that?"

"Munyika. Kim is a personal affront to him, a glaring reminder that some minorities *can* succeed."

Leland knew he was taking a chance offering this theory to a black man. Ronnie Newbert was black, but that didn't mean all blacks subscribed to her theory. He studied Hightower's face for some clue as to what he was thinking, but there was no emotion in that poker face, and he found it extremely irritating. He'd rather see anger—or even incredulity—anything except than those damn expressionless frog-eyes.

He continued. "Munyika hates Kim and everything he stands for. If we enforce the restraining order,"—Leland purposely used the pronoun 'we'—"we stop Munyika from destroying Kim; we reduce the level of intimidation for people who want to shop there; and we lessen the power he has over the people in the neighborhood. People in this city are waiting for us to take the initiative, Chief."

"Have you run this by Drum?"

"No."

"Why not?"

"He won't go for it."

Hightower finally smiled. "If he won't go for it, how are you gonna do it?"

"We just do it."

Hightower shifted in his chair and grimaced. "Damn knee injury is acting up again." He straightened his leg. "Dickie, I notice you keep using the term 'we.'"

"Richard, Chief. I prefer to be called Richard. And the 'we' is you and me."

Hightower rubbed his knee. "How much time do you got in the job, *Richard*?"

"Twelve years."

"I got thirty-seven and plan to do forty. If *we* do as you propose, I won't make thirty-eight."

"Afraid?" Leland threw the word out like a challenge. Up until last night, he'd been afraid, too. But no more. He was through being afraid.

Hightower's chuckle was a rumble from deep inside his belly. "You bet your ass I'm afraid and I'm not afraid to admit it. I've spent thirty-seven years building a career and I'm not gonna blow it all now." He studied Leland. "I'm curious. Why are you so hot to bang heads with Drum? I thought he was your hook."

"He's not my hook and I have no choice."

"You're willing to risk your career for a Korean grocer?"

"It's more than that, Chief. I don't want to get all warm and fuzzy, but this is an old-fashioned morality play. Good vs. Evil. You and me and Kim and hard-working people and the cops in the Five-five against Munyika and what that sonofabitch stands for."

A grim Hightower got up, stretched his leg, and limped over to a wall map of the Bronx. "Look at this"—he slapped his big hand on the map—"I command twelve precincts; thousands of cops and civilians in a borough that's known worldwide."

He stared at the map for a moment. "I've always been able to make the tough decisions and that's the sign of a good commander. All in all, I feel pretty good about myself"—he turned to glare at Leland—"until a moment ago. You've dropped a nasty moral dilemma on me, Captain, and I don't appreciate it."

"I'm sorry."

Hightower carefully slid back into his chair. "The hell you are. You know if you cross Drum, your career is finished."

Leland smiled weakly. "That particular thought kept me awake most of last night."

Hightower went on as though he hadn't heard. "Your situation is very different from mine. I'm at the end of my career; you're just starting. You might be able to survive this screwball scheme of yours. You can wait for Drum to retire and hope his successor doesn't hold it against you. Me? I don't have the luxury of time. I want my final three years to be peaceful and dignified."

Leland saw the turmoil in Hightower's face and almost felt sorry for him. He knew what the chief was up against. If he took part in this "screwball scheme," Drum would force him into retirement or humiliate him by burying him in some back office where he would spend his remaining days rotating the same papers through his in-and-out baskets. He understood the chief's dilemma, but he also needed his boss's support. He couldn't do it alone. "Chief," he said softly, "there are times when you have to stand up and be counted."

Hightower ran a big hand over his face. He was quiet for a moment, and then he said, "Is there a possibility you're making a bigger issue of this than it really is?"

Leland had considered that question last night, wondering if he'd become afflicted with some dangerous quixotic streak. But as he thought about it, the real reason slowly emerged. "Chief," he said, giving voice to that reason, "In the past year, I've seen my cops risk their lives and their jobs in order to do the right thing. I guess what I'm saying is that I want to be as good a cop as they are."

"Dangerous talk, Captain."

Leland tried for a grin. "I know. It scares the hell out of me."

Hightower studied the wall map for a long time and Leland tried to imagine what was going on behind that expressionless face. What did it matter? He'd given the borough commander his best sales pitch and he could only hope he'd convinced the chief that his was the only course to follow.

Finally, Hightower turned away from the map. "I can't do it, Richard, and I suggest you forget about it, too. It's the moral high road all right, but the euphoria you get from doing the right thing will quickly dissipate when you have to face the consequences."

Leland was stunned by the abruptness and finality of Hightower's answer. When he came in here, he knew it was a long shot, but, in his heart of hearts, he thought chief would agree with him in the end.

"Okay, Chief. I tried."

He left the chief's office angry and disappointed with Hightower. But, as he pulled up in front of his apartment building, a disturbing question suddenly occurred to him: If he had thirty-seven years invested in the department, would he be willing to go ahead with his plan?

He didn't know the answer to that question.

~~

A crestfallen Leland came to work the next morning convinced he'd have to forget about his whacky plan to enforce the restraining order. Without Hightower and the manpower that the borough could provide—and he would need—it was impossible to confront and contain Munyika's demonstrators. He did his best to put his ill-conceived plan out of his mind by riding with sectors for most of the day and burying himself in paperwork late into the evening. He even accepted a call from Paula Wheatley, the head of CUT, that lasted over an hour.

But, in spite of everything he did to stay busy, he couldn't shake the plan out of his head. The next day he was thinking about it again, and the following day he concluded that maybe, just maybe, he could do it with his own Five-five cops. It was certainly risky and there were a lot of "ifs" to contend with. But slowly he began to believe it could be done.

Over the next several days and nights he worked on his plan, adding and discarding ideas until it took on the proportions of an obsession. He made a long list of all the things that could go wrong and made detailed contingency plans for each of them. From his earlier experience with the Seaman Street drug operation, he knew he could not foresee every problem, but this time he would make certain he thought about the obvious ones.

One week after Hightower turned him down, he finally convinced himself that his plan would work. Everything was in place. The only question remaining was: When would he do it? And the answer to that question, he knew, was up to the Reverend Kawasi Munyika.

Chapter Thirty-Three

Two weeks before Thanksgiving, he came into the office for a day tour and found a note that the late tour patrol sergeant had left on his desk.

Captain Leland: Received word that Munyika is going to hold major press conference today at 1200 hours at Kim's. Many pickets, press expected. Borough notified.

Leland read the note again and his heart thumped in his chest. This is it. *Today was going to be the day.*

Five minutes later, Barry, Hanlon, Seidel, Engle, and Labonte were seated in his office.

"Lieutenant Hanlon, you have the Kim detail today. What are your numbers?"

"Me, two sergeants, and twenty cops."

"You'll need more. Jack, I want every cop in the building in uniform. How many can you give me?"

Barry's eyebrows went up. "Everybody?"

"Every cop that's not on restricted duty."

Barry made a quick mental count. "I can give you nine."

"How about you, Marv? How many do you have?"

The Anti-Crime sergeant chewed on his cigar. "I got five."

"Good. I want them all in the bag. You, too."

Seidel squirmed. "Cap, I'm not even sure I have a complete uniform."

"Borrow what you don't have. I want every cop and boss in uniform today."

Seidel squinted through a cloud of smoke and asked the question that was on everyone's mind. "Mind if I ask why?"

"We're going to enforce the restraining order today."

It was the first time Leland had ever seen his Anti-Crime sergeant speechless. But he wasn't the only one. The others stared at him open-mouthed. Only Barry seemed to have anticipated what Leland was going to say. His bright blue eyes twinkled and there was a slight smile on his lips.

After Leland finished describing his plan in detail, and the part each of them would play, he said, "You are the only ones who know about this. Secrecy is critical to our success. I will personally tell the troops when the time comes." Leland drummed a tattoo on the desk with his hands. "Okay, gentlemen, let's get moving."

Barry remained behind. When the others had gone, he said, "Captain, are you sure you want to do this?"

Leland studied his Operations Coordinator, who over the past eleven months had taken on the role of anxious uncle. Jack Barry was a man of few words, but he was always watching and listening. Leland had come to learn that whenever Barry asked: *Are you sure you want to do this?"* he was really saying: *"I think you're making a big mistake."* In the past, Leland had not always listened to that warning and had gotten burned as a result, but this time he was never more certain. "Yeah, Jack," he said. "I'm sure."

"Captain, I've watched you walk a tightrope since you came to this command. You've lost your balance a couple of times and slipped a couple of times, but you're almost to the other side of the precipice. Do you really want to risk everything now?"

Leland stared into Barry's pale-blue eyes that were now clouded with concern. "Jack, if you were me, what would you do?"

"I know what I'd want to do, but I don't know if I'd have the guts to do it."

"Yes, you would. You have the curse of all good cops. You have to do the right thing."

~~

Leland went directly to Kim's and watched from his car as additional cops—crammed into the back of radio cars—began arriving. In spite of the tension churning his stomach, he had to chuckle at the sight of the "palace guard,"—the station house clerical workers—most of whom hadn't worked in uniform in years, awkwardly adjusting unfamiliar gun belts and helmets.

Seidel, his bulging belly severely straining the buttons of a borrowed uniform shirt, climbed out of the back of a radio car and gave the finger to a wise-cracking cluster of cops who were making fun of him. The Anti-

Crime sergeant started to light a cigar, but Hanlon reminded him that he was in uniform and he stuffed the cigar back into his pocket.

Another radio car pulled up and Leland was surprised to see Lt. Barry emerge in full uniform. "Jack, I didn't mean for you to suit up."

"Captain, I wouldn't miss this for the world."

"Who's running the shop?"

"I've trained the civilians well. They'll do just fine."

There was no point in arguing. Clearly, Barry had no intention of going back to the station house. "What's our count, Jack?"

"Two lieutenants, three sergeants, and forty cops."

Leland scanned the roll call with raised eyebrows. "Where'd you get the extra people?"

"I took three sectors out of service."

"Who's gonna cover—?"

"I called the Ops-Coordinator in the next precinct. They'll cover for us. He owes me a favor."

Once again, the informal network of friends and "guys who owe me" had come to the rescue. "Okay," Leland said. "Check with Hanlon. Make sure everyone is properly assigned."

Barry saluted. It was the first time he'd ever done that. "Yes, sir."

Leland studied the pickets with growing concern. In the last fifteen minutes, they'd been arriving in clusters of twos and threes. Now there were more than thirty demonstrators crowding the sidewalk in front of Kim's.

It reminded him of Civil War battles he read about where, inadvertently, each side built up its strength and moved closer and closer to each other until the proximity became such that the two armies had no choice but to do battle. As he watched the ever-increasing number of pickets arrive, he wondered whether he'd be able to implement a plan which would require a superiority of forces. He prayed the pickets would stop coming.

He stood across the street, away from the TV cameras and reporters, and glanced at his watch. It was almost eleven-thirty. Munyika was never late for a press conference. He would be here in half an hour.

It was time to let the troops in on the plan. "Lieutenant Barry," he said into his radio, "assemble everyone over here."

When the entire detail surrounded him in a tight circle, he said, "I'm aware you all have been unhappy about how this boycott has been managed." There were a few angry murmurs and hard looks. "Without going into details, I just want to say that there's more to this complex problem than you could possibly imagine."

He looked into a sea of grim, hostile faces, wondering if it was too late to get them on his side. "But, as of today, things are going to be different. What I am going to tell you now is to be repeated to no one outside the Five-five." The group squeezed closer, suddenly very interested in what their CO had to say.

"The Reverend Munyika will be here in less than half an hour. When he arrives I am going to inform him that the police department is enforcing the restraining order."

No one spoke, but the grim looks gave way to raised eyebrows and even a couple of smiles.

Charlie Reece said, "Cap, what if he says he's not gonna move?"

Leland was suddenly aware of a great silence—as though their concentration on his response had created a force field that blocked out the ambient street noise. "Then," Leland said quietly, "we move them."

"*No shit!*" a voice gasped in amazement.

Leland looked toward the voice and, to his dismay, saw that it belonged to Billy Lafferty. When he'd said he wanted everyone in uniform, he'd forgotten about the mercurial and unpredictable Lafferty.

Aware that he had their undivided attention, he continued. "There is one word that I want you to remember today and that word is restraint. I know this has been a long ordeal. I know some of you have been cursed at and some of you have been spat upon, but what we are going to do today is not about revenge. It's about justice. If any of you exceed your authority today, you will make a mockery of the restraint you have shown all these months. Don't betray your integrity. Show the people of this city that you are professionals. Are there any questions?"

Mazzeo spoke up. "Cap, there's a lot of pickets and not a whole lot of us. Are we going to get reinforcements from the borough?"

"No," Leland said. "We're going to do this ourselves."

Reece scratched his double chin. "I've been to a lot of demonstrations, Cap, and I know a big show of force goes a long way toward convincing demonstrators that they should do what you say." He looked at the cops surrounding him. "This ain't exactly a great show of force."

Leland displayed what he hoped was a confidant grin. "There's not a lot of us, but we're all Five-five cops."

Over muttered, *"Damn rights!"* and *"Yeahs!"* Lafferty's plaintive voice was heard. *"Christ! I feel like I'm at the fuckin' Alamo!"*

Peggy Garrigan elbowed him. "Billy, will you shut *up*."

"Okay,"—Leland rubbed his hands together—"back to the barriers. And remember, restraint."

A curious reporter had been watching Leland talking to the cops but he was too far away to hear what was being said. He came over to Mazzeo. "What were you guys talking about over there?"

"We were picking this week's lottery numbers," Mazzeo said with a straight face.

Leland was troubled by Lafferty's presence. If his plan was to work, every cop had to be in full control and he wasn't sure he could trust Lafferty. He pulled Seidel aside. "Marv, I want you to watch Billy Lafferty—"

"Don't worry, Boss. I'm gonna stay real close to him. If I even think he's gonna get out of line, I'll personally cold-cock the sonofabitch myself."

Leland fervently hoped that wouldn't be necessary.

Seidel had been cupping a cigar in the palm of his hand but he wasn't fooling anyone. Nothing except burning tires could smell that bad. He took a quick drag of the cigar and squinted at Leland. "You're doing this on your own, aren't you?"

Leland nodded.

"Without Drum? Without Hightower? Captain, they'll rip your nuts off and feed them to the squirrels."

"Probably."

"Boss, I'm a pretty good judge of character, but you've been a hard one to nail down. At first I figured you for a typical headquarters mope, then I figured you for a guy who means well, but who always steps on his dick."

"So what do you figure now, Marv?"

"You're one of those Don Quixotes. In my thirty years in the job, I've met maybe three like you. I don't know what to make of you guys. On the one hand, I admire your balls, but on the other hand, you're hopeless dreamers. In the end you usually get your ass in a shredder."

"Think that's going to happen to me?"

Seidel studied the ash at the tip of his cigar. "I guess we'll both know before the day is out."

"I guess we will," Leland said, feeling a flock of butterflies take flight in his stomach.

Seidel looked over Leland's shoulder and said, "Well, I'll be goddamned! Here comes the cavalry."

Leland turned and stared slack-jawed as he watched six Borough Task Force cars coming down the street. They pulled up and five helmeted cops got out of each car. Leland was on his way to talk to the lieutenant in the lead car when he saw Hightower's black Ford come into the block. The car stopped in front of him and Chief Hightower, in full uniform, got out. He wasn't smiling, but then he seldom did.

Leland saluted him. "Chief—"

"You're going to do it today, aren't you? I got the message about the press conference and when I called your precinct, all I got was a bunch of civilians. They said you'd all gone to the demonstration."

"Chief, don't try to stop me." Leland was adamant. He'd backed down too many times and he was through backing down. " If you do, I swear to Christ I'll resign right here and now."

"Don't get your shorts in a knot." Hightower's practiced eyes swept the pickets and Leland's contingent of cops. "Just as I thought. You don't have enough cops. I brought six and thirty-six."

"I… I thought you didn't want anything to do with this?"

"I don't want anything to do with this lunacy." Hightower studied Leland's bewildered expression. "To tell you the truth, Captain, I didn't trust you when you first came to the Bronx. I figured Drum sent you here to spy on me and screw up my borough."

"And I didn't trust you," Leland said, still trying to grasp that Hightower was with him. "When you gave me permission to do the Seaman Street raid, I figured you were just giving me enough rope to hang myself."

"No, Captain, that's called delegating authority."

"When did you stop distrusting me?"

"After I saw you stick your neck out a few times. The Seaman Street raid and going to the press with the Poet Bandit—those are not the kinds of decisions a career-oriented headquarters man makes."

"No, I guess they're not," Leland said, suddenly realizing he was no longer that kind of career-oriented man.

Hightower watched Lt. Barry giving assignments to the additional cops. "You know, Richard, in my younger days I thought I was a black Wyatt Earp. I used to fantasize about being in blazing gun battles and making detective. Thank God my fantasy didn't come true." He grunted. "Now I'm too old to even have such fantasies. He looked across the street at Kim's Market. Kim and his family stood in the window watching all the cops in wonder. "But maybe this is as good a way as any to end a career."

"Does Chief Drum know?"

"He will. I had to notify Operations that I was mobilizing the Task Force and bringing them here. Maybe it'll be over before he finds out."

Leland asked the question that had been bothering him since this whole affair had begun four months ago. "Chief, why did Drum insist on this do-nothing policy?"

Hightower cocked his head. "Richard, I'm surprised at you. A sophisticated headquarters guy should know the answer to that question. Charlie Drum is terrified of Munyika. He wants to be the next PC and he's been laying the groundwork since Randall got here. It hasn't escaped City Hall's attention that Charlie Drum has been running the department for Randall. All he has to do is keep the lid on this city for another year. Randall has said he's going to retire and Drum will have the inside track for the PC's job. The only thing that could screw up his plans is a clash with someone like Munyika. That's why he insisted on you running this demonstration alone. He doesn't trust me, but he knew he could count on you to do exactly as you were told."

Leland suddenly realized that was why he'd been sent here in the first place. Munyika had been a thorn in the side of the city for years and it was only a matter of time before he found a cause that would give him national exposure. And when that happened, Drum wanted Richard Leland, the good, obedient soldier that he was to be in place to keep the lid on. The thought suddenly occurred to him: *He probably arranged for Inspections to give Sperling a bad evaluation so there'd be an opening for me.*

Before he could dwell further on that thought, he heard Hightower mutter an oath and turned to see what the borough commander was looking at. Chief Drum's black Oldsmobile, with the magnetic red light flashing on the roof, was racing down the street toward them.

The car screeched to a halt and Drum bolted out in full uniform. "What the hell's going on?" he growled at Hightower.

The borough commander remained unperturbed. "Did you come to assume command of the detail?" he asked blandly.

"No, goddamn it, I didn't. I came here to find out what the hell's going on. Lucian, I told you—"

"Look at the number of pickets, Chief. Captain Leland doesn't have enough people to handle them. *I'm* responsible for the safety of the people in this borough and—"

"And *I* am responsible for the whole goddamned city, and that includes the Bronx. I specifically told you I didn't want a show of force. I told you—" He stopped in mid-sentence when he saw Munyika's Escalade coming down the block. "Jesus H. Christ!"

Munyika, adorned in a bright red Dashiki, stepped regally from the back seat.

"Chief, do you wish to assume command of this detail?" Hightower asked again.

Drum watched in horror as the TV media people descended upon Munyika. "No. That won't be necessary." He turned to Leland and looked at him as though he were a total stranger. "Captain, you are in charge here. You will not attempt to interfere with the Reverend Munyika—"

"No," Hightower said firmly. "*I* am in charge."

Drum's face turned dark crimson. "Whatever. As long as everything runs smoothly."

Hightower turned to Leland and there was just a hint of a smile on his face. "Go ahead, Captain," he said. "Execute your plan."

Leland turned away and heard Drum say to Hightower, "Plan? What plan?"

As Leland started walking toward Munyika, a kaleidoscope of images flashed through his mind. He saw his ex-wife, Marilyn, and once again regretted the pain he'd caused her. He saw himself, holed up in his bedroom, studying for his three promotional exams, shunning family and friends until the exams were over, putting his life on hold. He saw his dejected father sitting at the dinner table, patiently explaining why he didn't get that promotion. And he saw Gloria's enigmatic, troubling, aggravating, and wonderful smile.

And he never felt more alive in his life.

Munyika stood in front of his entourage and motioned to the press that he was ready to make his statement. Dutifully, the TV press, augmented by national media reporters who sensed that this demonstration was about to reach a climax, closed in.

Leland stepped between Munyika and the press corps, keenly aware that every cop and demonstrator was watching him carefully.

Suddenly, he remembered the best 4x400 race he'd ever run in college. He'd been the anchor leg and he'd gotten the baton a full 30 meters behind the lead runner. He knew it was impossible, but something inside him said, *"You can catch him and pass him."* And his mind went on automatic pilot. He gave no thought to breathing, to the pain in his muscles, or pacing himself. Every fiber in his body concentrated on the number 26 pinned to the back of the lead runner. Slowly, the number increased in size until he was abreast of the runner.

Then, with an effortless burst of speed, he passed him and broke the tape three meters ahead of him.

Now, he was having the same out-of-body experience. He hardly noticed the crush of reporters surrounding him, the TV cameras, the lights, the shouted questions. He looked up into Munyika's smirking face and said, "Reverend Munyika, you can't stay here."

Munyika laughed. "Of course I can."

"No. You'll have to move."

Munyika's nostrils flared in anger at this cop who, until now, had been no more annoying than a troublesome gnat. Now he was interfering with his carefully orchestrated press conference.

"*Where* do you suggest I move, *Captain*?"

Leland pointed across the street to where Lt. Barry, at his direction, had set up a rectangular enclosure of barriers.

"There."

Munyika looked at Leland with contempt in his eyes. "Why should I go there?"

"Because it's fifty feet from Kim's Market and that's what the restraining order requires."

The contemptuous smirk gave way to uncertainty. "That's a *civil* order, Captain."

Leland was pleased to see self-doubt creeping into Munyika's eyes.

Strobe lights flashed joyously and the media pressed closer. At last there was going to be the confrontation that they'd been waiting for all these months.

Munyika was suddenly uncertain. This startling change in the mild-mannered police captain, and his threat to enforce the restraining order, threw Munyika's mind into turmoil, but he was enough of a professional to hide it.

"No," he bellowed, playing to the cameras. "I will not move from this spot. You"—he pointed at Leland with disdain—"are merely a captain. I want to speak to a superior."

Hightower appeared at Leland's side. "I'm Assistant Chief Lucian Hightower, the commanding officer of this borough. What can I do for you?"

Munyika grinned at Hightower. He was just beginning to fear that his cause might collapse on local *and* national TV, but now, here was a brother. Here was someone he could talk sense to—even if the brother was glaring at him as though he wanted to rip his lungs out. "Bro, tell this—" he almost said honky, but he caught himself in time—"this *captain* that I have a right to stand where I want."

Leland's senses were sharpened by the tension and excitement and he was acutely aware of everything around him. He saw the uncertainly in Munyika's eyes, he heard the calm determination in Hightower's voice, and, standing off to the side with a look that was a mixture of fear and impotent, was Chief of Department Charlie Drum.

Suddenly, Leland remembered his father again, and a thought that he'd harbored, but refused to admit to himself, came rushing into his consciousness. *He'd always believed his father was a fool for sacrificing his career for principle.* But now he realized that his father had been a brave and ethical man. Leland felt a surge of pride for that quiet, gentle man. He was also aware that he'd arrived at a major turning point in his own life and that no matter what happened this day, he would always be proud of himself as well.

"No, Reverend Munyika," Hightower said firmly. "We are enforcing the restraining order. You and your demonstrators will have to move across the street."

Leland didn't turn around, but he sensed that every cop standing behind him was leaning forward with restrained anticipation.

Munyika saw the resoluteness in the eyes of the captain and the traitorous black brother and knew there was no point in arguing further. He wished he'd known in advance that the police were going to do this. He would have mustered a hundred more pickets to beef up the ragtag collection of no-accounts fools who were now staring at him with dumb, bewildered expressions. He would have paid a handful of young thugs to start fights with the cops. It would have made a great photo op. But, it was too late for that now. He'd been outmaneuvered by a turncoat brother and a pain-in-the-ass captain. Or maybe not.

"We will not be moved," he bellowed defiantly.

Leland turned to Lt. Barry, who was now at his side. "Lieutenant, let's move these demonstrators across the street."

As the double rows of blue-helmeted police officers with nightsticks at the ready moved toward the demonstrators, Leland saw a horrified Charlie Drum scramble back to his car. As the demonstrators and cops came together, Drum's car screeched away from the curb and sped down the street.

The initial collision of police officers and demonstrators was dutifully recorded by a light-show of flashing strobes and swarming cameras. But the clashing of forces was surprisingly subdued. The quiet determination of the police, combined with the shock of the police suddenly enforcing the law, threw the demonstrators off balance and they meekly allowed themselves to be herded across the street.

Just when Leland thought everything was going to come off without a hitch, one of the demonstrators threw a sign at a cop. He held his breath, waiting for the nightsticks to fly, but Mazzeo and Reece rushed forward and quickly subdued the assailant.

Munyika was enraged that his people were allowing themselves to be moved back so obediently. *What the hell am I paying them for?* The cameras were trained on him. The reporters were watching him with puzzled expressions. He saw his reputation collapsing as quickly as his picket line. *"Hold your ground,"* he bellowed to his followers.

But the cops, shuffling forward in a slow, persistent line, gave the demonstrators no opportunity to resist. In a desperate attempt to regain the momentum of the moment, Munyika hurtled the barriers and stood in front of Kim's store with his arms folded in brazen defiance. He waited until the cameras caught up to him before he shouted, *"I will not be moved."*

Sergeant Marv Seidel, accompanied by his Anti-Crime team of Tom Kohler, the born-again Christian Stan Quigley, Carrington, and Soika, stepped up to Munyika. Seidel, who was a good foot shorter than Munyika, squinted up at the taller man. "Leonard"—he addressed Munyika by his real name—"you can go quietly or you can"—he jerked his head toward the massive Kohler and smiled evilly—"just go. Your call."

Kohler ground his nightstick in his ham-sized hands and studied Munyika intently. He may have been the gentle giant of the Five-five, but he was still a cop and he had little charity for lawbreakers. Furthermore, as a born-again Christian, he had even less charity for a man who made a mockery of religion.

Munyika glared back at the big cop, who was a couple of inches shorter, but at least thirty pounds heavier. The size didn't bother Munyika. He'd taken on bigger dudes in prison. It was the burning intensity in the big cop's eyes that he found unnerving. *That man is crazy!* Munyika had planned to be arrested in a violent confrontation, but looking at the wild-eyed, broken-nosed cop, he realized he could get seriously hurt. One thing he knew for sure: He'd look like a fool grappling with this big ox and there was no way he was going to look like a fool on national TV.

From across the street, Munyika's followers watched him from behind the barriers with an assortment of expectant and puzzled expressions. He glared back at them with contempt. They'd let the police herd them like cattle. He was consumed with rage and frustration. *All he needed was one more day.* He knew the Korean bastard was about to close his store and he'd come in triumph to remind the press—and the world—about his promise to drive the foreigner out of his community. But in a matter of minutes, all that had changed. Frantically, he struggled to think of some way to snatch victory from the jaws of defeat, but he couldn't think of any.

Unable to come up with a better solution, he sat down on the sidewalk. "Arrest me," he said to a grinning Seidel. "I ain't moving."

Chapter Thirty-Four

Richard Leland arrived at the precinct the next morning feeling an odd mixture of self-satisfaction—and dread. The night before, he'd watched both the six and eleven o'clock news on every channel, and was gratified that he and his cops had acquitted themselves well. He even thought he detected a subtle shift in the tone of the news anchors. For a change, they seemed to be more sympathetic to Kim and the police department. On the other hand, maybe it was just wishful thinking on his part.

Lt. Barry came in and dropped a copy of the *Daily News* and the *New York Post* on the desk.

Leland hadn't read the papers yet. "What do they say?" he asked.

Barry grinned. "If we were a Broadway play, we'd be a smash hit. Even Culpeper has nothing but praise for our restraint."

Leland's eyebrows went up at that news. Toby Culpeper was an acerbic columnist who, since his arrest for drunken driving five years earlier, had declared jihad against the New York City Police Department, and he'd been a scourge ever since. Praise from him was nothing short of a miracle.

The *Post* headline said: BRONX MARKET SIEGE BROKEN. The *News* declared: POLICE ENFORCE RESTRAINING ORDER. Leland chuckled at the front-page photos. Both papers featured photos of Munyika, his long legs and arms akimbo, unceremoniously being carried to a police van by four Anti-Crime cops with Sgt. Seidel leading the way.

He flipped thorough the papers looking for unflattering photos of his cops. Thankfully, there were none. "What's the tone of the articles, Jack?"

"Both editorials support the police. The Post is asking the PC why it took him so long to act. He isn't going to like that."

"No, he isn't."

Ronnie Newbert came in and she was smiling again. "How's it going out there?" Leland asked.

"Cool. Very cool. Only four pickets and they're across the street behind the barriers behaving themselves."

After Munyika had been taken away, Leland had announced to the remaining pickets that no bullhorns would be permitted and that they would not be permitted to harass customers who went into the market. Without Munyika to tell them what to do, they'd meekly acquiesced. Now that Leland had the momentum, he intended to enforce those rules and had left instructions with all supervisors to read the rules to pickets at the beginning of every tour.

"Boss, you turned the tide," she said with genuine admiration.

"We turned the tide," Leland corrected.

Newbert chuckled. "The cops who were off yesterday are really ticked. They all wanted to be in on the action."

That, Leland noted gratefully, was a sure sign of good morale.

Ronnie looked at her watch. "Gotta get back out there." At the door she stopped and turned. "By the way, Captain. I pulled my request for a transfer."

Leland nodded. "You sure?"

She pushed her glasses up on her nose. "I gotta stay. These people need me."

"So do I, Ronnie," Leland said.

The phone rang. It was Hightower. "Have you seen the papers?"

"Yes. I'm pleasantly surprised at the extent of the support we received."

"Before you dislocate your arm patting yourself on the back, I have some bad news. You and I are to report to Drum's office at 1400 hours today."

Leland hung up. He'd been expecting it. After what happened yesterday, he knew he'd get "Drummed." Surprisingly, he didn't care. He attributed his lack of distress to the new sense of freedom he was feeling. It was as though he'd spent his entire life tiptoeing under the threat of an imminent avalanche. Well, the avalanche had come down and he'd survived. He wouldn't have to tiptoe anymore. From now on, he would rely on his instincts and not his political antennae to tell him what to do.

At 1345 hours, Leland, dressed in full uniform, walked into the Chief of Department's Office. The same faces were still at the same desks doing the same tasks. He caught a glimpses of Timmy Frazer seated at his old desk. The newly-minted captain was having a meeting with three lieutenants and two sergeants. Leland caught his eye. Frazer nodded vaguely and quickly returned to his discussion.

Leland stopped at Frank Joiner's desk. "I'm here for my appointment with the Chief."

Drum's clerical sergeant recoiled as though Leland were a leper. Leland grinned. "It's okay, Frank. I'm not contagious. Just tell me where I should wait."

Joiner, a man completely devoid of humor, looked at him, perplexed. "The Chief isn't back yet, but you can wait in his conference room, Captain."

"Is Chief Hightower here yet?"

"No." Joiner buried his head in a report, effectively breaking off all further conversation.

Leland went around the corner to the men's room to freshen up. While he was washing his hands, a worried John Wallace slipped in. "How're you doin', Boss?"

"Good. How you doing, Johnny?"

"Still here." Wallace peeked under the stalls to make sure there was no one else in the restroom. "Boss," he whispered. "You're gonna get Drummed."

"I know." From the stricken expression on Wallace's face, he was taking it harder than Leland. "It's okay, Johnny."

"It ain't okay. You know, there's been grumbling around the building for a couple of months now about this Munyika thing. Everyone's been wondering when we were going to do something about it."

"How'd Drum take it?"

Wallace rolled his eyes. "You know he can go ballistic, but I'm telling you, I've never seen anything like it. He came back here yesterday ranting and raving about backstabbing traitors. I thought we were going to have to call the surgeon to have his gun taken away from him."

"I guess he was referring to me?"

"And Hightower."

Two men came in and Wallace slapped Leland on the back, "Hey, Boss. Good to see you again. You take care."

"Yeah, you, too, Johnny."

On his way back to the Chief's office, Leland ran into Captain Wolfe in the hallway. The short, gloomy man tried to effect an air of concern, but he was a very bad actor. "Richard, I'm so sorry."

"About what?" Leland enjoyed keeping Wolfe off balance.

Wolfe hesitated. "Have you spoken to Drum yet?"

"No."

"He's going to Drum you."

"Oh, that."

Wolfe was taken aback by Leland's lackadaisical attitude. "Don't you care?"

"There's no capital punishment in New York State, Harry. What's the worst he can he do to me?"

"But… but what will you do?" Wolfe couldn't imagine being in Leland's shoes.

"Go wherever he dumps me."

"You won't pack it in?"

"Nope. I've got big plans for this job."

Wolfe smirked. "Not as long as Drum is the Chief of Department."

"True, but I'm a lot younger than Drum and I'll be here long after he's gone. And like the mythical phoenix, I shall rise from the ashes." He tapped Wolfe's cheek. "I'd love to stay and chat but I have to go get Drummed. See ya around, Harry."

Leland came into the conference room smiling. Just seeing the expression on Harry Wolfe's face had made his day. A glum Hightower turned from the window. "What's so funny?" he growled.

"People, Chief, people. Did Drum get back yet?"

"No."

Leland was truly at peace with himself, but he felt sympathy—and some responsibility—for the tired and drawn man standing at the window. "Chief, what do you think Drum will do to you?"

Hightower shrugged. "Probably remove me from the borough and give me some make-work assignment down here."

Leland had seen that particular form of punishment used many times in the past. There weren't many places to dump an out-of-favor assistant chief, so the solution was to give him a no-authority, no-responsibility headquarters job. He earned the same salary, but for men who've achieved that rank, money was no longer the most important motivator. Most put in their papers and retired rather than continue in the demeaning assignment. Leland suspected that Hightower, too proud to accept such a humiliating fate, would resign on the spot.

"Chief, I'm really sorry I put you in this position."

Hightower waved a hand in dismissal. "Whoever said being a cop was easy? You play the hand your dealt. I just wish—" He stopped talking when he heard Drum's shrill voice bellowing from the other side of door that led to his office.

"He's baaack," Leland said, in a bad impression of Jack Nicholson.

They couldn't make out what the chief was saying, but there was no mistaking the anger and fury in his tone. Then, something that sounded buckshot—or a handful of miniature soldiers—thudded against the other side of the chief's office door.

"When he's really pissed, he throws things," Leland explained to Hightower, who was calmly watching the door.

A few minutes later, an ashen-faced Sergeant Joiner stuck his head through the door. "Ah, Chief Hightower, Captain Leland, you can go now."

"What about our meeting?" Hightower asked.

"Ah… it's been canceled." He ducked his head back and quickly shut the door behind him.

The two men looked at each other in astonishment. Then, Hightower stood up and said something he never thought he would say again. "Come on, Captain. I have a borough to run and you have a precinct."

∼∼

Now that Munyika's stranglehold on Kim's Market was broken, the newspapers began to ask troubling questions. Every day, the police commissioner and the mayor were besieged by reporters demanding to know why it had taken so long to enforce the restraining order. And every night, an amused Leland watched Commissioner Randall on the eleven o'clock news squirming as he tried to explain a policy he didn't understand.

The *Post* turned up the heat by publishing a three-day series on the department's history of enforcing civil injunctions and restraining orders. The thrust of the series was that—except for the Kim restraining order—the police department had never refused to enforce a civil order when public safety was an issue.

∼∼

A week after the confrontation, Leland went to One Police Plaza to attend a precinct commanders' meeting at the Chief of Patrol's office to discuss the Thanksgiving Day parade, which was just a week away.

The first three people he met couldn't wait to repeat the latest, hot rumors: The PC's head was on the chopping block. A massive shakeup in the department was imminent. And, depending on who he spoke to, Hightower was going to get fired or demoted.

Leland had been hearing these and other rumors for a week and gave them little credence. What troubled him was *his* future status in the department. He still didn't know why Drum had canceled the meeting, but he was under no illusion that everything was forgiven. Sometimes the disciplinary machinery of the department worked slowly, but it worked eventually. As sure as the sun rose every day, his—and Hightower's—day of reckoning would come.

~~

Edwin Gessler, the Chief of Patrol, chaired the Thanksgiving Day Parade meeting. As a leader of men, he was completely incompetent, but he was a shrewd political animal. The day of the confrontation at Kim's, he'd been ready to cast the first stone at Hightower and Leland, but as a groundswell of support for their actions grew, he joined in praising them. But now, in the face of all these conflicting rumors, he didn't know how to treat Leland. Unable to determine which way the political winds were blowing, he did the only prudent thing: He ignored Leland throughout the entire meeting, which, mercifully, ended quickly.

As Leland was waiting for the elevator, an ashen-faced Harry Wolfe lurched toward him.

"Harry, you really should get out in the sun more often. You look like hell."

Wolfe clutched Leland's sleeve. "Richard," he said, wide-eyed, "there's going to be a bloodbath."

"Let me guess. Drum is wielding the hatchet and Hightower and me are the turkeys."

"No"—his voice cracked—"*Drum* is the turkey."

Leland studied the panicked captain carefully. One Police Plaza thrived on rumors, most of which were the product of overheated imaginations. But Wolfe, who had raised gossip-gathering to an art form, was seldom wrong. Still, Leland couldn't imagine Charlie Drum being toppled. He'd done everything in his power to make himself indispensable to the police commissioner. "Harry, are you sure?"

"Positive. I've double-checked with my sources in City Hall."

"What happened?"

"All the pressure from the Kim-Munyika fiasco got to be too much for the mayor. He called Randall in and told him to fall on his sword—or find a suitable replacement. Randall came back to his office like a tiger with a hot poker up his ass. He and Drum had a hell of a row. That was the day you and Hightower were supposed to get Drummed."

Leland remembered Drum shouting and throwing things. Suddenly, all the pieces fell into place.

Wolfe looked over his shoulder as though he expected to see the police commissioner himself eavesdropping. "It took Randall most of the week to work up the courage, but less than fifteen minutes ago, he called Drum into his office and told him to put in his papers."

"Who's going to take his place?"

"I don't know. That's what's got me worried. A new Chief of Department will clean house. Where does that leave me?"

Leland nodded gravely and tried not to smile. It was typical of Harry Wolfe to worry only about himself.

"You know what happens when a slot of this magnitude opens, Richard." Wolfe wiped a bead of sweat from his upper lip. "It's like dominos. One man moves, another fills his spot. It can change the whole balance of power."

"Take it easy, Harry. We're talking about the police department not the Middle East."

"It's easy for you to make fun," he said bitterly. "You're in patrol. One asshole precinct is the same as any other."

The elevator door opened. Leland patted the distraught captain's arm. "Harry," he said with mock sincerity. "I'm so sorry."

A stricken Wolfe was still standing there when the elevator doors closed.

~~

That night, Leland went to Steve and Pam's apartment for dinner. He hadn't seen them since the christening in March.

Pam opened the door. "Well, hello stranger."

"Never mind that. Where's my godson?"

She gave him a peck on the cheek and pulled him inside. "At my mom's."

"What? I came to see him, not you two."

"Sorry, Godfather, but I need a break. Tonight, I may get drunk. For sure, I'm gonna sleep late tomorrow morning. You'll have to settle for pictures."

"You have many?"

"About four or five thousand," Steve said, coming into foyer with a martini in each hand. "I figured you could use this."

"You should work for the Psychic Hotline." Leland took his glass and followed them into the living room where they immediately began to bombard him with questions about the Munyika confrontation.

Pam became so engrossed in Leland's running account of the affair that Steve finally interrupted and said, "Oh, Pam, baby, were you planning on feeding us dinner *tonight*?"

"Yeah, sure. I just want to hear this first."

Steve lifted her out of the chair. "Why don't we all go into the kitchen. Richard can tell us the rest of the story while you throw dinner on the table."

The three crowded into the tiny kitchen and, while Pam finished cooking, Leland continued his story.

Later, after dinner, they went back onto the living room and the conversation moved on to non-police topics. It was just after eleven and Steve, a diehard Islander's fan, flipped on the TV. Ignoring Pam's disapproving look, he said, "Just for a second. I want to see how the Islanders did."

As he was flipping through the channels, Leland saw something. "Wait, go back to the news."

Steve clicked on the station and on the TV, a grave mayor, flanked by an equally grave Commissioner Randall, was saying, "… put this all behind us. Commissioner Randall has acted quickly and decisively in selecting a new Chief of Department. I'll let the Commissioner introduce him."

"Who's it going to be?" Steve asked Leland.

Leland moved to the edge of his seat. "Probably Edwin Gessler, the Chief of Patrol. He won't rock the boat and that's exactly what Randall wants."

Bruce Randall, blinking uncomfortably in the harsh lights and looking like *he'd* just gotten fired, cleared his throat and read from a prepared speech. "The position of Chief of Department is one of the most critical assignments in the department. The position requires intelligence, integrity, as well as a broad range of experience. After careful consideration I have chosen a man whom I believe embodies all these attributes. Ladies and gentlemen, I give you the new Chief of Department… Lucian Hightower. .."

A stunned Leland fell back in his seat.

"Hey, isn't that your boss?" Pam asked.

"Was," Leland said softly.

"What gives? I thought you two were in deep doo-doo."

"We are… I mean we were… I mean… I don't know what I mean…"

As Lucian Hightower began to speak about his plans for the police department, the picture cut away to a building collapse in Newark. Steve switched the TV off.

"What does this mean for you, Richard?"

Leland's head was spinning at the sudden and unexpected change of events. "I have no idea," he said. "No idea."

Steve took his empty glass. "You look like you could use another drink."

"Yeah"—Leland exhaled slowly—"that would be good."

Chapter Thirty-Five

The next morning, the precinct was buzzing with the news. Jack Barry, who'd spent the better part of the morning on the telephone checking with his sources, came in to brief Leland.

"Tony Pedula is taking Hightower's place in the borough."

Leland nodded with a grin. That was good news. Pedula, the exec in Manhattan South, was a rarity: A boss who was well thought of by both cops *and* supervisors.

During the next several days, Leland read the Special Orders with great interest as he followed the rise and fall of careers. Wolfe had been right about one thing: A new Chief of Department did create a domino effect. One opening created another opening and on it went. Some chiefs advanced, others stayed in place, and still others, seeing that their careers had come to a screeching halt, put their papers in. And that created a new opening and yet another round of dominos.

Except for Hightower, there weren't many surprises. Commissioner Randall, not known for innovative leadership, selected senior men for the higher positions and junior men for the lower positions. They might not have been the best choices, but they were the safest.

Hightower wasted no time in cleaning house. Harry Wolfe was transferred to a Brooklyn precinct as the executive officer—a move that Leland was certain would make the fearful captain put in his retirement papers. Tim Frazer was also transferred, but like a true headquarters denizen, he'd landed on his feet and secured another administrative assignment in the Chief of Patrol's office. John Wallace and most of the other clerical people stayed.

Life in the Five-five returned to some semblance of normalcy. No longer distracted by the Munyika boycott, Leland got back to the full-time business of running a precinct.

The picketing of Kim's Market continued, but the dwindling number of half-hearted pickets had little effect. No longer fearful of Munyika's wrath, a steady stream of customers flowed in and out of the market. And things returned to normal at the market as well—which was not necessarily a good thing. Kim still shouted at his customers and they still tried to haggle with him. A patient and supremely optimistic Ronnie Newbert spent hours talking to the suspicious Korean, convinced that one day she would acclimate him to the arcane mores of the Bronx shopper.

After his arrest and subsequent bad press, the Reverend Kawasi Munyika lost interest in saving the Bronx from foreigners. But Leland knew he wasn't finished. The next time Munyika saw a cause that would get him headlines, he'd be back on the street. Leland fervently hoped he'd be gone from the precinct by then.

~~

It was the day before Thanksgiving. Leland stared at the calendar, scarcely believing he'd been in the Five-five just two days short of a whole year.

He thumbed through the calendar that had been pristine on January first. Now, every dog-eared page was crammed with appointments, messages, and notes to himself. It had been a busy year. He'd accomplished a lot, but there was still much to be done.

Munyika had taken up more than four months of his time, time he should have been devoting to tweaking the precinct's operation. No matter. He had at least another year and he planned to make the most of it.

He flipped the calendar to the month of December. His eyes came to rest on December 25th and his stomach tightened. The thought of another holiday season alone was already beginning to weigh on him. Fortunately, this year he'd made certain he would get away. He'd confirmed his vacation slot with the borough and he'd made travel reservations.

He opened his drawer, took out the travel brochure, and studied glossy photos of the white, sandy beaches of St. Thomas. Just a month from now, he would be lying on that white, powdery beach drinking rum-and-somethings.

The phone rang. "Captain Leland, this is Sgt. Joiner in the Chief's office. How are you, sir?"

"Fine." The sergeant sounded a lot friendlier than he had in their last encounter. "What can I do for you, Frank?"

"Chief Hightower would like to see you at 1700 hours today."
"What about?"
"I don't know, Captain."

Leland looked at his watch. It was almost four. "I'm on my way. If I don't run into traffic on the FDR, I should be there in forty-five minutes."

On the way downtown, Leland got caught in the slow, creeping rush-hour traffic and used the time to reflect on his old boss. Since Hightower had been promoted, Leland hadn't heard a word from him. He'd sent the chief a congratulatory note, but he hadn't received a reply. Hightower was probably too busy to waste time answering congratulations notes, he told himself. On the other hand, maybe the chief was angry with Leland for having almost ended his career.

He looked at his watch. He had twenty minutes to get to One Police Plaza and it wouldn't do to be late for his first appointment with the new Chief of Department. He slapped the magnetic red light on the roof, hit the siren, and edged his way through the line of cars on the FDR like Moses parting the Red Sea.

~~

Leland walked into the office with five minutes to spare. A solicitous Joiner jumped up. "Captain Leland, can I get you a cup of coffee, sir?"
"No, thanks, Frank."
"Then, go right in. The Chief is waiting for you, sir."

Except for the four stars on his shoulder, Hightower looked the same. He sat behind Drum's old desk, which looked a lot larger without its legions of miniature Roman soldiers.

"Sit down, Richard," the chief said gruffly.
"Congratulations on your promotion, Chief."
"Thanks. I got your note, but I've been busier than a one armed paperhanger and I haven't had a chance to acknowledge any of them."
"I understand."

Hightower made a bridge with his fingers and studied Leland. "Well, Captain, did you ever think it would turn out this way?"
"Not in a million years, Chief."
"That's the excitement—and frustration—of the job. Sometimes being in the right place at the right time is half the battle."
"Competence has a lot to do with it, too."
"Randall didn't want to promote me," he said abruptly.
"Why not?"

"He's afraid of me—thinks I'm a loose cannon. He wanted Edwin Gessler, but the mayor insisted he promote 'the guy who broke Munyika.'" He looked at Leland for a long while. "He got the wrong guy."

"I couldn't have done it without you, Chief."

Hightower grunted. "Anyway, it's good that Randall's afraid of me. He'll stay out of my way and I'll be able to run this department the way it should be run."

Hightower got up and went to a large map of the city that covered most of the wall. Leland noticed that he was limping. His knee must be acting up again.

Hightower tapped the map with his big hand. "My dominion has increased from the Bronx to the entire city. It's a heavy responsibility, but you know what? I'm having the time of my life. Unfortunately, my wife isn't. She didn't think I could work more hours in a day than I did when I had the Bronx, but she's found out differently."

He turned away from the map. "Richard, I'm going to promote you to deputy inspector."

Leland was so surprised he didn't know what to say. A week ago, he thought he would lose the Five-five. Until a moment ago, he figured he had another year to go. And now—a promotion to deputy inspector. Oddly, he felt no great sense of joy. A year ago, he would have done anything for that promotion, but after what he'd been through, it just wasn't that important anymore. "Thank you, Chief," he said quietly.

"Don't thank me, Richard. I have plans for this department and I need people like you."

"Where will I be assigned?"

Hightower returned to his chair and stretched his stiff leg. "I have two choices for you, Richard. One, you can come back here and run this office."

Leland's heart thumped in his chest. This was the assignment he'd hoped Drum would offer him. Running the Chief of Department's office was a high-profile position and it would give him the opportunity to rub shoulders with the movers and shakers in the department. It was the ideal career move.

"What's the other choice, Chief?"

Hightower's frog-eyes blinked once slowly. "Executive officer in the tenth zone."

Leland's eyes shot to the wall map. *Patrol*. The tenth zone covered six precincts in the Bronx—including the Five-five. Supervising them would be a tough, demanding job requiring difficult and potential career-ending decisions on a daily basis.

A year ago, he would have had no problem deciding which assignment to take. But now, as he stared at the small horizontal and vertical rectangles that represented the streets of the Bronx, he thought of the people he'd worked with over the past year; Jack Barry, his quiet, competent Operations Coordinator; Eddie Mazzeo, a headstrong cop who sometimes shot from the hip, but who was, nevertheless, a good cop; Peggy Garrigan, who'd risked her shot at the Detective Bureau to try and save a young girl from her mother; the cigar-chewing Marv Seidel, the best cop he'd ever met; and the dozens of other police officers in the Five-five who, every day, went out into the streets and quietly went about the business of protecting the people of the Bronx.

Patrol was a frustrating, mostly thankless job, but it was the place where real police work was done. And right now he couldn't imagine working in the anemic environment of One Police Plaza. There would be plenty of time for that later.

He turned away from the map. "The patrol assignment sounds good to me, Chief."

Hightower's only reaction was a low grunt. "You'll be promoted a week from this Friday."

Leland suddenly thought of his vacation. "Chief, I've made plans to go away for the holidays. Will I be able to—?"

"No." Hightower's eyes narrowed. "I hope you bought travel insurance."

"Actually, I did—this year," Leland answered bleakly.

"You'd better do it every year, Richard. You're going to be moving up the career ladder fast and, while no one is indispensable, it will get harder and harder to find someone to fill in for you. Where were you going anyway?"

"St. Thomas."

"Too much sun," the chief grumbled. "Look how pale you are. You'd probably get third degree burns."

~~

Leland had just one week to put everything in order. But he worked around the clock and, by the following Thursday afternoon, he'd cleared up all the loose ends.

It was after six and he was all alone in his office, emptying the few remaining contents of his desk into a cardboard box. He hadn't said anything to anyone, but he was disappointed that, since his promotion had been announced, no one had come in to offer congratulations. It was also customary for the precinct staff to have a pizza and beer party to celebrate the promotion of their commanding officer, but that hadn't happened either. He knew he'd been a tough boss and his tenure here had been rocky at times, but still...

Jack Barry came in. "You about done, Cap?"

Leland slammed the empty drawer shut. "Yep. All done."

"You got time to stop off at Corr's? I'd like to buy you a beer."

"Yeah, Jack," he said, genuinely touched. "I'd like that."

~~

The little Irishman reached across the bar and pumped Leland's hand. "Congratulations on your promotion, Inspector."

"It's still captain until tomorrow."

The old man waved a hand in dismissal. "Details. Details."

Barry thumped the bar. "Enough of your blather, Paddy. I took the captain here to buy him a drink not stand around jawing with you."

"In a minute." He grabbed Leland's sleeve. "First, I want to show the inspector the improvements I've made upstairs. I've been getting it ready for the precinct Christmas party next month and I must say I've outdone meself."

With a shrug at Barry, Leland followed the old man up the stairs.

"Take a look at this now," he said, throwing open the doors. The lights came on and the crowd shouted: "*Surprise!*"

Leland stood in the door, blinking in amazement. Then he began to make out faces in the crowd—Eddie Mazzeo, Peggy Garrigan, Henry Engle, Jimmy Elliot, George Oliver, and Charlie Reece. "Who's minding the store?" he asked Barry.

"The next precinct. They—"

"Owe us. I know."

Paddy grabbed Leland's arm and propelled him into the room. A sea of smiling faces pumped Leland's hand and offered congratulations. Someone stuck a martini in his hand as he moved through the crowd meeting the wives, husbands, boyfriends and girlfriends of his cops. It was very different from the Christmas party of a year ago.

A smiling Peggy Garrigan hugged him. "Thanks for the recommendation, Captain. OCCB called me today. I'm going next month."

"So, you're on the way to the Bureau?"

"Yep. This is the first step."

"Good luck, Peggy."

"Thanks, Cap." She squeezed his hand. "For everything."

After a buffet, which everyone agreed was the best spread the parsimonious Paddy had ever put out, Jack Barry walked to the center of the floor and put his hands up for silence.

When he had their undivided attention, he said, "The first day Captain Leland arrived at the precinct he gave me a list of things that needed to be done in the station house. I questioned why we should be concerned with missing garbage can covers, dirty windows, and broken shades when there was so much more to worry about. The Captain's response was: 'We have a right to work in a neat and clean environment.' I didn't agree with him then, but I do now. Captain Leland has more than cleaned up our physical facility—he's cleaned up our act, too. My apologies to the ladies, but my sources tell me that the bosses downtown no longer refer to the Five-five as 'Camp Fuckup.'"

Barry motioned to Carol Mazzeo, who stepped out onto the floor carrying a small, gift-wrapped package. "Captain," Barry said. "If you'll please step up here, there's something we want to give you."

Leland came forward and a self-conscious Carol Mazzeo cleared her throat. "I... that is, we have something for you that we think you will really like."

Leland took the small package and shook it. "Well, judging from its size, it can't be a bronzed garbage can cover. Should I open it now?"

She nodded and he tore away the shiny paper and ribbon. Inside the box were four rectangular pieces of green stained glass. He knew immediately what they were: Replacement for the broken green light in front of the station house. "Where did you get this?"

Carol smiled shyly. "I made it. I took a stained glass course at Adult Ed. They fit. Eddie took the measurements."

Leland kissed her cheek. "Thank you."

She hugged him and whispered in his ear, "No, thank you, Captain. For everything."

Leland gazed out at the sea of smiling Five-five cops. His cops. A year ago, he didn't know one name, now he knew every man and woman in the command by first name. He knew the good cops, the slackers, the students, the ambitious, and he realized that he would miss them all—even, God help him, Billy Lafferty.

To shouts of *Speech! Speech!* he began, "There's an ancient Chinese curse that says, 'May you live in interesting times.' Well, my year in the Five-five certainly has been the most interesting of my life, but it hasn't been a curse. It's been a blessing and a great learning experience. You taught me that sometimes you have to take risks. You taught me what being a good cop is all about, and for that, I thank all of you."

After a standing ovation, Leland went to the bar with Barry. He handed the stained glass to his Operations Coordinator. "You know where this goes, Jack."

"Right, Boss. He took a pen and a wrinkled piece of paper out of his pocket and made a great show of crossing out something.

"What's that?" Leland asked.

"The list you gave me the first day you came into the precinct. The green glass was the last item on the list." He slid the list across the bar to Leland. "Now, everything's been taken care of."

Leland studied the yellowed paper. It seemed like he'd written it a million years ago. Now, it seemed childish and naïve and he could hardly remember why he'd done it.

He folded it carefully and put it in his pocket. "Jack, I'm gonna frame this and hang it up as a reminder the next time I'm about to do something stupid."

Jim Elliot and George Oliver came up. Oliver shook Leland's hand. "Hey, Boss, it was good working for you."

"It was my pleasure, George."

Oliver put his hand around Elliot's shoulder and beamed. "Did you hear? My partner, here, passed the sergeant's exam."

"Leland shook Elliot's hand. "Congratulations, Jimmy."

"Thanks, Captain. I scored pretty high and I should get made with the first batch."

Oliver leaned into Leland and whispered, "Hey, Boss. If you have any influence with the new CO, do you think that you could arrange it so I don't get stuck with Billy Lafferty?"

Leland grinned. "I'll see what I can do, George."

Leland made his way down the bar, pausing to talk with his other cops. Reece pumped his hand. "Hey, Boss, as a PBA delegate, I gotta say you were an OK guy."

"Thanks, Charlie. And you were an OK delegate."

Reece cringed. "Don't say that too loud. If the guys hear that, I'll get voted out of office."

Leland turned to Lafferty, who was sitting next to Reece. Over the past year Lafferty had done his best to avoid him. He didn't know if it was because the little cop didn't like him or if he was just trying to stay out of his way.

"Well, Billy," he said. "I wish I could say it's been fun."

Lafferty flashed his weasel grin. "Yeah, me, too, Cap. One thing I gotta say about you though. I got less CDs from you than any other CO I ever worked for."

Leland was already beginning to feel sorry for his successor. "Billy, let's see if you can break that record with the next CO. Okay?"

Lafferty scratched his head. "Jeez, I don't know. That's gonna be a tough one."

Marv Seidel was surrounded by his cops and, as usual, he was regaling them with war stories. He turned to Leland. "Well, Cap, I kinda hate to see you go. You were just coming around."

"Thanks, Marv. I'll take that as a compliment." He signaled to Paddy, who was tending bar. "I'm buying. What'll you have?"

Seidel blew a cloud of blue smoke in Leland's face. "It's your promotion party. I'm buying. Right after I get that cheap Mick leprechaun to buy us a drink."

~~

It was almost midnight by the time Leland left. The party was still going strong, but over the course of the evening, his initial euphoria had given way to a feeling of melancholy. Maybe it was because he was leaving the Five-five or maybe it was because he was anxious about his new assignment. Whatever the reason, he had to get away. He made his last rounds, shook hands with everyone, and slipped out the door.

As he drove through the streets of his command for the last time, he felt a surge of pride in what he, and his cops, had accomplished. He hadn't done as much as would have liked, but that wasn't possible. The work of a precinct commanding officer was a work in progress.

He drove through the Bulge and stopped in front of the Joy Lounge, which was now a Pentecostal church. Every Sunday, the sound of joyful voices, electric guitars and tambourines filtered through windows painted to look like stained glass.

He drove down Seaman Street with its rundown tenements and broken brick stoops. It still looked the same, but it wasn't. Since the raid, he'd kept up a police presence and the block had remained drug-free. Vera Roland had never thanked him, but she stopped attending Community Board meetings and that was thanks enough.

He drove up to the Hill and, although he'd done it a hundred times, he was still struck by the amazing contrast. It wasn't just the newer, more expensive autos parked on the street or the row after row of gleaming apartment houses with their well-lighted vestibules. Even the streets seemed to be cleaner, and it suddenly occurred to him that they probably were. The people on the Hill had more than enough influence to insure that they received the lion's share of the Sanitation Department's resources.

He looked up and was surprised to find himself in front of Gloria's apartment building. He hadn't seen her since the day she'd watched him tell Mr. Cohen—and the world—that the police department wouldn't enforce the restraining order. He'd seen her turn away in disgust and he couldn't blame her. Still, he was hoping he'd get an "atta-boy" call from her after the Munyika confrontation and was disappointed when it didn't come.

When he'd first walked into the party tonight, he'd searched the sea of faces looking for her. His disappointment had been somewhat assuaged when Barry told him that the cops had decided that the party should be for cops and families only. Even Heidi Vancamp had been turned away.

He looked at his watch. It was almost twelve-thirty. There was no point in going up there. She was probably asleep or worse—entertaining someone.

A minute later, he found himself standing in front of her door, his finger poised at the buzzer. He took a deep breath and pressed the button. There was no sound from inside the apartment. He was about to turn away when he heard footsteps. He knew she was looking at him through the peephole and it suddenly occurred to him that this had not been a very good idea.

He turned to leave, and then he heard the sound of the bolt being undone. Suddenly, she was standing there in the open door looking absolutely lovely in a New York Mets nightshirt that ended just above her knees. She was barefoot and her long black hair was pile high on her head.

She leaned on the door. "Hello, Captain."

"Hello, Gloria." He tried to read her mood, but all he saw was the hint of a smile on those beautiful lips.

"Congratulations on your promotion," she said.

"Thanks." She made no move to invite him in and he suddenly felt awkward standing there in the hallway. "Today was my last day in the precinct. I'm getting promoted tomorrow."

"So, back to One Police Plaza?"

"No. Exec in the tenth zone."

She raised an eyebrow. "Patrol? I didn't think that was in your game plan, Captain."

"My plan has changed."

"In what way?"

"My new plan is not to make plans."

He searched her expression for some sign that she might have some feeling for him, but she revealed nothing in those beautiful dark eyes.

Since his divorce he'd gone out with many women, diligently avoiding all but the most superficial kinds of relationships. He'd told himself that it was necessary because personal entanglements would only distract him from his career. That was why he'd stayed away from Gloria. At least that's what he'd told himself. But the truth, which he hadn't been able to admit even to himself, was that after Marilyn, he'd become gun-shy about establishing an emotional relationship with a woman.

Until now.

He couldn't lie to himself anymore. He wanted Gloria more than anything else in the world, but he didn't know how to tell her.

"Why did you come here tonight?" she asked.

"*Why*? Oh, because... that is, well, you know, to say goodbye... and—*because I wanted to see you*," he blurted out. He hadn't felt this inadequate since high school.

"Why?"

"Damn it, Gloria, stop asking questions like a lawyer."

"I am a lawyer."

He stepped forward and took her delicate shoulders in his hands. She didn't pull away, but she made no attempt to move toward him either. "Gloria," he said softly. "I want us to be together."

She looked into his eyes, searching. "What about your career? Doesn't that come first?"

"No. It's not that important anymore."

"What is important?"

"You, " he answered softly. "Me."

Now she stepped toward him and pressed her warm, soft body against his. He slipped his arms around her and kissed her.

"I want us to be together, too, Captain."

He held her away from him in exasperation. "Gloria, my name is Richard."

"I know that." Her smile was mischievous. "But, I'll always call you Captain, even when you're a chief. Even when you're the police commissioner. Is that all right with you?"

He smiled. "Yeah, that's all right with me. Aren't you going to invite me in?"

She took his hand and led him inside.

The door closed and the sound of the bolt reverberated in the quiet, empty hallway.

The End

About the Author

Michael Grant is a former member of the NYPD. He worked as a police officer in the Tactical Patrol Force and the Accident Investigation Squad. Upon being promoted to sergeant, he worked in the 63rd Precinct, the Inspections Division, and finally the Police Academy. As a lieutenant, he worked in the 17th Precinct and finished up his career as the Commanding Officer of the Traffic Division's Field Internal Affairs Unit. He retired in 1985 and went to work for W.R. Grace Company as a Security Coordinator.

Mr. Grant has a BS in Criminal Justice and an MA in psychology from John Jay College. He is also a graduate of the FBI National Academy.

In 1990, Mr. Grant moved to Florida where he wrote his first three novels: Line of Duty, Officer Down, and Retribution. In 2006 he returned to Long Island where he has written eleven more novels: The Cove; Back To Venice; When I Come Home; In The Time Of Famine; Dear Son, Hey Ma; Krystal; Who Moved My Friggin' Provolone; The Mentor; Appropriate Sanctions; and now Precinct.

He lives on Long Island with his wife, Elizabeth, and their Golden Retriever, Jack.

Mr. Grant can be reached at: www.smashwords.com/profile/view/mggrant

Made in the USA
Columbia, SC
25 August 2022